LOTUS

A Novel

C. K. DURHAM

Publishing Services provided by Paper Raven Books LLC

Printed in the United States of America

First Printing, 2022

Paperback ISBN: 979-8-9859477-1-7

Hardback ISBN: 979-8-9859477-2-4

Ebook ISBN: 979-8-9859477-3-1

For my brother Bob who stayed for a time in a cave in Laos during the Vietnam War.

And, of course, for the glorious spiritual teachers who point out the way with exceptional compassion and love.

PART I

Know all things to be like this:

A mirage, a cloud castle,

A dream, an apparition,

Without essence, but with qualities that can be seen.

Know all things to be like this:

As the moon in a bright sky

In some clear lake reflected,

Though to that lake the moon has never moved.

Know all things to be like this:

As an echo that derives

From music, sounds, and weeping,

Yet in that echo is no melody.

Know all things to be like this:

As a magician makes illusions

Of horses, oxen, carts and other things

Nothing is as it appears

—Gautama Buddha

Prologue

El Salvador

Her eyes fluttered and then flared open wide. The girl shivered, damp with sweat on the bamboo mat, both knees pulled up to her chest despite the stuffiness and overwhelming humidity of the second-floor room. Quickly, she rolled onto her back, her long legs extending now past the limit of the mat. A single sheet, grey and dirty, lay crumpled on the side. It was a still, windless night—not even the cicadas chirped. The girl was thin, but her silhouette, barely visible in the shadows beyond the starlight filtering through the window, emphasized the soft flow of her shoulder and slender, high-arched feet.

Off in the distance, a dog barked, followed by a series of sharp yelps closer by. Suddenly, the night was a cacophony of barking and howling. The distinctive rumble of a large motorcycle could be heard fast approaching. The girl bolted up and quickly switched on a lone light bulb that dangled from the ceiling on a single cord. She stood half naked, trembling, and her eyes darted, furtive. The room was bare, except for the mat and her clothes thrown in a heap. She bent to collect the blouse and skirt and quickly slipped them on.

There was no knock below, just the front door thrown open wide.

"¿Dónde está la chica, José?"

Voices wafted up through the plankboard of the flooring. The low one belonged to José, a large man whose belly overlapped low-riding pants by more than a few inches. He wore a tight T-shirt yellowed from rings of dark sweat under the armpits. The pungency of his strong body odor permeated the house. Most mornings, José, slow to awaken, stumbled into the kitchen to grab a can of leftover warm beer while lighting the stub of an unfiltered cigarette. His lips smiled—one front tooth chipped, the other missing—but his eyes were dull.

Without a moment's hesitation, the girl climbed up and into the open window. She grasped the frame and then lowered her body outside. Carefully, she walked her feet down the stucco wall and hung from the windowsill. She closed her eyes and let go, dropping the remaining two meters. Her shoulder hit the ground first hard. Slowly, she rose and wiped a thin layer of dirt from her body before bolting into the camouflaging forest, bending to avoid low-lying branches, bushes, and deep foliage. She glanced back without slowing her pace and then broke into a fast run, her stride reminiscent of the bounding leaps of a jaguar.

"I'll only say this one more time. Where's the girl?"

The intruder narrowed his eyes and moved from the doorway fully into the room, deliberately knocking a pack of cigarettes and a half-full can of beer off a shelf to his right. Warm beer trickled onto the floor.

The two men circled, vultures vying for roadkill, each anticipating a moment's hesitation in the other.

The girl took care to stay behind trees, out of sight, without slowing her pace. She covered several kilometers by the time the door to the upstairs room flew open and both men, in tandem, registered the open window and recently vacated space. José spat, squeezed his hand into a fist, and slammed it against the drywall.

The intruder's plain features revealed nothing. He would be indistinguishable in a crowd, except for a two-toned dragon tattoo that spiraled up and around his upper-left bicep.

"Looks like I won't be needing you after all. Hand over the cash."

The tattooed arm shot forward, its fingers reaching deep into José's upper-right pocket.

A few moments later, the front door banged against the building before slamming shut.

Chapter One

1960

El Salvador

*I*t was the same dream. Quiet whisperings that haunted into the morning easily, as if another world claimed her too. Her hands and feet were bound, entangled in a thick web of vine, and all attempts to break loose only exhausted her. The creeping weeds grew thicker, tighter, and reduced her movement to the pulsation of blood and the rapid blink of an eye. Particles of pungent earth clogged her nostrils and choked her throat, making it hard to breathe. Her heart thumped, ricocheting inside her chest.

Abruptly, the scene shifted. She was now enclosed on all four sides. Above, a dark wooden ceiling; below, two-inch thick oak flooring supported her weight. But there was room now to move her hands and feet, and her airways were clear. She drew in a full breath.

Rays of light flickered through a tiny crack. Suddenly, the ceiling flew off the enclosure followed by the front, back, left and right walls. She clung to the wooden flooring that floated in a vast empty space. If she let go, she feared a plunge into an inky abyss. Her fingers tightened around the edge of the wooden floor. She had been here many times before. This time, slowly, reluctantly, she peeled her fingers open one by one until only her thumb and forefinger clutched the wooden plank. With a sharp exhale, she released.

1

Awareness expanded to merge with undefined dimension and immensely open possibility. Solid forms arose from the void to populate the emptiness like endless stars fading in and out. A lone bumblebee crawled across the surface of a sunflower, fractals and geometric patterns spiraling. The insect sensed for the perfect location to extract nectar in a symbiotic relationship inherent within the whole of creation. The sweet smell of dew and a crystalline sharpness filled the air.

Images streamed in chromatic intensity, one after the other. Dozens of hummingbirds hovered in midair like tiny Christmas ornaments reflecting spectral light. A lake appeared, and clouds echoed on the mirrored surface. Dragonflies skated across the calm water.

The girl advanced across a meadow toward the turquoise lake where a white elephant frolicked, showering herself in a bubbly spray. The girl held out her hand as if she might reach across the meadow and touch the elephant's trunk. In a blink, the elephant morphed, minuscule now, no taller than her index finger, all four of its feet firmly planted in the center of her palm, its pale eyelashes curling in an arc. She lifted her hand to see. There was a pure gold anklet with a tiny mermaid charm on one of the elephant's hind feet. The elephant raised its little trunk and probed the girl's eyes, nose, and chin and blew its warm breath into her ear. She giggled. The elephant's skin was rough and prickly and made the hair on her arm rise, like dough.

Once again, the scene shifted abruptly. She found herself towering four meters above the earth, sitting precariously on the pachyderm's skin, directly behind its large ears, which securely pinned her legs. Every so often, the elephant opened its ears, and the girl quickly laid her head down, tightening her arms on its neck. It moved toward the water, eased into it, and then began to swim. Beyond the lake towered a pagoda with a golden roof and stones of turquoise, red, and black. The air was suffused with jasmine while light bells tinkled in the crisp mountain air.

The girl and the elephant were both intent on swimming to the other side. Superimposed, the rounded eyes of a jaguar watched, his whiskers vibrating with the elephant's strokes.

The dog leaped from the floor onto the girl's bed, whimpering and licking her ears. Isabela opened her left eye. The dog bit the bedcover, playing tug-of-war with the sheet. The young woman wrapped her arms around the bundle of fur and began to massage his neck.

"Shh, shh …"

Isabela closed her eyes, sinking back into the fading images of the lake, suppressing the all-too-familiar angst that threatened to disturb her morning. She never called for her mother, not even as a young child. She didn't have the words and somehow intuited her mother would have no jurisdiction there. "Arf!" The dog's bottom raised high above its head, its tail whipping left and right like windshield wipers on high speed.

"Bueno, Cesaro. Listo, listo."

She threw back the covers and stepped onto the cool tile flooring.

Several large decks of the spacious stone residence nestled up against the side of a green hilltop, appearing to merge with an abundant rainforest. West-facing bay windows afforded a panoramic vista of the Lempa River, winding through El Salvador to empty into the Pacific Ocean. Isabela sipped black tea with two spoons of sugar and took small bites of dark marmalade toast on the hacienda's wide veranda. The flowers of two large maquilishuat trees formed a natural canopy of tufted pink over the deck.

Isabela loved to awaken early and sit quietly to sketch the wild species of birds visiting the trees closest to her home. There were heavy-billed toucans, flocks of parakeets, and, most recently, a pair of vibrant green quetzals who worked tirelessly to excavate a nest in the bark of a rotting tree trunk. Every so often, the male, with a ruby abdomen and a long twin tail, poked his head out to purvey the latitude of the morning. The young woman was enchanted with its magnificence. The ancient Mayans believed the bird was a symbol of peace and light.

Isabela was slender and, at five foot six, already an impressive height for a Salvadoran woman, appeared taller due to her erect posture and relaxed shoulders, which seemed to extend her neck. Her dark hair shone, reflecting health and vitality, and fell easily down her back in soft waves.

Ivanna Marquez sat across the table from her daughter, reading the morning paper and drinking black coffee. She took a final sip from her cup and stood, folding the paper to place it securely under her arm.

"Isabela, don't forget your father is coming home this afternoon. I have organized a special dinner to welcome him back. The Chavezes are invited."

"Mama, remember, today is Thursday. I am at the university until eight."

"Tomás will be here. Try not to be too late."

Isabela smiled, rose, and kissed her mother on the cheek.

"I'll be back by nine. Don't worry. Tell Papa I can't wait to see him."

The moon rose, full and high in the night sky, softly illuminating the path as if on a dark cloudy day. The din of the cicadas, along with the roar of cascading waters, descended twenty feet to crash on the craggy rocks below and drowned out casual conversation. Isabela wondered once again why she acquiesced so easily. Dinner was always a long affair when the Chavezes visited. After a full day of classes, she was tired and searched for the perfect moment to excuse herself and escape to the glorious solitude of her room. However, her mother played her hand casually, as if the thought had just occurred to her.

"Why don't you take Tomás down by the river? It's a beautiful night. Leave us *viejos* with our coffee and brandy."

Tomás extended a hand and drew Isabela to his side, helping her across the small creek. A felled tree trunk made the perfect bench, and they sat silent, apart, listening to the roar of the waterfall, its mist light and refreshing.

The Marquez and Chavez ranches bordered one another like giant pieces of a jigsaw puzzle. Tomás and Isabela had played together as young children, but as they matured, their interests diverged. Isabela, a shy and quiet girl, was drawn into the magical world of story and the arts. Tomás, loud and boisterous, displayed an avid, reckless jocularity early on. At the age of twelve, he was rescued from the jaws of an immense crocodile. He had jumped into infested waters on a dare. His friends screamed and waved their hands frantically while the reptile surfaced its head to leisurely yet swiftly navigate the river to encroach on the other side within the blink of an eye. They dragged him out just in time, before the beady-eyed reptile lurched forward to attack the boy.

Tomás was of medium height and stocky build, his arm muscles clearly defined. He had soft brown eyes with thick black lashes. A small scar ran across his forehead from an accident when he was four years old. He had run full speed through a glass door that he thought was open. His mother rushed him to the hospital, where he received seven stitches. Although faint, the scar remained.

In her early teenage years, Isabela had withdrawn into the poetry of Octavio Paz and Pablo Neruda, later expanding to include authors from faraway places: Tolstoy, Austen, and Brontë, their characters so captivating that actual friendships often paled by comparison. Later, she began to dabble in watercolors, painting vistas of the rainforest and some of the wildlife that populated it. Paintings in varying stages of completion were haphazardly tacked to her wall or simply strewn across her work table. She often lost time, reverent to the curve of a toucan's beak or the quiet echo of branches whispering in the wind.

Tomás couldn't be sure when the girl next door began to intrude on his thoughts. Maybe it was the faint smell of jasmine that always seemed to accompany her or the way she moved so gently and unobtrusively. It was no coincidence that he offered to take on more responsibilities for his father, which just so happened to include frequent visits to the ranch that zigzagged along the border of his family's property.

Isabela was mesmerized by the exquisite night. Crickets dinned, accompanied by the occasional hoot of an owl. She felt comfortable and content, listening to the evening's chorus, when suddenly Tomás spoke. "There's room here. Sit closer to me."

He edged nearer as Isabela slowly turned to look at him. He laid his arm on her shoulder and bent to bring his lips to hers. Instinctively, she leaned back, but his forward momentum easily eclipsed her move. His lips were warm and tasted of salt, coffee, and brandy. Stray wisps of her hair caught between their lips. His left hand, lightly resting on her back, began to move, silently exploring, navigating the side of her ribs. She let his hand stray, intrigued with the sensation, but then abruptly sat up, definitively moving a few inches back. She smoothed hair from her face and looked down at her feet.

"Tomás?"

"You can't say you haven't noticed. I don't come to your house every day just to work with your father."

"We've always known each other. You are a brother to me."

He leaned in, kissing her again. This time, his tongue parted her lips and probed her teeth, tongue, and the inside of her mouth.

"Isabela, you are so beautiful. I want you to be my wife. Will you?"

"Tomás, what are you saying?"

"Isabela, I asked if you would be my wife?" His hand lay on her forearm, his fingers slowly tightening.

"Tomás, you have caught me completely off guard. I haven't considered marriage yet. We are both young. I know you will be the most wonderful husband to whomever you choose. I am touched by your offer. Please give me time to consider."

A golden, syrupy liquid swirled in the deep crystal goblet, forming tiny eddies that emitted a strong aroma of orange and anise. A mahogany pipe carved with small Arabic writing hung from Pablo Marquez's bottom lip, the tobacco pressed tightly into the bowl. He took small puffs, igniting embers to a soft burning red. He was a quiet man who genuinely listened with interest, his attention wholly with the speaker, contemplating the words spoken without undue commentary. It wasn't that he always agreed, but most visitors left with a feeling that their case had been heard without judgment. When moved to anger, Pablo simply stood up and walked away.

"Tomás has been visiting us quite a lot these days." He sucked on the pipe until embers glowed bright red.

"Oh, mi amor … I wondered when you would notice." Ivanna Marquez looked up, a triumphant smile playing at the corners of her mouth as she spoke. "I am dying to hear your thoughts." She paused imperceptibly. "Imagine, our beautiful daughter could live right next door. We wouldn't lose her at all. Our families would share everything. The babies can grow up right here! It's absolutely perfect." Ivanna Marquez's cheeks flushed as her voice rose to a light crescendo.

Pablo drew on his pipe as he quietly observed his wife. "Do you think they are compatible? She's an artist, our girl."

"Tomás is very handsome, don't you agree? Our daughter has several sketches of him on her wall. She may appear to be absorbed in the arts, but she is a young woman now. I've watched her. She lights up when he's here."

"But are they suitable for one another?" Pablo puffed on his pipe as small clouds of smoke formed and dissipated.

"Mi amor, what does a young girl need to know? Compatible, what is this? He is handsome, bright, and can make sure she never wants for anything. They will grow to love each other as we have."

Pablo continued to draw on his pipe pensively as his wife extolled the virtues of Tomás, the perfect prospective son-in-law for their only daughter.

Ivanna Marquez smiled broadly when she saw Isabela and Tomás approach the hacienda, holding hands and laughing. She lowered her head to nod once in the direction of her husband, eyebrows raised in anticipation.

Two months later, Tomás formally asked Pablo Marquez for his daughter's hand in marriage.

Chapter Two

Subic Bay, Philippines

Lance Jameson eased back on the airplane's stick, starting a gentle climb. Then, in an abrupt reversal, he pushed the stick forward, unloading the wings. Several pencils, papers, and a pair of flight gloves now hovered midair like hummingbirds suspended in flight.

"Jameson!" a disembodied voice screeched through the pilot's headphones. The radio intercept officer, or RIO, seated directly behind Lance in the tandem two-seat Phantom II jet fighter continued his plea. "Quit that! Too many beers last night, buddy. Having a hard time back here. Have a heart!"

Lance responded by banking to the right and then rolling the plane 180 degrees so ground became sky and the sky an open ocean below. The F-4 flipped back, now right side up, as the USS *Midway* quickly materialized from a dot on the radar screen to its huge, hulking mass.

"The most beautiful sight in the world, wouldn't you say?"

"Oh yeah!"

The F-4 slowed to 200 knots, lining up with the aircraft carrier that seesawed and shimmied with the ocean's waves. The tail hook snagged the third wire with ease, and the plane jolted to a stop. The hatch popped open, and Lance Jameson jumped out, followed closely by his RIO, Tom Johnson. Tom smacked his right hand flat across Jameson's chest.

"I promise you! You won't see it coming, Jameson."

Lance suppressed a grin and dropped his arm on Tom's shoulder. With his free hand, he took a small wad of gum from behind his ear to place in his mouth and ran his hand over his stubbly, light-brown crew cut.

"You know I've got eyes in the back of my head, Ace, I'm interested to see what ya got!" Lance began to mold softened chewing gum around his tongue as he squeezed Tom's shoulder.

The two entered the ready room, smiling and joining the pilots already assembled. The landing signal officer nodded toward the two and motioned for them to be seated. He continued to address the assembled group, turned, and directed his attention to the pilots just seated.

"Jameson, once again, good use of power. Perfect cut on the number three wire. Either you are the luckiest son of a bitch or the best pilot I've seen in this man's Navy in the last fifteen years, but for right now, I'm gonna go with 'lucky son of a bitch,'" the LSO said.

After the debrief, Lance and Tom stood as the operations officer approached.

"Jameson, the old man wants to see you in his stateroom, stat," he said.

Lance looked at Tom and shrugged his shoulders.

"I'm telling you, Jameson, the old man has eyes in the back of his head! He's going to have your ass for playing around with a $6 million airplane."

Lance beamed as he replied. "I should be so lucky to be kicked out of this hellhole. Let them send me home! I'll just settle in with my lovely new wife and live a life of ease and comfort!"

"You're one lucky son of a bitch, Jameson. I don't know how you do it!" Tom grinned and shook his head.

A few moments later, Lance knocked on the door to the commanding officer's stateroom.

"Ah, Lieutenant Jameson, come in." Lance entered and saluted.

"At ease, Lieutenant." The CO, still dressed in his flight suit, barely glanced up as Lance entered. He shuffled through several papers on his desk.

"In yesterday morning's message traffic, there was an interesting communication from Chief of Staff Captain Sharp, concerning you."

Lance reached to scratch the side of his face, but at the news, he straightened his head to look directly at his commanding officer. "Me, sir?"

"You are to proceed to Pearl and prepare for a possible permanent change of station. It seems like a Nigel Hawkes requested an interview with you." The CO now looked up fully from his papers to peer directly at the lieutenant. "Who the hell is Nigel Hawkes and why is he interested in you?"

"Nigel Hawkes, sir? If it's the same Nigel Hawkes, he was my Asian international affairs professor at Oxford. Hell of a nice guy and a great professor."

"Professor, my ass. I did some research. This guy has one hell of a background. Major with the 22nd Special Air Squadron in Malaya in the early fifties. That means British elite special ops. I checked him out, all right. I want to know who's stealing one of my best pilots."

Lance rolled his jaw in small circles as his eyes peered to the left of the CO. "It must be a different Nigel Hawkes then. My old professor is a shortish, bald gentleman with eyeglass lenses thick as a Coke bottle. He's only got one good leg. He lost part of the other one just below the knee to cancer about ten years back. We spent a bit of time together. He was interested in my background, growing up in Thailand."

"Well, I'll be goddamned. You're in for one hell of a ride, Lieutenant."

11

Chapter Three

1960

El Salvador

On the blackboard, bold cursive in bright yellow chalk listed guidelines for the upcoming art history research project. Isabela carefully copied the directions in her loose-leaf notebook, then gathered her books and headed down a long stone hallway to the library, where she quickly surveyed the room, zeroing in on her favorite table in a small corner alcove. She was happy to see that it was vacant. She dropped her books on the table and moved toward the back of the library, where hundreds of file cabinets lined the wall. She pulled out a drawer and skimmed through index cards alphabetized by subject, intent on finding reference books with information on her chosen topic: Michelangelo and the Sistine Chapel.

She jotted down several names and moved in the direction of the titled row of books. After selecting three she hoped were beneficial, she returned to her table in the alcove. Several minutes later, a metal cart rattled past her, the bottom shelf filled with books and the top strewn with magazines and newspapers. Isabela looked up. The librarian, wearing a pair of wide, tortoiseshell-frame glasses that dominated her rather thin, pale face, stopped the cart directly to the side of Isabela's table to answer a query from a student. The librarian left the cart parked in place and walked with the student toward the back of the library.

Isabela made a mental note to return to paragraph three on page twenty as her attention drifted to the cart beside her. She stretched her arm out and shuffled through the pile of periodicals on top and selected a recent 1960 copy of *National Geographic,* half-hidden underneath several newspapers. The magazine was in English, a language she had studied since grade school. Friends and acquaintances often complimented her on her extensive English vocabulary and well-formed words with an accent that was hard to place.

Her attention momentarily diverted from her assignment, Isabela began to skim an article relating to an archaeological dig in Egypt and its recently discovered mummified remains. She briefly glanced at the pictures without taking time to fully read the scientific study or its conclusion. Flipping the page once again, she drew in her breath. The title, "Exotic Thailand," hummed in her ear as she looked at the photographs of gilded temples, giant Buddhas, and hundreds of monks in silent vigil on a mountainside.

The images danced in front of her as one loomed largest—a lone elephant seemed to stare directly into her eyes. On its left hind foot was a brass anklet linked to a thick metal chain. The background of the image was entirely filled with stacks of processed logs. A thin, bare-chested, brown-skinned man stood to the side, barely reaching up to the elephant's shoulder joint. The man held a thick wooden stick with a brass hook that grabbed the inside of the elephant's front foot. Underneath the photograph was the caption "Logging in Thailand." The elephant's eye seemed to bore straight through Isabela's skin and reach deep down into the center of her chest. Images of her dream elephant flickered like waves of heat in the desert. Suddenly, she felt the texture of rough skin on her fingers and the sensation of a tiny trunk tickling her ear.

"Disculpe." *Excuse me,* the librarian said.

Dark eyes peered at Isabela behind her large glasses. The librarian stood directly in front of the alcove. Isabela looked up and tried to focus on the woman waiting expectantly for her response.

"Would you like to keep that magazine? Otherwise, I will be moving along." Isabela smiled and assured the woman she had what she needed. She lowered her gaze and deliberately turned the page, abandoning the elephant and its sad, haunting eyes.

Her mind wandered to the Michelangelo Fresco she was studying in school. Her hand rhythmically flicked pages, the content of which she barely retained. Images blurred, one running into the other. The page was half turned when a flash of turquoise and gold danced in the corner of her eye. Slowly, she let the page fall back open to a pantheon with a gold-leaf roof and walls of intricate, inlaid stone, turquoise, black, red, and gold. The shrine sat upon the green side of a white-topped mountain with hundreds of prayer flags stretched above and below. Isabela's heart began to race as an invisible rainbow bridge drew nearer, and an urgent whisper echoed in her ear.

Chapter Four

1976

El Salvador

Thick, dark lashes accentuated her mossy green eyes, which reflected glints of copper with just the right angle of light. Santiago Rodríguez called Mera, his youngest child, a gift from the angels. He loved his daughters and his sons equally, he was fond of saying, but whenever he came back from a visit to the big city, he always brought something special for the girls—a piece of candy or a small toy he knew would bring a smile to their sweet faces. Gracias a Dios, their small farm, produced well. The livestock were healthy and the crops plentiful over the past few years. This year had all the indications of another robust harvest. Santiago sighed. The children were all almost grown now. Evenings, when they were still small enough to hold, he'd often have one on his lap while the others tried to climb up on him until he made room for them all. Nonetheless, his favorite time of the day was still when the sun dropped behind the horizon and all his loved ones gathered to eat the evening meal and discuss the events of the day.

Mera slept entwined with her brothers and sister. The children shared a large straw mat placed at night to the right of the cooking area where they all slept in one big comfortable heap. When asked

15

their favorite food, one by one they replied, "Arroz y frijoles, arroz y frijoles!" *Rice and beans, rice and beans!*

Maria Rodríguez loved her youngest daughter as she loved all her children. However, she kept a subtle distance not noticeable to many. She was afraid and, therefore, prayed fervently to the Virgin, the angels, and all the saints to protect this wild and intractable girl.

Maria was soft and round, with her hair plaited in two thin braids that reached down to the small of her back. She rose before the others in the dark and lit a candle to walk the dark hallway to the cooking area where she started mashing corn for tortillas. By the time the sun began to peek over the horizon, the children stirred. Their bodies, like a giant octopus waving its limbs, stretched an arm here and a leg there. Maria descended upon the sleeping mass, her handmade broom tapping a buttock or back, throwing back blankets, as if to sweep them all up into one big pile. Like synchronized fireworks, the children shot up and lined up out the door to relieve themselves in the outhouse.

Eight chickens and a rooster entered the cabin at will when the front door opened and they were freed from the henhouse. The bedding was folded and stored as each of the Rodríguez children began their chores for the morning.

Mera and David, the closest in age to her, were inseparable. David had jet-black hair and dark brown eyes that appeared almost black but were nonetheless warm and inquisitive. The two looked out for each other, as they shared an intense curiosity about nature and animals that was considered somewhat odd to the others. In the late afternoons, when all the work was done, they ventured down to the river to observe quietly any animal that approached for a drink.

Mera was enchanted with butterflies and hummingbirds, especially the fluorescent Blue Morpho, with a wingspan that dwarfed its smaller relatives. She secretly believed that the giant butterfly had a peculiar ability and would one day lead them to a magical spot that could only be seen by those with extra eyes in their heart.

Mera lay on her belly and brought her finger to her lips. David squatted next to her, straining to see where she pointed and what new mystery might be revealed. Almost completely merged with its leaf, a praying mantis blinked its bulging eyes in acknowledgement of them both. His wings blended perfectly with the color and texture of the leaf. Mera held out her finger, and the insect graciously stepped onto it as if he had been waiting just for this meeting.

"Qué hermoso." *How beautiful,* she said. She remained quiet for several moments and then whispered, "He says to tell you this is the home to the ones we cannot see … they've been waiting for us! We are the invited guests, just you and me. No one else can know. Promise not to say a word, not even to Mama!"

David nodded, as always, impressed by his youngest sister's vivid imagination. He loved to glimpse the world through her eyes, a unique universe where each creature had its own language, purpose, and way of communicating. She urged her brother to stay quiet and reminded him of their highest objective: invisibility.

A rustling in the ferns turned both heads to the east. In between wavering plants, golden eyes peeked out. Instinctively, David put his arm in front of Mera, pushing her back. Mera resisted, curious.

"Shhh, he's just a little one."

"Little ones have big mamas. We need to go!"

Mera remained still, her finger to her lips once again. David turned 360 degrees, scanning the area before crouching next to his sister. A spotted jaguar cub pranced into the clearing, followed immediately by his black sibling. The rosettes of his dark fur were muted but visible. The black one pounced on his brother, and soon, the two rolled and jostled each other with playful snips and mewling growls.

Suddenly, the black one went flying over his sibling and landed within arm's reach of the two adolescents. Mera and David held their breath and instantly froze where they crouched. The young cub arched his back and hissed, staring directly into Mera's eyes. She softened her gaze and made quiet mewling sounds. Slowly, the cub lowered and turned to once again pounce onto his sibling.

David motioned quickly. Mera, dazed by the encounter with the cub, reluctantly backed up at the silent pressure of her brother's hand between her shoulder blades. Up on the road again, David took Mera's hand and pulled her toward home. A loud growl reverberated through the ferns and trees.

"Do you hear that? She is calling her babies home."

"And Mama will be waiting for you with a broom if we don't get going."

David lightly slapped her on her bottom, and she responded by jumping onto his back and wrapping her long legs around his waist. David staggered under his sister's weight but kept moving forward. They fell into a laughing heap, tumbling very much like the young jaguar cubs as Mera broke free and cried, "Race!" She was already running. David trotted after her, knowing any attempt to catch up was futile.

The Rodríguez family ate the evening meal seated around a wooden table, hand carved by Santiago and his two boys. The two daughters, Rosita and Mera, served steaming plates of chicken, rice, and beans from the kitchen and placed the food in the middle of the table. Often, the first serving disappeared in moments, so the girls served the men a second helping before sitting down themselves.

Santiago patted Marcos, his oldest son, on the shoulder. "Marcos tilled the entire right field," he said, chewing a mouthful of rice. "The soil is rich and ready, so we need all four of you kids to plant maize tomorrow. No school, no promenades. I mean you too, Mera and David. No disappearing, understand?"

"Papa, there's talk in town. There's been trouble in some of the villages," Marcos said.

"Marcos, we spoke of this. I told you to stay away from those meetings. There is more than enough work on the farm. The government will not disturb hardworking families. We are farmers. I don't want my family involved. Do you understand?"

"Papa, come to town tomorrow night after the planting. At least hear what's been going on. People are being killed."

"Marcos, I understand you are a young man and feel passionately about such things. That is good, but the best way is to stay neutral. We have crops to tend and food to put on the table. I've heard the talk. Believe me, we need to stay out of all that."

"Papa, you are putting your head in the ground. They are killing women … children, people just like us."

"Santiago, what is Marcos talking about? Do we need to leave? Who will take care of the crops?" Maria's voice rose as she took her husband's hand and squeezed it hard, her eyes anxiously searching his face.

"Maria, no te preocupes, no te preocupes." *Don't worry, don't worry.* "No one will disturb us."

Santiago looked at his oldest son with a piercing gaze. "Marcos, you are upsetting your mother and the children. No more of this talk!" He turned abruptly and faced his younger son.

"Now, David, where did you and Mera go off to today? I had Rosita down by the river looking for you."

"Papa, we saw the most interesting …"

Mera aimed a kick under the table at David, but Marcos, seated across from him, received the blow instead. "Mera," Marcos shouted, "why did you boot me?" He raised his eyebrows and shook his head. David, interrupted for a moment, glanced their way and then continued, intent on corralling his father's attention.

"… the most interesting animals today. There was …"

Two black beans catapulted across the table, one landing in David's hair and the other right above his eye. He stopped abruptly and faced his younger sister. Mera bounced up and down, her face reddening.

"You can't tell. You promised."

Maria stood and began to collect the dishes from the table and stack them one on top of the other. On her way to the kitchen, she spoke over her shoulder.

"Mera, stop throwing food and eat. You are too thin."

Chapter Five

1959

Honolulu, Hawaii

It wasn't that Lance was unaware of the time. On the contrary, he was consistent, like the second hand of a watch. He usually arrived at least five minutes before any appointment or meeting, but this time, he needed his contact to show up first. He stood in the doorway of the open-air restaurant at Honolulu International Airport and surveyed the diners, oblivious to the soft breeze that swayed the tops of the palm trees lining the terrace. In the background, the melodious notes of a ukulele accompanied the silent, undulating hula dancers welcoming travelers on the warm island walkways.

Ignoring the din of excited chatter among travelers, Lance scanned the crowd and then settled on certain individual details. At the table to the far right, a heavyset Polynesian woman in a green-flowered muumuu ate alone. To her left, a young couple spoon-fed dark pudding to their curly-haired toddler. Even from where he stood, Lance could tell it was poi. He grimaced, remembering the one and only time he tasted the fermented taro root.

An immaculately dressed Japanese businessman with a Buddhist flag pin attached to his lapel nodded to his business associate, a man of Middle Eastern descent. Before Lance could step to the side, a

21

group of American tourists, each of them with a fragrant lei dangling around their necks, swelled in the entranceway and pressed him firmly into the restaurant, the sweet aroma of plumeria redolent in the air.

A second later, he identified the lone man. He sat in the far corner dressed in dark khaki pants and a beige Hawaiian shirt with orange orchids. A fedora lay on the seat beside him. His thick eyeglasses were noticeably missing, replaced by a pair of sharp Ray-Bans pushed to the top of his shiny, bald head. Lance approached the table.

"Damn, Professor, it's good to see you!" He grinned and extended his hand. Nigel stood, pushed his chair back, took Lance's hand, and laid his other hand on the younger man's shoulder. "Professor, I am way beyond curious. What's with this British Special Air Service business? What the hell is going on? Two days ago, I was flying training missions off the USS *Coral Sea* near Subic Bay, and now, here I am in Honolulu, talking with my old professor from Oxford."

"Sit down, Lance. Sit down. I hear the steak is quite good here." The professor handed Lance the menu, indicating he should take a minute to review it and order.

"Professor, I am at a loss. I received orders for a possible military move and was directed to this interview with you."

"In a minute, Lance. Let's have some lunch, and then we'll take a walk. In the meantime, you can tell me about those jets you've been flying."

Chapter Six

1959

Honolulu, Hawaii

The turquoise ocean lapped gently onto Fort DeRussy Beach in Honolulu, contrasting sharply against the brilliant cerulean sky. White clouds hugged the horizon, but the upper atmosphere remained luminous and clear. Palm trees wavered in the light breeze as several groups of well-conditioned and scantily clad youth played volleyball along the shore.

From his military buzz cut and tailored khaki pants to the olive-green crocodile shirt and dark sunglasses, Lance was just as well dressed as the shorter man walking beside him, their heads bent together in deep conversation. The professor walked with a considerable limp, but due to his poised bearing, the impediment was not easily noted by the casual observer.

"Cancer?"

"Actually, I lost my leg in Malaya in '52 while on a deep penetration mission. I took a bullet in my left calf. Not too bad a wound actually to start, and then bloody gangrene set in before we could hike out."

Lance raised his eyebrows but remained quiet as Nigel continued.

"My good fellow, I have a bit of interesting work for you to consider, to which British intelligence and your government very much hope you will agree. I've been told to tell you it would be a 'good career move.' It requires, however, the resignation of your commission, to be reinstated upon successful completion of the mission with appropriate promotions. I think with your current skillset and a bit of training from the British SAS, we just might bring you up to speed and get you into the southeast Asian theater of operations. You would work for me. That is, British intelligence. We are an 'advisor' to the U.S. Studies and Observation Group on your chaps' side. Don't let the name fool you. These blokes are serious professionals, and this is a highly classified mission."

Lance pushed his dark sunglasses up onto the top of his head, removed the piece of gum from his mouth, and stuck it behind his ear. He watched his old professor with unwavering attention.

"Where?"

"Northeastern Thailand to start. How much do you remember from your old Asian studies classes?"

"It was quite a while ago, Professor. We covered a lot of ground. But if you're asking if I've kept up with what's going on in southeast Asia, I'd say communism is a hungry beast, ready to devour some tasty appetizers."

"Spot on. Thailand is getting very nervous. She's surrounded on all sides. Laos, Cambodia, and Burma are all more than receptive to Mao's ideology. The theater's blown wide open. Thailand risks a lot to align herself with the West and the United States in particular. The situation is precarious. To avoid a rapid unraveling of democracy in southeast Asia, we have to act quickly and under the radar. Eisenhower tried the way of negotiation at the Geneva Convention. Laos, to his mind, wasn't a threat. Currently, intelligence is more than concerned."

Nigel paused a moment to look directly at the younger man. Lance nodded for him to continue.

"One small country falls to communism, and it becomes a domino effect. We need positive intel that the Chinese are behind the surge in rebel activity along the northeastern Thai border. Your fluency in Hmong could prove quite useful. More importantly, we need to make friends with the Hmong. It turns out they are central to our mission. They are fiercely independent, and, as I said, they don't like the Chinese at all … nor, for that matter, the Laotian Pathet Lao and North Vietnamese, which makes them our new best friends."

Lance observed his old professor for a moment and said, "That's what this is about? The Hmong?"

Nigel nodded and continued to speak. "In part. We are going as an advance to the U.S. Special Forces. Your language skills and close kinship with the Hmong, as well as your photographic recall, elicited this meeting and the SAS's strong interest in you."

"The languages are less than proficient at this point, Professor. I haven't been back to Thailand since before high school. I went to college in the states, Oxford, and then on to the Navy. There aren't many Hmong to converse with in an American squadron. I learned French on the streets of Bangkok when I was a boy. You know better than I do that the French were all over southeast Asia and had colonized half of Thailand in the early 1900s. I studied Mandarin in college, but more to the point, how did you know I speak a Hmong dialect? I don't remember sharing that with you. In fact, I never speak about that."

"My good chap, how about you fill me in now?" Nigel scribbled a few notes on a small yellow pad he extracted from his orange-flowered shirt pocket and then opened his hands as if to receive a blessing.

"Professor, my childhood? Is it relevant? That's a world I've worked hard to forget. Nothing but ghosts there." *What the fuck is he expecting to learn?* Lance forced his left hand into a fist, commanding the slight tremble to still.

"I'm afraid it's very to the point, old chap. Your past is why we've gone to such extreme measures to recruit you. It wasn't easy, you know, extracting you from the U.S. Navy."

Lance took the wad of gum from behind his ear, popped it back into his mouth, and began to chew. His eyes opened wide as the muscles of his jaw tightened.

"Where do I start?"

"Let's have a seat." Nigel indicated a park bench located a few meters off the beach. "And please start at the beginning. That's always the best place. That way we're sure not to leave out any less-than-obvious details."

Lance opened his mouth and relieved the tension in his jaw. He hitched his shoulders almost to his ears and then pulled them back, opening his chest wide before dropping his head from side to side to stretch his neck in each direction.

"All right, Professor. If it has any relevance, which I sincerely doubt, I'll cover the basics."

Nigel hinged forward, giving his entire focus to the younger man.

"I was born in Bangkok in 1932. My father, Robert Jameson, was from Philadelphia. My grandfather, when opportunity arose, never failed to bring up the family's strong American heritage, several generations born in the USA, originating from good old Irish and Norwegian stock. My mother, Meredith, was somewhat of a mixed breed. She was part English, and the other half was a mix of Thai and Japanese. They met in Singapore, where she worked for the Red Cross and my father traveled for business. He was a gem dealer. Actually, he traveled extensively, all over southeast Asia. After they were married, they lived in Bangkok, where I was born."

Lance glanced at the small yellow pad on Nigel's knee. There were just two notations on it.

Nigel nodded for him to continue.

"My mother died a year after my birth from diphtheria. I have no memory of her. My father was devastated and took his time to acknowledge my existence. I was raised by a nanny, an old Hmong woman. Her husband died, but she wouldn't leave us to go back to her clan. There was a backstory there, but I was a kid and given a revised child version." Lance paused as his mind drifted back twenty-five years.

The memory was clearer than most because, during the twelve years he had lived with his nanny, it was the only time he ever remembered her crying. "Why are you crying, Amah?" he asked. Slowly, she opened her hand to reveal a large green stone that sparkled. He reached out, and she dropped the heavy stone into his palm and allowed his small fingers to close around it.

"Hold it gently," she said. "It's a very special one."

He slowly opened his hand to look at the stone from every angle. "Why does it make you cry, Amah?" he asked. For some reason, the answer she gave him was still easily recalled.

"The people never understood that wealth is an illusion," she said.

Nigel closely observed the younger man as he revealed the memory. "Go on," he said finally.

"She told me she left her village because the ancestors said there was a little boy who needed her. So, she followed the signs and found me. Being a kid, I didn't think to ask anything more. Later, though, when I was grown, I wondered what really made her leave her people to live with strangers in the city."

"Did the subject ever come up again? When you were older?" Nigel shifted his weight and stretched his prosthetic leg. Lance glanced at it before continuing to speak.

"No, I didn't think to ask her when we were still together. Then, of course, it was too late." Lance shook his head as the memories flooded his mind. "From the outset, my father was never home. I realized later he didn't have any idea how to care for an infant. He was grieving. He buried himself in his work, but he did provide for me, for us. I called my old nanny Amah, and she was the closest I ever came to having a mother. She nursed me, fed me, and told me stories, creation myths, and the history of her husband's clan. She brought me to gatherings and ceremonies of the Hmong. I only knew a spattering of English until I was about seven." Lance's gaze shifted from the professor out across the adjacent beach. He remembered his father's deep-set eyes, rounded shoulders, and sallow skin from long hours in poorly lit rooms examining gems with a jeweler's loupe attached to his eye. Lance visualized the door to his father's study, a door that he never saw open. The sudden recollection of the strange and shocking day his father miraculously emerged from the dark cloud of heartbreak burned like a brand on his skin. It was almost a full minute before Lance spoke again. "That was the year my father came home after traveling for almost a year. He was horrified to learn I spoke English with a strange tonal accent."

"How did you react to that?"

"It took some time … I was shy at first, but Amah helped us. And then began my formal English education. I was sent to private school and immersed in my father's culture. My father began to spend time with me whenever he returned from trips. He tried to enroll me in boarding school, but I yelled and made our home life quite miserable for all of us. In the end, he relented and sent me to a private day school in Bangkok. I was able to stay with Amah at night and weekends. Amah was home."

The first day of school wavered in the back of his mind in a black-and-white montage. He remembered Amah walking through the tall iron gates with him tugging on her arm and begging her not to leave him there alone, past children in the playground and up the steps to the main office. Lance watched scenes from his childhood rise and dissipate only to rise again. He watched himself, as a tow-headed boy, glare at a teacher, answering first in the tonal Hmong dialect he spoke at home and then reverting to French as the teacher threatened to have him stay after school. School was a culture shock for him. He didn't fit in and kept to himself for the first few years.

"And then?" Nigel spoke quietly.

"I was a rebellious kid who pushed back daily at what I believed were extreme deprivations to my liberty. As an aside, I didn't like the school's food much either. After a while, though, I just wanted to fit in. I was tormented by the older boys at recess before and after school. I was the lone sheep in a den of lions, or that's how I viewed it. It wasn't until age eleven that I found a doorway in: rugby. I took to rugby and excelled beyond my wildest hopes. My father and I finally shared an interest and became comfortable in each other's company. I think, looking back, I was finally old enough for him to relate. It's the time I remember best. All the rest seems a lot like images from an old photograph album."

Lance paused, immersed in thought. He imagined a rattling old movie projector clicking through sound bites like a drumroll. Images from the past reflected light like a display onto a blank white screen. Then in Technicolor, they swirled by. The boy stood by his father on the side of a riverbank learning to cast his reel. Father and son bent over the workbench assembling tiny pieces of a model airplane splayed on a blanket on the floor in numerical order, and the boy questioned the father, "Is this the right piece to go here?" The boy, in his white rugby shirt with "JAMESON" printed in bold red letters across the back of his shirt and a big number seven underneath, ran toward the ball, aimed, and kicked. The ball flew through the air, a perfect missile, straight through the goalposts. Lance could almost smell fumes of fried fish from the restaurant next to the rugby field, hear the shrill whistle and the roar of the crowd, and see the long arm of the referee point his arm towards the center circle, indicating the location of the next kickoff. He remembered the exact moment he noticed his father in the crowd.

"For almost a year, my father made it to almost half of my games," Lance said, "and he traveled less. Our team entered into the Asian semifinals. It was a big deal to a kid. I played halfback, and goddamn, I was good. My father promised he wouldn't miss the date. But it turns out I never saw him again. He was run over on the streets of Singapore … just crossing the street. It was a hit and run, they told me." It felt, suddenly, like thick smoke replaced the air inside his lungs. Lance coughed once and took several short breaths. Like a mantra, he silently repeated the Navy's core values—honor, courage, commitment. He willed his mind to detach and recount the story as if it happened to someone else.

Nigel lowered his voice as he said, "How old were you?"

"It happened a week before my twelfth birthday."

"One hell of a birthday present."

Lance met his old professor's unwavering gaze. "At first, I was mad that he did not show up for the match. I was quite sure he had forgotten. About a week later, I learned he was never coming back. I was called out of class to the principal's office at the Bangkok Patana International School. They were kind. There's really no way to break news like this. They just sat me down, and there you have it. It doesn't make sense, but instead of feeling sad, I was furious. I was angry with him for leaving me. I stormed out of the office and roamed the streets until late in the night."

The yellow pad lay on Nigel Hawke's knee, still with only two notations on it.

"I left school. My tuition was paid through the end of the year, but I didn't have the heart to go back. The school reminded me of him. Amah and I packed our few belongings, boarded a bus, and never looked back. We moved to a small village. It was not exactly a Hmong settlement, but there were Hmong who lived there. I worked with local boys herding goats. Amah worked in the fields. In the evenings, she did laundry for several families. We grew our own vegetables. Honestly, we didn't need much. I recall being quite happy."

"And then?"

"It was a year before the American came. He arrived in the village asking noninvasive, indirect questions, I imagine. Otherwise, we would have had warning, and no one would have directed him to our door like it happened. Apparently, this hired agent had been searching for me since the day I disappeared with Amah. It turns out my father had not left me destitute. In fact, there was a sizable inheritance, but one I would not have access to until I turned twenty-one. I was told the inheritance was managed by my paternal grandfather. This foreign man told me I needed to go with him to a foreign country to live with unacknowledged relatives. I was suspicious and scared out of my wits. There was no way I was going to leave everyone I loved. I told Amah I wouldn't go. I planned to run away. The Hmong guard their liberty above all else. Amah said, 'Let's run away together!' She said we could return to her husband's clan on the northeastern border. No one would find us there. She said she'd find a way to ease the tension with the clan. She'd do that to keep me safe. It sounded like a great plan to me. We told the American to come back in a week, packed our belongings again, and left. But they were on to us straightaway. The police apprehended us on a bus headed north to Chiang Rai. They had my photograph and a copy of my passport. Of course, we stuck out. I was a towheaded boy traveling with a Hmong woman. In the end, Amah was arrested for child trafficking and kidnapping. I clung to her and screamed bloody hell. They pulled us apart, but it wasn't easy. I wouldn't let go. Her face in that moment is not easily erased from my mind. They threw her on the ground, handcuffed her, yanked her to her feet, and pushed her away from me. There was no way to find her after they separated us. I knew what happened was because of her love for me." Lance coughed and then breathed out slowly. "Damned if that wasn't another life, like a dream that pops up in my mind once in a while."

"Quite," Nigel said quietly. "Please continue."

"I was shipped off, signed, stamped, and delivered to my grandfather's door. He was a cold man. I wavered between sheer terror and absolute defiance. He felt it his duty to Christianize the little heathen and almost immediately sent me to a military boarding school. I graduated early from the academy, a place I imagined more than once to be its own kind of prison. I tolerated it because I understood pretty quickly it was preferable to life in his cold mansion. Yale was a big improvement. My father's inheritance became accessible my last year of college. If it had been left to my grandfather, he would have kept control, but luckily, my father's will was precise. Full access to the funds transferred to me at twenty-one. I could have dropped out, lived the good life, bought a boat and sailed the seven seas, but all my military training left its mark. I graduated from Yale magna cum laude. School was easy and had its rewards in the end. You know the rest. I studied at Oxford for two years and then joined the Navy. It was in the military academy I started dreaming of flying jets, and my path was set. I'd like to make admiral one day, and I think I might just have what's required."

"And Amah? Did you ever try to locate her?"

"When I first came to the States, I wanted to find her. She's all I thought about. My heart was broken. I felt to blame for what happened to her. I was afraid they locked her up, and that absolutely would have killed her. I worried every day … if we had only left earlier as she had wanted. At thirteen, I had no power and was on the other side of the world. I was deported from Thailand like some kind of juvenile delinquent, basically lied to, and told I was a persona non grata. My grandfather was completely unapproachable on the subject of Amah. He called her a child trafficker and worse. He informed me that I was incredibly fortunate to have been located by the American he hired. Otherwise, I might have been sold to an Arab harem and become a eunuch. Anyway, you get the picture. Slowly, my attention was diverted. Once I had access to my inheritance, I thought about trying to find her again. But how do you locate a person you know simply as *Amah* nine years later? A person who has no address or phone on the other side of the planet? Anyway, that life, with a little influence, was permanently erased. I became focused on the future. The past is not a subject I revisit. The door is closed. Well, let's just say I threw the key away a long time ago."

"We hoped you might reconsider oiling the hinge a bit, you know, for the ol' red, white, and blue. Or at least for that trajectory up the military ladder. This just might be the fast track you're looking for."

"Where do we begin? What's the mission?"

"Like I mentioned, you resign your commission … for the time being. We need you back in England for covert ops training and to polish up those language skills. You'll be grilled on the cultural aspects of what you experienced as a child with the Hmong. It's not personal. We need to know everything about the Hmong, particularly how to make friends with them. We need people who can travel easily in and out of Thailand. A diplomatic passport will keep you flexible and untouchable by government agencies. To start, the U.S. government needs accurate strategic positioning, village locations, known identifiable friends and foes. For that, we may use you in a bit of undercover work and make use of that photographic recall of yours. Once they drop their troops in there, there's no turning back. American cadres will ultimately train the indigenous tribes to rescue fallen pilots. That is the mission."

Nigel laid his hand on Lance's arm.

"Before we proceed further, I need an affirmative. I'm afraid you won't get time *to think it over.* There can be no hesitation. We'll throw in a visit to your lovely new wife, either way. I heard you shipped out a week after the wedding?"

"I'm in, sir. And, yes, sir, a visit to see my wife will go a long way to smooth things over before this gets rolling."

"Jolly good! Once we have you in theater, we will send you and a medic to make friends with the first Hmong village. Later, the Americans will have several teams conducting the same mission. The first order of business is to get to know the leader. Identify the needs of the village. We anticipate they'll want arms to fight their enemy, the Pathet Lao, but we don't want to assume. Find out what earns their trust. We need to make the first village a strategic operations center, install radio operations, listen in to action near the border, and identify the players on the international front. The mission will entail covert activities across borders, which, fortunately for our purpose, are not enforced or even policed. However, if anyone is apprehended by the bad blokes, we'll deny any association. Of course, we'll send in our best to rescue any fallen officer, but there's no guarantee. We need to know if the Hmong will help us voluntarily. During the First Indochina War, when most of Laos was still a French protectorate, Hmong villages fought alongside the French.

But we can't be sure of their current loyalties. We need to develop our own relationship. Once this operation has a green light, we'll need friends who know the land. Airplanes will go down, and we need to extract the survivors as quickly as possible. We believe the Hmong will be a great ally. The Pathet Lao are no friends of theirs. It will be your job to communicate our mission and assure our friendship with these people. Once they agree, the Americans will send in the first cadre to train them."

"Is there anything else I need to know?" Lance's eyes did not waver from the Englishman's face.

"From time to time, we'll use you as an operative. You will work with a team on the ground. We need to know all the players on the international front. This mission is highly classified until the Americans show their hand."

Nigel rose from the bench, and after a meaningful glance, walked away and joined the crowd at Waikiki Beach. Lance rolled his jaw in small circles, chewing until the gum in his mouth was soft and transparent.

Chapter Seven

1960

Bangkok, Thailand

Lance braced his left foot against the bench as a rolling progression of wakes stirred by heavy river traffic wobbled the small wooden skiff. The boatman, a local Thai hired for the day, grinned and commanded the small craft in and out of the congested waterway, looking over at his client to see if he should stop here ... or there? Lance scanned and captured the bustling scene into panoramic images with a rapid-fire succession of clicks. He then removed the telephoto lens from the F/4 Nikon camera and set both carefully into a silver case.

Bangkok's floating market bristled with activity, splashed with reds, yellows, oranges, purples, and greens. Locals hawked exotic fruits, vegetables, and fish from just about every angle. Old ladies with wide-brimmed bamboo hats haggled for the freshest of the best. The tourist boats mingled and bumped with the locals, invariably charged two or three times the normal price, which was still dirt cheap.

Lance wiped sweat from his forehead, his white T-shirt already soaked. Damn, it was hot, even at barely nine-thirty in the morning. He woke with the sun and was in the boat by six a.m. The photographs, however, would be sensational. He was quite sure they would sell, and hopefully to one of the better periodicals. In between taking photographs, he took time for a little shopping. Juicy mango, sweet papaya, and a cluster of bananas filled his wicker bag to the brim. He let the boatman negotiate, and he still paid more than the fisherman would have on his own.

He pointed his boatman in the direction of the dock, and the Thai seamlessly maneuvered the small craft back through the crowded waterway to the shore. He added a generous tip, hoping to guarantee the service of such an experienced local, if needed, in the future. Stepping onto the dock and back into the street, he hailed a tuk tuk, the ubiquitous and cheap Thai ground transportation, for a ride back to his guesthouse. He needed a cool shower and a shave.

Once cleaned and refreshed, Lance wandered the streets in search of a meal, eventually heading for the German restaurant and bakery that was favored by ex-patriots. The place was always full of English, French, Americans, and Germans, with a spattering of other nationalities. Breakfast was served twenty-four hours a day, with unparalleled pastries. He entered the restaurant and grabbed a crumpled *International Herald Tribune,* clearly read by at least half a dozen regulars before him. He approached the counter, ordered a coffee, scrambled eggs, and an almond croissant, and then slouched into his preferred seat. The table was situated in the far corner of the café and afforded an unimpeded view of the entrance. He purposefully raised the paper high to discourage unsolicited conversation.

He heard the cough, ahem, and a plop onto the seat across from him. He continued to read the paper, folding it in close and then snapping it open wide. Whoever didn't get the message was an idiot. Five minutes passed with heavy, insistent breathing from the other side of the table.

"What?" Lance lowered the paper to just below his eyes.

"Jimmy ... James Calhoun, you're just the person I was looking for. Go on, read your paper. I'm not in a rush. I'm more than happy to wait until you're done."

Lance sighed and lowered the paper halfway.

"Yes?"

"Now, where's that Southern hospitality I hear so much about? I want to do business with you, my man. My people want to do business with you. Like I said last time we met, it's a very lucrative proposal. All I'm asking is that you hear what they have to say. Just pick the time and I'll take you to them." The speaker was another American, pale-faced, with platinum greased hair that adhered to his scalp like a thin layer of glue.

"Avery, thanks, but no thanks. I have a job—a good one. Go bother someone else." He raised the crumpled newspaper up to screen his face and hopefully end any further conversation.

"All right ... for now. But you know, I have a warm and fuzzy feeling about you, Jimmy. I told my people about you, and they want to meet you. Catch you later."

Known as Jimmy to locals and expats alike, Lance shook his head and attempted to read the paper for several minutes. He swore under his breath, folded the paper, and left it for the next patron. He grabbed the last bite of croissant, dropped some baht on the table, and moved quickly toward the exit.

Outside, he reached into his back pocket for a stick of gum and placed it in his mouth. He stood for a moment outside the restaurant rehashing the recent encounter and wondered if he should be concerned. His mind replayed the time when he first encountered Avery. After several failed attempts, Lance was granted a brief rendezvous with the Hmong military leader, Vang Pao. In the fifties, Vang Pao led the northern Laotian Hmong to fight with the French against the Pathet

Lao. His insight, cooperation, and leadership were considered crucial to the CIA as a fulcrum to unite the diversified Hmong tribes of Laos.

Lance had done his research before the meeting took place. He knew that Vang Pao's growing influence was, in part, due to his command of the country's lucrative opium business. He remembered thinking that engaging the cooperation of a military man immersed in the cultivation of drugs was a land mine sure to explode down the road. *Shit, it's un-American. But hell, who am I? I'm just the lowly messenger. My job is to set up the meeting with Vang Pao and proffer an invitation from the American CIA.*

They met in an outdoor eatery outside the city of Chiang Rai. Lance purchased two bowls of spicy, hot noodles at a local noodle stall and sat down to wait for the Hmong leader. At precisely three p.m., the prearranged meeting time, Vang Pao arrived, flanked by two army officers. Lance immediately stood and extended his hand in the formal Western greeting. The Hmong leader received his hand and waved it loosely. He motioned for Lance to sit down as he took a seat himself. The army officers remained standing on either side of Vang Pao.

Lance offered the bowl of noodles and said in fluent Hmong Daw, "I thought you might appreciate the extra spicy." Vang Pao smiled, without acknowledgement or surprise at the ease in which he spoke a Hmong dialect similar to his own. He accepted the bowl and a pair of chopsticks, slurped the noodles with a grin, and consumed several more mouthfuls before looking up from his bowl. Lance briefly stated the U.S. intelligence community's interest in meeting with him. He supplied a location, date, and contact information for a possible rendezvous.

He remembered the Hmong leader as friendly and surprisingly warm. Van Pao had wanted to know if he had a son and if his family was healthy. While they we spoke, Lance became aware of someone watching them. He felt the riveted, hawk-like attention as clearly as if the man stood an inch behind him and breathed hot air onto his neck. The hawk had pale skin and blond, slicked-back hair and was now unabashedly staring in their direction. He was too far away to hear anything, but the man repeatedly glanced their way with undisguised interest. Lance completed the interview with Vang Pao, all the while keeping the man in his sights. After Vang Pao took his leave, Lance waited and observed the man with the oily hair saunter casually up to his table.

"A fellow ex-patriot lost on the streets of Chiang Rai!" the man said. "I see you have some interesting friends. What brings you to this faraway corner of the world? The name's Avery, by the way. Yours?"

"Jimmy Calhoun," Lance said without extending his hand. "If you will excuse me, I have an important engagement I must attend to. It's a pleasure to meet you."

Lance replayed the scene several times and assessed the risk. *That lowlife has the uncanny knack to show up in out-of-the way places and at the most inconvenient times.* If there was a sycophant, Avery was one. He was harmless on his own, but his associates might not be. He made a mental note to stay clear of the man and focus on the job at hand.

Chapter Eight

1960

El Salvador

Isabela exited the university engaged in animated conversation with her friend Kate. Kate's father had extensive global business interests, and by the age of twenty-two, she had lived on four continents and was fluent in Spanish, French, and Japanese. Isabela, who purposely avoided university socials, took special care to spend time with this self-professed "free spirit." In sharp contrast to Isabela's quiet and secluded life, the young American woman offered a grander view of the greater outside world. She was scheduled to return to America at the end of the semester, and Isabela would miss her crazy, redhaired friend with skin like a porcelain doll.

"¿Tienes tiempo para tomar un café?" *Do you have time for a coffee?*

"Si, porqué, no? Me encantaría!" *Yes, why not? I'd love to!*

The waiter brought them each a café con leche, milk still steaming, with warm buns, butter, and strawberry jam on the side. The two sat outside on the restaurant's patio at a table under a wide green umbrella, whose shade offered protection from the sun's harsh afternoon heat. Kate spoke first.

"When you left the room today, I saw the professor looking at your painting, *Parrots in the Jungle.* I know he gives you a hard time, but I really think he admires your work. In my humble opinion, that's one of your best. The image stays with you. I've watched you mix the washes and the colors, but I always miss something. How did you do it? It's mystical."

"Katya, querida, I've told you. Painting is my escape and allows me to retreat into my own special world. I don't understand the injustice of children growing up on the street with not enough to eat, while others have everything. It's been a dream to learn these techniques and study such incredible artists, the ancients as well as the contemporary ones, but I'll be getting married soon. I hope I'll have time to keep it up."

Kate let out a breath and then slowly began. "There is still a whole year before the wedding. You and Tomás are so young. Why don't you postpone the nuptials? Then you and I can go on a daring adventure!" Kate paused and looked directly at Isabela, who only shook her head and smiled wistfully. Isabela changed the subject.

"What happened with Cristina and you today? She seemed upset."

"Oh, that. She crossed a line one too many times. You know how I am. If anyone betrays my trust, I sever the link."

Isabela reached across the table and placed her hand on Kate's arm. "Whatever it was, I'm sure it wasn't intentional. Cristina loves you."

"That's what she wants everyone to believe. The girl is a snake and only looks out for her own best interests, believe me."

Isabela patted Kate's arm a few times and then withdrew her hand without comment.

"Enough about Cristina. I have news to share!" Kate said. "I discovered a school with this amazing master artist … watercolors. His paintings sell for thousands of dollars. He only takes ten students, but I just know, or to be more honest, I'm hoping, to be one of them."

"Katya, I am so happy for you! Professor Perez loves your watercolors. You are so fortunate. One day, I'd love to study with a master

painter. I wish I knew a few months ago, before the wedding …"
Her voice trailed to a soft reflection.

"Isabela, you told me yourself the date hasn't been set, and the venue is on hold because nobody can agree on the number of guests. This is the perfect … no, the only time!"

"What would I say to Tomás?" Isabela tilted her head to one side and looked into the distance. She paused a moment before giving voice to her thoughts. "Well, Tomás I might persuade … but Mama, never. Katya, go for us both and then come back with your masterpieces. I'll see them through your eyes." She smiled and once again let her hand fall gently on top of her friend's.

"You're sure? We could have the most fabulous adventure!"

"Estoy segura!" *I'm sure.* "It would be like trying to swim the Amazon against the current."

"To be honest, I didn't think you'd agree, but I wanted to suggest it, just in case. I'll be headed back to the States next month to see friends and family. Then off to Thailand."

"What did you say?"

"Thailand. You know, Thai … Land—land of the free, far east Asia? Once Siam? Thailand. That's where he is, the master. Chiang Mai, Thailand."

Isabela steadied her hand on the table, her head suddenly light, nearly dizzy. Her friend continued talking, opening her mouth to form words that made no sound. Isabela felt the bun she had just taken a bite of stick in her throat as a steady vibration hummed inside her head. Kate stopped talking.

"Bela, are you all right?" Kate jumped up and was instantly at Isabela's side, offering a glass of water. Isabela took a sip, pointed to her throat, swallowed hard, and took a second drink.

"Thailand?" Isabela finally managed to pronounce. She leaned on her elbows and began to cry, quietly at first and then more heavily. Her shoulders lightly shook.

"Are you sure you're all right?" Kate repeated. "You gave me such a fright. I thought you were choking! What is your issue with Thailand?"

"How can I explain it? I will go to Thailand."

"What just happened? What do you mean? You just said that it would be impossible for you to go. I'm not following."

"Nothing changed. It's still impossible, but I am meant to go there. I have no idea how I will manage it. If I try to explain it all, even to you, you'll think I'm crazy."

Kate straightened her spine, the knot between her eyebrows softened by a wide grin.

"Well, this is fantastic. My mind is racing. I'll get the information to you as quickly as I can. Do you have a passport? What about Tomás and your mother?"

Chapter Nine

1976

El Salvador

From the moment she took her first step at nine months old, baby Mera Rodríguez was determined to master the mechanics of balance and locomotion. She stumbled, wavered, fell, and pulled herself up to start the whole process again. Within a few days, she had the basics and moved easily around the small farmhouse. It was only a few weeks more before the house became too small for her. Her mother's cry became "¿Dónde está la bebé?" *Where is the baby?*

Invariably, the small toddler escaped to the great outdoors and could be found chasing chickens, butterflies, or whatever inspired her imagination. She hardly ever cried, but cries of indignation reverberated around the house when anyone tried to restrict her movement. By the time she turned twelve, no one could remember a time when Mera didn't run. Late evenings, she returned to the house, face glowing and flushed, from the river or several loops around the maize fields just for the joy of it. Without fail, whenever Maria looked out the window and saw her daughter running, she'd gently lift the gold cross that hung around her neck and kiss it.

"Santo Dios," she whispered. "Protege a esta niña." *Holy God, protect this child.*

On Sundays, the Rodríguez family washed and scrubbed until no trace of the farm's rich red soil was underneath their fingernails or in between their toes. Maria brushed Rosita's hair until it shone inky black and gathered it, knotting underneath the length of hair. She sighed as she bent over Mera's thick head of hair, applying wide brush strokes in an attempt to contain the girl's wild, dark-brown locks into neat and presentable strands. No matter how tightly she held the hair in her hands, stray wisps defied restriction.

Sunday was a holy day. The girls wore white blouses with wide lace trim colorfully embroidered with delicate flowers over the shoulders. The men wore plain bleached white shirts and black trousers. The family walked toward the village four miles away, chattering merrily, like a flock of boisterous parakeets. Mera ran to catch up to David, who was always first out the door. Inevitably, the two ended up lagging behind, easily distracted by an insect, bird, or beautiful flower.

Early morning and late afternoon, there were crops to be tended and numerous other chores. However, in the time in between, on God's special day, farmers joined villagers to congregate in the small chapel to hear Father Guillermo's Sunday mass. On the third Sunday of the month, the women came together to prepare food outside the church, cooking on the coals of a huge bonfire. They gossiped, laughed, rolled out tortillas, peeled vegetables, boiled beans, and made rice. Occasionally, the women sent their sons to chase down some chickens. Young children played down by the creek while the men enjoyed a beer or two, sharing stories of the harvest.

And yet it was on a Sunday that the world turned upside down.

Faint wisps of clouds hovered along the horizon. The sky was a clear and cornflower blue. Marcos, Santiago Rodríguez's eldest son, had remained on the farm to tend the almost-ripe harvest. It was two weeks before Mera's fifteenth birthday, and preparations for her celebratory quinceañera were already in the works.

The last of the villagers straggled into the church as the bell tolled in the chapel. The congregation sat atop hard wooden benches, like birds huddled together on a telephone wire, except the church was stifling hot. Sweat ran down the faces of the men and under the armpits of the women. The pastor, Father Guillermo, leaned in to speak to a young pregnant woman. It was a normal Sunday, and the room was abuzz with the chatter of friends.

A muffled disruption echoed through the church from the entrance. Almost as one, the curious congregation strained to look back. Strategically positioned to fill the only entrance of the sanctuary, six young men, a few still with peach fuzz on their cheeks, intimidated the parishioners with rifles aimed directly into the crowd. One lunged forward to speak. His face was pale, his hair clipped close to his scalp, and there was acne on his chin and forehead.

"Attention! We are here from Fuerza Armada de El Salvador. This is a mandatory recruitment. We are enlisting volunteers! The rebels threaten to overrun our country. Volunteers . . . NOW!" His eyes scanned the room, noting the men and older boys. No one moved. Suddenly, Esther, a plump, grey-haired woman who ran the small grocery store in the village, rose from her seat.

"Carlos, is that you?" she asked. "Don't worry," she spoke to the crowd and then turned back to face the men with guns.

"Carlos, you are frightening the people. Put the guns away!"

The two shots rang out sharp and clear—ping, ping. Esther dropped, falling backward onto the row of seats behind her. The crowd breathed in as one. Carlos turned slowly and looked to his left, where a short adolescent grinned, the tip of his rifle hot to the touch. Carlos jerked and then visibly straightened. Father Guillermo took a step toward the young men, his hand outstretched.

"This is a house of God … please." His voice caught.

"As I was saying," Carlos said, "we need volunteers."

Carlos strolled past the pastor and up the center aisle, his rifle pointing to one man and then another. Mera's father slowly edged closer to the girls and yanked hard on Mera's arm, pulling her down toward the ground. Without a word she fell to her knees, her sister directly behind her. They began to crawl under feet and benches toward the front of the church and the pastor's private room. The people opened their legs or stood to the side, hiding them as best they could. They began to slide on their bellies.

Up above, the young soldiers grew bolder, stepping into the rows of benches and sticking hard metal in between the shoulder blades of several older men. Hands flew up in the air, the universal sign of acquiescence and surrender. The benches began to thin. The boys made their selection, and Santiago and David Rodríguez were among the first chosen.

The "volunteers" were pressed into a tight formation. Stepping into the bright morning, David squinted outside. A shove to his back pressed him forward to join the reluctant recruits. At the periphery, older soldiers surrounded the village. The leader barked a command while the young soldiers prodded their quarry and disappeared into the surrounding jungle like raindrops on parched pavement.

Inside the church, no one moved. Mera was still on her belly when the harrowing and deep, wrenching sobs of women burst the silence. Children scattered in all directions, some running outside. Mera and Rosita slowly rose to stand, frantically searching for their mother. Mera's hair flew free now as she lost the bandanna somewhere in the pews. Her face was streaked with a river of sweat. She pushed through the women, not caring who she knocked out of place, intent on reaching her mother. When she found her, Maria sat in the front pew with her head resting on her ample bosom. Every few minutes, she breathed out a soft, muffled wail. Together, the two girls reached under their mother's arms and strained to lift her upright, but her collapsed body was unresponsive and seemed to weigh one hundred kilos of solid stone. Rosita fired a succession of quick, precise instructions.

"Go home! Get Marcos! Don't take the road. Stay hidden. I'll make sure Mama gets up. We'll wait for you to bring Marcos. GO … NOW!"

There was no way Mera was going anywhere. She refused to look at her sister. Rosita repeated the instructions, speaking each word clearly, as her voice rose to a command.

"Mera, run … NOW!"

Mera shook her head forcefully, intent on staying close to her mother. Rosita grabbed her by the shoulders and shook her until tears ran down both their faces. Rosita wiped her sister's face with the bottom of her skirt.

"We need Marcos. Marcos will know what to do. Run, Mera!"

Mera nodded her head up and down without moving. Rosita squeezed Mera's shoulders hard and then pinched until her sister jumped.

"I'll go."

Mera kissed her mother on the top of her head. Her eyes were slowly drawn to the back of the church, where several women surrounded Esther's lifeless body. Mera suppressed a sob that threatened to overwhelm her. She clutched Rosita's hand and searched her eyes for reassurance. Instead, mirrored back were eyes like those of a frightened animal. Mera abruptly let go of her sister's hand, turned, and bolted down the outside aisle, purposefully avoiding Esther's corpse and the wailing women who surrounded it. Once outside, she began to run without slowing her pace until the familiar rows of maize were in sight. She stopped to gather her breath.

Marcos bent over to assess the health of a young plant and slowly stood back up, his right hand above his eyes to shade the sun. He was used to his sister running, but not on Sunday, not on God's precious day.

He took a few steps while Mera bolted into a sprint. Her breath came sharply, and her incoherent words garbled.

"Espera, Mera, cálmate ..." *Wait, Mera, calm down.*

Mera began to cry. Her eyes were wild and unfocused. For the second time that day, Mera was taken by the shoulders and pushed back and forth, hard.

"What is the matter, hermanita? Please calm down and talk to me. Tell me what happened."

"They are gone ..."

"Who is gone, Mera?"

"Papá and David. All the men. They took them!"

"What?" He shook her in earnest now. "What are you talking about, Mera? You are not making sense. Who is gone?"

Chapter Ten

1960

El Salvador

"¿Papá, estás ocupado?" *Papa, are you busy?*

Pablo Marquez glanced up with a warm smile when he saw his daughter hovering indecisively at the doorway.

"Nothing that I can't put aside until later. Please, come in."

He set down his pen, moved papers to the side, and walked to the couch.

"You know I've missed you these past few years," he said. "Since university, your studies have demanded too much of your time. Ay, everything changes, does it not? My sweet girl is all grown up. But remember, to me, you are always my little princess, twirling and dancing just for the joy of it."

Isabela walked into the room, wrapped her arms around her father, and kissed him lovingly on the cheek.

"I remember that day, Papa. I felt so grown up and beautiful."

"And so you were!"

Isabela approached the bookshelf where her father's pipe, tobacco, and matches lay. She handed them over, and her father began to press tobacco neatly into the bowl of his favorite pipe. He drew quietly until the tobacco glowed. Grey puffs of pungent smoke filled the office with a familiar and pleasant aroma.

The two sat side by side, comfortable within the silence, neither needing to hurry conversation. Pablo leaned back and closed his eyes. His salt-and-pepper hair resided on the sides and back of his head, but the top was noticeably bare and shiny. Isabela took his hand and felt the familiar peace her father always seemed to bring. It had been quite some time since they spent an afternoon in each other's company, so Isabela sank gratefully, happily, into the comfort of his reassuring presence. Once initiated, the conversation grazed easily in the quiet of early evening. Isabela referred to a painting she was working on in school.

"Papa, I have never painted this way. I know I am in school to learn, and I have so much I want to absorb, but when I begin something, there is … an immersion and feeling that only the shadows and nuances of color come close to revealing. It feels as if the professor is instructing me to restrict or conform to an area within the lines. I am left trying to contain a force of nature. My professor singles me out as an example of what not to do. I want to learn. I need good marks, but it is a conflict." Isabela spoke quietly, relating details of her experience at school and the broad spectrum of philosophies she gleaned from fellow students. The embers of her father's pipe brightened and then faded as he puffed on his pipe and listened intently to his daughter.

"Students love to gather and debate, especially politics," she said. "It often gets quite heated. Personally, I favor the Christian Democratic Party. I think they care more for the people. The National Coalition Party speaks thoughtfully enough, but underneath, there's an element of repression. Honestly, neither side is willing to compromise for the benefit of the country and the people."

Pablo observed that Tomás and the wedding were noticeably absent from his daughter's conversation. He leaned forward and took his daughter's hand in his own.

"And why do you think that is?" he asked.

"Opinions and contrasting views," she said. "It seems like they are six sides of the same stone. Each political group invests in their particular representation of what is best for the country ... really, what is best for their own political advancement. All of them ignore what doesn't fit. They will say any lie to get elected, and if they are chosen, the power of office overwhelms and bewitches them. Nothing changes for the poor, no matter who wins."

Pablo shifted in his seat to look more closely at his daughter as he gently released her hand. His thoughts withdrew momentarily inward. *How the years fly by! Our Isabela is not only a beautiful young woman. She is thoughtful and kind.* His eyes softened with his smile.

"When did my beautiful daughter become so wise?"

"Oh, Papa, you always see the best in people." She leaned her head on his shoulder before continuing to speak. "Volunteering at the orphanage has opened my eyes a lot. There is so much poverty. It's not fair."

"You have a big heart, Isabela. That is good. We wouldn't want you to be any other way. But remember, throughout history, there have always been tyrants. And there will always be those who extend a helping hand. In our little corner of the world, we see the worst and best of human nature. It is the same everywhere. Try to live your life without harming others, and it will be a good life. Incidentally, your mother told me you stopped going to the children's center? She is relieved, as am I. I know you love the orphans, but we hope you can find another avenue to help that doesn't expose you to harm in that part of the city."

"Papa, it's not as dangerous as you make it seem. There are many volunteers. We are well looked after. But don't worry. It will be some time before I'll have a chance to get back there." Isabela paused and looked directly at her father. "May I talk to you about something totally unrelated?"

Isabela rubbed her earlobe between her middle finger and thumb, a habit since childhood. Her fingers unconsciously moved up to stretch and massage her left ear. Pablo straightened, noting the subtle shift in his daughter's posture.

"Remember the friend I told you about? The American girl, Katya?" Pablo nodded.

"We have several classes together. She challenges the professors and brings up elements I've never even considered. She has our esteemed faculty backpedaling more often than not! We've become good friends. I've wanted to invite her to the ranch, but because we're so far out of town, it never worked out. I know you'd like her."

"Well, then, we will have to arrange a dinner in town. I am always interested to meet bright young minds. You are our hope for the future."

"Well, that's just the thing, Papa. She is leaving soon." Isabela's face was lightly flushed as she continued. "She is going to study in Asia with a master painter."

Isabela paused and looked directly in her father's eyes. He puffed on his pipe, completely present.

"I want to go with her. For a year."

It was hard to surprise Pablo, who easily navigated conversation with awareness and foresight. He noticed the set of his daughter's jaw and her clear, direct gaze. He didn't need her to repeat her request. She was absolutely serious, so he said the first thought that came to his mind.

"What of the wedding?"

"Ay, I haven't had time to consider it. Papa, I need your support. I'm sorry. I know this is asking a lot. It's not an easy thing to explain, but I am convinced that if I make this trip, I will finally find some peace. I need to go to Thailand. The answers are there. I've spoken to the university, and I can receive credit for the classes I take while there, so graduation would only be delayed one semester. I suppose I will have to ask Tomás to postpone the wedding. I hope he will understand."

Pablo stared out the window. He heard, precisely, his daughter's words and was unaccountably alarmed. Had his daughter felt distressed her entire life?

"Pablo, this is entirely unacceptable. We simply cannot allow Isabela to go. I have a wedding to plan! How do you imagine I would be able to do that with Isabela halfway across the world? What will the Chavezes think? I will simply not tolerate this crazy idea. Everyone knows about the engagement. No, no, I absolutely forbid it! I know the wedding date has not been finalized, but I am quite close to having the guest list completed. I have calls out to vendors and a thousand and one details to consider. Absolutely, no! What are you thinking to encourage her in this insanity? We have perfectly good art teachers here in El Salvador."

Isabela's mother, Ivanna, paced the room. She stopped directly in front of Pablo and pointed her finger at the middle of his chest. She paused, took a breath and continued.

"Yes, I realize Isabela can be quite determined. We will have to come up with an interesting distraction. We'll take a trip up the coast. All of us can go … No, she wants to study art. Yes, I have it. We can all visit the mountains. I think I've heard of some kind art school. It will be difficult for me to plan the wedding from up there, but I will manage. Perhaps we might ask your brother, Jorge, to coordinate the details? Better yet, a short trip to Paris. Isabela always dreamed of visiting Paris."

Pablo Marquez pushed his chair away from the table and quietly walked out the door. Ivanna glanced at his retreating figure as she considered her options and the difficulties each presented.

"Your mother will need some reassurance, mija."

Pablo sat next to his daughter on the veranda as both sipped cups of steaming café con leche. Pablo Marquez was in familiar territory: negotiations. And he was a master.

A tree needs to be flexible. Too stiff and the branches crack with the first harsh wind; too weak and it cannot stand on its own.

He felt that he could not deny her this trip. He wished he could take her in his arms and make everything all right, but he realized she was no longer his little girl. She lived in a universe of her own. She was a young woman now who needed room to explore and find resolution and peace for whatever had disturbed her.

"I promise to call home as much as you need."

"I have contacted the consulate in Thailand and called in a few favors. They have assured me that you will be well looked after. I can only begin to convince your mother if you agree to these terms."

Isabela jumped from her chair onto her father's lap, kissing him first on the left cheek, right cheek, forehead, and chin.

"Papá, gracias! Te amo, Papá." *Papa, thank you! I love you, Papa.*

Chapter Eleven

1960

Bangkok, Thailand

The air-stairs at Don Mueang International Airport, Bangkok descended into an overwhelming heat. A torrid blast greeted passengers and crewmembers alike. The two women waited their turn to disembark amid the crowd of international travelers. Isabela grasped the handrail with her right hand, steadying herself while balancing the blue-and-white tote bag on her left shoulder. Carefully, she descended the metal steps onto the tarmac and turned to look back at the Pan American 707, where a stewardess in a blue pillbox hat waved goodbye to the descending passengers.

Suddenly, an eerie premonition squeezed her like a vise, and she felt a cold urgency that called her to return, to find her seat on the plane, and fly safely back to El Salvador. Back home to a secure, peaceful future with Tomás, her family, and the country she knew so well. A light nausea swelled her stomach into a solid, knotted mass. Here was the axis, the crossing point. The two lines intersected for a brief moment, and then each catapulted through space in polar opposite directions. She stopped and took a deep breath. Kate, with smeared makeup and wrinkled clothing, passed her bag from her left hand to her right and then back again, shifting her weight from one foot to the other.

"Bela, are you okay?"

Isabela hesitated for only a moment. "I am better than good. Let's go!"

The two young women merged into the swarming crowd of passengers that wound slowly toward immigrations and customs.

Chapter Twelve

1960

Chiang Mai, Thailand

The Chiang Mai Sunday evening market bristled with activity as Lance entered Tha Pae Gate to weave in and out of children, bicycles, and vendors. He waited until the crowd dispersed to snap a quick succession of photos and then continued deeper into the crowd. His blond hair was pulled back in a short ponytail, and although dark sunglasses entirely hid his eyes, there was no mistaking his nationality. He was dressed in a pair of faded blue jeans and white T-shirt, damp with perspiration. A Nikon camera with a telephoto lens dangled around his neck.

An old Thai seller peddling an array of colorful paper lanterns motioned him closer. Lance approached, held up his camera, and pointed from the camera to her. She responded by holding up a hand-painted red lantern with a green-and-black dragon spewing golden fire from its mouth. He nodded and held out more than the required baht, leaving the lantern where it was. The old lady smiled, exposing a mouth with only four teeth and crinkling her cheeks into an intricate matrix of lines. She was now entirely framed by splashes of red, green, blue, and yellow lanterns. A rapid fire of clicks angled from left and right, after which Lance nodded and smiled.

He turned to leave, the camera once again hung across his chest, when a bony finger tapped him on the shoulder and pointed to where the red lantern had, moments before, been set on top of a display of small trinkets. Instead, the brightly painted piece was held at arm's length and studied with obvious appreciation by an attractive young woman. Light beads of sweat lined her brow.

He had the photos he'd come for, yet something about the young woman made him turn for a second look. She was slender with thick dark hair that fell loosely down the middle of her back. Her skin glistened. Her posture was beautifully aligned. A cream-colored linen dress conformed easily to her body. He paused, magnetized almost, with his eyes drawn to the woman.

Apparently, she did not have the same effect upon the Thai seller, who grabbed the lantern from the younger woman, admonishing her in rapid Thai. The seller then shoved the lantern toward Lance, who was just regaining his equilibrium and his manners. The seller reached back among the shelves to extract another lantern, this one painted with planets and stars, and displayed it to the young woman, who murmured politely, "No, thank you," and turned to leave. Lance shook his head once, as if trying to remember a dream that slipped like sand through splayed fingers.

"Miss?" He tapped her lightly on the back. She stopped and slowly turned around.

"Sí?"

She spoke in accented English, choosing her words carefully, yet with a pronunciation that was clear and bright. Lance held out the lantern in dispute.

"I believe you were interested in this lantern? I'd be most honored if you would take it. I was just lookin' to take some photographs of the seller. I bought the lantern, you see, to get the photographs. I am quite willing to part with it."

He spoke slowly, enunciating a Southern drawl, watching closely to see if she understood his English. He placed her somewhere from South America from the few words she spoke. She was young, about twenty years old, and from the look of her attire and overall appearance, she came from an aristocratic family. What he couldn't decide, finally, was what a young woman with such obvious good manners and breeding was doing here, alone, in Thailand. Then she smiled, her lips softly opening. Reaching into her purse, she extracted several colorful bills, Thai baht. She extended her hand and offered the money.

"If you will allow me, I'd like to buy the lantern from you." She handed the money to him, but he shook his head.

"Have a cup of tea with me and the lantern is yours. Ah, I forget myself," he said, extending his hand, "James Frank Calhoun from Charleston, South Carolina. Everyone just calls me Jimmy. I can't quite break 'em of it." He smiled.

Isabela looked at him but didn't take his hand.

"I am sorry, I cannot take tea. It is a pleasure to meet you, Mr. Calhoun. Por favor." Her hand extended the money a few inches more toward the man. "I cannot take the lantern without paying for it."

He sighed and reached toward her hand, his fingers lightly brushing her skin. Seconds passed. The colorful Sunday bazaar was suddenly reduced to a background watercolor landscape.

"You crush a gentleman's heart, señorita," he said. "Please take my card, if you ever happen to need a photographer extraordinaire."

Isabela took the card, quickly scanning the inscribed letters, and then placed it in her purse. "Thank you, Señor Calhoun."

She turned and tucked the red lantern under her arm but did not look back. Lance, however, watched until the young woman disappeared into the Sunday afternoon crowd. When she was finally out of sight, he slowly exhaled, a sudden heaviness pressing into the center of his chest. He forced his breathing to resume its normal pattern and was not quite able to shake a strange feeling that his life was a lie.

"Focus on the business at hand," he mumbled to no one in particular.

Lance sat across from the freelance agent, Dennis Nadeau, in the ten-seat Thai restaurant, tucked down a narrow alley off Chang Khlan Road. His leather portfolio lay on top of a thick wooden table, open wide.

"It looks like you've done it again, Mr. Calhoun. Last year, I submitted your photos of the elephant and its trainer to *National Geographic's* editorial staff. Honestly, I didn't think you had a chance in hell to get picked up by one of the world's finest publications. But it was that incredible photo of the temple with its fluttering prayer flags on the mountainside that sold them. This time, they know your name. While it may be a while before they print another article on Thailand, I think these will sell." He flipped decisively through the portfolio. "Your photo of the elephant bathing in the waterhole is sensational, but the one of the old Thai woman with her lanterns might just be a cover piece down the road. We'll see if we can get a story linking the two. How about that? I can't promise anything, of course, but I've been scouting photographs for twenty-five years, and I know what sells. I'd like to come by your hotel tomorrow afternoon and have you fill out some paperwork. I think the magazine is going to be very excited about what you have here."

"Unfortunate timing," Lance said. "I have to leave town early tomorrow. I'll tell you what. Go ahead and keep the copies. The hotel receives my mail. If the magazine can use the photos, tell them to go ahead. We'll settle up on my return. I'll sign a waiver saying they have permission to use whatever they want."

Chapter Thirteen

1960

Thai-Laotian Border

Lance lay on his belly and peered through a pair of high-powered binoculars across the Mekong River into Laos. His face was camouflaged with a thick stripe of black paint across his nose and forehead and green smeared across his cheekbones, chin, and neck. A pair of khaki pants and an olive, long-sleeved T-shirt also helped to merge his large frame with the colors of the landscape. A small village nestled on the hillside just across the water. Houses with bamboo walls and roofs of nipa palm were set in rough circular groupings with pigs, chickens, and small, naked children running freely amongst them.

Miles, the medic, was tucked inside a large cavern several kilometers away. His ivory-white skin glistened with sweat. There was not an ounce of fat on his muscular body. He sat on his haunches, slowly turning the knob on the radio to scan bandwidths. He heard a series of squawks and whistles and static followed by a low-to-high screech. Suddenly, a voice pierced the cave in sharp contrast to the undifferentiated radio noise.

Lance stayed low to the earth and inched back the way he came. As he moved, he recognized a slight rustling immediately before him, and he froze. Then a pair of brown feet clad in simple rubber sandals became visible through the tall grass. He held his breath. An adolescent boy cleared thick brush with a long, sharpened stick. Lance let out his breath as quietly as he was able and peeked out through the tall grass that hid him. He willed his turbulent thoughts to slow.

It's just a boy, and a young kid can't pose much of a threat. Still, it's unknown where he comes from. Does he come from the village across the river? If so, this could be a decisive encounter. If not, I risk exposing our presence to unknown entities.

Lance decided to stay under the natural cover and observe as the boy continued moving forward toward him. He lowered his head, attempting to blend in with the grass, slowly edged his chin up from the ground, and stole a glance. The boy was skinny, measuring just a little over one meter. He wore a pair of baggy, light-green pants and no shirt. His black hair was closely cropped. The boy lowered himself on the ground, curious as to the animal that moved the grasses. Carefully, he inched himself forward and, in a matter of moments, found himself directly opposite a green-and-black-striped giant. There was a sharp intake of breath as the boy recognized not an animal but a human. Quickly, he squirmed himself backward.

Fuck! No choice now!

Lance slowly reached into his pocket. He extracted his last stick of gum and extended his hand. The boy froze and looked as if he might cry. He was rigid, trembling like a rabbit aware of imminent danger. Lance began speaking in a soft Hmong Daw. The boy looked confused, but slightly calmer. He raised his head slowly from his prone position and studied the giant man with the paint-streaked face.

"Are you a spirit from the ancestors?" the boy asked in Mong Njua, a dialect similar to Hmong Daw.

Lance took gum from behind his ear, popped it into his mouth, and chewed. He unwrapped the stick of gum withdrawn from his shirt pocket and pointed to his mouth, indicating to the boy to put it on his tongue. The boy inserted the piece of gum into his mouth and then slowly grinned, exposing a wide smile and white teeth, the prominent incisors crowding the others in front. The boy reached out to touch Lance's hair, curiosity now stronger than his fear, and inched back a little. Lance smiled and patted the ground before he spoke. "Where is your village?"

The boy rolled onto his side to point back across the river. Lance remained quiet as his mind raced.

Hot damn! We have contact!

Lance's attention did not leave the boy. He nodded a few times to the south, indicating from where he came, reached into his pocket, and offered the boy a small pocketknife. "A gift. I will be here tomorrow." He pointed to the earth and to the position in the sky where the sun would be when he returned. "I am a friend."

Lance smiled again before slowly backing up. He waited to stand until his new friend was out of sight of the opposite riverbank, then walked across the grassy field toward the cave. The boy stood and watched the tall stranger disappear beyond the palm fronds. Only then did the boy stand and scamper down the riverbank.

A small wooden canoe was hidden in the bushes. He pulled it out and jumped in, paddling as fast as he was able across the churning dark waters.

Lance ducked and pressed aside the foliage that acted as a natural camouflage to the cave's entrance. From even a short distance away, the entrance to the cave appeared to be just more jungle and vines.

"Bloody hell, about time you showed up." Miles removed his headset off and handed it to Lance. He spoke in a clear, clipped English. The medic bent his head to avoid hitting the ceiling of the cave. His eyes were a very pale blue, and his hair was a curly eggshell white.

"Here, have a listen. I picked up a radio transmission. It's some kind of Chinese." Lance lowered himself to the ground and squatted next to Miles, cocked his head to the side, and nodded once.

"Mandarin."

The following evening, Lance and Miles were again deep inside the cave, preparing rations to eat. A small fire emitted minimal heat, just a little more than embers, on top of which simmered a pot of black beans and rice. Miles chewed on a dried strip of beef jerky, while Lance leaned against the cave wall.

"What do you make of it? The Chinese, I mean." Miles glanced at the radio hidden under a tarp as he spoke.

Lance poked the dying embers of the small campfire with a stick, making room for a few more pieces of wood. Several minutes passed before he responded, his thoughts returning to his pre-mission briefing.

"It appears the Chinese are also backing the Pathet Lao, and that little Laotian communist organization works very closely with the North Vietnamese. With both groups backed by Mao's army, the Hmong villagers across the river don't stand a chance on their own. It's bad news for the Hmong and any other peace-loving people.

But for our purpose? It's quite auspicious. Shit, help from the Big Brother across the sea!"

Lance continued to rake the embers of the small fire that emitted the only light in the otherwise darkened cave. Miles bit off another piece of beef jerky before standing. Outside, a quiet rustling echoed at the entrance to the cave. Both men, fully alert, reached for their weapons.

Miles whispered, "What kind of animals did you say live in this jungle?"

Chapter Fourteen

1976

El Salvador

"I need you to stay here!" Marcos held Mera by the shoulders.

"No! Don't leave me alone! I want to go back with you to help Mama."

"I warned Papa! Why didn't he listen?" Marcos swore under his breath and then looked his youngest sister directly in the eyes. "You'll be more trouble than help. Do you understand?"

Marcos yanked Mera's arm toward the farmhouse, kicked open the door, and forcefully pulled her toward the bodega. "You need to hide here!" he said. "I'll send Mama and Rosita back. We'll decide what to do when we're all together."

Mera bobbed her head up and down obediently, but once again, her body remained rigid. Marcos clenched his jaw as his eyes narrowed. He pushed her into the bodega and said, "Stay here! Do not leave this closet!" He shut the door firmly. Mera fell two steps backward and stumbled, knocking a five-pound sack of cornmeal onto the floor. A cloud of yellow-orange dust filled the food closet. She coughed, straining until she could no longer hear the crunch of her brother's footsteps on the dirt pathway outside.

Mera slid down the side of the wall to sit with her arms hugging her knees. Her every sense was on high alert. She heard a light scurry across the floor and felt a quick dusting at the bottom of her foot. She pulled her foot in closer but wasn't alarmed. Small rodents often came in looking for food. After several hours with her body in a tight, cramped position, her back began to ache. She stretched her legs out in front of her. Slowly, she scrunched her toes, then straightened them, finally making abstract shapes on the floor over and over again. She willed herself to stop and began to knot a tress of hair between her fingers, toying and pulling, releasing it, just to braid it again. Time seemed without dimension. It was impossible to tell if she had been there an hour or for five. *Marcos must be coming soon!* Her head bobbed, dropped onto her chest, and shot back up again, three times, then four. Finally, her head, heavy, swayed down to rest on her chest.

With a jolt, her head flew up from a semi-conscious sleep as she strained to remember—ping, ping. Images flashed sharp and clear across the screen of her mind of Esther, her mother's friend, first pressing a sweet into her hand and then falling forward as a stain of red broadened across her white blouse. Mera's heart began to pound. She pushed herself up to stand and heard whispers of conversation in the distance. Slowly, she pushed the door open a small crack, only far enough to assess conditions. Particles of dust swirled on the waning sunbeams of late afternoon. She edged the door until it opened fully and banged against the wall. Mera crawled like a toddler across to the cooking area to peek out the front window. She strained, ready to bolt in the direction of her brother and mother once verified, and pulled back quickly from the window.

The men emerging from the forest on the other side of the maize fields had guns. Imperceptible heartbeats now grew to giant thumps pounding like an ocean wave. She scrambled to the back of the house and opened the rear window wide enough to crawl through and quietly closed it behind her. Once outside, she dropped onto all fours and crawled across the small field, taking care to keep hidden and out of sight from the fast-approaching threat. When she reached the storage shed, she stood, bent low, and ran into the dense jungle that bordered their home.

It was a constant battle to keep the jungle from reclaiming the farm. Vines and roots wound deep into the earth. Troupes of spider monkeys, and even the large, reclusive mantled howlers, shared the space. Daily, the spider monkeys crisscrossed the route. Often, mothers carried tiny babies on their backs, and adults and youngsters swung from tree branch to trunk. You could set the time of day by their comings and goings. They were mischievous and artful thieves. Any food left unattended was swiftly snatched, only to be seen a moment later high up in a tree. Maria often threatened the intruders with a broom. The small thieves would retreat quickly to a nearby tree to merely bide their time until Maria moved away from the kitchen, busy with other tasks. Then, quicker than a ruby-breasted hummingbird diving to impress his mate, the rascals would swoop down to steal the prize. Mera, however, was enchanted and often waited outside to watch the parade cross from east to west. She spoke to them in soft tones, and, if lucky, a young one might scamper down a tree branch to check her out.

Snakes and spiders were common houseguests. Mera's daily chore was to check all the corners of the cottage for the poisonous ones. She knew how to capture a spider and release it away from the house. She would gently edge the spider into a container and bring it to the edge of the rainforest to set it free. For the poisonous snakes she called one of her brothers, and they inevitably killed the snake. She knew their venom was deadly, but even so, she felt sorry to kill the beautiful creatures that slithered so close to the earth.

Mera hid at the jungle's edge, where she could see her home in between large palm fronds. The air was humid and thick with bugs, and after only a short while, her legs became covered in small red welts. She crouched, occasionally sliding her hand down to scratch at her leg, but otherwise kept absolutely still. The men moved in and out of the house, with sacks of flour and bags of food hoisted on their shoulders or slung under their arms. She was grateful there was no sign of her family's return. Mera kept her eyes on two men who walked behind the house closer to her hiding place. Instinctively, she crouched lower.

"Get the men. We are heading out," the apparent leader yelled.

"The men ... we need to keep the men happy, Dino," a short one with oily black hair challenged. "There must be women who live here. They're probably hiding nearby."

Mera's attention constricted, focused now solely on the man named Dino. On his left bicep spiraled a two-toned tattoo, twin serpents separated at the elbow to rejoin at the shoulder. Mera's gaze fixated on the black and red serpents, their image etched into her brain.

Dino aimed his rifle just to the left of the short man's foot. A loud bang burst forth as the short one flew back against the side of the cottage.

"I said we are leaving ... now! Vamanos!" *Let's go!*

The short one straightened and shifted from left foot to right to regain his equilibrium. He dusted himself off as he murmured, "Lo que digas, jefe." *Whatever you say, boss.* He called over his shoulder, "Vamanos."

Grumblings and curses sounded from the men as they reassembled and headed back down the dirt road, a bulbous unit toting the rich bounty from the farmhouse. Mera waited a long time after the men disappeared, their voices no longer audible, before she emerged from her hiding place. She reentered the cottage the same way she left, by opening the window in the back. She couldn't say why, but she was hesitant to enter through the front door. Inside was in shambles. Wooden chairs were overturned, and the bodega was ransacked of all food items the family had worked diligently to plant, harvest, and store. Mera crawled into a corner and hugged her knees in close to her chest as the sun crept toward the horizon, the remnants of an aqua-and-pink sky consumed and recolored by the dark grey of advancing night. Sleep took a long time to come.

When the first light of dawn peeked through the window, Mera opened her eyes. Her body was stiff from her hunched position in the corner. The crowing of the rooster was eerily absent. She stepped outside and gazed to the north, south, and as far to the west as the eye could see. All was quiet, still. She ran to the back and pumped the small well, filled a jug with water, lifted the container to her lips, and allowed the water to splash onto her cotton blouse. Her hair was a maze of knots and tangles, with interwoven pieces of jungle leaves.

Pressing her feet into her sandals, Mera left the farmhouse at a slow trot until she passed the neat rows of maize and then broke into a fast run back toward the village. She stayed off the main road, well concealed behind trees and forest growth. It was slow going. Her long-legged gallop was not always possible as logs, debris, and hanging vines impeded her passage. Still, she reached the village before the sun fully rose, yet the early morning was already hot and sticky. A dog barked twice and then was quieted. The street was empty of the usual early-morning traffic and people beginning their day. Mera kept her eye on the church, but did not approach. Instead, she sat at the edge of the forest and watched, waiting. Finally, as the sun rose high, the door to the church creaked slowly open, and Father Guillermo stepped outside, squinting in the now-bright sun.

The padre was of average height but his body thin. He had snowy-white hair cropped in a straight line across his forehead. On Sundays, his warm brown eyes enfolded his flock from the pulpit. Mera bolted from her hiding spot to race across the square and jump into the startled pastor's arms. Father Guillermo scanned the area in front of the church, holding the girl with his left arm. He pushed the church door open with his right hand, and both disappeared within. Once inside, she cried out.

"¿Dónde está mi mamá?" *Where is my mother?*

"Mi hija, lo siento! Lo siento muchisimo!" *My child, I am sorry! I am so very sorry!* He stared at the floor and slowly shook his head.

Mera's eyes swept the church for a sign of her mother. Slowly, she forced her attention back, and her eyes drew to the large swelling on the side of the padre's head and the black-and-blue halo around his left eye.

"¿Dónde está mi madre? Por favor, padre!" *Where is my mother? Please, Father!*

Father Guillermo raised his eyes past the girl across the empty rows of benches. He stared blankly at the back of the church. His voice barely above a whisper, he said, "I'm afraid it's too late. There's nothing more to do. Your mother is gone."

Mera watched the padre's lips move. She leaned in closer, straining to hear, but it seemed as if he whispered in some foreign language.

"Those men, some of them were just boys. The one from San Salvador is so young. Maria tried to protect Rosita. That's what they told me. She did not suffer. You must have faith. Find peace in that."

Father Guillermo continued speaking, but his words were hushed and slurred. Mera grabbed him by the arm and squeezed it.

"I don't understand you! Where is Mama?"

Father Guillermo continued his self-interrogation, barely cognizant of the girl attached to his arm like a wild dog refusing to loosen its bite.

"I've known young Alberto since he was a baby, like all of the children." The pastor shook his head and closed his eyes. "Marcos and a few other young men, the few who weren't in church when the first boys came, were strongly encouraged to join the rebels against the government-sanctioned locals. Your brother Marcos volunteered, I'm sure, to look for your father and young David. He told Rosita to take your mother home. He wanted all of you to wait for him at the farm. He said he would be back soon. But I don't know. I don't know." The pastor rubbed the crucifix around his neck with his fingers.

Once again, the padre's attention drifted past the girl into empty space, appearing to plead with a phantom congregation. "How was I to know they would come back? Why did they come back? The women looked for reassurance. I got on my knees with the mothers and grandmothers, and our prayers rang out. One woman began to sing. One by one, the others joined her until the whole sanctuary resounded with the people's soulful, haunting lament. It is something I will never forget. But that is just when the boy soldiers came back for the second time. I should have taken them all away. Why didn't I hide everyone in the forest? They took Rosita and two others. Three young women from our peaceful village are now gone! I am a man of peace, a man of nonviolence. The Lord tells us to love all our brothers and sisters, and I have taken a vow. I cannot raise my hand against my fellow human beings, no matter how vile they become. I invoked the Lord's name, and in his name, I stood in front of the women to protect them with my body and with my prayers. That is the last I remember. When I regained consciousness, they were already gone."

He looked up to the sky and began to pray, continuing to rub the crucifix around his neck. He let the crucifix drop before continuing. "Mija, listen! I just remembered. It happened a long time ago, so I don't know. Let's see if it can be of use. Follow me, please."

Father Guillermo shook his head and then moved towards his private room. Mera remained in the sanctuary, sweeping her eyes up and down the aisles. Her chest pounded. When the pastor realized the girl did not follow, he took a step backward to grab her hand and pull her into the room where he slept and conducted all his affairs.

A large wooden crucifix hung on the whitewashed wall above a handmade teak table holding a Bible, the thin pages worn and yellowed with use. A thin mattress covered with a blue woven blanket was positioned in the far corner, directly on the plain wood floor. Three metal shelves were attached directly to the side wall. On the top shelf, a painting of Mother Mary holding the bleeding Jesus in her lap was framed in gilded gold. The remaining two shelves were filled with hardcover books with titles printed in gold or black.

Mera remained in the doorway where the padre had dropped her hand, with her eyes downcast. Father Guillermo moved several volumes to the side. He stretched up onto his toes and peered behind the books until his fingers grasped a rectangular metal box with a brass latch and small lock. He took the box and set it on the table. The girl was breathing hard and did not look up until she heard a sharp crack as the pastor wedged the lock open.

"I lost the key a while ago, but haven't needed to open it," he said, more to himself than the girl.

Mera stared at the padre and opened her mouth as if to speak, but no sound emerged.

"Mija, listen carefully. A long time ago, a strange man, a foreign man, came into the church and gave me this."

He rummaged through the contents of the metal box, through papers of various sizes and a stack of colorful Salvadoran colones bound with string, along with several small objects all crowded together.

"Ah, here it is." He held out a small card, yellowed with age, with raised black letters and numbers written across the front. On the back was a notation in ink with a handwritten number. "This distinguished gentleman came to me when you were very small."

Mera regarded the padre's outstretched hand as if it were a bug to sweep away.

"You were just a baby, understand? He came into the church wanting to speak to me. He asked me if I knew the Rodríguez girl. I said, 'Of course. I know all the children in this village, but there are two Rodríguez girls. Which one do you mean?' The man replied, 'The youngest. The baby.' At the time, I wondered why this foreign, well-educated man would want to know about a farmer's baby girl, but he waved away my question and then added something quite peculiar. 'Please have the child contact the number on the back of this card if there's anything she might need.' He was out the door before I could ask him anything more. You were barely three years old, at the time. I didn't want to bother the family with this strange incident. I put the card in the box, and even though I wondered about it from time to time, I didn't want to cause worry for your family. Your family is such a good family …" His voice trailed to almost a whisper. "Please, child, take the card. It may be helpful."

He placed it in the palm of Mera's hand, and she dropped it immediately as if it burned her skin. The small card fluttered to the floor. All of a sudden, her body lurched forward.

"I want to see Mama."

She stared now at Father Guillermo, who only shook his head.

"Mija, no, por favor, your mother is gone. Think of her. Remember the good. We will bury her, bury all three of them, and then go to the gravesite and say goodbye." The pastor retrieved the small card from the floor and once again pressed it into her palm. "Find this man. Perhaps he can help, mija. I know it's been a long time, but at least it is something."

She threw the card as hard as she was able, turned her back, and quickly moved out of the pastor's small room, down the aisle, and out the door of the church. Father Guillermo made no attempt to stop her. Once outside, she stepped hesitantly as if crossing a field with a thousand shards of broken glass. A few villagers gathered around the back of the church, where an old man leaned on a shovel. Flies buzzed black like a tornado. The droning was all around her now. It overwhelmed the birdsong and the quiet whispers of the villagers with its incessant, persistent buzz.

The three bodies were laid neatly in a row, all covered in woven blankets of bright red, with green and yellow stripes. The old villager who leaned against his shovel gently set his tool aside when he saw the girl. He quietly approached her and took her by the hand, kneeling beside the middle blanket. Their hands were stretched to the maximum as the man knelt and Mera stood straight. The old villager looked up at her. His brows raised, eyes open wide. Reluctantly, she nodded, and he pulled the blanket back from the body. Her mother's face was peaceful, serene, as if she was merely asleep. Thin black plaits lay across her breast, and the beautifully etched lines across her cheek and forehead seemed achingly lifelike in the still moment of death. Mera fell on her mother's inert body, and a haunting, strident wail pierced the quiet afternoon.

"Despiertas, Mamá! No me dejes! Te quiero!" *Wake up, Mama! Don't leave me! I love you!*

The girl continued to shake her mother's corpse as warm tears fell. The villagers left the girl alone, keeping a respectable distance. It was the old healer woman, Analena, who separated the distraught child from the body. She came to stand on the side of her and gently pulled the girl to her feet. Mera took a few steps forward, but her head still turned, looking back. The old woman whispered in her ear, but all she could hear was the incessant, resounding buzz inside her head and deep within her chest.

The three bodies were buried late in the afternoon. Villagers slowly emerged from their homes, braving the great outdoors to attend a simple service. Everyone cried. Although only three died, everyone had lost someone and could not be assured of their return.

Analena lay a blanket around the girl's shoulders and guided her to the edge of the village. Analena's waist-long yellow-grey hair was plaited and rolled into buns that looked like small roses. Her face was light brown and etched with deep crevices. No one knew how old she might be. It was said that she was pure Nahua Pipil. She appeared in the village one day as a younger woman and began to build a dwelling with her bare hands. The villagers, seeing her tireless endeavor, provided wood and building supplies and then helped her complete the construction of her dwelling. She rarely spoke, but people immediately recognized her as a healer. They came to her for swelling feet, back pain, and heartache. Analena knew every plant and herb indigenous to the region. There was no clinic within many miles of the village, so people paid her as they could, sometimes with a piglet, eggs, or vegetables from a garden. Often, the gifts she received were shared with those most in need. However, if you came to her with a frivolous matter, she always knew. She would simply sit and stare into space, ignoring the petitioner as if he had no more substance than a gnat or a fly. Inevitably, he would grow restless and back out of the room, later complaining about the crazy, old woman who lived in the village.

Analena guided Mera into her small cabin at the edge of the rainforest, just outside the village perimeter. She motioned for her to lie down on a bamboo mat. Analena's deep brown eyes were turned inward, as if the day's events were merely a reflection. Her eyes rested slightly above and to the right of the girl. Several village women entered. Mera felt wisps of sound floating around her. Words were indistinguishable from the cries and whispers of the women and accompanied by the strange buzzing that resonated all around and inside her.

"Poor child, what can we do?" the women lamented.

The sun set when Analena gestured the women toward the door. They rose obediently, muttering vague objections that they would return. She closed the door firmly after the last one departed and lit candles and herbs around the cottage. A sweet aroma now pervaded the room. Wooden shelves lined the walls of the small dwelling, on top of which were containers with a multitude of dried plants, sticks that looked like common tree branches, and dried leaves and flowers with yellow, orange, or purple petals. Along the ceiling, plants of all shapes and sizes hung upside down. Analena lit the small stove in the corner with a match. She poured water from a jug and reached up to snap herbs from the line hanging from above.

She placed the dried herbs and roots in water over a low heat, stirring constantly with a wooden spoon. The herbs simmered on the stove for an hour and eventually bubbled into a thickened, viscous liquid. Analena drained the herbs, poured the remainder into a tin cup, and brought it to Mera. She guided the girl's head up and quietly placed a spoonful of hot liquid into the girl's trembling mouth. Mera managed to swallow several spoonfuls before dropping her head heavily back onto the mat. Analena spoke quietly in her native tongue. Her words were shaped with tones and sounds aligned with the rhythms of nature.

Mera was falling. Her body felt transparent, weightless, dropping through the mat into a universe of planets, suns, insects, animals, and sound. She tried to hold onto something, anything. But as soon as she grasped for an object and felt its solid edges, it immediately disintegrated. She fell deeper and more assuredly into an inky abyss below. Bugs crawled into her eyes and ears. A rat gnawed her belly, separating flesh from the bone as dark red juice splattered its whiskers. She tried to scream, but no sound emitted. Suddenly, her eyes flew open.

Her mouth formed a silent word: "Ayúdame!" *Help me!*

A hinge squeaked, moaned, and amplified beyond limit. Mera's hands flew to cover her ears. Deep inside her belly, she felt a stirring as a river of golden energy began to rise up her back. A giant serpent's eyes now merged with her own. Her perception expanded, warm and loving. What was discordant and foreign began to soften. Converged, the eyes probed and explored. Sound reverberated. Light burst forth. Slowly, the scenes of the afternoon replayed in vibrant Technicolor and flashed and shimmered, bathed in benevolent sweet honey love. She remained untouched, even as insects devoured the cells of her body.

The sun rose, and the cabin was bright when Mera first opened her eyes. She was enveloped in a radiant warmth that emanated from the center of her being. She almost nodded off to sleep again. The front door squeaked as Analena entered, carrying a sack of freshly cut vegetables and herbs. Mera stretched and shook her head to focus her attention. Holographic, horrific scenes began to overwhelm her thoughts, yet the warm feeling in her belly remained. She felt strangely calm and at peace. Slowly, she pushed herself into a sitting position and watched the diminutive, old lady with the strangely straight posture begin to dice and prepare the plants.

Analena, intent on her task, pinched, chopped, and hung the herbs to dry. Mera pressed herself up slowly to stand and stepped toward the wooden table covered in an array of dried plants and flora. Analena pointed to a few dried pieces of bark and then indicated her stomach. The girl tentatively extended her hand a few inches from the plant, and the old woman snipped a few pieces more and began to mash the bark into the bowl, demonstrating the correct motion to grind dried bark into a fine powder. She handed another small bowl to the girl, added some more herbs, and nodded for the girl to give it a try. Mera fumbled, some herbs spilling onto the ground. The old healer smiled, snipped a few more pieces, and indicated for her to try again, this time taking her hand on top of Mera's and actively demonstrating the correct motion.

Both women remained intent upon their task until the afternoon's light faded. Then Analena motioned for the girl to follow her outside to a small garden where there were rows of vegetables. Spinach, peas, carrots, potatoes, and cucumbers grew thick and in abundance. She handed a basket to the girl and quickly gathered some of the vegetables. The girl dropped down onto her knees as the old healer woman placed the items, one by one, into the basket.

Once again inside, Analena set a pot on the stove to boil and added some rice. She gave a knife to the girl and laid the vegetables on a wooden board. Mera began to chop each into small, bite-size pieces, looking up at Analena for verification she cut them correctly. The old woman merely motioned with her hand to continue.

As soon as the sun sank under the horizon, Analena lit several candles. She carefully ladled out two bowls of rice topped with vegetables and handed one to the girl. They sat together, shoulder to shoulder, each lifting a spoonful of food to their mouth while cicadas chirped the evening's lullaby.

And so it was that Mera came to live with the old healer woman.

Chapter Fifteen

1960

Thai-Laotian Border

Four men, shadowy in the campfire light, materialized straight out of the cave walls. They wore billowing black trousers and black shirts brightly embroidered with patterns of animals and plants. Each shirt had its own design. The oldest one, distinguished by a red, woven bandanna wrapped around his forehead and hairline, moved to the front of the others.

Lance and Miles remained quiet, careful not to disturb the air with their breath.

A silhouette of the men wavered in the firelight like a shimmering oasis. The medic at full height almost hit the top of the cave with his head. The villagers were nearly half his size.

It was the old one who broke the trance. He smiled, exposing yellowed teeth, a thousand deep wrinkles, and piercing, dark-brown eyes. Lance returned the gaze as warmly as he could muster in the face of being so easily approached inside the cave.

The old one began to speak. He told them his grandson led them here. Lance slowly lowered onto his haunches, followed quickly by the medic. The elder motioned to his men to sit as well, until all sat around the fire in a circle. The Hmong stared openly at the tall, phantom-like man, hypnotized by the vision of this strange being who seemed to suddenly appear in their midst. Miles did his best to appear nonthreatening and responded with a friendly smile. Everyone smiled and nodded to each other.

The old one commenced the formalities, introducing the lineage of his clan and then himself, Xob. Lance reverted to the dialect of his youth in response, presenting Amah's husband's clan as his own, followed by his name. Only then did he attempt to explain their presence in the cave.

"We come as messengers from our people across the ocean. We are a strong tribe with many gifts. We understand the menace from the north that threatens your villages. We want to send the intruders back where they came from, and with your help, this is what we will do. Is there anything your clan needs? Cows, water buffalo, chickens?"

The old one shook his head, and his gaze assessed the fair-haired stranger. A young Hmong, the tallest of the four, stood and began to speak.

"The enemy from the north kills our men, steals our women and children, and burns our villages. They are a people without honor. We wish to cultivate our fields, live peacefully, and see our children grow strong. Our lives are threatened by constant danger from the north. They are like locusts that devour the land and leave nothing. We have no choice. Here we fight. Now, we become the aggressor. We want firearms. We need many guns to protect our people and fight the enemy. Can your people help with this?"

"Our enemy is the same," Lance said. "My people want to help you because the beast that destroys your villages also threatens many people of good will. Soon, there will be airplanes in the sky to help us. This is your home. We want to help protect your land and expel the intruders, permanently. We'd like to learn to work with your men. In turn, we will expose the locusts and send them running far away from here. We are a strong force. We will be powerful with your help."

The young Hmong rocked from one foot to the other.

"Guns. Many guns. You have these?"

Lance nodded and motioned toward Miles. "He is our healer with strong medicine that can help your people when they are injured or sick." Miles reached behind him for a large canvas bag and unzipped it. Inside were rows of syringes, gauze, ointments, antibiotics, morphine, and first-aid supplies. "My friend would like to come to your village and help the sick ones. Later, we will talk of guns."

Xob, the old one rose, followed immediately by the other three. He nodded once, and all four disappeared into the darkness as suddenly as they had appeared.

Miles, hands still on the medic bag, blurted, "Shit, what just happened, mate? My jaw is sore from smiling. That felt like a bloody dream. I can't believe you actually understand that gibberish!"

"They know we're here. It's their move," Lance said.

The boy appeared just as a thin, grey light penetrated the darkness inside of the cave. Lance and Miles slept spread-eagle atop camouflaged sleeping bags. The boy rested on his heels, quietly waiting. Lance abruptly sat up, silently reaching for the pistol that was always within easy reach. Miles rolled over, saw the boy, and instantly popped to his feet. Lance intentionally softened his voice to tranquil and warm.

"Young friend, what's your name?"

"I am Fue. My grandfather asks that you come with me to the village. The elders want to speak with you and ..." He looked up at Miles. "They want him to come and heal the sick people. The people want to see your medicine."

Lance translated. "Miles, this is it ... our window. We'll follow the boy. Bring everything you have, and we'll pray to God antibiotics and morphine will alleviate some of the villagers' ailments. Grab whatever medicine you have. If we heal the people, the elders will respect and honor us."

Miles swung the tote bag over his shoulder and bowed his head, barely avoiding scraping his head along the top of the cave as they emerged from darkness into the first light of dawn. Fue disappeared into the jungle, and Lance trotted in the direction of the wavering leaves that closed behind him. Miles followed close behind. The boy weaved, cutting back the thick vegetation with his stick. Lance followed the newly made trail and the swoosh that echoed for a moment from east and then north. After an hour of slow forward movement, they reached an embankment that led to the turbulent river. The rich foliage closed behind Fue. A second later, the boy emerged, pulling a small dugout canoe from its hiding spot. Lance grabbed the other side of the boat, and Miles waited, staring intently at the small craft while shifting uncomfortably from one foot to the other. The canoe was carved from the trunk of a single tree, and the carved-out center was easily large enough for two diminutive tribesmen.

Fue spoke rapidly to Lance.

"He'll paddle across with you first and then come back for me. Be fluid, like you're sitting on the back of a motorbike, mate!"

Fue pushed the canoe into the river and climbed in. Miles waded in behind him and placed one foot in the canoe with a hand on either side of the light craft. It swayed to the left as he added his weight, hovered vertically for a moment, and then flipped over with a decisive slap. Fue, light and agile, jumped free into the water and took a few steps to regain his balance, all the while watching Miles somersault up in the air and land back into the muddy water with a mighty splash. The boy doubled over as light, staccato hiccups burst from him, and laughter rose from deeper in his belly and reverberated across the water in the now-bright morning. Miles, fully drenched, looked up at him. The boy was unable to stop his infectious laughter. Lance's shoulders trembled with mirth as he waded into the water and reached for Mile's hand to help him up.

"Shit, you all right?"

Having accepted the extended hand, Miles was halfway to standing when Lance's body began to shake in earnest. The two teetered for a moment before they fell into the water, soaked head to toe in a tidal wave of river. Lance stood, dripping wet, to splash Fue with armfuls of chocolate brown. Fue returned fire with equal exuberance and glee until all three were dunking, swimming, and vying to reach the optimum angle and vantage point in the grand water melee.

On the far shore, Xob watched, while the younger ones fanned about him in a protective sheath. He nodded to the tribesman to his left, an indication to follow, then turned and walked up the embankment, the young ones close behind.

Across the river now, Lance and Miles scrambled up the steep embankment several meters behind Fue. A small throng of villagers moved toward them with Sawm, one of the village trackers, in the lead. He spoke quickly to Lance, pointing toward a large hut situated in the center of fifteen to twenty smaller but similarly constructed bungalows.

"They wait for you there," Sawm said and motioned for Miles to follow him in the opposite direction.

Lance ducked into the bamboo house with the thatched roof and dirt floor. Xob sat on the ground surrounded by what appeared to be the entire male population of the village over the age of twelve. Lance's gaze adjusted from the bright sunlight of the morning to the dark interior of the dwelling. He scanned the room, singling out an open space between two elders, directly across from Xob. He moved quietly to the spot, lowered into a cross-legged seat, and waited.

The old man's voice reverberated in the hot humid morning.

"We are a free nation and a peaceful people. We grow food to feed our people. That is all. Now, we grow opium. It is the exchange for the basic needs of our people. Our ancestors have lived close to the mother for as long as the rivers have flowed, I am told. We came here from another land, far away from this place. We have endured and struggled to live peacefully, away from the locusts and their incessant, foolish destruction. To live as a free people, we left our home and traveled far from the world that we knew. I cannot say how many times my people were forced from their land, for I cannot see into the times of the ancestors, but we believe it has been many, many times. The trouble for our clan is not over. It is here we must stand and fight the angry beast that devours everything in its path."

Lance's voice rose to match the tone and timbre of the village chief.

"I will communicate to my chief the words you have spoken … the big brother will bring firepower from the sky. He has many guns and ammunition to help send your enemy running back the way he came. Together, we can be a force that prevails."

Xob nodded and then turned his head to stare fixedly forward. The interchange was complete. Lance slowly stood, bent to avoid hitting his head, and moved toward the entrance. Outside, Sawm squatted and chewed. His teeth were bright red from what Lance assumed was betel nut—a bitter, spicy, sweet, and salty seed that produced a narcotic effect and was enjoyed by locals all over southeast Asia.

When he saw Lance emerge from the hut, he grinned, stood, and motioned with a flick of his wrist for Lance to follow him. They wound around the edge of the village to another hut elevated onto wooden stilts. Lance climbed up the three-step ladder that leaned up against the entranceway and entered the abode. Inside, Lance saw Miles on his knees, leaning over a mat to cradle the arm of a very old man. He gently wiped the man's arm with a clean cloth saturated with disinfectant. The man's wife, equally old but seemingly in good health, perched on the opposite side of the mat, her face tight with concern. Miles injected a shot of morphine and looked up as Lance squatted next to him.

"Not much I can do for this bloke. He's got two feet out the door. The shot will ease his pain, but I doubt he'll make it until sunset. Bloody well hope our new relationship is not dependent on a miracle!"

"Don't worry. The meeting with Xob went well … I think. It's the first step, but I believe we are moving in the right direction. Do your best for the patient and make him comfortable. I fly back to base in a fortnight. They'll send in an agent, another Brit, to help out with the radio while I'm away."

"Don't leave me here in a shambles. Get your arse back quick! They never send anyone who speaks the lingo." Miles slapped Lance on the back and grinned. "Besides, you're my mate."

The funeral lasted three days. During the requiem, every hour like clockwork, the elder's wife wailed, cried, and fell to the ground for exactly ten minutes while the rest of the village stood apart, quiet and respectful. The remainder of each hour, everyone laughed, conversed, danced, and thoroughly enjoyed each other's company in celebration of the life of a respected elder of the clan. The elder's wife was often the loudest and most boisterous celebrant.

The elder was a man of means in the village, clearly displayed by a fence made of hundreds of old Coca-Cola tin cans. The Coca-Cola fence surrounded the open, simple, wooden casket. Inside, the old man was dressed in his finest clothing, as if he too attended the festivities.

Every hour, the ritual repeated. The elder's widow, on cue, began to wail as the villagers became quiet. Just before dawn, one by one, people disappeared into their huts. Then, late morning, the people reemerged and carried on where they left off the night before.

On the fourth morning, the simple rhythm of village life resumed without pause.

Chapter Sixteen

1961

Chiang Mai, Thailand

Situated on the banks of the Mae Ping River, the white-columned house was brilliantly lit against the dark night sky. Dark-haired servants dressed in starched white shirts moved silently among the fifty guests, serving bacon-wrapped ginger soy scallops and pear chutney bruschetta. Eric and Melanie Hartman, the American hosts, smiled brightly as they mingled among their guests. The echo of light conversation swelled and abated as if synchronized with the water lapping along the shore below.

Lance sipped a scotch and leaned casually against a stone railing as he looked down at the river. In stark contrast to the formal dress code of the evening, he wore a faded green shirt with a square collar, khaki pants, and leather sandals. His blond hair was pulled back in a short ponytail.

He observed the well-heeled crowd from the terrace, standing apart yet very much present. A mini-United Nations was in attendance. He scanned the crowd, noting the French attaché to Thailand nod once in the direction of a Japanese businessman. To his right, the Thai army lieutenant general leaned easily across the bar to speak with the bartender, his rank insignia patch of three stars and a golden crown displayed prominently on the epaulet on his shoulder. Lance noted the Japanese businessman glance every so often in the Thai lieutenant general's direction and then slowly make his way toward the bar.

Melanie Hartman approached and lightly laid her hand on Lance's arm.

"Jimmy, you are being absolutely antisocial. My friends are dying to meet you!"

He bowed to his host and smiled warmly, holding up his drink in a toast-like gesture. "I'm afraid I spend too much time alone in the jungle. I have been remiss."

"Well, darling, no offense taken. I, for one, would love to hear about your adventures."

"Alas, the mundane can appear exotic from the outside looking in. There's not a lot to tell. I can assure you, spending eight hours a day in the backwoods as fodder for mosquitos and leeches alike is unbelievably dull. On a good day, I might catch sight of a rufous-necked hornbill and snap a few photos when the light's just right." His attention appeared to be entirely focused on his host, and Melanie basked in the warmth of his gaze.

"I am sure it's far from boring," she said. "Your presence brings a bit of excitement to the usual embassy business crowd. I am delighted you came … Ah, new arrivals. Duty calls! Don't you go anywhere! I will be right back!"

Lance's gaze naturally followed her retreating figure to the arriving guests. His eyes widened as he pressed himself straight from the railing.

Isabela walked out onto to the terrace accompanied by a redhaired young woman in a black evening dress and a slim Thai male in Western evening attire. The trio was obviously new to the gathering, as many eyes now turned their way. Isabela wore a simple black skirt with a side slit to just above the right knee and a green silk blouse.

Her dark hair flowed down her back and over her shoulders in soft waves. Simple pearl earrings and a small gold bracelet were her only adornments.

He downed the reminder of his whiskey, left the glass on the railing, and exchanged brief pleasantries with the French attaché, all the while keeping the young woman in the periphery of his vision. He continued to angle through the guests and waited until the Thai companion retreated to the bar. The redhaired young woman was animatedly engaged to the right. He grabbed a glass of white wine from a passing waiter and inserted himself in the place of the retreating Thai companion to proffer the wine with a bow.

"Our paths cross again, señorita." Isabela turned to face the tall American.

"Disculpe." *Excuse me.* "Have we met?"

He knew she recognized him, as her face was lightly flushed and her words slow and overly enunciated, even for a foreign speaker.

"I trust you found a good place for the lantern? Or was it a gift?"

She smiled and slowly took the extended glass of wine.

"Si, gracias." *Yes, thank you.* "You are very kind. I sent it home. It will hang in the garden."

"I forget myself, once again. Jimmy Calhoun from Charleston, South Carolina." His hand reached across the space between them, and this time, she offered hers in return.

"Isabela Marquez from El Salvador. I am pleased to meet you."

A warmth began in the pit of his stomach and expanded throughout his body. The occupants and the noise of the room muted, and again, there was only the girl. Their hands touched in a formal greeting but neither pulled away.

"If you will permit a personal question, Isabela Marquez from El Salvador? I have to wonder what a beautiful, young woman from

Central America is doing all the way across the world in Thailand, Chiang Mai, for one, and then this particular gathering for the other?"

"I am a simple art student." She hesitated and then began again. "My father's business connections are quite extensive. My mother was opposed to my year in Thailand. Before she gave her blessing, she made my father promise to contact everyone he has ever met from this part of the world." She laughed and lightly shrugged her shoulders. "And I agreed to attend a few parties. It is a small compromise to have the opportunity to see this part of the world and experience the colors, the people, and the beauty. It's a country that otherwise would remain only pictures in a magazine. I have been here two months only, and already I am in love with the food, the textiles, and the gracious Thai people."

"When we met in the bazaar, you had just arrived?"

"The Sunday bazaar was my first outing onto the streets of Chiang Mai. Thailand is an inspiration for my watercolor paintings. Sometimes, before I fall asleep, images of water buffalo, rice fields, and boats filled with colorful fruits won't leave my head until I've sketched at least a few of them. When the time comes, I don't think I will want to go home."

Isabela's Thai companion returned from the bar with two iced glasses filled with passion fruit and vodka. White plumerias floated on the top. He noticed Isabela held a glass in her hand, so he extended one to the redhaired young woman, Kate, and took a sip from the other.

"Isabela, Kate, I must introduce you to our host, Eric Hartman," the Thai gentleman said, nodding once in Lance's direction. He guided Isabela with a light pressure on her right elbow, and Kate followed the lead.

Isabela paused and turned back briefly. Lance bent over in an overemphasized bow, and his eyes gravitated to hers. She returned the bow with a quiet smile before following her companions. Lance watched her retreating figure for several moments more and then moved to the back of the room where he was better able to survey the occupants of the party. On his left, a heavily accented French man spoke intently to someone whose head was bowed. Lance was unable to see the man's face. He kept the two in the periphery of his vision, edging in their direction. He waited until the French gentleman was alone and positioned himself in the place of the retreating figure.

"Can I buy you a drink?" Lance said.

The French man laughed. "You are American. What brings you to Thailand?"

"I'm a freelance nature photographer. *National Geographic* picked up a few of my better photographs. And you?"

"A small-business man. There's plenty of opportunity in this corner of the world, if you know the right people."

"What is your business, if I may ask?" Lance said.

"A little of this and a little of that," the man replied. "Mostly information."

"I'm a history buff," Lance said. "It's a side interest. I like to keep up on current events wherever I am. For instance, my newest diversion is the little country of Laos. I'm interested in its history and politics."

The Frenchman laughed, "Laos? Hardly a country."

"What do you mean?"

"It has no infrastructure, et communication from one place to another is very, very … problématique. Try to get two villages to agree on even one purpose. You will fail, mon ami. Much of the country is pure, wild jungle and barely civilized from a Western perspective. After independence was declared in 1953, the new, so-called government divided the area into five military regions. This has done little to improve the situation."

"Corresponding to the thirteen provinces, right?" Lance said.

"I see you have done some reading. But have you learned that besides the capitol, there is really no centralized governmental influence? Each district, or village, is quite autonomous. That is why it is so difficult to get them to agree. Rich and powerful families rule their own areas like tiny kingdoms. Each has its own, shall I say, priorités. It is one of the reasons my countrymen had such a difficult time here."

"You seem to know quite a lot on the subject," Lance said.

"Did you know, in the fourteenth century, little Laos was called Lan Xang? You see, I am an encyclopedia of useless information!" the Frenchman laughed.

"What does it mean?" Lance asked.

"Kingdom of a million elephants!"

For some unknown reason, images of the young Salvadoran woman, Isabela, flitted across Lance's mind. He shook his head and returned his gaze to the Frenchman.

"It sounds poetic."

"Voilà, the réalité is far from poétique, I am afraid. The civil war between the Royal Lao government and the Pathet Lao is beginning to rage in the country. Very bad for business."

"Do you care who wins?" Lance asked.

"Mais bien sûr, mon ami." *But, of course, my friend.* "Like I mentioned, I am a businessman, and the communists do not appreciate free and honest trade."

"What is your interest in Laos?"

"A friend of mine does business with a Laotian family in the panhandle. That is, southern Laos. They think of themselves as the royal family of their district, but the truth is they are only very rich and so control their area like a small Byzantine Empire. For myself, I take care of a few mundane affairs for my friend."

"Sounds interesting," Lance said.

"The North Vietnamese, with the backing of their friends the Chinese, of course, are moving into the panhandle and trying to take control of the area. This is also bad for business, but what can we do?"

"You mentioned that each area has its own pursuit. What are the family's needs? Desires? I may be in a position to help."

"Eh, for that discussion, we would need to meet more privately," the Frenchman said.

"Je peux vous contacter?" *May I contact you?* Lance slipped easily into French.

"Je suis désolé. Je ne me souviens pas de votre nom." *I'm sorry. I don't recall your name.*

"Bien sûr, les présentations d'abord. Je m'appelle James Calhoun de South Carolina, USA." *Of course, introductions first. I am James Calhoun, from South Carolina, USA.* Lance smiled and extended his hand.

"Je suis enchanté de faire votre connaissance, Monsieur Calhoun. Je m'appelle Jules Arsenault." *I am delighted to meet you, Mr. Calhoun. My name is Jules Arsenault.* The Frenchman scribbled a number onto a napkin on the table before continuing, "Si vous voulez bien m'excuser? J'attendrai votre appel." *If you will excuse me, I will wait for your call.* The Frenchman stepped back, laid his hand briefly on Lance's shoulder, and sauntered into the crowd of ex-patriots.

Lance swung swiftly around as he felt a hard bump to his right shoulder. The unmistakable palomino, slicked-back head slithered past him. *Avery? What the hell is he doing here? That's an encounter best to avoid!* He quickly moved toward the front door.

Melanie Hartman noticed her guest's imminent departure and rushed to intercept him, almost leaping across the floor to interlace her arm through his elbow.

"Please tell me you aren't leaving? You simply must stay. We are about to light and release one hundred paper lanterns for the beginning of Makha Bucha next week. It is a magnificent sight."

"Melanie, thank you for the invitation. Next time, perhaps. I have a few projects that need tending before I leave town. I am most honored to have made the guest list." He lightly kissed her hand and continued toward the door.

The Triumph kicked into gear as the engine revved. Lance glanced back over his shoulder before shifting, crunching pebbled rock as the bike sped down the driveway and back onto the main road.

Three days passed since Eric and Melanie Hartman's evening affair, and time was running out before Lance was needed back on the border with the Hmong tribe. He had called the number scribbled on the napkin Mr. Arsenault gave him, but there was no answer. He turned the corner onto the street of his guesthouse and entered the foyer. The front desk clerk extended a neatly folded note.

"Mr. Calhoun, a gentleman stopped by earlier this morning asking for you and left this note."

Lance quickly scanned the contents and stuffed the note into his shirt pocket. *Hot damn!*

"ขอบคุณ, Somchai." *Thank you.* "Did the gentleman mention if he would return?"

"No, sir, he did not. He asked a peculiar question, however. He asked if any American Marines were staying here. I told him no, sir.

No military from any nation. Mr. Calhoun is a famous photographer from America."

"Very good, Somchai. Ring my room if he stops by again. I don't plan to go out again today."

The phone rang four times before Lance lifted the receiver. "Hello?"

"Mr. Calhoun? Monsieur Arsenault here. Would you be available to accompany me for a short excursion? I am downstairs in the lobby."

"Mr. Arsenault? This is a welcome surprise. I tried reaching you, but it looks like you found me first! Can you give me a minute? I'll be right down." Lance lightly placed the phone back in its cradle, opened the drawer to the nightstand, and retrieved a small pistol. He checked the reload cartridge and then strapped the gun beneath his shirt and under his arm. He swept the loose baht and his room key from the top of the table and stuffed it all into his shirt pocket. Before he left, he picked up the phone again and dialed. A voice answered on the other end, "Yes?"

"Contact has been made." Lance once again set the receiver back in its cradle before exiting the room. A few minutes later, he stepped out of the elevator and moved across the foyer.

"A pleasure to see you again, Mr. Arsenault. How did you find me?"

"My friend's business empire is quite extensive. And Chiang Mai is not very big, n'est-ce pas? My driver is waiting outside. Shall we?"

Lance accompanied Mr. Arsenault and stepped into the Frenchman's black limousine. The automobile swerved in and out of traffic and navigated the outskirts of town before opening up and speeding north onto a double-lane road. Both men kept the conversation light while Lance took note of the direction and passing landmarks. His mind replayed the events of the past few days and noted how easily the Frenchman had located his hotel. *He has done his research,* Lance thought to himself. *It's the reason for the three-day delay and not answering my calls!*

After an hour, the limousine swerved onto a rutted dirt road. Lance could just make out an orange-and-white windsock fluttering in the distance.

"Local airport?" Lance turned to face Mr. Arsenault while he quietly assessed the pros and cons of traveling to an unknown destination with a person of questionable purpose.

"My private landing strip. I hope you did not have anything planned for the afternoon?"

"Free as a bird. I look forward to an interesting history lesson."

"You have a fascinating background, Mr. Calhoun. The Laotian friend I mentioned at the party expressed an interest in meeting you. The distance is not far, mais. There are no roads, I am afraid. I hope it is not an inconvenience?"

"On the contrary. I'm intrigued."

The limousine sped alongside the landing strip and then came to a quick, jolting stop in front of a small two-aircraft hangar. The driver jumped out and opened the rear door for his employer. Lance stepped out, signaling with his hand there was no need for the driver to proceed further. Inside the hangar, a crew readied a four-seat Cessna for flight. Parked beside it was a Grumman Gulfstream aircraft.

"I used to be a pilot in the Marines. I'd love to fly one of these one day." Lance nodded in the direction of the Gulfstream. "Where are we headed?"

"Maybe you might buy one of your own, n'est-ce pas?"

"One day, maybe," Lance said.

"I thought you might like to see a small kingdom in the making."

"My curiosity is piqued," Lance said as he climbed into the aircraft.

"I must tell you the commander is quite particular about who he invites to his home."

"I am flattered, but I doubt my limited perspective will be of much value to him."

"Life is quite unfair, do you not agree? At the bottom, the masses slave away entire lives and barely eke out an existence. The top players, however, flick a finger, and millions are instantly at their disposal."

"The inequities of existence have always confused me. I am just an ordinary man, so I hope I will not waste your commander's time."

"Please do not be concerned. Our commander requested this meeting with you, and he is familiar with your particular history."

"What is his interest in me?"

"Your connections, mon ami—the people you know. Dark clouds are assembling over Vietnam, Laos, and Cambodia. The communists are preparing, as are your American compatriots. For us businessmen, however, there are excellent profits to be made in arms, intelligence, and drugs. Unfortunately, our commander is not as forward thinking as we businessmen are. He thinks only of the moment. He doesn't realize there must be a vision and plan for the future. Unfortunately, our commander will align his interests, and his district, with those who provide the best financial backing and protection."

"I've been told the U.S. government is in an ambiguous situation," Lance said. "President Kennedy does not want to continue the confrontation in Laos. If he is successful in his endeavor, the U.S. government's hands may soon be tied as far as conventional warfare is concerned. Like I said before, I am a history buff, and I am fascinated to watch history in the making. Rumors are circulating. A peace settlement between the Russians, Chinese, and Americans regarding little Laos may be in the works. I've heard the push is to declare it a neutral state."

"The North Vietnamese will not honor it! They are moving into the panhandle at an alarming rate."

"Do you know anything about a road through the jungle? A supply route from the south of Laos into Vietnam?"

"The Pathet Lao are very determined, and unfortunately, our little district lies right in the path of their endeavors," Mr. Arsenault said. "The commander needs strong support from the West, or he will align himself with the adversary."

A small dirt runway loomed in the distance as the pilot dropped altitude for the landing. An open-air jeep drove onto the landing strip as the Cessna came to a jolting stop. Lance and Mr. Arsenault exited the aircraft and climbed into the seat of the waiting vehicle. The driver immediately sped off, speeding down the deeply rutted road. Neither spoke, as each held on to the side of the jeep to avoid bouncing out. The driver came to a screeching halt in front of a heavily forested area, beyond which the outlines of a palatial home were just visible.

Two servants greeted Mr. Arsenault and Lance outside, each dressed in a crisp white, square-necked, cotton shirt and billowing embroidered trousers. The servants bowed and politely showed them down a long pathway. Beautiful flowers adorned the sides of the road, but Lance noted outlying buildings in the distance that appeared to be barracks. Groups of men engaged in some kind of training activity in a nearby field.

The Frenchman nodded in the direction of the men and said, "Oui, oui," *Yes, yes.* "The commander's small private army."

The large audience room was lavishly adorned with furnishings reminiscent of a fourteenth-century French castle. A heavy baroque gilded armoire, thick Persian carpets, and a white sofa with gold-accented wood trim filled the high-ceilinged space. In the front of the room, a large throne-like seat, all gold with plush crimson cushions, set on a riser. Lance briefly wondered at the expense of bringing such lavish and impractical items to this jungle home.

The two men sat on cushions directly below the golden chair and were served a sweet, ice-cold lemon drink spiced with fresh mint. The commander emerged from behind a curtain, just to the left of the throne-chair. Lance breathed out slowly, cognizant of every detail in the room as well as the man who just entered. The commander was of broad face and thick build. His small eyes darted back and forth and then stopped abruptly to fix on Lance, who immediately stood up, followed by Mr. Arsenault. They both bowed, with their palms lightly pressed together. The commander sat down in the large, gilded chair and, with a gentle wave of his hand, indicated the cushions in front of him. Lance noted the advantage the man established by virtue of sitting above the petitioners and looking down on them. *He is used to calling the shots,* Lance thought to himself. *I wonder if he speaks English?* The commander began to speak in a Lao dialect, and Mr. Arsenault quickly translated.

"He is delighted to make your acquaintance. He has been told about your background and has a strong interest in learning what, perhaps, you might know about America's interest in southeast Asia."

"Laos is a land far away from America and, therefore, of little concern to the American people," Lance said. "For those of us who know history and the interdependence of free world trade, it is quite another matter. The communists are stretching their influence and power. They are strengthening, and little Laos is an important strategic point toward their ultimate goal: domination of the Asian theater."

"Yes, yes," the commander said. "What is your opinion of the American CIA? Do you believe they would willingly lend support to an important strategic area such as ours? Several Hmong villages in my district grow opium. Up until now, they were merely small, local farms with a negligible distribution. Of course, we collect our fair share from their earnings. But we are interested in expanding their production and entering into the global market. It is of no consequence to us which country supports our endeavors."

"I can't speak for the CIA and its purpose. Like I said, I am just a photographer. But I have friends. My friends may be in a position to direct your interests to the American government."

The commander stared hard at Lance. Without taking his eyes off him, he spoke rapidly in Lao. Mr. Arsenault did not translate, as both the commander and Mr. Arsenault continued to stare in Lance's direction.

I wish I understood the lingo, Lance thought. *Being at the discretion of an interpreter is never optimal.*

"May I assume you are negotiating with other players?" Lance asked.

"Of course. But it would be bad business to take the first offer on the table. And we like the Americans—if they are willing to provide a package that satisfies our basic needs."

"I see," said Lance.

"Perhaps you might convey our sincere greetings to your American friends. Please educate them on the situation in our area. In exchange for military protection, we can assure cooperation and support for their cause."

"As I said before, I can only speak as a messenger and convey your wish to meet," Lance said. "Whether or not they choose to negotiate is out of my hands."

"Very well. Time is of the essence. There is pressure building in the south of Laos, and we must carefully choose our alliance."

"You can be sure your message will be delivered promptly, and a reply will be imminent."

"Very good." One of the commander's beady eyes stayed locked on Lance while the other eye seemed to wander to the left.

"Please go now. I have business to discuss with Mr. Arsenault. Allow my associate to show you around our grounds."

Almost instantly, a man appeared through the curtained doorway behind the commander. Lance slowly stood. "Thank you for allowing me to visit your beautiful home." He bowed slightly and followed the man out the door.

They crossed a small field, beyond which several barracks-like buildings were strewn. Groups of slender men practiced calisthenics, target shooting, and, oddly, some kind of wrestling. Lance followed his guide, and as they drew nearer, he noticed the fight was being supervised by a large German man with thick, black chest hair and a chunky gold chain that hung down the middle of his bare torso.

The two wrestlers stepped gingerly in a slow circle around their opponent, each eyeing the other suspiciously. When sunlight glinted off the silver blades each fighter clutched in his left hand, Lance realized the high stakes of the match. As he neared, he realized the wrestlers were not the full-grown slim men he came to associate with most Laotians. They were young boys, perhaps only about fourteen or fifteen. The German looked up just as one boy lurched into an attack. Blood splattered onto the ground as the injured boy dropped to the ground. His pant leg was sliced open just above the knee.

The German laughed and said in English, "Good match!" Lance assumed the English was for his benefit, as the German quickly walked over to his side of the circle. "The American has come! I have been looking forward to our meeting again."

"You have me at a disadvantage. I don't recall running into you, and I never forget a face."

"Ach, such a triviality. Let's just say I have a very large network, and your name has come up more than a few times."

The German laid his thick, stubby fingers on Lance's shoulder and squeezed it hard. Lance winced internally, suppressing the urge to knock the intrusive hand away. Instead, he smiled and allowed the hand to remain.

"Please, let me introduce myself. My name is Volker. I believe you and I will be good business partners. Everyone makes a little on the side, here and there."

"A pleasure to meet you, Mr. Volker. My interest is with the commander. Any involvement I undertake will be through him."

The German laughed again. "How do you think he conducts his trade? I am in charge of the distribution of his assets. And there is plenty of cash for all!"

Lance eyed Volker for a moment and then brushed past him without bothering to respond. He quickly knelt by the injured boy lying on the ground holding his leg. Blood oozed through his fingers.

"This boy needs medical attention. Are there any bandages? Antibiotics?" Lance leaned over to look at the wound as the boy winced. He saw that the knife cut reached across the boy's thigh and penetrated deeply into the thick muscle. "Il y a quelqu'un qui peut m'apporter de l'eau?" *Would someone bring me some water?* Lance tried French, and still there was no response.

Suddenly, another boy, no older than about ten, darted out from the crowd around Lance and the wounded adolescent. He pulled on Lance's sleeve, motioning with his free hand toward the barracks-like building. Lance scooped up the injured boy and followed the wisp of a child, his face red and his heart beating like a snare drum. *What the hell are they doing here? They treat these boys like animals!* The small boy dashed around the building, still motioning with his hand for Lance to follow. Off to the right behind the building, a bright red water pump poked out from behind thick vegetation.

Lance set the injured boy down, opened the water flow, and helped him onto his one good leg, allowing the boy to use his arm as a crutch to approach the pump. Lance removed a small knife from his pocket. He carefully slit the boy's pant leg further and gently held his leg under the water. The boy sucked in his breath.

Water showered the wound, bringing into view the thick muscle of the quadriceps. Lance lifted his shirt over his head, exposing the gun strapped under his arm and across his chest. He picked up the knife and began to slice the fabric for a bandage.

"Komm, komm," Volker said, suddenly appearing from behind them. "Please do not destroy such an expensive and handsome shirt." Volker extended his hands. He carried antibiotic ointment and white linen bandages. Several boy soldiers surrounded the German, with their rifles openly pointed at the American. Lance reached under his arm. With one liquid movement, he unsnapped the pistol from its holster and laid it on the ground.

"I see you are an intelligent and respectful man," Volker said.

"Right." Lance snatched the medical supplies from the German's hands and laid out a bandage across his upper thigh and gently applied the disinfectant to the boy's wound. As the ointment penetrated the open, oozing laceration, the boy gasped, his eyes glued to Lance's face. Lance applied the bandage over the wound.

"Tell him to wash it every day and apply the ointment. He has to keep it clean. Change the bandage twice a day. If he doesn't, infection will set in, and he'll lose the leg."

"You have many talents, Mr. Calhoun," Volker said. "You will be most useful to us."

"Just take care of him, all right?"

"Ach … weakness presents omens of failure and perhaps even death. But don't worry. I am prepared to overlook this small deficiency.

Please, think no more of this young soldier. He is becoming a man. The wound will strengthen him."

"If you don't kill him first." Lance looked into the boy's eyes and recognized the dullness and fear in them.

"I wish I could take you with me, son," he murmured. Lance slowly stood, brushed dirt off his pants, and pulled on his ripped shirt. He glanced briefly at his pistol on the ground.

Volker bent, retrieved the gun, and said, "Thank you for the gift."

"Yeah, right." Lance walked back toward the jeep parked outside the commander's home. Mr. Arsenault emerged, almost simultaneously, from the front door. Lance climbed into the back seat of the car, a steady stream of profanities just under his breath. He barely noticed when Mr. Arsenault climbed in beside him. "Let's get out of here."

Chapter Seventeen

1977

El Salvador

Analena moved with a grace and ease that belied her advanced years as she moved between bushes and plants, inspecting each one as if it were a sacred object. Hours passed. Mera stooped in a squat behind the old woman as she watched her carefully select each herb. It was almost as if the old healer woman politely asked permission to separate members of a family for a greater benefit. She wondered why the old one never touched certain plants, and Analena replied to the unspoken question with one word. "Madre." *Mother.* She pointed to a particular one that must have had a strong root system to give its leaves such a deep green color, much darker than the other leaves nearby.

Mera tried to keep near the old woman, but she often disappeared into the shrubs and heavy foliage of the rainforest to seek some special plant that after careful observation she knew only grew in between crevices or beside gnarled roots. When Mera lost sight of the old healer, her throat would suddenly constrict, and her hands became clammy. She'd remain rigid, with her eyes glued to the last spot she'd seen the old woman. Only when Analena reemerged into view was Mera able to relax her breathing and command her legs to move again.

Village life sputtered and then resumed with older boys filling in for absent fathers. One day, several months after the attack, a distant Rodríguez relative came to town and was directed to Analena's door. She marched into the old healer's cottage, with lips set in a firm line. She took Mera by the hand, first trying to coax and then dramatically pressing her toward the front door. Mera, mute since the day of the attack, broadcast her response louder than a chorus of howler monkeys. She yanked her arm up and out of her relative's grasp and leaped to hide behind Analena, awkwardly attempting to disguise her lanky body behind the tiny old woman. The relative reluctantly retreated, directing a barrage of insults at the old healer woman as she huffed out the door.

Father Guillermo, harangued by several women in his congregation "to do something about the Rodríguez girl," visited next. On seeing his approach, Mera backed out of the cottage, pantomiming with quick hand movements that she was going to get water. She remained just outside the perimeter of the old woman's yard and refused to return until the padre's retreating figure finally disappeared. Finally, everyone just let her be.

Mera was open and curious and began to identify a few plants. She learned how to dry and grind the herbs into powder and boil roots into a dark brew. However, the art of combining one herb with another remained a mystery to her. Mera imagined there was a unique and special bond between the old woman and the plants she cultivated. Other times, she felt quite certain Analena was more than a little crazy. Yet, on the periphery of her own mind, a haunting whisper stirred. She intuited a vibration of light hidden deep within the rainforest that was, somehow, not separate from her own being. When she quieted her mind, magic happened. But when anger threatened or images of violence consumed her, a dark veil dropped, decisive and absolute, leaving her feeling empty and alone. Most days, she simply missed her mother, her father's warm embrace, and, most of all, her brother, David.

Chapter Eighteen

1961

Chiang Mai, Thailand

Three forty-five in the afternoon. She was on time and waited for a response to her light tap on the wide-open studio door. She knocked again, this time a little louder, and then stood awkwardly to the side, alert for any indication that she should enter. Prapat, the artist, stood back from the easel and quietly studied his drawing, an outlined sketch of the Buddha at the foot of the Bodhi tree and a line of monks bowing at his feet. The sketch was exquisite, inviting the observer to come close and inhale the moist, rich fragrance of the lotus flower.

Isabela entered but stopped midway, hesitant to disturb the artist. He looked up and motioned with a flick of his hand for her to approach.

"What is needed here to complete?" He pointed at the sketch and then continued to devour it with riveted attention, her presence all but forgotten. Invisible, she leaned in. Her hushed words emanating from an unknown source.

"A spiraling road. A journey everyone must take ... home," she exhaled softly.

"Yes, yes, my dear! And here?"

His hand waved, indicating the upper-right quadrant of the canvas, still virginal. The shadowy dance of his fingers were like a magician coaxing images to appear. His eyes bored into that corner, and the drawing revealed itself to both in the same moment. Isabela's finger lightly caressed the empty space.

"There's a woman. She holds a white flower—a flower with hundreds of petals. It's in her left hand. The young woman is on her knees, with her head bowed behind the monks who block her view. You can see she's come from very far away. The lines around her eyes make her seem older. She's tried to separate the root from the flower, but the stem stays attached. The root, it hangs down. The woman lifts the gift with both hands. Her face is simple. Pure."

"Ah, the thousand-petalled lotus, yes."

The penciled images danced on the white paper. A puissant and alchemistic link bonded the Thai artist and the young Salvadorian woman. A knock turned both their heads from the painting to the door.

"Prapat, you have five minutes to conclude the interview. There are four more waiting." The assistant held a notepad in his hand.

Isabela bent to gather her portfolio. She quickly opened the large black binder to reveal the watercolor of the parrots in the jungle. Prapat came up behind her and gently closed the leather-bound satchel.

"That won't be necessary. Please be here Wednesday at nine in the morning." He called out, and the assistant appeared at the door. "I'll see the others together. Send them in now."

Isabela hesitated, unconsciously rubbing her left earlobe between her forefinger and thumb. She hedged a step closer to the artist, attentive to further instruction, but clearly, the interview had come to a close. Isabela took a deep breath, hoisted the satchel strap onto her shoulder, and stepped quickly toward the door and into the hallway. Seated on both sides of the corridor, several young petitioners awaited their interview to be considered for the chance to work with the famous and gifted watercolor artist. Kate, among those waiting, leaped off her chair and intercepted Isabela.

"Well, how did it go? What do you think? You were in with Prapat less than ten minutes. I am devastated. If he doesn't accept you, then there's absolutely no hope for any of us."

The assistant, Kasem, motioned to Kate and three others to come forward.

"The master will see all of you together."

"Isabela, don't wait. I'll see you back at the hotel. Everything will be all right. We'll still have our adventure. Te lo prometo, querida!" *I promise you, dear.* "Meet me in the bar, okay?"

The lobby bar was quiet for a Friday night. Just a few residents lingered over a cocktail or a mug of local beer. Isabela reached into the side pocket of her purse and pulled out a pale pink lipstick. She glanced across the bar into the lobby and did a double take at the sight of the tall, lanky man in the faded jeans and dark sunglasses. His blond hair was pulled back in a short ponytail. She was quite sure it was him. Her lipstick forgotten, she watched as Jimmy spoke to the front desk clerk and extended a thick manila envelope. Isabela's neck rose two inches as she craned to the left to see past the bulky German businessman directly blocking her view. She barely took notice as Kate sank down on the stool to her right. But then she reluctantly withdrew her attention from the lobby and focused on her friend. Kate's words burst forth in a fluid rush.

"Prapat is only taking one student. That's what the assistant told us. He said the person has already been chosen. The remaining nine will work with him, Kasem. I'm sorry—he's the assistant. The master will give a class once a month. I am so sorry, Isabela. I have been rash and impulsive, not one of my better traits. I dragged you, my beautiful friend, far away from your fiancé and family without knowing the details. You know, the small print nobody reads. Kasem met with us afterward and read the names of the students who will study with him, an incredible artist in his own right. I … don't know how to say this, so I'll just come out with it. Your name was not mentioned. You are not one of the nine. I can't believe it. It's so unfair. You are an unbelievable artist. Maybe his style and yours are not compatible. That's all I can think of for a reason."

Isabela hesitated, glancing one more time at the front desk before bringing her attention back to Kate.

"Katya, querida, no importa." *Katya, dear, it doesn't matter.* "I am happy. It is my dream to see this beautiful country. You are my inspiration."

She touched Kate lightly on the shoulder, smiled, and raised her glass in a toast.

"You're sure you're not upset?"

Isabela blew a kiss as her eyes moistened.

"I am so relieved. I have been going crazy with worry. I can't believe he didn't choose …"

"I am going to meet him Wednesday. I don't know what he is thinking. He didn't look at my work. Maybe there is still a chance? Perhaps they will take ten?"

Kate stared at her feet, a vermilion red broadening across her white abalone cheekbones. *The artist made his choice!* Abruptly, she pushed the stool away from the table and looked left then right, anywhere but directly at Isabela.

"Isabela, look, I am drenched with sweat and need to take a shower. I am going to stay in tonight."

"Katya, go. We'll talk later?"

"Yes, let's talk later."

Isabela's gaze moved slowly, inexorably, back to Jimmy, who now stood in the lobby staring into the bar directly at her. She returned the gaze, and for a brief moment, neither moved. As if it had a will of its own, Isabela's arm lifted to wave. He moved across the lobby in a few long strides.

"Señorita Marquez, it's a pleasure to see you again." His eyes, intent, piercing. "May I take you to dinner?" he asked. "I know a local restaurant along the river just outside of town. It's very authentic. We'd be the only foreigners. It's one of my best-kept secrets."

"I ..."

He touched her hand briefly and then wrapped his long fingers around her narrow slender ones. The gentle pull of interlaced fingers invited her to stand. Once outside, they walked along the sidewalk without speaking. Jimmy indicated with his hand a motorcycle parked on the side of the road.

"My transportation. If you would prefer, we can take a tuk tuk?"

"The motorcycle is good, Señor Calhoun."

Isabela smiled, feeling very much, she imagined, like the baby swallow she once rescued, mothered, and one day set free. She had taken the cage to the veranda, opened it, and extended her finger into the cage. The little bird stepped up and wrapped its tiny, clawed feet around her finger, trembling in the infinite expanse of a now cage-free reality. It opened its wings wide while tightly gripping her finger. Open, close, open, close. On the third attempt, it relaxed its feet and sailed up, up and out of sight.

"A tour of Chiang Mai then, before dinner?"

Isabela had never ridden a motorcycle, but lifted her leg easily over the seat to sit behind Lance. Her white linen slacks fit comfortably, but her low heels did not.

"These won't do. Come with me," he said.

Isabela slid off the bike and followed Jimmy barefoot into a shop, where he proceeded to purchase a pair of cheap white tennis shoes. He then crouched to place them on her feet. After they climbed back on the bike, he revved the engine and maneuvered the motorcycle effortlessly in and out of the thick traffic. Isabela wrapped her arms loosely around Lance's waist. A distinctive smell of sweat mixed with aftershave permeated her senses. She settled in closer and set her head against his slightly damp green shirt, feeling the quiet rhythm of a steady heartbeat. The warm wind blew softly across her cheek as they passed red-roofed temples and giant golden Buddhas. Isabela suddenly remembered Kate, and she realized she had left without leaving a message. She tightened her arms around Jimmy's waist as thoughts of her mother and Tomás faded with the setting sun.

The traffic was thick and smoky. Vendors sold noodles on the side of the road next to exotic fruit sellers, and mini-bar carts hawked scotch, rye, and bourbon. Bald and greying foreigners sat atop bar-stools, leering at the young Thai prostitutes who meandered the street in high heels, mini-skirts, and bright red lipstick. The motorcycle slowed almost to a halt as congestion consumed the street ahead. An old woman, with brown, rheumy, watering eyes, sat on the sidewalk. She held her hand out to Isabela, who freed her arm from around Jimmy and reached into the purse slung across her chest to extract a few baht. The motorcycle idled at the traffic light as Jimmy reached back to block her offering mid-action.

"It's a business, Señorita Marquez. Chances are that woman has a big house outside of town with servants of her own or else she answers to a cartel that takes any possible benefit from her. Either way, it's a bad idea. Watch."

He reached into a side bag on the motorcycle and extracted a packet of dried fruit in wrapped cellophane and extended the food toward the woman. She spat in response and looked in the other direction.

"There's a lot to learn on the streets of Chiang Mai, Señorita Marquez. Nothing is as it seems."

Isabela remained quiet but turned to look behind her as the distance between the old woman and the motorcycle grew larger. The congestion abated beyond the outskirts of town, and the motorcycle sprang forward as Isabela's thick hair blew in a dark halo around her head. A sharp turn to the right sent dust and pebbles spraying in every direction as they began a steep climb up a narrow, serpentine road, just wide enough for one at a time.

The motorbike slowed to a stop in front of a small restaurant at the top of a hill that offered a spectacular view of the Chao Phraya River and the sprawling city of Chiang Mai. Isabela slipped off the bike to stand beneath a broad-leafed fig tree with wide branches that spread like a canopy across the graveled road. Little green puffs of birds with white eyes that blinked and shivered like wind in the leaves blended with the verdant foliage.

"Qué lindo!"

She held her out her hand, and one little bird took flight, followed by the flock. Dozens of tiny wings rose in a whoosh. Isabela stood mesmerized. Between the branches, a proteinaceous silk web of intricate geometric pattern expanded and shimmered in a dizzying array of fractals.

"Quite a sight! Is it not, Señorita Marquez?"

"Mira!" *Look!*

Isabela pointed at tiny, crocheted angles and light-refracting prisms. A spider with a cream-colored abdomen moved slowly across the corner of its creation toward a tiny ant, immobilized in its silky threads.

Lance peered at the web that seemed to so captivate the young Salvadoran woman's attention, thinking to himself, *What the hell is she looking at?*

The scent of African gardenias billowed around them. Small, round pebbles pressed into the mound of her right foot through the thin sneaker bottom. Isabela sensed Jimmy's approach and leaned back into his body as if they were still connected on the motorcycle. With warm lips, he lightly kissed her shoulder. She turned around slowly. He raised his finger, softly outlining the twin mountain peaks that formed her upper lip.

Isabela was still as she watched his face. Her mother's eyes, her father's voice, Tomás, were all a mere background whisper. As if he suddenly remembered something, Lance suddenly straightened up and stood back.

"You must be starving, Señorita Marquez. Let's go inside. You won't be disappointed. The food is excellent."

"Por favor, my name is Isabela."

There was a deep tapping inside her ribs, so strong she was sure the waves moving through her chest must have been visible.

"Señorita Isabela, I am honored."

He followed her to the restaurant's outdoor patio and sat down across from her at a small table overlooking the dark river, twinkling now with reflected light. Rows of lights formed a ceiling of stars on the outdoor patio, and a small candle burned on top of the green-flowered plastic tablecloth.

"May I suggest ..."

"Please, can you recommend a specialty of the house? I am not very familiar with Thai food yet, but so far, I have enjoyed everything I tasted," she said.

The waiter brought a scotch and dry white wine and set them on the table. He took their orders and disappeared silently. The outdoor patio, empty when they first arrived, now filled with a local clientele. No foreign language was discernible outside their own.

Isabela leaned forward, as the space between her and Jimmy seemed huge. She felt as if she might only recapture an essential, vital part of her being within the vicinity of his touch. Mirroring her action, Lance leaned on his elbows to narrow the space between them.

"Señori… Isabela, why did you choose to come to Thailand, really? It's a very long way from Central America, and I'd imagine many of the great art maestros are elsewhere. Not that I am an expert by any means, but when art is mentioned, I think of Paris and Italy. Thailand would be far down the list, even though I'm sure there are masters here. I cannot help but wonder how a young woman like yourself chose to study in this exotic corner of the world?"

"Do you remember my crazy, redhaired friend from the party? You see, she was looking around for an art teacher. A watercolor artist, specifically. My friend has traveled all over the world. I think she wanted something different from the usual European schools. The whole trip was her idea. I wasn't planning on coming, but …"

"May I ask what changed your mind?" he said.

She glanced quickly across the table, her words barely above a whisper. "A dream … I came because of a dream."

She straightened her spine, and her gaze was open and direct. Lance considered the young woman seated across from him, with receptive and unwavering eyes. He waited for her to continue. His facial expression remained curious, yet relaxed.

"Have you ever wondered what is real and what is imaginary?" she said. "Maybe you wake up and aren't quite sure if you are awake or dreaming and still asleep."

Lance slowly breathed out. Isabela's voice was a hypnotic melody that rocked him like a baby. His attention did not waver from her face. He nodded, but it was only afterward he realized that he knew exactly what she meant.

Isabela continued. "Since I was a very small child, I've had a dream that will not go away. The scene might be different each time, but I always know I am back there. I never talk about it, not to my father, even though we have no secrets between us. But there are no words for this ... world. What I imagine is, it can be known, but never told. This year abroad was not convenient for my family. I am supposed to marry in a year. But my father is a very kind and considerate man. He knew I needed this time. He arranged my visa, booked flights, and secured my rooms at the guest house. I am so grateful for his support. There's something here in Thailand. Something I have to catch? See? Meet? I'm sorry. It is difficult to find words." She paused and then spoke slowly, "I suppose I'm looking for peace ... freedom."

Lance observed her. Her eyes were slightly glazed and unfocused. Suddenly, he felt both raw and exposed as he breathed in the very essence of her. A shimmering image flitted across his mind, like a wisp or a fragrance. Someone in the past had looked at him that way. He pushed the image firmly back, willing her soft brown eyes to melt away. The Salvadoran woman was to be married. Good!

He remembered the fond farewell at the airport that came sharply into focus. His wife was beautiful and poised, yet somehow now she seemed two-dimensional in black-and-white. He had specifically chosen her. He bought the cute, three-bedroom house outside Washington, not that she was a domestic type. She graduated at the top of her class at university and immediately went to work with her father in his international consulting firm. Her father often joked that his only daughter was a rarity among women. Smarter than a man, he'd often say. One day, she would inherit the business, and he wanted to make sure she was knowledgeable in all areas of the enterprise.

Lance was on his own track, focused on a successful career in the Navy, and Anne was the perfect woman to have as a partner at his side. The future was intricately envisioned and set for both of them. Yet the vibrant, three-dimensional young woman seated across from him was strangely familiar. He realized she presented a dangerous diversion from his carefully laid plans. And he never before let anything interfere with his future.

He was in unfamiliar territory. No stranger to romantic liaisons, he was, however, extremely careful where women were concerned. He strove to avoid any emotional entanglement. That's why he chose Anne. She was intelligent, practical, and ... a little distant. It was a trait he came to appreciate. But he sensed, there was something quite different, yet eerily familiar, about this woman sitting across from him.

Careful, ole boy, you have a wife at home, a future that is all but guaranteed, and objectives to accomplish.

"You came all this way because of a dream?"

Isabela smiled and bit her lip.

"Sometimes I get this feeling that everything we see or touch is only a reflection, like foam settled on the top of the ocean. Many worlds are inside and out, like the little dolls that nest inside each other from Russia?"

His hand had a life of its own as it reached across the table and stroked her cheek.

Just then, the waiter approached with two steaming pad thai dishes. He set them down and returned to fill her wineglass, offering to fill one for the gentleman. Lance nodded without taking his eyes from Isabela.

"Tell me about the dream."

Isabela began slowly, tentatively, noticing his relaxed shoulders and how his eyes looked directly into hers. Suddenly, words tumbled one over the other, and her English became jumbled, almost incoherent. He missed a word, several of them, whole paragraphs even, but the force with which she attempted to communicate seeped into his skin and seized him like a vise. A magnetic switch pulled on him and beckoned. Without warning, memories mixed with and stacked one in front of the other like they played leapfrog. A vivid dream from early childhood loomed, urgent and salient.

A strong perfume wafted and trembled the insect's left antenna. He dropped the load he carried to rush away from a steady and driving demolition, joining a rabid exodus of workers. There were multitudes of ants! Yet he knew some of them. He recognized Amah, his father, and even his mother, whom he had never known in this life. From up above, a giant human boy shoveled deep into the earth in an excavation that crumbled the foundation of his world. He searched frantically for his family among the dispersing horde, all forced to abandon and move helter-skelter away from the devastating undulating earth that convulsed and rocked.

Lance momentarily abandoned the present to a flood of suppressed memories. He remembered awakening to an all-encompassing fear. His entire body dripped with sweat. When he opened his eyes, Amah was beside him, rubbing a cool cloth across his forehead. She began to speak to him in her low, soothing voice, this time about the kingdom of the ants, as if they had actually been there in his dream. He recalled her words precisely.

"All beings want to be happy. You are a special boy to have been given a vision outside of your own familiar world." He remembered how his old nanny looked directly into his eyes, smoothed his forehead with her cool cloth, and whispered, "Do not forget! Treat all creatures with respect and do your best not to bring harm to even the smallest ones."

For just a moment, the border between memory and reality blurred. Lance glanced across the table as images and memories were superimposed upon the present reality. It was as if Isabela's next action wove directly into the fabric of memory. The timing was utterly precise. She reached out and lightly placed her hand on his damp forehead. It was as if Amah's whisper echoed through the years and drew her near. Lance exhaled, took Isabela's hand from his forehead, and brought it to his lips. He willed his mind to focus on the present moment—the green checkered tablecloth, the small red candle on top, the ubiquitous chatter of conversations from neighboring tables, and the aromatic odors of chilis and garlic wafting throughout the restaurant. Isabela gently smiled, and her eyes connected to his without any need to look away.

Old dreams and the present moment fused into one giant montage. Like an intricate origami form slowly unfolding, buried memories arose, one on top of the next. The first was of Lance just arriving in the United States for his first year of military school. Everything was strange—his grandparents, the infrastructure, and the food. His grandfather bought eight pairs of shoes, socks, underwear, and trousers for the academy. They had his bag packed and ready to go in a matter of days, depositing him into the beige leather seat of the long black limousine. Charles, the chauffeur, escorted him up the steps to the headmaster's office, dropped his suitcase in the back of the room, and then disappeared with a nod to the boy. Lance experienced the room again, smelling the strong disinfectant on the gleaming black-and-white linoleum floor, the pungent aroma of cigar smoke, and the distinct mixture of whiskey and mint on the headmaster's breath when he leaned across the table to point at the school motto framed in black, the only adornment to the stark white walls, copied almost verbatim from West Point. They were proud to model themselves after the highest in military standards, he said.

"A cadet will not lie, steal, cheat, or tolerate those that do." The headmaster's hair was cropped short in a crew cut, his only compliance to a military standard. Circles of sweat lined his armpits, and white particles dusted his shoulders. He handed Lance a thick folder. "You are expected to be knowledgeable of all school rules by tomorrow morning. I suggest you read this cover to cover. Any upperclassman can and will test your knowledge and compliance. We have very high standards here. You are dismissed."

Lance shook his head once again, attempting to reorient himself back to the present moment. He glanced across the table at Isabela, whose outline seemed to waver in the candlelight. He hovered, present in disparate realities like a long row of passenger cars on the red-eye train from Baltimore. He observed the separate events with curiosity. It seemed so easy to pop into any car and believe its dimension, the smells, the texture, and even the taste of it. One moment and his mind was utterly absorbed by the soft curve of Isabela's neck, and in the next, a choreography of still film images burst forth.

He was assigned a double room with just one student, Cody from Michigan, a resident of the academy since the sixth grade. His first week, a fragile spider, a garden spider perhaps, wove a finely spun web in the corner of the dorm room. Cody grabbed a paperweight in his right hand and moved with zeal to smash the insect against the wall. Lance jumped off his cot and lunged across the floor, pushing his roommate to the side. He gently gathered the insect in his bare hands, and carried it gingerly out the door and down the stairs to the outside courtyard, and placed it on the branch of a tree.

Cody, of course, ratted him out. That very night he was yanked out of bed at two in the morning and doused with a bucket of ice water. Upperclassmen grabbed his arms and pushed him against the wall.

"Sissy! Mamma's boy!" The irony of the comment barely registered in his consciousness.

He instantly remembered the collection of glass jars in varying sizes that lined the shelf above his cot in the dorm of his new school. Inside the small rectangular jar were two spiders. The round jar contained several ants and in another three lightning bugs. The largest receptacle held a single monarch butterfly. He was ordered to kill them one by one, culminating in pulling the wings off the butterfly. He refused and locked his hands under his armpits. They, in turn, held him down and made him watch while they mutilated the insects. The nightly torment continued over several weeks. He never knew when, or if, they would come. Would he sleep the night? Would they wake him with ice water or a sharp jab to his feet?

He realized the mutilation would not stop until he complied, but that was not the end of it. One night, groggy from just-awakened sleep, he was presented with a small box, a gift they told him, wrapped in a lovely, rose-colored paper and tied with a sweet pink bow. Inside, a small grey mouse scurried back and forth. Its tiny nails scraped the bottom of the container. He was told to poke out the eyes and cut off the tail. He held his breath as the color drained from his cheeks and he passed out. Another bucket of ice smacked him to a disheartened revival, and the scene repeated again.

It was naïve, he realized later, to let down his guard. He thought they would finally leave him alone, become bored with him perhaps. But after two weeks of blissful, uninterrupted sleep, he was once again yanked awake at three in the morning. In a large cardboard box, undecorated this time, a brown rabbit with an oblong patch of white on its nose trembled, and its marbled eyes quivered. They forced his right hand into the box, and an upperclassman's fingers guided his to stroke the animal's head gently from ear to tail. The upperclassman tightened his grip, his fingers coercing the younger cadets to close around the neck. In his hand, he felt the animal's heartbeat, as a blurred vibration synthesizing the pounding beats from within his own rib cage.

It was the rabbit that wavered in and out of his awareness during his time at the academy. He pushed the memory down, commanding the horror of it deep into the shadow. However well-hidden, though, the memory of it slipped into his dreams well into his twenties.

The upperclassman, Dexter, announced, "Your pre-training is complete."

Isabela reached out her hand. "Are you okay?" she said, as her eyes searched his. Strangely, she felt an urge to lunge across the table and wrap her arms around this strange man, who seemed, in this moment, so vulnerable and boy-like. She wished she might hold him and keep gently rocking until the angst inside them both lifted. Lance let his fingers slide along the outline of her jaw. He, too, was silent and thoughtful. Defying reason, the heaviness inside him began to lift like a dark cloud dissipating into a wide-open sky.

The waiter, aware his presence might intrude, silently approached the table to politely stand to the side until he was acknowledged. Isabela looked up first as the waiter pointed toward the bar. There, a bald man with black-rimmed glasses and a loud, orange Hawaiian shirt held up his glass in a gesture of a toast. He was the only other foreigner in the restaurant. Lance straightened, immediately wide awake and alert. Nigel Hawkes had entered, sat, and then ordered a drink, and Lance was oblivious to his arrival. It was a grave lapse in attention. He swore under his breath, instantly breaking the almost magical trance that enveloped him and Isabela. She noticed the change, and her eyes naturally followed Lance's. Nigel Hawkes walked toward them, with a smile toying at the corner of his lips.

"Jimmy Calhoun! Such a fortuitous encounter. I hoped I might run into you. Heard you were in Thailand somewhere. I just arrived myself this morning. May I join you? And please introduce me to your lovely companion."

"Miss Marquez, Nigel Hawkes. Nigel is an acquaintance of mine from England. Miss Marquez and I briefly met a few months back at the Sunday bazaar. She is from El Salvador but is here studying art." Lance's attention was now riveted on the Englishman. "Nigel, it's great to see you. I was—we were, however, just leaving. Do you have time tomorrow?"

"No need to rush off on my account. Stay and finish your coffee. Let's grab a lunch, as you Yanks say, tomorrow. How about late morning? Eleven thirty, say? Are you staying at the same hotel as last time? Might I meet you there?" Nigel smiled.

"Yes, it's the same hotel as always. I'll leave a message with the front desk if I run out for a minute."

The two men shook hands; then Nigel extended his hand to Isabela. "Miss Marquez, it was a pleasure to meet you. I hope your stay in Chiang Mai will be most interesting."

Isabela's posture was aligned and poised, but as Nigel Hawkes approached, her height increased a millimeter, instantly aware of the change in electricity, especially the abrupt shift she'd witnessed in

Jimmy. She watched Mr. Hawkes return to the bar and noticed the slight drag of his left foot. She was quiet, trained by her father to sit silently, attentive yet unobtrusive, when business was discussed. Her father often solicited her perspective as a key element in considering possible options and their subsequent consequences. Every choice, he was fond of telling her, rippled and spanned beyond the scope of human prediction. The best one could do was to be well-informed, approach each decision with insight, and consider the subject from as many vantage points as possible.

Isabela quietly sipped her espresso and waited for Jimmy to speak. He, however, pushed back his chair and motioned to the waiter to bring the check. He paid without a word and propelled her toward the exit with a light squeeze to her elbow and a quick nod toward the Englishman sitting at the bar.

"Thank you for a beautiful dinner. It was delicious," she said.

"You are most welcome, Señorita Marquez. I hope you enjoyed the view."

It was as if a bucket of ice water was thrown over them both when Nigel Hawkes walked over to their table. Isabela felt the dramatic shift from warmth and intimacy to a cold formality down into her bones. The man, Nigel Hawkes, was someone important to Jimmy Calhoun. She could see it in the set of Jimmy's eyes and the tightness of his jaw. Isabela knew it was none of her business, yet after the shared closeness of this night, she could not prevent her mind from returning to the strange and abrupt ending.

Neither spoke on the ride back into the city. She wrapped her arms around his waist and laid her face against his back, listening to the same steady heartbeat. He came to a stop in front of her guesthouse, revving the engine without moving. She continued to lay her head against his back with her arms around his waist. After a few minutes, he turned off the engine and lifted her from the seat. He drew her to him and wrapped his arms around her, pressing her close against his chest. He smoothed hair away from her forehead. He bent down to touch her lips, pausing just a moment, and then straightened and turned her by the shoulders toward the hotel entrance.

"Isabela." She stopped, turning to face him and ready to jump back onto the motorcycle with him. He straddled the seat, and the engine purred. "Isabela … Señorita Marquez, I am leaving town in the morning. We can't meet again."

Chapter Nineteen

1961

Chiang Mai, Thailand

It was still dark outside when Nigel rapped on guestroom number seven. He pushed the door open, entered, and sat on the edge of the bed. The sheets were tucked into perfect hotel corners and evenly stretched, without a wrinkle. A voice resounded from the bathroom.

"I'll be right out!" Lance emerged from the shower, rubbing his head with a towel and wearing only a pair of khaki shorts. He quickly slipped on a navy T-shirt.

"I ordered us some coffee and a few pastries. I figured you'd be here early. I hope you're hungry." Lance went to the door and opened it just as room service appeared in the hallway with a cart. The aroma of coffee and freshly baked bread wafted into the room.

"You can leave the food on the table. Thank you." A small pile of baht and coins lay strewn on the nightstand. Lance reached for the cash and offered it to the room service man, who smiled graciously and quietly closed the door behind him. Nigel moved to the table and poured two cups of black coffee.

"We have a mandatory meeting in Chiang Rai this morning at nine a.m. All the big brass will be in attendance. I'd like to go over, again, what you observed from the party last week and, in particular, your visit to the panhandle. Terribly sorry you've been given the runaround, but it's necessary. It was nothing less than a stroke of luck to have so many players under one roof. Up until now, we were unable to negotiate with the commanders in southern Laos. Your visit with Mr. Arsenault and the panhandle may be the most promising development we have experienced in establishing friendly relations with a prominent family in the south."

Lance combed his fingers through his hair. "It's a complex situation," he said. "The commander has his own small army, if you can call it that. From what I could see, most of the soldiers were terrified boys of fourteen or fifteen. One kid was no more than about ten. The rifle was bigger than he was. If I had my way, I'd send in a team to rescue those kids, not negotiate with criminals. Damn it, they should have a fucking chance in life."

"Quite," Nigel said.

"It's a high-stakes chess game, I understand, but will the CIA really support this kind of criminal activity?" Lance said. "It pisses me off."

"Quite right, old chap. Unfortunately, international politics is a multi-faceted game. Certain injustices must be overlooked to secure the objective."

"Well, it seems un-American. The commander's region is definitely not Xob's peaceful Hmong village, with the sole purpose to protect the land, women, and children. What I witnessed at the commander's residence was a calculated move to increase drug production and a power play to gain Western support for it. The commander was not shy in expressing his intention," Lance said.

Nigel noted the tension in the younger man's shoulders and the tightness of his jaw as he spoke. He paused before replying. "It takes upward of six months for anyone or anything to get through the jungles of Laos. It's a certain death trap. Malaria, wild animal attacks, and starvation are just a few of the deterrents. If the Pathet Lao gain more ground in southern Laos and create a supply infrastructure, our efforts to stabilize the region will become that much more difficult. Opium production is a way of life over here. We won't interfere."

"If the CIA provides military support for these local commanders, they will become powerful and extremely dangerous. I think they need to reconsider doing business with potential drug warlords."

"To stabilize the region, we have no choice. Either we work with the regional commanders, or the communists will certainly prevail. Time is of the essence. If the American public gets a whiff of war in a faraway land too soon, Congress will close the purse strings. We'll lose our chance at stabilizing the region."

"I know I am just the messenger, but I see the dire implications of these alliances."

Nigel reached for a second croissant, took a bite, and then continued in an abrupt reversal of subject.

"Intel has been quite thorough in providing you with an interesting backstory. You were briefed on the details," he said. "Disgruntled Marine officer working undercover with an axe to grind, whose allegiance might be manipulated for the right price. It's always a good idea to make the interested parties dig a bit for their information. What we have supplied them with is just enough truth to be believable and keep them sniffing in the wrong direction."

"It's the German who makes my skin crawl," Lance said.

"Don't worry. Your part in the negotiation is done. The team will take it from here. I am sending you back to the village."

"Hanging out in the cave is starting to look like a vacation." Lance grinned.

"When you get to the village, I'd like you to do a little scouting. Take a few of the village men and see what you can uncover regarding construction in Laos. Intel mapped a few roads in the area, but if they are expanding their network, the Americans will need to know." Nigel took a final bite of croissant and left the rest on the table. "Let's go. The helicopter is waiting."

Nigel and Lance strode out of the hotel and onto the street. A car waited for them at the curbside, engine running. They climbed into the vehicle from opposite sides of the car and eased back into the rear seat.

"What is your estimation of the village leader, Xob? Can we be assured of his cooperation?"

"I'm confident he's onboard. It's just a waiting game until the elders have the opportunity to raise objections, consider risks and benefits, and allow everyone's voice to be heard. It's the democratic process in its idealistic state. We have to support that!"

Nigel laughed. "You have done an excellent job all around. After the scouting mission, and once we are reasonably sure the elders of the village are on board, you can take that well-deserved R&R I have been promising you. In the meantime, keep a low profile. I don't like the German fellow's insinuation and interest in you."

"Yes sir! And thank you, sir."

The meeting lasted two hours. As they exited the building and walked toward the aircraft hangar, Nigel placed his hand on Lance's shoulder.

"Old boy, I hope there will be no further need to mention the woman you dined with last night. A lovely young woman by any standard, but given the present political environment and the mission at hand, I must insist on no further contact."

All at once, the subtle scent of jasmine seemed to suffuse the air around him. Lance hesitated, a brief second, and quickly replied, "It was a chance encounter. We won't meet again."

Nigel noted the pause, stared hard at the younger man, lifted his hand in farewell, and then turned and walked away.

Chapter Twenty

1961

Chiang Mai, Thailand

The maestro rarely critiqued. Instead, he approached the student-teacher dynamic with respect, careful to ignite and inspire curiosity rather than restrict. Under his tutelage, the scope and breadth of Isabela's work deepened and took flight. Her art transformed into a mirrored expression of her inner world.

One evening, the maestro rolled out a long sheet of white paper that ran across the width of the studio floor and motioned for Isabela to come close. He placed a large chunk of chalk in her hand and asked her to draw without any purpose in mind. "Allow the energy to express without criticism. Let the curves, lines, and spiraling figures guide you."

It took some time, frustrating minutes, away from her art. *What is the purpose of this?* After only a short while, however, her thoughts calmed, and her lines became fluid. Separation between herself and the flow of black chalk on white became muted and mysterious.

Prapat asked questions, not to impart his vision but to excavate her subconscious and the wells of her hidden creativity. He'd place an object on the table and ask Isabela to describe the contours, its form, and, more importantly, the feeling it invoked. Invariably, she returned to the piece she was working on more open and able to see. She learned to see the beauty in the ordinary and simple. The maestro hired models, some nude and others fully clothed, but refrained from hiring the traditionally good-looking or even ordinary types. He preferred souls exposed to the raw and harsh reality of living. One day, he brought in an old woman with a severely hunched back, no teeth, and gnarled hands. Another time, he found a young beggar woman with a prematurely wrinkled face and dirt jammed under her fingernails. She was discovered hugging an equally filthy baby to her breast. Blood seeped from a wound just near her left nipple. Nonetheless, the baby clung to his mother's bony frame and sucked. The young beggar woman sealed her lips tight as her suspicious eyes darted around the studio. She squeezed the baby in against her rib cage as if the child might be snatched at any moment from her grasp. Isabela sat down and began speaking softly in Spanish, a language the beggar could hardly have known. She laid her arm on the woman's shoulder and did not pull away at her pungent stench. Eventually, a timid smile edged across the beggar's cheeks, and the woman's hand flew up to conceal an abyss of rotted teeth. Isabela eased the woman's arm down and lightly ran her fingers across the woman's forehead, arranging her greasy hair behind her ears. Quietly, she reached behind her to take up pencil and paper. She looked into the woman's eyes, at the haunted intelligence of her gaze, and for just one moment, she imagined their roles reversed. What would it be like to live on the street with nowhere to call home and a child to care for? Isabela immersed herself as she became the other. She smelled menstrual blood ooze down her leg and felt a gnawing pierce inside of her stomach. She gazed down at the sleeping child and was overwhelmed by a universal tenderness and love. She felt the baby nestled close to her skin and its mouth sucking on her emaciated breast as an all-consuming need to defend and protect this tiny human engulfed her.

The finished watercolor elicited a rare response from her mentor. Isabela stood back from the painting with brush poised in hand. Should she add a splash of shadow under the women's eye or perhaps brighten the ray of light from the window to illuminate the child's face? Prapat touched her arm gently, stopping it mid-action. His gaze bore into the luminous dark eyes of the mother. He spoke softly, "There is nothing more to be done."

Chapter Twenty-One

1977

El Salvador

It was early. Cumulus clouds painted the sky with puffs of pillow-like cotton. Mera sliced papaya and slathered butter on a piece of rye bread before passing the plate to Analena, who took the food and began to eat. They both looked up as the front door swung wildly open, and a woman entered in obvious pain, her shoulders supported by her husband on the one side and her brother on the other. The woman moaned as the two men gently lowered her onto the mat Analena indicated with her hand. The husband's words sputtered and tumbled. His wife was normal and healthy when they went to sleep the night before. This morning when she woke up and when she tried to stand, she collapsed onto the dirt floor, screaming. Her foot was swollen to twice its normal size. The old healer motioned Mera closer to see how the skin of the woman's left foot was engorged and bright purple with internal bleeding. The woman gasped as Analena palpated the foot lightly with her left palm, feeling the pulse and allowing her fingers to gently move over the surface of the sole and around to the heel. She observed the woman's foot.

"Araña," Analena said, nodding toward the front door in indication of the rainforest.

"Go. Find the plant. Be quick about it," she said without looking in Mera's direction.

A sudden heat overwhelmed Mera's body, and her cheeks darkened to a deep red. The woman's leg, perhaps her life, depended on whether she could find the plant with the precise antivenom chemistry to counteract the poison of this one particular spider. All she thought she learned about nature and healing disappeared in an instant. Mera froze halfway out the doorway when Analena spoke to her mind as clearly as if she'd shouted out loud. *Stay here then if you are unsure. Take care of the woman. I'll go.*

Shocked from inertia to action, Mera bolted into the rainforest with absolutely no direction or plan. She cleared the cottage and the vegetable garden and splashed across a small stream without slowing her pace or stopping to collect her thoughts. Tears streamed down her cheeks.

I am only a girl. Why did she send me out here alone? Tears dried as a sudden crippling rage constricted her breath. *The woman needs to see a real doctor! What am I doing with this crazy, old woman?*

Images from *THAT DAY* materialized. Solid and heavy, they sucked the very oxygen from her lungs. Her feet were numb, and she stumbled and fell into the shallow water. Immediately, she pressed herself back into an upright position to once again run like a horse along the creek's edge. Her foot slipped again, and she fell backward, knocking her head on a sharp rock. Blood oozed from the back of her skull and dripped down her neck. She dragged herself to the shore, panting, and her eyesight blurred. Her breath recovered, and she realized the creek tumbled into a cascading waterfall. She brought her hand to the back of her head to explore the large swelling with her fingers.

Mera scrambled down the steep rocks of the rapids. Mist sprayed upward in a giant arch and transformed into tiny beads of iridescent light in the afternoon sun. Her blue flowered dress, dirty from falling and dampened by the water mist, clung to her body. She dropped into the deep pool of water fully clothed, submerging her head into the pristine water to let it soothe the bruises and cuts on her arms and legs. After a short while, she climbed out of the water, sat down on the bank, and wrapped her arms around her knees. *I need to go back now so we can take the woman to the medico! I need to tell the old woman I don't know where to look for the plant! How does she expect me to know where to find the right one? There are so many everywhere! Which one? What color? What should the leaves look like? It's impossible! I'm so afraid! Please don't let it be too late!*

Mera's body rocked back and forth, and then she cried out, "Mama, please help me! Come back, Mama. I don't know what to do!"

The sound of her own voice, silent for so many months, sounded strange in her ears. Sweat oozed from every pore in her body. Stark images from *THAT DAY* threatened to overwhelm her. She closed her eyes and took a long breath in, held it, and willed the images to disappear. She passed out.

The air was still as Mera lay inert on the forest floor, unconscious. A numinous presence, freed from its tight constraints of physical form, gazed down at the unresponsive body, yellowish and suffused in a soft, dull light. *Is that person breathing?* Curious, it moved in closer. Recognition dawned. *That person is me!*

Mera drew in her breath and instantly found herself back in her body. Tears spilled onto the dirt as giant sobs racked her torso. She cried until there was not an ounce of liquid to squeeze from her eyes. She lay prone on the ground watching swaying branches and the changing geometric patterns of blue sky and green leaves as the forest inhaled and exhaled.

It might have been a few minutes or a half an hour. She wasn't sure. A faint light flashed twice as the sun danced between wavering leaves, and then again slivers of light shot out stronger and brighter. She pushed herself up onto her elbows and became aware of a faint tinkling of bells and flutes. She cocked her head to listen. There it was again, coming from the direction where the sun rose. Slowly, she stood and tentatively stepped in the direction where she last heard the music. The tiny light that flashed like a pinprick expanded to fill her entire peripheral vision. The source of the light was a grouping of plants showered with purple, spindly flowers. *Of course!*

She bent down, chose one young plant, and snipped a cutting. She continued to the next array, careful to select just one plant. She left the others intact and said a prayer to the largest—the Mother. She began to see the forest with renewed wonder. *Life is precious! Every seed, every sparrow, and every little creeping, crawling creature!* She felt lighter and in tune with the forest around her. It was as if her whole being had suddenly taken residence right in the center of her heart. A voice seemed to whisper in her ear, *It's not about you!* Knowledge that was nonexistent the moment before suddenly became sharp and focused. If this body ceased to exist, there was no worry. Every plant, animal, mountain, and stream was in constant flux and change. The woman with the swollen leg suddenly flashed across Mera's mind. Carefully, she placed the herbs into her pocket as she stood and began to run back the way she came.

The sun painted the sky in flamboyant orange when the girl finally burst excitedly into the cabin and reached her hand into the wide pocket of her dress for the plants. The light in the cabin was suffused by the setting sun, and just a few candles burned. Otherwise, the cabin was empty and silent. Mera slowly withdrew her hand from her pocket and sank to the floor. She was sure it was the right plant, exactly what was needed. But what was the use? Half a day had passed, and fatal infection would have set in hours ago. Images of the woman and her husband burned onto the surface of her skin like a brand on livestock. Analena had trusted her!

The girl took a breath and quickly began to gather her few belongings, intent on leaving the cottage before the old healer returned. She couldn't bear the thought of the old woman's deep, fathomless eyes. She took one last look around the cabin, taking in the pungent smell of herbs and rows of plants in various stages of drying. Then slowly, as if pulled by an invisible cord, her eyes zeroed in on a spot to the left. Suspended lightly from the ceiling, she saw dried purple flowers with feather-weight spindly blossoms. She stepped closer and reached into her pocket to extract the flowers. She held them next to the ones hanging upside down. A match! Relief flooded her awareness as if a soothing balm.

Analena entered the cabin as Mera hung purple plants upside down next to the older dried ones. Mera leapt across the room and dropped onto her knees. She opened her arms and hugged the woman tight against her chest. She spoke aloud for the first time in nine months.

"Gracias, gracias, te amo mucho, gracias." *Thank you, thank you, I love you so much, thank you.*

Chapter Twenty-Two

1961

Chiang Mai, Thailand

"Miss Marquez, what a pleasant surprise!"

Isabela looked up sharply from the article she was reading with the American president, John F. Kennedy, in the headlines. She considered the man in the tailored beige business suit standing in front of her with his maroon bow tie and clean white shirt. The clothing was in stark contrast to the casual attire he'd worn when she was first introduced to him.

"May I join you?"

"Of course." Isabela indicated the seat across from her and smiled. Her mind, however, raced. *What is he doing here?* Isabela straightened her spine and sipped her cup of coffee. She smiled as politely as she was able, under the circumstances.

"I see you keep up with American news?" he said. "What do you think of their president? A handsome fellow by most accounts, especially the ladies … although, a bit of a womanizer, I've heard tell."

The conversation meandered. He asked about school, art, and her impression of Thailand and its people. He proposed several recommendations to visit sites seldom uncovered by the casual tourist.

"Be sure to visit the Doi Suthep monastery outside of town," Nigel said. "It sits on the top of a small mountain. Quite inspiring, they say, to art students and laymen alike. There's a legend about a white elephant and the origins of the monastery."

"So, it's true? There is such an animal as the white elephant? I thought it was a myth. Mr. Hawkes, you seem to know the city well. Do you live here?"

"I'm here on and off for business. Of course, over the years, one tends to pick up bits of interesting lore. Actually, the albino elephant is shown in art as pure white, although in reality, it's a reddish-brown color. Only the toes and eyelashes are light. The Thai term is Chang Samkhan, or auspicious elephant. It means purity. The Thai buy into all these metaphysical myths. There's nothing solid about it. The elephant, however, is real."

"I will make sure to visit this temple."

"And you, Miss Marquez, when will you go back to your country? How long do you plan to stay?" Isabela noted the expression on his face subtly shifted. She sat up and reminded herself to pay very close attention. "How long have you known Jimmy Calhoun?" Nigel asked without waiting for her answer. "He's a bit of a womanizer as well, I'm afraid. Decent sort of chap from a man's point of view, but not the reliable sort where women are involved. I've known Jimmy for years, and a lovely young woman like you would do best to keep her distance."

Isabela willed her heart to steady as she quickly considered her response. Obviously, Mr. Hawkes did not want her and Jimmy to meet again. She chose her words carefully. "Thank you for your concern, but we only met once. I don't expect to see him again."

Nigel noted the small white lie. The two had met at least twice. He shifted in his seat and changed the subject.

"Well, my dear, where was I? Ah yes, the white elephant myth. There's a legend about it. As the story goes, there was once a common monk who was a sincere spiritual aspirant. He went to sleep one night and had a special dream, wherein he was instructed to look for an unusual object. When he woke up the next morning, he immediately began to look around, and before long, he happened upon a bone and picked it up. This was not any bone, mind you. This one was a magical bone that glowed and had a special charmed ability. It was able to disappear at will. The magical bone was given to a king, who was a dull and unimaginative sort. In this king's possession, the bone displayed no magical powers. The king wanted to discharge himself of the item as quickly as possible, thinking it would bring him bad luck. A second king, more of a visionary sort, heard about the relic and was intrigued. He asked if he could have it with the first king's blessing. And so, the second king gained possession of the bone, which immediately glowed and split in two, according to the myth. The smaller piece was enshrined in a temple in Wat Suan Dok. The king placed the larger piece on the back of a white elephant and released him into the jungle. The elephant is said to have climbed the mountain at Doi Suthep and trumpeted three times before dying at the site. It was interpreted as an omen and is why, some say, the temple was constructed there. Some believe the relic was actually half of Buddha's shoulder bone." Nigel paused before continuing, "You can read all this up on the hill when you visit. I am an agnostic myself."

"I'd like to paint this magic elephant and his temple. Gracias, it is a beautiful story." The gap between what she wanted to ask and what she actually said was widening.

"Alas, my dear, I must take your leave. Thank you for allowing me the pleasure of sharing your breakfast table. And please, if I can be of any assistance to you while you are here in Thailand, I'd be most obliged. I am very familiar with the city and might direct you to a few hidden gems."

Nigel extended his business card.

NIGEL HAWKES, *CEO,*
International Paper Imports
Chiang Mai, Thailand

"Gracias, Mr. Hawkes." Her question remained silent in the space between words.

Chapter Twenty-Three

1961

Chiang Mai, Thailand

The change was subtle, yet definite, when Isabela began her apprenticeship with Prapat. Isabela and Kate still met for an occasional glass of wine or to attend a social event, but the easy familiarity they had enjoyed in El Salvador became conspicuously absent. Neither mentioned the subject of art. It was a bridge inevitably burned where once there had been wide passage. Isabela tried to tell Kate about Jimmy Calhoun. Three times she stood outside Kate's door with her arm poised to knock, only to drop her hand and walk away. Instead, she stayed late at the studio, often hours after the master himself had left for home, immersing herself in the textures and colors of Thailand. Her dreams were cast with the fragrance of lotuses and the hazel eyes of Jimmy Calhoun.

"That's all for today. You may go home now."

Isabela glanced up from her piece, a white elephant standing in turquoise water. Prapat's willowy voice instantly jolted the two-dimensional world of easels and paint into sharp focus. Last

Sunday, while perusing the local library, she came upon a travel magazine. One of its articles extolled the virtues of northern Tibet with accompanying photographs. One in particular highlighted a remote lake with brilliant, turquoise-blue water high in the Himalayas. She used the photograph as an aide, although the designs and colors of her painting looked nothing like the original image. Her elephant was a creamy white, and the outlines of its body merged and seemed evanescent with the material world beyond.

"The eyes … I don't see the eyes. They're …"

"Take a little time, my dear. A day off will do you a world of good. Go out with friends. Sometimes, we have to leave in order to see. Come now, it's almost seven."

Isabela cleaned the last brush and placed the tops back onto the watercolor tubes. She moved in slow motion, willing Prapat to take his leave so she might return to her piece. Prapat, however, had his hand on the light switch and looked in her direction. She hurried to put her brushes and paint away and exited the studio with her mentor, but her mind still filled with turquoise hues and an orange emblazoned sky. Together, they walked down the steps as Prapat wished her good night. Isabela turned and moved toward the corner, the spot easiest to grab a tuk tuk. A loud rumbling startled her, and her eyes naturally moved in the direction of the sound. Down the street to her right, the revving of a motorbike overpowered the clatter and clang of the evening's heavy traffic.

Straddling the seat, a man shifted the handlebar of his motorcycle without moving from his parked position. Isabela walked toward the tuk tuk stand and the man on the motorbike, still distracted by her painting and the washes needed to achieve the effect she wanted to create. All at once, her eyesight sharpened, and her attention was stirred to an outward pull. She stopped mid-step and stared at the man on the motorcycle as his facial features became suddenly recognizable.

It had been almost three months since he'd dropped her off at her guesthouse with the parting words, "We can't meet again." Isabela tried to steady her breath.

Lance swung his leg over the bike and walked toward her, narrowing the distance between them in a few easy strides.

"Hello, Isabela. It appears I am unable stay away from you after all. You have been haunting my dream, you and Amah."

"Amah?" she said, a quizzical expression forming on her face.

"Amah is my old nanny, a Hmong woman who looked after me when I was a boy. Of course, you don't know who I am talking about. I never mentioned her to you when we met. You could say she was like a mother to me. You don't look remotely alike, but somehow when I'm dreaming, there's no separation between an old Hmong woman and your beautiful face. Damned if I know what the hell it means!"

Lance took the small wad of gum from his mouth and stuck it behind his ear and narrowed his gaze down to his boots.

Isabela gently pulled on her earlobe. She hesitated before saying, "At first, I knew you would come, but then after such a long time, I could only hope."

He raised his head to look at her and said, "You came out of nowhere, damn it! Like a bullet. There's no place for you in the world I live in. The trouble is I'm unable to get you out of my mind. What are we going to do, you and me? I haven't considered the happiness of anyone in a very long time, do you understand? All I've wanted is to be the best and to hell with anyone who gets in my way. It's all unraveling and gone to shit. I have no idea where that leaves me." He reached out and lightly touched her hair. "Will you give me a minute to figure things out?" he said. "Let me walk you home. We can stop on the way and get something to eat."

He parked the bike on the side of the road and took her hand, which slid within his fingers easily. The night was calm, with the afternoon's heat just abating to a more comfortable temperature. The traffic, however, still bustled. Horns honked, and taxis wove precariously in and around each other, defying any rational purpose. Lance released her hand and rested his arm comfortably around her shoulder.

"I'm only in town today," he said. "Then I'll be gone for at least a month, but I'm hoping to have a few days off when I get back. There's no telling when I'll be free, but there's a place I'd like to take you. It's an incredible island in the south of Thailand where my father took me as a boy. I remember it as a veritable paradise. Would you be able to get away? We could meet there. There are things I need to explain."

"I don't know …" she said.

Thoughts of her mother, father, and Tomás came briefly to her, but they faded into the background as she leaned into Lance's shoulder. She was silent for a few moments, and then words burst forth of their own volition.

"I'd like to see your island."

Chapter Twenty-Four

1977

El Salvador

The girl was gone for most of the day. The sky darkened to a deep purple hue as the first star of the evening pricked through the velvety magenta above. Analena stirred thick chicken soup over the wood stove, and a delicious aroma filled her cabin. She glanced over her shoulder and out toward the direction where the girl had left that morning, as if she could see through the closed door. It was much later than usual. Suddenly, the door burst open, and Mera entered. A sack filled with roots and herbs was slung over her shoulder, and her cheeks flushed from the heat.

"Analena, I have never seen this plant before. Please tell me its purpose. I think it is a special one!"

The old healer filled two earthenware bowls with soup. Orange and green vegetables floated on the top of the steamy chicken broth. She motioned for the child to sit on the dirt floor beside her. They ate silently side by side. The old healer's voice crackled, piercing the silence.

"Where did you find this, mija? I have only seen this root once before, when I was a young woman. A curandero, a powerful healer from a far-away village, brought it to where I lived with my family. The root's presence among the village preceded terrible things.

Afterward, I never saw my family again. No, I don't work with this medicine, although others do." Analena paused for a moment before continuing. "It was not the plant, you understand. The root simply showed the elders what was coming. That it has found its way here to us is important. You must be ready, mija, for I am an old woman."

Mera listened, and sweat beaded on her forehead. Her hands began to shake.

"Abuelita, por favor!" *Grandmother, please!* "We need to go into the forest! The trees will hide and protect us!" Her voice cracked, and her heart raced.

Analena gazed across the fire. Her eyes were dark and bottomless.

"Your journey will not be an easy one, mija. We are here now sharing this time and this place, but the doorway is closing. You will wander lost and broken, traveling far, far away from here. You will try to come back, but the forest will no longer welcome you …" Analena stopped mid-sentence, placed her hand under Mera's chin, and looked into her eyes. "You must be strong and overcome three things. Only then will you learn that life is like a shadow."

Mera's eyes began to well. "I can't. I want to stay with you."

Analena's gaze did not waver as she continued. "Remember, fear eats the spirit whole. Turn around and face the demons. Don't back down! You have lost confidence, but don't worry. Your feelings of powerlessness and frailty do not run deep. You have great strength inside of you. Your heart is shut down from such a great pain, but this is not the way. Let your heart beat with the rhythm of the birdsong and the whisper of the trees. Let the rivers teach you to move while standing still."

Mera's body trembled. "Abuelita, what are you saying?"

"Learn to overcome your fear. You must find the strength that lives inside you!"

Analena set the soup bowl down and began to chant prayers in an ancient tongue until a familiar peace enveloped both the old one and the girl.

"Don't worry, my child. You are not going to die," the old healer whispered, her words soft and soothing like a lullaby.

Mera closed her eyes and slept curled up on the ground. Analena covered her in a blanket and continued to pray.

Chapter Twenty-Five

1961

Chiang Mai, Thailand

*T*he man sat in an oversized chair holding a small dog on his lap. His features were shadowed and indistinct. The dog carefully licked a raw, open wound that zigzagged up the entire length of his front forepaw. The girl flung the bathroom cabinet door open wide and slammed dresser drawers in and out. She stood up on her tiptoes to reach the shelf above the icebox. She was sure there must be some ointment, antibiotic, or bandages somewhere. It was definitely the man's dog, but the owner appeared uninterested in its well-being. "The dog is fine," he said. She continued to scrounge every corner of the house. Then she understood she was not at home, and here in this foreign country, no store sold the necessary ointment. She ran up and down the streets, intent on finding anything that might be of use.

The phone rang and startled her awake. Isabela rolled on her side and glanced at the clock on her nightstand. It was 3:33 a.m. She switched on the light and lifted the phone receiver to her ear before falling back onto the bed. She settled comfortably onto the pillow, assuming she'd hear her mother's voice and the almost-certain plea for her daughter to return home on the next available flight.

"¿Hola?" *Hello?*

"Isabela?"

"Si." *Yes.*

"My sweet girl, I am so sorry to wake you. I am only near a phone for a minute. I won't be able to come to Chiang Mai, but we could meet at the island. Might you manage to get away? You'll need a passport."

"Jimmy? It's you?"

Suddenly, Isabela was wide awake. Her heart thumped erratically.

"My driver can pick you up at the guesthouse Thursday morning at eight in the morning. I'd like to take you to the island I told you about. It just might inspire a painting or two! Please, don't worry. My intention is honorable, and you will have your own …"

Crackling static ensued. His voice was indistinct and faint. The connection weakened and then went completely dead. She held the receiver in her hand to jiggle the buttons on the base.

"Ms. Marquez, how may I help you?" the front desk clerk politely inquired.

"I am sorry. No, I do not need anything."

Mera gently set the receiver back into the cradle. She sat up and wrapped her arms around her bent legs, resting her head on her knees. After a short while, she fell asleep with her head still on her knees.

At six, the phone rang again, sharp and clear. Her eyes shot open, and she quickly reached across the nightstand, only to hold the receiver against her chest and take a deep breath. Slowly, she brought the phone to her ear.

"Jimmy?"

"Isabela, es tu madre! Quien es Jimmy?" *Isabela, it's your mother! Who is Jimmy?*

Isabela sank under the covers. "Nadie, Madre, nadie. Como estás?" *No one, Mother, no one. How are you?*

"I am fine, but I will be much better when you return home! When may I tell the Chavezes you will be back? Tomás says he hasn't heard from you in weeks."

"Thursday I am going on a little trip to see an island in the south of Thailand. I've heard it's very beautiful. Please, Mama, this is my last opportunity to experience a little bit of the world before marriage. There is still so much to see and learn!"

After listening to her mother share all the gossip from home and promising she'd be in touch soon, Isabela quietly set the telephone back in its cradle. A light vermilion spread slowly across her cheek, and her entire face felt hot to the touch. She held her head in her hands and lightly swayed back and forth. A polite refusal to the island invitation was the proper and correct response. What would Papa think? Memories of her father's kind eyes and his warm hand lying atop hers rushed to the forefront of her mind, while an unfamiliar voice whispered in her ear.

You will never have this chance again. Beyond right and wrong, just take this moment to be young and alive. Experience whatever this is with Jimmy. Then go home and live the life you're expected to live. It's not for three days yet. You have plenty of time to decide …

Isabela fell back onto the bed and pulled the light blanket up to her chin. She rolled to her side and nestled into a tight fetal position.

Chapter Twenty-Six

1961

Ko Pha Ngan, Thailand

Sweat rolled down her back as incipient, tiny monsters nipped at the lining of her brain.

What if he's not here? Why did I come? Stupid girl! Traveling to meet a foreign man in a strange land, far away from anything familiar and comforting.

The note she'd received was accompanied by precise instructions. Flight information and airline and ferry tickets were all delivered to her door. Even as she packed her bag and arranged for a few days off from the studio, she didn't really believe she would go through with this. But, from the day she wandered into the Chiang Mai bazaar and her path crossed with his, she knew the decision had already been made.

Isabela observed the crowd that moved like a wave toward the ferry exit as her eyes shifted to the right. Weaving upstream, he towered above the five-foot Thais. Dressed in khaki shorts, a light green T-shirt, and leather sandals, he moved toward her with a warm smile. He waved and indicated with his hand to stay put. He would come to her. Her shoulders dropped as she breathed out, and the tension in her face relaxed. All of those inner voices suddenly quieted. She allowed the crowd to separate on either side of her as a space naturally opened. Jimmy came to a stop and extended his hand. Instantly aware of the heat and pressure of his long fingers wrapped around her smaller ones, Isabela returned the smile.

"I was afraid you might not have come," he said.

Thick, wooden pillars lifted the one-story bungalow easily above the water. The charming, three-bedroom house with its living room and extended terrace was almost one with the clear turquoise bay below. A Thai servant in a red flowered dress greeted their arrival with palmed hands and her head bowed. She guided them into the house and then left. In a moment, she returned holding a small tray with two iced papaya drinks. White plumerias floated on the top. She lowered her head once again and faded into the hallway.

"I hope you don't mind the house. You have your own room, of course. Take some time to clean up and settle in. Perhaps we can take a walk along the beach before dinner?"

"It's beautiful here. Yes, thank you."

Isabela's bedroom door remained closed as the sun lowered toward the horizon.

Jimmy approached the closed door and then abruptly turned to step onto the terrace overlooking the sea. He stared out over the open waters, and his forehead gently knotted. He pushed against the railing and turned back into the house. This time, he knocked and spoke through the closed door.

"Isabela? Is everything all right?"

He edged the door open a crack, then a bit wider. Isabela sat on the side of the bed, with her eyes lowered and focused on her feet. She glanced quickly up when the door creaked open and dropped her head into her hands.

Jimmy remained halfway in, with a light fist pressed against the doorframe.

"I am a crazy, stupid woman. I don't know why I came. I will marry Tomás. How can I be here?" Her voice cracked.

Jimmy paused, let out a breath, and made his way into the room. He took hold of her hand in a soundless encouragement to move up and out of the bedroom. Outside, an orange sun dipped low, kissing the ocean. The clear, warm water lapped gently against the thick, wooden pilings as a school of brilliant blue fish, now greyish in the fading light, swarmed around the wooden posts. As if on a choreographer's cue, the entire group of them spun ninety degrees and headed back out to deeper water. Isabela sat down on the edge of the terrace and allowed her feet to dangle over the edge. Her attention was diverted and captivated by the foreign world below.

"Qué mágico!"

"Quite something isn't it? My father brought me here when I was a boy."

Isabela looked up, "Aquí?" *Here?*

"Yes, this house. It is the best of my childhood memories. My father rented this place for several months one summer when I was eleven years old. It was a time I remember being sublimely happy. We fished, I swam, and we both dove for crab and lobster. In the evenings, we'd sit here on the deck and watch the sun go down. He always sat with his cocktail and a fresh-squeezed fruit juice for me." He paused and added, "I've never been back."

Isabela reached for his hand. His fingers instantly closed around hers, and a warmth and ease permeated the space inside and around them. Isabela leaned her head against his shoulder and felt the light drumming of her heartbeat ricocheting in her ear. She skimmed her toes over the surface of the water and was aware of the fragile transition of daytime into twilight. The sun disappeared below the horizon as a faint star appeared in the darkening sky.

"I wish there was a way to hold onto a moment like this one. The smell of sweet flowers, the changing patterns in the sky, and the temperature which feels just right. All of it together." She spoke softly, but even still, the sound of her own voice intruded. She immediately wished she had remained quiet and let the evening continue to envelop them both in its rich blanket of warmth.

"Maybe that's the point," he said. "Even the most beautiful experience inevitably passes away."

They remained quiet, listening to the sound of water gently lapping against the shore and feeling the soft breeze caress their bodies.

It was several minutes more before Isabela quietly said, "Tell me something about you."

Jimmy looked out over the water and thought, *What the hell can I tell her that's not a lie? Without betraying honor, mission, country ... and a wife at home?* Several moments passed before he spoke.

"To the folks back home, I am all American—a southern boy. But I wasn't born in the United States, even though my father was American. I was born right here, in Bangkok. It's where I lived until I was twelve. I was raised by my father. But the honest truth of it is my father was away most of the year traveling on business. So the responsibility for my care fell upon a wonderful Hmong woman, the one I mentioned to you last time we met. I just called her Amah. After my father died, I was forced to move to the States, so I lost touch with her. One day, I'd like to find her and thank her. Have you heard of the Hmong?"

Isabela shook her head. "Y tu madre?" *And your mother?*

"My mother? She died a year after I was born. I never really knew her. She was a mixture of English, Thai, and Japanese. My father, although born in the United States, was of Scottish descent. He had a Norwegian great-grandmother, and I seem to have inherited her Scandinavian fair eyes, light hair, and height. My father was surprised. He told me they expected a dark-haired baby, but instead, there was this green-eyed infant with long legs. Where my father was tall and angular, my mother was petite and fine-boned. Just the shape of the eyes is all she gave me. I know he wished I looked more like her. He adored her. What little I know of my mother is from the rare moments he let down his guard. I realized very early on that I could never fill the void she'd left. When he spoke of her, he always called her Mera, although her real name was Meredith. My mother was a dedicated and sincere Buddhist from what I have gathered. My father, at least from the time I knew him, was a pure and simple agnostic. Any religious or spiritual tendency he might have entertained died with her. However, certain Buddhist and Hindu myths captured his imagination, especially the mythical Mount Meru."

"Is this a real place?" she asked.

"There is a mountain in the Himalayas called Meru, but I don't believe there's any connection to the mythical one."

"What does it mean, then?" she said.

"It's considered by the Buddhists, and I believe Hindu mythologies as well, to be the center of the physical and spiritual universe. It is supposedly a golden mountain that, according to the myths, reaches high into the heavens and deep into the lower realms to symbolize infinite layers of existence. I researched it in college."

"What is the connection to your mother?"

"That's a good question, and one I've often wondered about myself. In Hebrew, Mera means 'light.'" He paused a moment and said, "Do you like the name? If I ever have a daughter, I'd like to name her Mera."

"It's beautiful," she said.

"My mother was the center of my father's universe. She was his light. It is the name he always used when he spoke of her to me. Maybe Mera was just a nickname or, as I used to fantasize, a metaphor." Jimmy gazed down at the darkening waters and took a small wad of gum from behind his ear and put it in his mouth.

"I'm sorry you never had the chance to know her. What of your father?" she asked.

"My father died in a car accident when I was twelve. So, you see, I'm an orphan." He smiled and kissed the top of her head. "Life is eerily strange," he continued. "We're completely blind to what's just around the corner. Out of the blue, the wind shifts, and you are presented with an irrevocable situation that makes your world completely unrecognizable."

Isabela leaned into Jimmy's shoulder.

"There's a temple on the hill overlooking the island that my father took me to when I was a boy. I remember it as a very special place. I'd like to take you there to see it."

They followed the trail up the hillside to the temple that dominated the highest point on the island and from where a sweeping view of inlets, bays, and rugged coastline prevailed. Inside, a gigantic golden Buddha dwarfed monks and visitors alike. Isabela stood before the massive statue, admiring its huge construction and intricate detail.

Along the back wall, a line of saffron-robed monks bent over ancient texts, chanting a monotone prayer that filled the room with its echoing incantation. A gong bellowed three times. Isabela began to rock with the vibration of sound. All at once, her normal perceptual state loosened its grip. She heard Jimmy and felt the deepening pressure of his fingers on her shoulders. But her mind was suddenly clear like sky, with no constraints. She found herself above, looking down upon the masses of people, and her heart ached for the indiscriminate suffering. She saw the exquisite beauty and fleeting fragility of all existence. She felt she could let go of it all, right now! Jimmy dropped his hands from her shoulders and wrapped them around her. His voice rose above the chanting of the monks.

"Isabela, are you okay?"

His voice sounded far away, as if on the other side of a telephone wire with a weak connection. Her perception expanded out beyond the limits of her physical form. She knew she could leave her body like a worn-out shoe. The gong sounded again while a single thought dropped her down into the thick soup of humanity and experience. *Jimmy.*

"Are you all right?" he asked again.

She responded by pressing her face into his chest, and her words were muffled. "Take me to the water. I want to swim in the ocean. Take me somewhere where no one is."

She began pulling him away from the Buddha, away from the center where she could so easily disappear.

He searched her face for some indication or explanation, but she only smiled and curled her arm around his elbow as they walked down the hill and back the way they came.

"There's a place my father brought me once. It's an incredible spot. I'll have to ask around. I was just a kid so I didn't pay attention to how we got there."

Jimmy steered the rented motorcycle along a narrow, serpentine road that hugged the blue coast. The directions received from the local fish restaurant were sketchy, but it was a small island. He felt confident he would recognize the turn onto the dirt road that narrowed and dropped steeply to the beach, if the road still existed.

He realized he had probably long since driven past the turn after exploring several small dirt lanes, each time to head back the way they came and finally arrive at a dead end at the island's edge. He swung the cycle in an arc, sand spraying in a thick cloud of dust. Isabela coughed and held on tight. They continued down the main road, and then suddenly, he stopped the bike. A small road was almost completely camouflaged in thick vegetation and barely visible ahead on the right. Jimmy maneuvered the bike along the narrow trail and told Isabela to duck her head. The passageway was just wide enough for the cycle to pass, and the lane was thick with sand. They proceeded slowly forward, and then he stopped again.

"You better get off. I need to get the bike through this patch. I'll pick you up by the tree over there."

Isabela slid off the bike and jumped back, covering her face with her hands as the motorcycle's front and rear tires spun out and sprayed fine particles of sand in a 360 degree cloud that penetrated her eyes, nose, and mouth and only embedded the motorcycle deeper into a rut.

"Get back!"

Isabela retreated behind a tree in a vain attempt to shelter herself from the upcoming sandstorm. After several more tries and rising clouds of sand and dust, Jimmy let the bike fall on its side.

"Cheap excuse for a vehicle!" Jimmy kicked the back tire twice, took a breath, and clipped it again, hard.

Isabela felt the top of her head. Granules of sand were embedded in her scalp, which felt like sandpaper. Her face was covered in a thick film of dust. Jimmy was equally beige from his dust-filled hair to his sand-covered toes. His eyes narrowed and were keenly riveted on the motorcycle stuck in the sand. Isabela began to rock from side to side. She bit her lip, but the corners of her mouth couldn't help but widen. She laughed, quietly at first, and then louder until she held her knees and shook with the craziness of the moment. She was so very far away from anything remotely familiar. She felt raw, vulnerable, and joyfully awake. Jimmy turned his attention away from the stuck motorcycle and was irresistibly drawn to the woman doubled over and shaking with merriment.

"What's so damn funny? It could be a very long walk back," he snapped.

The sharp rattle of an orange-beaked kingfisher turned both their heads up toward the trees. The blue-breasted bird rose from the tight branches toward waves that crashed along black coral.

"Well, I'll be goddamned!" Jimmy lifted his sunglasses onto his head and squinted toward the horizon. "This is the place. I'd know it anywhere. Come on."

He grabbed Isabela's hand and pulled her toward the sea through a mesh of overgrown bushes and trees. No trace of a road remained from his childhood memory, but the small inlet practically shimmered and beckoned an invitation to descend.

Isabela found the lack of a path through the heavy brush impassible. Thorns scrapped her fingers, and a superficial cut caused a thin film of blood to ooze from her forehead, dripping blood into her right eye. Jimmy made it down to the beach and glanced back. Isabela had only advanced a short distance. Immediately, he turned and climbed back to where she stood captive in a maze of branches.

A tress of her thick dark hair was entwined with pieces of leaves, thorns, and berries.

"Looks like the rainforest wants to keep you too! Give me a second. Stand still, and I'll untangle this."

Isabela winced as the last strands were free.

Jimmy threw her up and over his shoulder. He stumbled, repositioned her weight higher up, and burst down the side of the hill, bulldozing his own path through the thick vegetation and finally dropping her onto the beach.

"Why did you do that?" Isabela swept her hands through her hair, still sitting in the place she was deposited.

Her gaze swept past Jimmy and out to the turquoise water at the shoreline. Powdery white sand strewn with tiny shells contrasted sharply against the clear azure waters and the deep green of the trees. Out across the bay, a small island dominated by a cone-shaped mountain seemed to rise straight from the ocean's depth and swell into the clouds above.

Isabela shaded her eyes and threw off her shoes. She was completely unprepared for the exquisite beauty of this place and of this moment. She unbuttoned one pearl, then another, and allowed the cream-colored dress to fall in a heap around her feet. She stepped over it, clad now in only white silk panties and a delicately laced bra. Slowly, her hands reached behind her and unhooked the bra. Jimmy stood five feet behind her and sucked in his breath. She stepped out of the panties, completely and utterly at peace. She turned to look behind her and held out her hand. Jimmy threw his shirt over his head and dropped his undershorts. Together, they walked toward the water as effortlessly as if the moment had been rehearsed a hundred times.

The water was velvety warm and crystal clear. They stepped deeper into the water, holding hands until the water reached her shoulders.

Isabela dropped his hand and ducked underwater. Her dark hair streamed behind her as her arms parted the small waves in a smooth breaststroke, and she moved away from him. Jimmy watched for a moment and jumped up into a shallow dive. In several quick strokes, he swam directly over her submerged form. She stayed near the sandy bottom as long as her breath could hold and then burst through the surface, with her hair smooth against her scalp. He moved toward her. The water resisted his forward step, but his eyes stayed locked with hers. She waited, aware that the perfectly manicured life her mother envisioned for her was rapidly and decisively unraveling.

His arms encircled her. She stood absolutely still and allowed his thumb to trace the outline of her shoulder, and up along her cheekbone. Every cell felt completely alive to his touch. Slowly, she reached her hand to lightly stroke his face, feeling the rough stubble along her jawline. Jimmy lowered his mouth to her shoulder, which tasted of sweat and salt. He reached under her arms and lifted her so her chest rose out of the water, dripping beads of salt water upon her skin. His lips wandered down. Her legs, free now of gravity, opened and wrapped around his hips.

"Don't go back to work. Stay with me," she said.

"That is a very tempting offer," he said, kissing her shoulder, her cheeks, and then slowly on the lips. Isabela broke free and looked him in the eye.

"Whatever happens, tell me you will come back."

"I'll do my god damn best. I promise you that."

Isabela lay with one leg draped over Jimmy's thigh and her head nestled against his chest in the warm sand. The sun had completely vanished, but its light still illuminated the sky in a soft haze. He swatted at the no-see-ums and gently buried his head into her neck.

"You need to put some clothes on. The bugs are out in full force. I am so sorry, but it looks like we are here for the night. I wasn't prepared for a night on the beach, but at least I can make a fire. I have water and a lighter. That should keep most of the insects away."

Isabela stood and walked toward the water, bending to pick up her dress and underclothes, as well as Jimmy's shorts and shirt. She dropped the clothes by Jimmy's feet. He shot up and swept her in a giant half circle. Their clothes remained in the sand, and they fell together, their bodies merging into one.

A billion stars and a sliver of a moon shed negligible light. Isabela was draped across Jimmy's bare chest. The delicate outline of her body blended with his own so that he couldn't say where she ended and he began.

He kissed her lightly on the top of her head and gently shifted.

"Put some clothes on. I don't want to share you with the bugs!"

He slowly extracted his arm and stood up to put on his shorts and shirt. It was dark now. There was just a shaving of light from the moon to collect firewood. He returned from the edge of the tree line with an armful of branches, and within a few short minutes, a giant bonfire lit up the beach. Isabela slipped on her dress, leaving her underclothes in the sand. He continued to collect large branches until a huge pile was amassed. When he was done, he encircled Isabela, gathering her in his arms as she leaned against his chest.

"Where should we live? Near the mountains or by the water? What say you?"

"My home is with you. I will go where you go, but please, not El Salvador. I can't go back there now. My mother, you see, she will not forgive."

"All right, we'll travel the world, then. How about Australia, New Zealand, South America, maybe an island in Indonesia? We'll keep exploring until we hit upon the perfect place. Just you and me and damn to the rest of the world. We might just have a kid along the way. Would you like that?"

"Sí, a boy to look just like you. And a daughter. I would like to have a daughter and teach her to see the shadows and colors of the world."

"Okay, with two kids we'll need a house. What sort of house? Stone, wood, or bamboo?"

"A little house where we can live all together, with a big veranda near the sea. I will make beautiful art in this house."

"And a dog. There should be a dog. All kids need a dog. We'll name him, what? Admiral?"

"Qué? What is this name?"

"Okay, a Spanish name then. Hhmm, something simple … Amigo? Amigo will keep you safe when I have to be away."

"Sí, a dog named Amigo. Me encanta!" *I love it!* She snuggled her body closer to his and continued to speak, but her tone was softer now. "I had a brother once. The baby died before I was born. Perhaps my mother was *más suave antes*?"

"More gentle before?"

"Sí."

"Listen." He kissed her shoulder and her neck and tasted the salt on her lips. "Finish what you came here to do and complete your studies with the master. Then go home and make peace with your mother. How can you be happy or free unless you do? The time here, this moment on this extraordinary island, has to last us for a while. I don't know when I'll be able to break free again. I have to complete what is already in motion. I have commitments. Once the job, or my part in it, ends, I have to leave Thailand and return to the States. I need to untangle a web of wrong turns and poor choices. It may take a while, but I need to know that whatever happens, you'll be okay. I need to know that you'll wait for me and we'll live this life by the sea in the little house with two kids and Amigo."

"Sí, mi amor." *Yes, my love.* "I'll wait for you."

Isabela stood up to run, tossing her dress once again to the sand. In two leaps Lance bounded ahead of her and dove into the velvety waters.

The sharp cry of a macaw jarred Isabela wide awake. She sat up abruptly. There was sand in her ears, nose, and just about every crevice of her body. She glanced over at Jimmy, who lay spread eagled on his back, completely naked. Red welts covered his legs and arms. Isabela looked at her own arms and saw they were also spotted with red, swollen bites. She again looked down at Jimmy. His eyes darted left and right inside his eyelids. His body jerked several times, and his jaw was clenched. Isabela quickly placed her hand on his shoulder gently.

"Wake up, mi amor! The bugs keep biting!"

Jimmy shot straight up and looked indiscriminately around him as if the sea, the beach, and the sky confused him. He slowly put his hand to his forehead, closed his eyes again, and then ran his fingers through his hair. He remained still for another moment and patted the sand to his right as if he were verifying its solidity. He rolled over, brushing the air with his fingers until he found Isabela's arm.

"There you are!" He gathered her down and onto his chest and held on so tightly she struggled to catch her breath.

"Jimmy, let go. I can't breathe. Qué pasa?" *What's going on?*

Jimmy released his half-nelson-like hold and repositioned himself to encircle her in his arms. She nestled against his shoulder and stretched her arm across his chest.

"That's better," she said.

"That was one weird dream." He patted her arm again and gripped his fingers around it.

"What is it?" she said.

"I need to feel that you are real and here with me."

"Tell me about the dream," she said.

He breathed out slowly. "You were with me … let me see if I can remember all of it …" Jimmy relaxed to quiet his thoughts. "Yes, that's it. You were riding behind the ears of a very large elephant, and I was seated on the back of a wild, muscular cat. Maybe a jaguar? We were moving through the jungle together, listening to the sounds of the birds and watching the sun filter through the trees. The elephant was walking very purposefully, slowly moving aside anything in the way with its trunk. You were smiling, and I … when I looked up at you, way up high on that elephant, your eyes bored straight into my heart."

"Qué hermoso." *How beautiful,* Isabela murmured.

"Everything was crystal clear, right down to tiny dewdrops on shimmering leaves and the humming of the insects. Somehow, we were part of all of it. I can't remember feeling so at peace since I was a boy."

Isabela withdrew a few inches so she could see his face. She whispered, "Te amo." *I love you.*

She immediately buried her head deep into Jimmy's neck as he kissed the top of her head. "Me, too," he said. He tightened his hold around her and gazed out beyond the beach and across the bay. Lance repeated, softer this time, "Me too, damn it."

The swooshing roll of the sea onto the shore soothed like a lullaby. Neither spoke for several minutes as they listened to the sea's rhythm, accompanied by the croaking of two egrets hunting for their breakfast along the coast.

"Is there more?" she said.

"Yes. At first, my ride, the jaguar, walked alongside you and the elephant, but all of sudden, it broke into a run. I was startled but not afraid. I wanted to get the beast to turn around, to come back to you, but it flew up through the trees. I held on for the ride of my life. I whispered in its ear, and it turned back down the way we had come."

"The elephant and the jaguar. Maybe that's you and me. I think your dream is beautiful."

"Yes, the first part is. Listen to the rest of it."

"Sí, go on."

"When we came back, you were still on top of that huge elephant. Did I mention the elephant was blue?"

Isabela shook her head. "When I was a little girl, my father took me on a trip to New York. We went to the zoo. Ever since, I've been fascinated with elephants. They are such giant, intelligent animals. I felt so sad they were locked up like that. Did you know they mourn their dead like we do?"

"Yes, I remember reading something about that."

Isabela murmured, "I never imagined a blue one, though. I wonder what it could mean?"

"Who the hell knows?"

"And?"

Lance chose his next words carefully, as if the dream unfolded with his telling of it.

"The elephant was still walking slowly, but now it was coming out of the forest, down onto the beach, and moving steadily toward the water. My jaguar stopped dead at the water's edge, and I slid off, motioning wildly for you to get down. But the elephant kept walking into the water. The shoreline led to a deep blue ocean. You were holding a bundle of something I could not see close to your heart, protecting it. I kept calling out to you to jump off. You were shouting something back at me, but you sounded so far away. I couldn't make out a word you were saying. I waded into the water and started swimming out to the middle of the ocean toward you. But you and the elephant kept getting farther away, growing fainter and fainter until I couldn't see you at all. In the end, I was just swimming in circles out in the middle of a deep, black ocean. That's when you woke me up."

Lance hugged her in closer.

Isabela whispered, "I know that place."

Suddenly, he swatted at his arm and sat straight up, knocking Isabela from her position on his chest onto the sand.

"Damn bugs! Come on. We need to get going."

It was an hour before Jimmy freed the motorbike from the sand. They pushed it another half a kilometer onto more solid ground and arrived back at the house famished and with their hair and clothing full of sand. They jumped into the shower together, Isabela rinsing Jimmy's back with a thick sponge dripping with warm suds. He turned around and grabbed the sponge from her hand, leaving light particles of soap along her neckline. The soapy sponge encircled a breast, her slim waistline, and then down to the triangle between her legs.

"Thief!" she said, plucking the sponge away from him and allowing it to absorb warm water. She stood on tiptoe and squeezed the warm water over his head, bringing her arm to naturally fold around his neck.

A loud, booming pulse resounded across the bay. The sound originated from the nightclub built on stilts up over the water. Isabela allowed the music's beat to move her body in slow, undulating spirals as she neared the barstool where Jimmy straddled his seat. He sipped a scotch as he watched her, hypnotized by her body's fluidity and grace. She took his hands and quietly pulled him toward the dance floor.

"I don't dance. There's been no time for it."

She continued to pull him toward her, standing on her toes as she pulled his head down to touch his mouth with her lips. He encircled her in a giant bear hug, and together they allowed the music to envelop them, moving to a quiet rhythm in the blasting vibrations of a fast-paced bass. The music slowed to a haunting melody and then swelled, quickening its tempo and pitch. The two kept swaying, lost in a shared trance, oblivious to the raucous crowd around them and unaware that the music, as well as its very composition, changed into something high-pitched and hard-driving. As if on cue, they simultaneously broke from their shared stupor. When the smoke-filled room and smell of sweat registered on their senses, they moved without a word toward the terrace for fresh air and a view of the quarter moon.

Jimmy leaned against the railing and looked out over the darkened waters. Isabela stood next to him, looking at the crescent moon with her head resting on his arm.

"Cuando vayas, ver la luna, como este noche. I will be thinking of you."

Jimmy leaned down and lightly kissed the top of her head. "Luna means the moon. Yes, we can both see the moon wherever we are."

All of a sudden Jimmy's head shot up, and he pushed Isabela abruptly to the side, away from him. A single foreign man moved across the wooden terrace and closed the distance between them. Jimmy turned his back on the man's approach and looked straight ahead to loudly whisper in Isabela's direction, "Go!"

There was no way to avoid the encounter. There was no back door. The man approached Jimmy and slapped him on the arm.

"Jimmy Calhoun! I hate to intrude and break up such a sweet moment, but I have to know—what brings you to this tropical island paradise?"

Jimmy allowed a small smile. "Hello, Avery."

Jimmy turned to face Avery, intentionally drawing the man's attention away from Isabela's retreating figure.

"And who might your lovely companion be?"

"A date for the night. A little fun."

"A ladies' man? I didn't take you for the type. Do you believe in fate? Running into you tonight makes a believer out of me! How about we meet tomorrow and discuss business? My boss has been looking for you."

"What do you mean? I don't recall any business I might be interested in that includes you or anyone you might work for."

Avery reached into his pocket and withdrew a small pocketknife, with which he began to carve out small chunks of wood from the railing.

"It's hard to forget my patron, the big German, Volker. He is a powerful man and doesn't appreciate being ignored. He wants to meet with you."

Jimmy stared hard at Avery. "I have no interest in meeting with him."

"Let's just say Volker gets what he wants, no exception."

"Best of luck with that. Goodnight."

Jimmy headed back into the nightclub without a backward glance.

Isabela stood just inside the doorway, looking out onto the terrace in his direction. He took her elbow and guided her towards the exit.

"Let's get out of here. The music is boring holes in my eardrums."

Isabela's hand slipped easily into Jimmy's as they walked along the water's edge. She removed her sandals and placed them under her arm, feeling the warm sand beneath her toes and the lick of salt water roll up to her ankles and retreat again.

"Can you stay a few more days? I don't want to leave this beautiful place," she said.

"Damn it, there's been a change of plans," he said.

"What do you mean?"

"We need to leave tomorrow. I'll book a flight for you early afternoon. You'll have to get the ferry first thing in the morning."

"I'm not ready to leave."

"I'm sorry. Something came up. We have to cut this short by a day, but the quicker I get back to work, the faster I can complete the assignment, and the sooner I come back to you. I'll be away for a while and completely out of contact. The company sends me to some very remote areas. Remember, for the photographs? Will you be all right? Immerse yourself in art and don't you dare forget me! I'll be dreaming of you."

Isabela's words tumbled out in a hurricane of Spanish.

Jimmy took a step back as a few easily translatable words, "Loco, sin explicación y mierda!" accentuated an otherwise blast of rapid Spanish, their meaning inherently clear to any person regardless of what language they might speak. Isabela calmed slightly and responded in a Spanish-English mix.

"Qué pasa?" *What happened?* "You are planning to leave, sin decirme porque?" *Without telling me why?*

"I'm sorry. It's an unfortunate turn of events. The man I ran into at the club tonight has been trying to recruit me. He deals in drugs, arms, and other contraband. He targeted me as a potential asset. He's a lowlife but a potentially dangerous one. I can't risk him seeing us together again. He will use you to get to me, don't you see? I can't let him know you mean anything. I need to get you on the first ferry tomorrow morning. I'll follow a few hours later. We can meet in the Chiang Mai bazaar tomorrow night before I head out again. So, this isn't goodbye, and we have every single minute until then."

Jimmy ordered two bowls of steamy noodles, extra hot, from the Thai vendor at the Chiang Mai bazaar, exactly as Isabela requested. He elbowed his way through the thick crowd and around to the wooden table where she sat sipping iced tea.

"Sunan has the best noodles in all of Chiang Mai. Better than the finest restaurant. They might burn a hole in your stomach, though. I've never tried the extra spicy before," Jimmy said. He watched as Isabela wound the noodles around her chopsticks.

"Me encanta. Es delicioso!" *I love it. It's delicious!*

Jimmy took a bite, and immediately, his eyes began to water as the pungent spice burned his throat, his esophagus, and down into his stomach. He quickly downed a glass of water.

"How can you eat that?"

Isabela laughed, wound noodles around her chopsticks, and offered a second bite across the table.

Jimmy shook his head. "Hell no!"

He pushed his bowl of noodles to the side, and popped a piece of gum in his mouth, and reached across the table to take Isabela's hand in both of his.

"Will you be all right? Tell me you'll make beautiful art while I'm away. No matter how many twists and turns there are in the road, I'll make it back." Jimmy laid his hand lightly on her arm before continuing. "I'm sorry. I hoped we might have a little more time, but I got the call. I have to leave first thing in the morning. It could be days, weeks, or months before I'm free. There's no way to know. If you have to leave the guesthouse before I get back, I need to know how to contact you. Will you leave me a note where to find you?"

"Mi amor, no te preocupes." *My love, don't worry.* "I will stay in Chiang Mai and study, paint, and think of you." Jimmy rose and maneuvered around the table to sit next to Isabela, inhaling her light scent of jasmine. He knew he shouldn't, not in this public place, but he was unable to stop the impulse to stay close and feel the softness of her skin. He enfolded her in his arms as the crowded Sunday evening bazaar was reduced to a sea of indistinct colors and sounds.

Chapter Twenty-Seven

1961

Bangkok, Thailand

Isabela drew her finger down the B column in Bangkok's telephone directory.

"Aquí está!" *Here you are.* She jotted down the number and address and dialed.

"Bangkok Patana International School, may I help you?"

"Yes, please, my name is Isabela Marquez. I want to speak with the headmaster."

"Do you have a child you wish to enroll?"

"No, I don't. I am looking for information regarding a child who went to your school about seventeen or eighteen years ago."

"Well then, our headmaster only arrived from England in 1953. You will need to speak with our French teacher, Miss Cécile Bérnard. I believe she is the only faculty member who dates back to that time. Let me think. Yes, Mrs. Bérnard has been an educator here since the thirties or early forties. You have to understand, though, in that many years, thousands of students have passed through our doors. Although we keep a record of every child who attended our academy, it's quite improbable she will remember your student."

"Please, may I visit and speak with Señora Bérnard?"

"Just a moment. Let me ring her office and see if she can set aside some time later in the week."

Isabela knocked lightly on the open office door. A thin woman with slightly rounded shoulders glanced up, her wispy grey hair coiled into a soft bun on the top of her head while a pair of gold spectacles lay as an afterthought on the bridge of her nose. She set down her pencil and motioned for Isabela to enter. Piles of papers, school reports and partially graded tests, books, and general office supplies comingled on top of her desk.

Miss Cécile Bérnard sighed. "I know. It's quite the mess. However, despite all appearances to the contrary, I am most efficient this way. Every once in a while, a well-meaning soul comes and tidies up for me. Then chaos ensues, and I am at a loss. I can retrieve any student's work in this miscellany in a blink. But I digress. Miss Marquez, you are researching for an old student of mine? How may I be of assistance?"

"Bueno, yes. A boy, he went to this school. I do not know when, maybe … " Isabela stopped and counted on her fingers. "I think maybe 1938? He was here four years."

"His name?"

"Jimmy Calhoun."

"Are you a relative?"

"No, señora, a friend. I want to surprise him and find the woman who cared for him like a mother."

"Under normal circumstances, we cannot disclose student information to anyone but family, but since this was such a long time ago, I don't see how any harm can come of it. I will visit the archives down the hall. I'll just be a moment."

Isabela waited for what seemed like a long time before Miss Bérnard returned.

"I am sorry, Miss Marquez. We have no record of a student by that name during those years or, for that matter, at any time in the school's history. Are you quite sure you have the right institution?"

"I am staying in Bangkok this week to renew my visa. I hoped I could surprise my friend and find his Amah. My friend told me he went to a British international school in Bangkok. I thought he said the Bangkok Patana School, but I must be wrong. Thank you for seeing me today. I am very sorry to have taken your time."

"If I can be of any further assistance, please don't hesitate to stop by. It was a pleasure to meet you, Miss Marquez."

Chapter Twenty-Eight

1961

Thai-Laotian Border

Crouched low, his silhouette magnified to epic proportions by the light of the campfire, Sawm grinned and pointed in excitement to the front of the cavern, where a distant yet rising commotion just made itself known. In the distance, a gaggle of village men could be seen earnestly moving a barrel in the direction of the cave's camouflaged access, in and around tree trunks, bushes, and roots. Like clockwork, one man dropped off the front of the heavy vat to be instantly replaced by another man.

Lance set down the headset, interrupting a daily exercise to intercept and interpret possible enemy communications along the Laotian border. He followed Sawm out the door, pistol in hand, and stopped just outside the doorway of vines to watch a slow procession of men maneuvering the large, bulky object. He couldn't quite make it out. He viewed the activity for several moments more and then eased the pistol back into his shirt, out of sight. *What in the hell are they doing?* He watched closely as one man dropped off the front of the vat and retreated to the rear. He was replaced in the front by a familiar and towering figure. Lance shook his head. He jogged to close the distance between the cave and the crazy, festive mélange of Hmong men and Miles, who by all estimation was thoroughly enjoying himself. Xob stood to the side, pointing ahead and advising the most direct and seamless route.

"Xob said to turn to the right. The path is freer over here!"

"Miles, what the fuck?" Lance quickly blinked twice, his eyes adjusting to the bright sun.

"Not bleeding likely, I know. I was hijacked when I got to the village. These blokes are stronger than piss, and they are determined to get this contraption to the cave."

"Why? It must have taken all day to move that thing all the way up here."

"It's a stumper, isn't it? But everyone's in a jolly ol' state of mind. I'll be buggered to know what it's about, but you can't help but get caught up in the fun of it. You want to have a go, mate? There's a system to it. Move in when you see that bloke drop off."

Miles indicated the slight fellow who was now at the front of the pack. Within a few minutes, the villager eased off his position. Lance quickly sidled up behind the last man to sync his movement with the others. After a while, he realized there was a fluidity of movement to the unit as if an unseen voice commanded the men, directing them as one wholly interdependent entity.

It was a full hour before the container finally rolled into the cave and settled in by the small cooking fire, yet somehow it felt as if only a few minutes passed. Camaraderie and good cheer abounded. Every man had put forth his best effort, with no need to be better than anyone else. Miles noted the lack of competition, so inherent in Britain and the West in general. It wasn't until the vat was firmly established in its final resting place that Lance learned the objective of this wild endeavor. He quickly translated the essentials to Miles as an effervescent Sawm threw his arm around Mile's waist, giggling buoyantly.

"They want to celebrate our alliance and brotherhood! All the men will gather here tonight. Shit, the ancestors must approve!"

The men sat in a lopsided circle around the giant cask filled with a deep, purple wine. Lance scooped a metal mug into the dark liquid and offered the first cup to Xob, who did not extend his hand to accept. Immediately, Lance turned and proffered the cup to Sawm, who eagerly took the cup and downed the entire contents in several giant gulps. Wet magenta dribbled down the sides of his mouth. Sawm dipped the mug back into the vat and handed it back to Lance, who inhaled the sharp fumes. Instantly, his eyes watered, and the insides of his nostrils burned. He sloshed the liquid around before taking a careful sip.

"This stuff will curl the hairs in your nose!" Lance spoke out loud in English. Several men neared and slapped him on the back, motioning wildly for him to drink more.

"Damn, here goes," he said.

He took a larger swig, quickly emptied the remaining contents, and passed the cup to the next man. The process was repeated twenty to thirty times during the night. Miles, his back propped up against the cave wall, remained quiet and attentive, content to laugh and share the mood of the evening without the need to understand the particulars. Lance made a languid attempt to translate. However, as the night wore on and the mood became more boisterous, no interpretations were needed. Suddenly, Sawm stood up and swayed side to side, grinning widely.

"Let's make a trade!" he cried out. His lone finger wavered in wild circles and then focused and settled in on the giant figure hunched against the stone wall of the grotto.

Miles waved back, grinning.

"We give you two very fat water buffalo for Big Brother!"

Lance faltered and pressed himself up into what he hoped presented a more dignified posture, translating to Miles, who tilted his head back and roared, a broad grin spanning across his face.

As the night turned into the early hours of dawn, alcohol continued to flow. The villagers howled and shrieked, and a few stood up to throw their bodies into an enthusiastic and delirious dance. Several drummed a beat onto the tinny backside of metal pans.

All the while, Xob stood apart and watched.

Rays of sunlight flickered into the interior of the cave, announcing the full light of morning. Xob and the villagers were gone. Miles lay on the ground and stretched his arm above his head.

"What the fuck happened?" he mumbled. "My head is pounding!"

"Don't you remember?" Lance said. "We traded you for two water buffalo. I wonder if the good ol' USA's state department will adopt our bargaining method?"

"Brilliant. Sod off. You're not serious?"

"Not one, but two of their finest plump ones! When you get back to base, I'd definitely ask for a raise."

Wincing as he raised himself up, Miles took a drink of water and suddenly burst into a fit of laughter. "Fuck!" He tottered toward the cave entrance to relieve himself. Fast as the drift on a rapidly flowing river, he was back. His eyes were wide, and the corners of his mouth were drawn down.

"Shit, it's a bloody fuck-up," he said.

With a pounding head and aching muscles, Lance slowly rose, trying hard to clear his head and regain a modicum of alertness. He followed Miles outside of the cave and squinted in the bright light. Sawm and another villager sat on their haunches, each holding a thick twined rope in their hand. *What the fuck?* Slowly, his eyes followed the rope from Sawm's hand and along the ground to the object it was attached to. A fat and healthy water buffalo grazed lazily, his huge horns protruding from either side of his head. Several meters away, a second buffalo stopped grazing and stared directly at him, pawing at the earth with its hoof. Lance took the wad of gum from behind his ear and placed it in his mouth, chewing as if each close of his jaw might clarify the murky events of the past night.

"Damn it, Miles, get your things. You'll be staying in the village until we sort this out."

Chapter Twenty-Nine

1961

Thai-Laotian Border

Lance adjusted the antennae camouflaged in the thick vegetation. Triggers hid in a 360-degree circumference around the antennae. The devices were extremely sensitive, and even the most delicate touch activated them. Loud clicks would instantly be broadcast to the occupants of the cave in the event of enemy encroachment. Lance carefully surveyed the outlying area for the best possible escape routes, each dependent upon the particulars of any given circumstance—how many, from which direction, or how much time? The equipment, the AN/GRC 109 OSS radio fondly referred to as the Angry 109, had been carried on Lance's back in from the drop, all fifty pounds of it. All outbound communication required a second party to hand-crank the generator. With Miles living in the village now, young Fue became indispensable to Lance's everyday operations.

The incoming Morse code communication was brief.

"Transport Jameson oh-eight hundred hours Sunday eleventh. Jackson stand-in interim."

Lance set down the headset and murmured to the walls.

"Damn it, just a month to extract Miles from his new family. I sure as hell don't want to explain this mess."

Miles worked daily with the people in the village. He cleaned wounds, set broken bones, and taught basic hygiene. He observed the midwives' administering herbs to a woman in labor and retreated quietly during the birth, leaving the delivery to the women. The villagers were in awe of him. The women smiled shyly, and children stared unabashedly. When Miles moved to the village, young children hid behind their mothers or raced behind a bush to peek out at him. Then one day, a little one, his curiosity larger than his fear, suddenly left his mother's side, ran up to the giant man, and touched his leg. Miles leaned over and scooped the boy up and onto his shoulders. He trotted around the village and gave the boy the ride of his life. After that, all the children fought to be near him.

In the meantime, Lance trained Fue as a runner. Initially, it was just between the cave and the village, but eventually, he taught the boy skills he would need once the cadre arrived. He stressed the importance of communication. Where Miles had a gaggle of kids surrounding him, Lance and Fue were practically inseparable. Lance taught the boy how to handle weapons, load and clean them, crank the generator, and work the dial of the radio. He began to teach him a few English words as well.

One evening, after the day's work was done and it was too late for the boy to return safely to the village, Lance laid out a sleeping bag next to his own. During the following weeks, Fue stayed in the cave more often than he went back to the village. The reason Fue told his grandfather and his family, Lance never knew, but there was never any trouble about it. Each night Lance unrolled a sleeping bag for the boy, and the two sat around the fire laughing and telling stories. Lance did his best to describe how airplanes fly in the sky, the nature of grocery stores and banks, and the separate lives of Westerners. He wondered, as if hearing these concepts fresh and from the boy's eyes, how Western civilization had wandered so far away from what makes a person human. Fue was fascinated by all of it, especially the mechanics of airplanes. How did such a big metal object rise up in the air and travel from one place to another?

"It's the way air moves around things, little brother, and the shape of the airplane's wings. You see here how the wings are curved, like a bird's? They're rounded on the top and flatter on the bottom."

Lance ripped out a piece of paper from his journal and blew across the top of the paper. Instead of dropping down, the paper rose as his breath passed over it. He then demonstrated with his curved hand how the heavier pressure from below lifted the airplane up, just like the piece of paper. He patiently described the mechanics of weight, lift, thrust, and drag again and again to a delighted audience of one.

In turn, Fue recounted the many tales of the ancestors he so admired, such as communal gatherings of the clans and of the strength and courage of his elders. Lance whittled with his pocketknife while the boy talked. He found he enjoyed the precision and peace of it. He started without any idea of what he intended to make, and then magically, each unique piece of wood began to reveal an animal. The first to emerge was a tiny elephant. It seemed to Lance like faint wafts of jasmine fluttered in the air as the small carving took form.

He carved it for her, for Isabela. Yet the boy was overcome with such a sparkling enthusiasm as the tiny elephant emerged that Lance didn't have the heart not to give it to him. *I have plenty of time to create another*, he thought. Over time, a jaguar, a dhole, and a serpent raising its head to strike took shape from his knife. Fue lined the miniature carvings along a ridge in the cave wall and held lengthy conversations with them, as if they were living creatures.

The entire village participated in assembling Miles's new domicile, which was larger than average. With three days of fervent effort by the people, his new home quickly became livable. The elders watched and offered advice, and women wove strips of leaves around bamboo to reinforce the walls and ceiling. Camaraderie and goodwill permeated the village.

Miles returned to the cave once a week to report on events in the village.

"You are a sight for sore eyes, my friend. I miss you!" Lance slapped Miles on the back and offered him a tin cup of instant coffee. "How are you holding up? I feel guilty that you have to bear the brunt of our mutual fuck-up," Lance said.

"I'm the bloke who drew the long end of the stick." Miles grinned. "You are busting your ass, and I get to sit on mine! I envy these people, mate. There is something so universal and natural here. All the modern conveniences are somehow a burden to our humanity, aren't they? It wouldn't be such a bad idea to stay put, find a good woman, and put down roots with the Hmong! Fuck, in another life! I'm buggered. Television, fast cars, and Sainsbury have got a hold on me! There's no way out!"

Lance hopped out the open back door of the light aircraft that just landed and ran into the building. Inside, Nigel motioned with a flick of his hand.

"I've told the pilot to get a cup of coffee and fuel up. What the hell is going on out there? Do I have to remind you of our objective? Make friends and gain the people's trust. What is required to clean this mess up?" Nigel took a large swallow of tepid, stale coffee and shook his head.

"Yes sir. I take full responsibility for the problem with Miles and the buffalo. It should never have happened. I'm requesting a fortnight to rectify the situation. On the positive side, our Hmong are ecstatic to have Miles living among them. They believe he is a blessing from heaven. Extracting Miles will be delicate. The village elder, Xob, is the key. Once he agrees, the people will come to terms immediately. Our problem is that there is no one there, just little ol' me, and I am considered way down on the political stratum or tribal hierarchy.

"In their view, I am the messenger. The person of power will come after our preliminary negotiations are complete. For negotiations of this kind, we need a warrior Xob deems his equal, which can only be another village chief or one of our esteemed generals. The more Purple Hearts and colorful insignia, the better. They go for shiny objects in a big way. But don't think you can fool Xob with an actor. He is extremely perceptive. It's uncanny. He'll size up your life and the sort of man you are and hand it to you in a nutshell. The negotiator will have to be experienced in war and a true leader. Then there has to be something valuable to barter with. Make no mistake—our village chief is very shrewd."

"Damn it, Jameson, you have the extra time, but I trust the situation will be resolved and cleaned up without offending these people. Then get back here!"

"There's a local boy I've made friends with. He's been staying in the cave with me. I've been teaching him to be a runner and to work the radio. He's keen to learn and is quite smart. He'll know who is most respected in the area. Look, it just might work in our favor. Maybe we can enlist the cooperation of two villages, instead of just the one, before the Americans come. It's going to cost us, though. More guns and ammunition. You can bet that will be one of the demands. For a couple of staunch allies, it's a small price to pay. If that fails, you know of a general in the area you can call in for a short visit?"

"You're treading on thin ice, Jameson. I want this resolved stat!"

The acrid stench of burning maize stalks, remnants of the just-reaped harvest, smoldered in the early afternoon. Fue entered the cave carrying a bamboo box, in which two plump chickens squawked. He set the handmade crate down and opened the wooden latch. One bird was a brilliant splash of gold, blue, red, and black. The other was a baby-powder white speckled with chestnut brown splotches. One at a time, the birds bobbed their heads up and down to peek out, hesitant to brave the open door into unfamiliar territory. The multicolored one with the golden head was the first to gingerly step beyond the now-open access. Once free, she immediately began to peck at the dirt floor, followed shortly by her white, mottled, roly-poly companion.

"The gift is from Xob's woman's own stock. No bird is superior. You will have many eggs—twelve to fourteen a week when the big brother comes!"

Lance swore under his breath. A virtual farm was developing. So far, they had two water buffalo and a pair of chickens!

"Xob's generosity is unequaled. They are the most magnificent birds. Later this afternoon, we can go out by the buffalo and build a solid henhouse for these birds. What do you say? Then tonight, when we're done, I want to review the escape routes one more time."

Lance and Fue sat shoulder to shoulder by the small fire, the only light in the cave. Lance held a long stick in his hand and, with it, began to draw a crude map in the dirt. Each time he drew lines in one direction, he looked at the boy to make sure he understood the direction he intended and then quickly smoothed out the dirt to erase the lines he made.

"Remember, if you hear those clicks, the same ones we heard the night the wind blew the old tree over, you have to leave immediately. The clicks are a warning that the ears of the big brother, those ears that hear like a bumblebee bat and speak to faraway places, were encroached upon. You won't know if it's animal or human, as either could trigger the clicking. Like I showed you, cover the fire, and make it look as if no one has stayed here, and move to a safe place. Outside, in between those first rocks, is a good spot to see who it is. You need to stay hidden and alert. Be ready to leave the instant you are sure of the best route to safety. Leave immediately. Double back if necessary and then head out again. Don't come back here. Never return to the village."

"Don't worry. You have said this many times. I remember," Fue said.

"And I trust you, young friend. Big Brother is very pleased with you!"

Fue beamed and inched taller, looking not so unlike the fluffy chicken out by the water buffalo.

"Where is the fiercest village? The village with the strongest leader? Who is equal in strength to Xob?" Lance asked.

"Xob is the strongest and the wisest."

Lance immediately reframed and restructured his question. "Is there someone Xob esteems? When Xob seeks help against the ones who have no honor, who does he confer with?"

"There is a big village with many warriors, but it is far. It is a hard, two-day journey. Tswj Fwm, the village leader, is unafraid.

I have only seen him once, but I have heard the people tell of his bravery. A long time ago, Xob and Tswj Fwm were warriors, and they fought together against the wicked ones."

"Bingo." Fue looked up quickly. Lance broke a piece of gum in half, popped the first half into his mouth, and offered the second half to the boy, who smiled shyly. "Fue, I want to pay a visit to Tswj Fwm. I need you to stay here and watch out for the big brother's ears. You will be doing a very important job. You will be responsible for everything here. I am counting on you."

Fue leaned in, his eyes intent. He straightened his spine, and his chest puffed out like ruffled feathers on a bird. He grinned and made the thumbs-up gesture his American friend had taught him.

"Who can show me the way to this village?" Lance said.

"Sawm. Sawm will take you there. His woman is from this village. Sawm knows the way."

Lance pulled Fue toward him in a quick embrace, disheveling the boy's hair with his free hand. Several seconds passed in mutual warmth and affection. Abruptly, Fue ducked under Lance's arm and came back in a low dip to knock him off his feet. Lance jumped up. The two now hovered in a crouched position, circling slowly. Lance towered over the boy, but Fue was quick and agile and maneuvered the martial arts movements Lance had shown him with ease. Once again, Lance was thrown onto the dirt floor, only to slowly rise and reposition himself for his next move. He lifted Fue high and threw him onto the ground, but the boy rolled like a tumbleweed and landed firmly on two feet. Both were breathing hard. Fue sat on his haunches and smiled widely.

Lance shook his head. "All right, you win this time, but I don't like to lose! Back to work, my young friend. I want to make sure you remember. There are four main escape routes. If the enemy comes from this side, go in the direction where the sun rises. Be quick and cover any sign of passage. Move away from the village. Hide out until you know it's safe."

Once again, Lance drew lines in the dirt with a stick, indicating the home base and routes that fanned out like a network of tributaries from a main river. Fue picked up a stick and drew finer lines that crisscrossed in and out of the deeper ones Lance just made. The boy knew the territory, the bushes, the trees, and the curves of the river. Lance squinted, leaning in close to examine the marks.

"What's this?"

"A den of a dhole and her three cubs. It's big enough for me to crawl in, but not you, my big brother!"

Before the sun graced the horizon, Sawm appeared at the entrance to the cave. Lance packed provisions for four days and made Fue repeat the instructions until he was satisfied there was no confusion. He moved outside and glanced back into the cave. He felt a slight gnaw, like mice nibbling on cheese. *What am I forgetting? I've gone over every possible scenario. Fue is smart and quick. What am I worrying about?*

Fue stood still, with his hand held up in a silent farewell. Lance thought of his old Amah as her eyes briefly flitted across his mind. He called Fue to the entrance of the cave and laid his arm on the boy's shoulder, surveying the high cheekbones, his light brown complexion, and those dark brown eyes that reminded Lance oddly of a young fawn.

"Any sign of trouble, get out! Forget taking the radio, okay?"

It was already very hot and sticky. They had a long day's trek ahead of them through heavy jungle terrain. Sawm told him the path would be overgrown at times, and in those places, they would have to create a path of their own. Lance's gaze drifted back toward the cave as he began to follow Sawm, who was already moving at a fast clip.

The sun was sinking fast, and now just a crescent of light remained on the horizon. Fue entered the cave after feeding the buffalo and the chickens. It was dark inside, so he switched on the battery-powered floodlight left out for him. As a precaution, there would be no fire while the big brother was away.

Tick … tick … tick … tick. On, off, on, off. Fue was enchanted. There was total darkness and then an explosion of light! Emptiness and then bright and clearly defined objects! The big box of light was magical. Fue unwrapped beef jerky and bit off a large chunk, excessively chewing until the meat became a soft mass. He removed the small wooden elephant and the jaguar Lance had given him from the grotto wall.

A low-frequency rumbling arose from the back of Fue's throat. He perfectly mimicked the elephant's sound. He held the tiny wooden elephant in his left hand and the diminutive jaguar in his right hand, hidden behind his back. A booming growl burst forth and echoed throughout the cave, followed by a sharp trumpet wail. The tiny animals now faced each other head-on. His reproduction of the call of each animal was indistinguishable from those in the wild.

A click echoed in the cave, sharp and exact. Fue sat up, instantly alert. He held the small wooden elephant in his left hand. The jaguar fell to the floor. A second click shot through the cave and bounced back.

Fue quickly covered the radio and cooking gear with branches and shut off the floodlight. Within a minute, he was outside the cave. He peered toward the antennae from behind the cropping of rock, watching for unusual movement in the greying light.

The night the wind toppled the old tree over, ripping it up by its roots, Lance and Fue had been sleeping when they were abruptly awakened by the same loud resounding clicks. They quickly jumped into action. The equipment was camouflaged in seconds before they exited and made their way to the concealed vantage point. From there, they could see a lone, curious elephant calf who had crossed into the inner circle and was quietly checking out the antennae with its trunk. Lance doubled over and let out his breath. Fue slapped him on the back. A loud trumpet summoned the diminutive calf, who turned and trotted in the direction of its mother's call.

But this time was different. There was no elephant calf and no loud trumpet to call it home. In its place, Fue heard voices—two or maybe three in a language he did not understand. Lance had made him repeat his next actions precisely. There was no question as to what he should do next. Leave immediately along one of the escape routes. He'd rehearsed it a dozen times, yet Fue hesitated. He was responsible for the safekeeping of the buffalo and could not allow the prized animals to be stolen.

Fue sank down low and retreated slowly back until he determined he was a safe distance away. Then he broke into a run, not toward any planned escape paths but forward toward the buffalo. He let out a sigh of relief as he saw the two animals grazing peacefully. He approached the animals, untethering one and then the other. He held the lead to both animals in his left hand and spoke quietly into the first buffalo's ear.

"Come. I need to take you to a safer place."

He gave a strong yank on both tethers and made a soft clicking sound to coax them into forward movement.

Suddenly, he felt a hard round object press into the small of his back. He froze.

The Pathet Lao surrounded him. There were ten, maybe fifteen of them. The muzzle of the rifle pressed him into a walk. The buffalo walked meekly behind him. One of the Pathet Lao forcefully ripped the ropes from his hands amidst a flurry of rapid instruction from the leader. The soldier pulled the buffalo in the opposite direction, heading out with several men. Fue let the tiny, carved elephant drop from his hand and forced himself to look forward, away from the cave. Without resistance, he allowed his hands to be tied behind his back while suppressing the intense urge to cry out, "Goodbye!" to his father, his family, his friends, and the beautiful land he called home. Farewell to the big brother with hair the color of yellow flowers. Farewell to all he had learned. He knew too well the fate of those taken. You never saw them again.

A few years younger than Xob and a good two inches shorter, Tswj Fwm exhibited the same eerie sense of knowing, a characteristic Lance began to associate with being the chiefs of the Hmong. It was as if the depth of your soul was as easy to read as a bold-print book for both tribal leaders. Lance spent two days in Tswj Fwm's village, and as best as he was able, he presented details about the sequence of events that had led him there.

When Lance finished his telling, Tswj Fwm continued to gaze as if the air itself held information only he could see. Finally, Tswj Fwm smiled, exposing blackened teeth and eyes bright with intelligence.

"Give us a school for our children. Send us teachers to instruct our youth in the reading and the writing. This knowledge they will need to navigate the changes that are coming."

Jesus! Lance thought to himself. *Every damn village has their own prerogative. How the hell can anyone unite these crazy diverse peoples?*

"How many children are in your village?" Lance asked. "I need to know how big the school needs to be and how many teachers will be needed. There are also school supplies and books to consider, but I feel confident that your request will be granted. Can we also be assured of your cooperation against the Pathet Lao?"

"Light-haired stranger who speaks our tongue with familiarity, I will speak with Xob on your behalf and help return your friend to his village. In return, you must express our needs to your chief. We welcome the big brother!"

Lance had been away a full twenty-four hours longer than planned. The overwhelming responsibility he entrusted to the young boy began to weigh on him as he pushed Sawm to move at a faster pace. He was mystified. He realized nothing could have pressed Tswj Fwm. It had been several weeks before any negotiation at all had been possible with Xob and the village elders. He imagined some mysterious telepathic link between the two elders. How else would Tswj Fwm and his village have agreed to his request so easily?

Retracing the trail, was much easier, but with each step, Lance's anxiety grew. Suddenly, Sawm stopped and motioned for Lance to get down. Both crouched behind a large outcropping of rock. Cautious and alert, Sawm moved first as the path opened to reveal a lone man rapidly moving down the trail in their direction. Sawm trotted openly to intercept the man, who was breathing hard. Lance recognized the man as one of Xob's best trackers. The man spoke rapidly, gesturing behind him amid a flurry of rapid hand movements.

"Fue is gone. The buffalo are gone."

Lance bolted, his pace relentless as branches of low-lying trees scraped his arms, legs, and face. He pushed aside the verdant covering to the cave opening and entered. Inside, all trace of human habitation was erased, just as he had instructed. Breathing hard, he headed towards the antennae and found the area undisturbed. It was several minutes before he decided to check on the buffalo enclosure. The fencing was intact and undamaged, but the gate was wide open.

Lance felt his boot step on a hard object and looked down. He bent to pick up the small elephant carving from the ground just outside the open gate. He gazed beyond the pen into the forest while rubbing the small carving between his fingertips and then slipped it into his pocket.

The chicken squawked indignantly. Mindlessly, Lance unlatched the wooden lock and set them free. Sawm and the runner squatted outside the cave, waiting. Lance motioned for Sawm to follow and instructed him on how to crank the generator for the outgoing Morse code message. He checked the machinery and properly adjusted the key before clamping it to his knee and holding the key to transmit the standard test word: Paris. The light movements of his hand signaled in a smooth, rhythmic flow. The spacing of the letters and empty pauses were precise so the message on the other end would be read exactly as he intended. Lance often compared a skilled radioman to a brilliant musician whose technique flawlessly disappeared within the notes of his song.

"The enemy encroached the operation. The cache is pristine. We are still virgin. Village youth captured. Request immediate assistance to rescue."

The return message came almost immediately. "Request for assistance denied. Over."

"The boy was working for us. Protecting our interests."

"Permission denied."

Lance unclamped the key from his thigh and threw it hard onto the dirt floor.

Chapter Thirty

1961

Chiang Mai, Thailand

Isabela leaned in and watched as the blank canvas exploded into evocative and vibrant images. Prapat's art, just one stroke of his brush, communicated a delicate poetry that easily allowed the viewer to consider infinite dimensions of interpretation.

The wave of nausea came from nowhere. Isabela's face whitened, and she swayed to take hold of the back of a nearby wooden chair. Prapat looked up from the painting and quickly set his brush down.

"What is the matter, my dear?" he asked. He approached and gently helped Isabela to release her grip on the back of the chair. He quietly guided her around the easel and into a seat. "The color has completely drained from your face. Please, I will have my driver take you back to your guesthouse right away. I hope you did not eat any spoiled food."

Prapat moved across the floor and opened the door from the studio to call for his assistant, who immediately rushed in.

"Please have the driver take Miss Isabela home. She is not feeling well."

Isabela tried to protest when yet another wave of nausea threatened to overwhelm her. She stood up slowly and nodded.

"Please take good care of yourself and come back when you are feeling better. If you prefer, I will have my physician come to the guesthouse," Prapat said.

"You are so kind. I am fine, really. I am tired only. I have not been sleeping well."

When Isabela arrived at the guest house, she dropped her portfolio in the middle of the floor and sank onto the bed without bothering to remove her shoes. Within a few moments, she was fast asleep.

Prisms of light streamed through the windowpane. Isabela's eyes flew open. The image of a sweet, young face with clear hazel eyes, surrounded by a halo of thick, chestnut hair, burned bright and clear into her brain. Wide awake now, Isabela's heart began to pound.

Chapter Thirty-One

1962

Thai-Laotian Border

The wide channel twinkled with the reflected lights of a thousand stars and a pale-yellow moon. Lance dragged the dugout canoe down to the river, where he waded out a few feet before balancing his hands on both sides of the craft and stepping carefully into its center. He began to paddle with deep, even thrusts to counteract the heavy current opposing his forward movement. Once he reached the other side, Lance jumped out, splashing his feet and dragging the boat up onto the bank. He climbed up a hill. The light of the moon illuminated the now-familiar route. Lance walked through the village to where Miles's hut stood on the periphery. His was larger than the average, a tribute to his body size and newly acquired status in the village. Proposals to him for matrimony were an almost daily occurrence. Fathers displayed their daughters in brilliantly embroidered garments that showed off their child's skill and dexterity. Miles threw up his hands with a wide grin. So many beautiful women, what was he to do? And that was his saving grace.

Miles's hut was pitch black in contrast to the moonlit night. Lance clicked his flashlight on, letting the beam flicker across the room to locate Miles's large frame, prone on the military sleeping bag.

A light, wheezing snore disturbed the otherwise still night. Lance softly laid his hand on Miles's shoulder, then tapped a little harder.

"Mate, sorry to disturb you. I need your help. Meet me at the cave first thing in the morning. Sawm will come for you before daylight."

"Sure thing, mate." Miles lightly patted Lance's arm, rolled onto his side, and instantly fell back to sleep.

A thin light nudged the horizon, announcing the forthcoming dawn. Sawm, dwarfed by Miles's hulking mass, followed the larger man into the cave, quiet as a shadow. Inside, Lance sat on his heels among a mélange of camping items and firearms. A large flashlight hung from the wall, flooding the camping gear with a wide beam of light. Strewn across the cave floor were rescue essentials—water, knife, a pair of binoculars, several small pistols, canteens, flashlight, first aid kit, compass, matches, mosquito repellant, and dried food.

"I can't tell you how glad I am to see you!" Lance said. "Damn it, I'm sure you know by now that Fue was taken captive by the Pathet Lao, yes? You've no doubt noticed the increased activity in the village?"

"I wish I had come over sooner, mate. I saw things heating up, but without the ability to communicate, I wasn't sure what the fuck was happening. I figured you'd fill me in if it was important," Miles said.

"I'm sorry you've been kept in the dark. Everything happened so fast. I was trying to figure out a way to get you back to the cave without causing a split with Xob. One thing led to another, and long story short, I left Fue alone in the cave for too many days. I thought the kid understood my instructions. Damn it, I went over every possible scenario three or four times. But shit, I didn't consider the damn buffalo! Fue was captured trying to save the damned water buffalo."

"You know what they say. One man's treasure is another man's rubbish. As much as I try and blend in over there in the village, there's a huge cultural gap," Miles said.

"To bring you up to date, I was ordered to mop things up in a fortnight, from the whole drunken trade. I thought to enlist the negotiating power of a neighboring village, but as it turns out, the village was a full two-day trek through the jungle."

"I am not a prisoner, mate," Miles said. "I can leave when I want. I just didn't want to add another fuck-up to the major mess we had already created, so I've stayed on. Don't get me wrong—the Hmong want me to stay. They have been increasing the enticements. They built me the fanciest hut, prepared their finest delicacies, and paraded an unlimited number of eligible young women past my hut. Quite the situation, isn't it? I've never felt so popular! But, let's get back to the problem at hand. What's going on?"

"The tribe is set on a revenge attack. Xob and the boy's family are resigned to his fate. There seems to be no way of talking them out of their belief that he is already dead. They are set on retaliation, to crush the wicked ones. I've pleaded for this small window to free the boy before they strike. Xob has given me four days, and then it's out of my hands. I asked for just one man. Sawm here volunteered his scouting services. He is an excellent tracker by all accounts."

"Good man," Miles said softly.

"Before I go on, you have to know the operation is unsanctioned. I've been commanded to stand down. What the fuck happened to leave no man behind? You'd be stepping out on a fragile limb with me here, mate. Your participation could put your career in jeopardy. And there'll be no medal to show your family and friends at the end of it."

"You're dead set on this?" Miles asked.

"Our new friends have given us their trust, and I am quite certain that actually means something to them. Maybe I've fallen between the cracks. I don't know. If the situation comes down to a court martial, I'm prepared to take full responsibility. I can't logically justify disregarding a direct order. It never would have occurred to me in the past. But somehow, the military goals and achievements I've been working so hard toward these past years, they just don't measure up to saving the life of one skinny Hmong boy. I have this gnawing apprehension that the war, once initiated, will not be easily won. What will become of the ones left behind? They're our dear friends when we need them, but when we're done, what then? I am beginning to question the sanctity of our presence here. Are we the good guys?"

"I hear you, mate." Miles said. "What's the plan?"

"We go in under the radar. The boy was working for me, and there's no way I will abandon him. This happened on my watch. It's my responsibility. No hard feelings if you want to bail."

"Fuck, happy to oblige. I never cared too much for establishment anyway. An added plus is the much-needed vacation from a horrendous stampede of matrimonial proposals!"

Miles raised his hand and met Lance's with a hard slap.

"I owe you one. My firstborn child! Now here's the plan. Sawm will follow the tracks. Let him lead. We'll keep a good way back and hidden. When we locate the enemy, we'll need to assess their number, where the boy's being held, and what kind of weapons they are carrying. We have to devise the best extraction plan for whatever situation we encounter. Under no circumstances do we use weapons unless we're in a life-threatening situation. You know the drill. I've packed enough provisions for the four of us for three days. Let's hope to hell we can get in and out without causing a scene."

Sawm led the way and followed the subtle indications of the Pathet Lao's passage: a broken twig, light indentations in the earth, and his uncanny sense of the enemy's presence. Both men wore long sleeves, full-length pants, and wide-brimmed hats to protect them from a virulent mosquito infestation. As tiny insects whined around his head, Miles stepped cautiously into a fast-running river with his backpack held up above his head. Lance followed a few meters behind. Once they reached the other side, they continued to follow the river. A series of small waterfalls finally led them down-hill until the river seemed to come to an end. Both men stopped at the edge and looked down. Water flowed swiftly over the precipice into a massive cascade that gathered momentum and exploded like thunder down below as it converged with another river. Fine mist sprayed in every direction and rose on updrafts to where the two men stood watching.

"Impressive! That's got to drop at least twelve or thirteen meters. I wonder if there is an underwater spring?" Lance said.

"Shh …"

Miles dropped suddenly onto one knee, motioning with his left hand to get down, and carefully opened his backpack without making a noise. He extracted a pair of high-powered binoculars and raised them to survey an area of swooshing grass off to the right of the waterfall that was accompanied by strident monkey shrieks.

"Have a look at that," Miles whispered out of the side of his mouth just as Lance dropped down behind him.

He passed the field glasses to Lance and pointed to the northeast, where the disturbance appeared to initiate. Lance scanned the area and saw only a dark blur and then a flurry of white. He adjusted the focus as the color orange, punctuated with brilliant black stripes, crystallized into view. The massive tiger crouched low, concealed in the tall elephant grass. Lance passed the binoculars back to Miles. "He's got to be at least 225 kilos. Those are some muscles!"

Miles readjusted the focus, his sight straying to the left as the animal changed position. "This is as close as I want to get. How do we stay clear of him?"

A quick scurrying ensued as a large lizard slithered through the bush. The tiger pounced on the scaly reptile, who instinctively maneuvered out of its claws. The tiger bounded once again to slap its prey as if playing a child's game of hide-and-seek. Lance reached into the backpack and withdrew a pistol, indicating for Miles to do the same.

"I hate to destroy a magnificent beast like that. Just our luck to end this whole thing as fuel in the belly of a tiger. Let's stay upwind of him. Beautiful creature, isn't he?" Lance whispered.

Sawm, who was scouting the territory up ahead, doubled back and silently appeared. He indicated with quick hand motions the proximity and location of the enemy. Lance quickly reverted to Hmong to alert the tribesman to the position of the tiger and motioned for Sawm to stay close. They proceeded cautiously, with Swam once more in the lead. After only a kilometer, Sawm indicated a recessed area in the abundant brush that could easily camouflage their presence. Miles followed the tracker back the way he came while Lance stayed behind to set up an abbreviated central command center. Within twenty minutes, Miles was back.

"Damn it, you're not going to like it. They've got the boy, and he's in bloody bad shape. It's barbaric. Arms and legs are pinned to the ground, and he's being eaten alive by bugs. Not bloody likely he can withstand that kind of torture for long. If we want to bring him back to his family breathing, the extraction has to be tonight."

Lance dug his boot heel into the ground. His eyes were glued to the marks he'd just gauged in the earth.

"The opposition. What's the count?" he asked.

"Twelve, all armed. There could be more. As soon as it's dark, I'll go have another look and get a more accurate picture."

The Pathet Lao congregated around a glowing campfire. Their mood seemed jovial and relaxed, most likely brought on by the large jug being passed around the circle. Voices rose as the jug traveled round and round. Fue was on the ground to the right of them, spread-eagled in the dirt and tethered to the ground. He moaned softly. A bare-chested soldier with a rifle slung over his shoulder walked past the swollen, semi-unconscious boy and nonchalantly kicked him in the shin, laughed, and joined the group by the campfire. Fue jolted, but remained quiet.

Sawm whispered to Lance. "They are careless. It is good for us!"

"Fuck, I hope you're right." They retreated slowly. "We'll have to wait to see how this plays out. With any luck, the main players will drop off to sleep. We have to assume there will be guards. Sawm and I will tape their mouths and immobilize them. Miles, you will only all have seconds. Cut the restraints and extract Fue. The Pathet Lao won't likely have seen anyone that looks as giant or as pale as you! Hopefully, it will all work in our favor."

One by one, the Pathet Lao disappeared into a tent or curled up on the ground, seemingly dead to the world. The fire was reduced to reddish embers. Lance glanced at his watch. It was three thirty-three in the morning and just two soldiers remained awake. One leaned against a tree, a rifle slung across his lap, and the other, a plump soldier by Laotian standards, walked around the boundary of the encampment and peered occasionally into the black jungle. He kept his hand on a rifle that hung under his right arm.

Lance motioned for Sawm to place himself near the soldier against the tree and indicated for Miles to be ready. Lance's objective was the sentry walking the perimeter. When both guards were secured, Lance would make the agreed-upon call—the natural hoot of an owl three times. That would be Miles's cue to dart in and cut the boy's hands and feet loose, throw him up onto his shoulder, and head back into the night to where the rivers converged, the rendezvous point.

Time slowed. The sentry circumnavigated the perimeter every twelve minutes. Lance studied his movements, alert to any sign of sleepiness. He watched as the sentry's pace slowed slightly and determined that he would make his move on the guard's next round. Lance, clad entirely in black with green-and-black camouflage paint covering the white of his face, poised to jump as soon as the man passed by him. He waited for the crunch of the sentry's boot on twigs directly in front of him. The moment had to be orchestrated with exact precision, or the whole camp would instantly wake. He heard the man's shallow breathing as he approached and then the snap of a twig. In two steps, the man would be directly opposite Lance's concealed position. The element of surprise was an advantage. Lance leaped out from his hiding spot, knocking the sentry down. He swept his hand over the enemy's mouth and dragged him quickly into the jungle. Sawm silenced the guard leaning against the tree, moving with synchronistic precision in tandem with Lance. He held a knife to the man's throat and covered his mouth with tape before pulling him into the forest and tying his body to a large eucalyptus tree. Miles stole into the campground and, within seconds, severed the ties that bound the boy to the earth. He threw the lightweight child over his shoulder and disappeared into the night.

Miles reached the convergence of the two rivers and unpacked the lightweight stretcher he'd hidden earlier under thick brush. He gingerly laid the boy down and secured him. The boy moaned, and his body was hot with fever. Miles opened his small backpack and took out a syringe of antibiotics. He wiped the boy's arm with disinfectant and injected the liquid. He extracted a second syringe of morphine and administered it into the boy's thigh. He nodded when he saw the boy relax. Miles quickly scanned north from where they had just come. A few minutes later, Lance appeared, breathing hard.

"Good job, mate," he said. "Let's get the hell out of here! Where's Sawm? Did he scout up ahead?"

"Just me and the boy here. No sign of Sawm yet."

"God damn it! He should be here by now! I'll have to circle back and see what's up. Just keep heading back the way we came. Follow the river. Leave the stretcher. We'll try and catch up to you."

The grey light of morning began to spill through the trees as Lance headed back. He stopped every few minutes to listen and make the bird call, but the forest was eerily quiet. Moving forward, he slowed and crouched low. Through the thick underbrush, he saw his friend—and the enemy. Sawm stood still as a statue with a gun pointed at his right temple. The Pathet Lao soldier holding the pistol appeared to be waiting for something, and only a moment later, Lance saw what it was. Two Pathet Lao soldiers approached from the east.

Lance calculated his advantage. He could easily take out the enemy holding Sawm hostage and maybe one other, but in the process, he would lose his friend. It was not an option to rescue the boy only to lose this very loyal and dedicated man. Sawm's life dangled before him, dependent on his next move. Suddenly, a deep rumbling echoed and reverberated to the right, and all eyes moved in the direction of the rustling branches. The Pathet Lao soldiers turned and aimed their weapons toward the disturbance, but it was seconds too late. A blur of muted orange and black flew through the air to dig its claws into the back of the Pathet Lao soldier holding a gun to Sawm's head. The tiger's gleaming white incisors sank deep into the nape of the soldier's neck. The pistol pointed at Sawm's temple dropped decisively onto the forest ground with a soft thud. A high-pitched shriek burst forth from the approaching Pathet Lao. One soldier bolted, with his eyes wide with horror. He was followed closely by his comrade. The tiger crouched over its prey as blood oozed through its wiry whiskers.

Sawm seemed unable to assimilate and respond. He was paralyzed by the scene millimeters from him. Lance whistled the agreed birdcall that indicated his location. Sawm jolted upright and cocked his head as if awakening suddenly from a bad dream. He swerved in a half-circle, listening for the direction of the bird calls, and moved quickly to follow the guidance and sound of the last owl hoot. Lance emerged from his cover and let out a sigh of relief when he saw Sawm quickly trotting toward him. Together, they paused for just a moment to watch the huge beast drag its prey into the sweeping grasses. A shot rang out from the north and landed in the trunk of a tree as the tiger disappeared with its mangled prey, limp and unresisting.

Lance thrust Sawm forward as they began a quick retreat through the jungle, away from the scene. It was another thirty minutes before they reached the confluence of the two rivers. Lance waded into the water and crossed to the other side as Sawm trotted in the shallow creek's edge and moved with the flow of the fast-paced water. Lance bent his arm and indicated an easterly direction, away from their return route. It was the first of many maneuvers to conceal their intention and destination from the enemy.

Dark splotches of sweat stained the backside of his khaki shirt, while the front was dripping wet. Lance didn't remove it because the insects would have eaten him alive. He moved through the jungle, slowly and laboriously. Every few minutes, he slowed and cut back the heavy branches and vegetation that blocked his passage. He almost stumbled over a thick tree trunk concealed beneath the voluminous plant life. Instead of stepping over it, he lowered himself down onto the log and dropped his backpack with a thud onto the ground. *Where the hell am I?* He had backtracked and moved in the opposite direction of his destination so many times now, he was uncertain if he actually achieved any real progress. He reached into his pack and withdrew his compass. He knew the Pathet Lao were excellent trackers. Nonetheless, he felt confident that he had successfully eluded them so far.

Where is Sawm? And fuck! For that matter, where are Miles and Fue?

Lance closed his eyes, intending to rest for just a few minutes. All of a sudden, he shot straight up, hand on his pistol. A surging, swooshing buzz echoed from beyond the perimeter of his view. *It can't be Sawm. His step is as quiet as the breeze. Pathet Lao?*

Subdued voices reverberated in the distance. Lance reached into his backpack and withdrew a green paste, which he quickly smeared over his face. He crouched low to the ground and moved stealthily, as near as he could imagine a tiger or jaguar might do. As the voices grew louder, he stopped. He pressed his ear close to the ground and listened. He removed the pair of high-powered binoculars from his pack and adjusted the sight.

Hundreds of men were spread out beyond the scope of his vision. In the first group, rows of slight Laotian men cut back thick vegetation with scythes, the blades catching glints of sunlight that flashed into the trees. Just behind them, swarms of men followed. In the second group, men removed large rocks and set them to the side. A third group was made up of women. The women pulled out roots of plants, one by one.

What the fuck are they doing? The men covered the area like ants building their colony nest. He stayed low and readjusted the binoculars to razor sharp. He watched the process for the next twenty minutes before he finally realized their endeavor. So much for intelligence! *The Lao don't have the machinery to build an infrastructure that amounts to anything,* he heard on more than one occasion. *They're building a road, one millimeter at a time.*

He slowly retreated, away from the army of road builders. When he was sure he passed any possible range of sight or sound, he stood up and checked his compass again. Fortunately, the work was being done to the north, and his intended direction was southeast.

Where is Sawm?! Lance almost shouted to himself.

He hiked through the day and into midafternoon. Going was slow, but this time, he was sure he moved in the direction of the village. Another flash of light caught his eye, off to the left. In between the trees, he could just make out an old temple glittering in the sun. Its ancient walls were in varying stages of decay. He crouched low and edged closer to the perimeter of the rainforest, where he could view the area and remain undetected. He listened closely for voices and human activity but instead heard only bird calls, shrieks of monkeys, and water flowing down and dripping off leaves.

He moved stealthily, crab-like, darting, and then burrowed into the crumbling structure. The stone walls were orange-red, weathered in places to shades of greyish-black. He darted behind the walls and into the central courtyard. The inner circle was overgrown with wild tangles of vines and flowers. There was a quiet hush about the place. Lance immediately sat down and surveyed his surroundings. Carvings of female and male deities were covered in an emerald-green moss and seemed to observe him with benevolent smiles. To his right, a life-size elephant was perfectly chiseled deep into the stone. It stared out at him with eyes direct and piercing. It was so lifelike, Lance felt the animal might walk out of the stone and lay its trunk on his shoulder. Isabela's face faintly fluttered in front of him.

What's wrong with me? I am beginning to hallucinate! Focus! He closed his eyes. Heat and exhaustion overwhelmed him. He drifted into a semiconscious state and relaxed. *Stay alert! Don't fall asleep!* He repeated these commands, like a mantra.

Sunlight filtered down through the open-air ceiling. He opened his eyes. The scene in front of him wavered, dream-like. "What the fuck are Western forces doing here? What am I doing here?" he whispered to himself. He rubbed his eyes and dared the images around him to solidify. Instead, the deities gazed from the walls of the temple and seemed to become even more transparent. One appeared to fly out of its stone enclosure and fill the open room with a joyous, haunting song. Two luminous beings neared, with radiant faces.

He felt himself lift up and out of his body. His view expanded. It was as if he had, all at once, removed clothing that was three sizes too small. Now, he was able to see and inhabit multiple perspectives all at once without an attachment to his own. He sensed humanity, with its infinite masks and disguises, and lives that vied for acceptance, power, relevance, and love. Farmers, drug dealers, lovers, Americans,

Lao, and Hmong. In an instant, he understood how so many were trapped in their own tiny prisons. A wave of sorrow engulfed him as he understood the futile endeavors of countless beings. He was filled with a wish for all of them to be free.

The sun beat down on his face, but still, he didn't stir. Four Lao men gathered around him, talking among themselves. At the command of the leader, one man bent over and jabbed a syringe into the upper arm of his sleeping form, right through the sleeve. Lance jolted and immediately relaxed.

The leader motioned to the others to lift his body. Two grabbed Lance under the shoulders, and two each took a leg. They moved as one unit, carrying the unconscious man out of the temple and down a narrow trail. Every so often, they stopped and lowered him onto the ground. After ten minutes, they reached their destination. A wooden trapdoor was partially visible under several large bushes. One Laotian moved the cover to the side, while another lifted the trapdoor, which opened down into a narrow tunnel. Easy enough for the slight Laotians to navigate, but it was infinitely more challenging to maneuver the giant foreigner through the cramped passageway.

The Laotian quartet whispered among themselves for several minutes more. Decisively, one man crawled ahead, took Lance under his arms, and pulled. The others pushed from behind. Loose dirt dropped into the tunnel. Lance's eyes flew open, and he immediately suppressed a scream. *Am I being buried alive? Negative.* He heard voices and felt the pressure of hands under his armpits. *I am being taken somewhere. Why?* He quickly closed his eyes to feign a continued unconscious state and better assess his surroundings, as well as the men bringing him here.

The pushing and pulling stopped. He felt two hands lift up his head and a canteen press his lips to open as water poured down his throat. He gagged and sputtered liquid in all directions. There was no way now to feign unconsciousness. The two men up ahead yanked his arms and began to drag him through the tunnel. The third pull nearly ripped his arm out of its socket and was accompanied by a sharp command. He quickly understood he was to move of his own accord and follow.

It was not possible to stand up in the tight confines of this underground passageway, so he adjusted his body onto all fours and followed the men, like a toddler learning to crawl. Every so often, he stopped to wipe dirt from his eyes, nose, and mouth. After ten minutes of struggling, the passageway opened into a giant cavern. It took a moment for Lance's eyes to adjust to the light of the underground space and several moments more before he was able to take in the immensity of the underground world that now appeared before him. He saw an entire underground village. The large cavern was partitioned into many open rooms. He was able to differentiate living quarters, storage units, workshops, and kitchens. Some of the rooms were filled to the brim with burlap sacks. *Rice or opium?* He blinked hard a few times. Several pairs of dark eyes bore down upon him. In the subdued light, it was all but impossible to determine the facial expressions of his captors and, therefore, their intent. Somehow, he intuited, he was in no immediate danger. He attempted a weak smile and heard laughter. The canteen was once again pressed up to his lips. This time, he gratefully accepted the water. *I must have passed out from heat and dehydration. Or I've been drugged.*

Lance gazed out across the underground world and took snapshots with his mind. The row of rooms on either side of the great underground village extended as far as the eye could see. Slowly, he pushed himself up from his crawling hands-and-feet position to stand.

The blow came from out of nowhere and struck him perfectly on the backside of his head. He immediately crumpled into a heap on the ground.

Voices echoed in a semicircle around him. He opened his eyes as his hand moved instinctively to the back of his head. Several hands poked at him as he strained his focus. *What happened? Where am I?* He struggled to recall the sequence of events that led to him lying on his back with his legs immobilized. He tried to move his hands and found they were also bound. *This is bad! Assess conditions, location,* and *my captor's intent. Then make an escape plan.* He listened closely to the voices around him. *What are they saying? And how the hell do I get out of here?* He quickly ascertained that the language being spoken was not one he knew—Laotian. He forced his mind to focus and remember. Oh, right, he had been in the ruined temple and fallen asleep, maybe? Images of the temple and mossed-covered deities suddenly rushed across his mind. Something essential and with far-reaching implications flashed in his memory, but like a wisp of a cloud blown by the wind, it dissipated. It was instantly replaced by another—the smell of wet, moist earth and the claustrophobic confines of the narrow tunnel. Lance lifted his head and coughed in a futile attempt to expel the dust and debris in his dry, scratchy throat. Two slight Laotian men bent down. Each grabbed a shoulder and lifted him into a sitting position. Together, they propped his body up against the cavern's stone wall. He felt a damp cold seep into his back.

"Ne vas nulle part." *Don't go anywhere.* The men laughed.

"Y a-t-il quelque chose je peux faire pour vous?" *Can I do something for you?* Lance said, suddenly remembering his backpack left on the temple floor.

The two men giggled amongst themselves and withdrew. Several minutes later, they returned, followed by the German from the commander's compound, Volker.

"Ach, the American has turned up! You appear in the most unexpected places!"

"I'm glad to see you," Lance said as he slowly exhaled.

"I am happy to be of service. It appears you are in a bit of a jam. My Asian friends here had a plan for you, but I informed them that you are my friend." He nodded to his two Laotian companions to untie the bonds that restricted Lance's movements. In a few minutes, his arms and legs were freed. He rubbed his wrists.

"Thank you."

"Ach, not so fast, my young friend. I am a businessman, and as such, a good deed requires an act in kind."

"What do you want?" Lance said.

"It is not what I want, my friend. You are an eyewitness to this extraordinary network of underground villages and routes. It is a secret that cannot be disclosed. I'll need a guarantee that you work for me."

"And how would I convince you?"

"Loyalty. We collected your things. Inside your backpack, you'll find $10 thousand in U.S. currency."

"That's a lot of money. I imagine it would be bulky to carry."

"I am confident you will manage. The money is in $100 notes. Return with the package to Chiang Mai and deliver it to the address which you will also find in the backpack. Our contact will give you ten bags of pure heroin, processed in a lab from opium grown right here in the panhandle. You will take the heroin and deliver it to our contact in Bangkok. Quite simple."

"Would there be a second option?"

"Of course, there is always a choice, but if you would like to leave these premises alive, then I strongly suggest you comply with my request."

"Okay."

"We'll take you back where we found you. You have one week to fulfill your obligation and pick up the heroin. Another week to deliver the product to Bangkok. You see I am quite generous with your time. Also, when the product is delivered, you will receive $500 in U.S. currency."

"I accept the terms," Lance said immediately.

"It is as I thought. You are an intelligent man. I foresee a prosperous working relationship."

"How do you know I won't disappear in the jungle and run away with your cash?"

"I wouldn't advise it. I have an extensive network of spies, mercenaries, and executioners. It would be a foolish endeavor. By the way, I am curious. What are you doing here?"

"Let's just say I was helping a friend who got himself in a mess."

"Did you succeed?"

"I believe I did."

He patted Lance on the top of the head a few times and turned to leave.

"Gut, gut. I appreciate a man who helps his friends. My colleagues here will show you the way out. I trust you can find your own way back."

Chapter Thirty-Two

1977

El Salvador

It was a beautiful day. The sky was a rich, cobalt blue in vivid complement to the deep greens of the tropical forest. Analena's strange premonition, exposed now to the broad light of day, seemed the mere mutterings of a kind but ancient old woman. But to be on the safe side, Mera intended to put the root back precisely where she had found it. She sliced a thick piece of bread, slathered it with butter, and took a bite. She finished off her breakfast with a bright orange mango and let the sweet juice dribble down her chin. Afterward, she grabbed a large woven sack, filled it with a few necessities for the day's trek, and made her way out the door. In a moment, she was back. She had almost forgotten the root. If she brought it back to exactly the place where she had found it, she was sure the protection of the forest would make things right and keep the terrible world of men and their guns far away from here.

Every morning, Analena rose before the sun and disappeared into the forest, reciting prayers to the spirits of the forest, expressing her gratitude and requesting their collaboration in her healing work. It was the one time Mera was not welcomed to accompany her.

Mera hesitated. She scanned the edge of the clearing for the old woman. She didn't like to leave without telling her where she was headed, but it was getting late. There was a long way to go. *I'll be back before she has time to worry!* She searched the edge of the clearing one more time and turned to run, making her way around fallen trees and gnarled roots.

Mera felt awkward and out of sync with the forest's natural rhythm, but she was nonetheless determined to move forward with her plan. She was certain when she returned the root to its place of origin, the world would be set right again. Careful to retrace her steps of the day before, she still worried she wouldn't recognize the place. Twice, she thought she had found it, only to realize that a rock, a tree, or the surrounding bushes were different. Several hours passed as she alternated between a fast walk and an outright run, and she was tired. She sat down to lean against a tree, closed her eyes, and dozed. After barely ten minutes of a light sleep, her eyes flew open. Directly across from her was a unique, oblong stone that dominated the small clearing where she fell asleep. *How did I miss it? Yes! There's the cluster of bamboo and the moss-covered rock with the crack in it.* She moved closer and felt in between the sides of the crevice. *There it is!* She felt the stub of the root she cut only the day before. The root was no longer alive, but there was nothing she could do about that. Tenderly, she laid the root back in the crevice.

"Por favor, let me learn the secrets of the plants and help the people live peacefully like the old one does."

Mera knelt on the rough ground. A sharp piece of bark dug into her right knee while a stone pressed into her left. She ignored the pain and continued to pray. When she was done, she rose and swept dirt from her dress. Her original plan had been to return to the cottage when the root was restored to its place of origin. Instead, she meandered deeper into the rainforest to look for herbs, flowers, and rare plants she knew the old healer would be especially pleased to see displayed on the kitchen table at the end of the day. This time, she was very careful to avoid the cuttings of any plant she didn't recognize. Crouching low, she examined a cluster of yellow flowers that looked like the ones Analena had been searching for, but she wanted to be sure. *Sí, éste es el que cura la respiración! Yes, this is the one that helps the lungs to breathe!* She bent low, reciting a prayer of gratitude and appreciation as Analena taught her. A slow recognition dawned on her. This was love. The plant sacrificed in an act of healing.

The sun hovered just above the edge of the tree line as it began its descent down toward the horizon. With her sack full of healing plants, Mera turned westward to retrace her steps in a trot, hurrying to reach the cabin before dark. She knew the old healer had an uncanny intuition and would not be overly concerned about her whereabouts all day, as long as she made it home while there was still light. She looked forward to coming back and displaying all the plants she collected. She imagined the old healer's soft "mmm" each time she recognized an herb with a particularly powerful healing property.

Mera's mouth began to water as the taste and aroma of a warm stew filled her senses with anticipation. The old healer always cooked something delicious when she was out all day. Now, it was almost dark. Mera stopped abruptly. A sharp, stinging odor filled the air, but a soft breeze quickly blew it away. Her senses alert, she advanced cautiously, periodically stopping and sniffing the air before continuing on.

Closer now, she peeked through the trees and saw black wisps of smoke coiling in the distance like phantasmal snakes. Mera broke into a run toward the village, breathing hard as she neared the outskirts. Several buildings smoldered and emitted a strange orange light, but the old healer's cottage, a structure set apart from the rest, stood intact.

Mera rubbed her eyes and willed herself not to cry out.

"No, no, por favor, no!"

She darted behind the cottage and entered through the back window. The cottage was dark. No candles were lit. No warm stew simmered.

"Abuelita?" *Grandmother?*

Her whisper echoed in the silent chamber. Mera felt for matches on the windowsill and lit one. She lit another and another until she found a small candle that sat below the window. The cottage was intact, just the way she had left it. Plants dried and hung from the ceiling. She saw her sleeping mat rolled up in the corner.

Slowly, Mera creaked the front door open and let it bang behind her. She stepped outside as her heart beat erratically and echoed in her ears. There was just enough light to see the wreckage. Some structures were completely burned to the ground, while others stood, intact. Mera made her way toward the church. There was a figure draped across the doorway, face down. Black flies swarmed around its head. Mera forced herself to move forward, but it was as if she was being blown backward with each step. Finally, she reached the front of the church and recognized the man spread-eagled across the step. Slowly, she bent down next to the inert figure and rolled the man onto his side to reveal the padre's snow-white cropped hair and his hand clutching the silver crucifix that usually hung around his neck. Mera crouched lower and placed her ear next to the padre's nose and mouth. There was a labored wheezing as the padre sucked in air. He opened his right eye halfway as blood oozed from his right temple.

"Mija, por favor, ayuda!" *Please, help!*

His right eye remained open as the pastor breathed out and did not breathe in.

Instinctively, Mera reached under the pastor's armpits and tugged. She dragged him into the small church and up the single aisle, sweat mingling with tears that ran down her cheeks. She stopped just below the wooden crucifix, repeatedly wiping her face with her arm. She leaned over and, one by one, unbent the stiffening thumb and fingers clutching the crucifix. She gently placed it around his neck.

"Padre, estás tan frío. Te traeré una manta." *Father, you are so cold. I'll bring you a blanket.*

She crept into the office to snatch a blanket off the bed. It was only then, as she came back into the sanctuary, that the awareness of other bodies strewn amongst the pews began to register with her. She saw neighbors and old friends. She stared into space and past them all. Back in the sanctuary, she gently placed the blanket on top of Father Guillermo. Slowly, she rose to stand, but her legs buckled beneath her. She collapsed down next to the padre and lightly patted his shoulder.

"No te preocupes. Me quedaré aquí hasta que despiertes." *Don't worry. I'll stay here until you wake up.*

Her eyes drifted out over the pews as a flash of red caught her eye. Slowly, her gaze moved back to the center pew to a familiar red serape shawl and the light brown curve of a cheekbone. She lunged up in a gathering force. Money. There was money in the padre's box. She burst into the office and in one gigantic sweep knocked all the books, lined neatly on the shelf, onto the floor. The small metal box dropped down with the dozens of leather-bound books and clanged onto the ground. Mera lunged for the metal box. The front lock was intact, but the back hinges were still unattached from the day Father Guillermo wedged it open. On top of the money was the small yellowing card with embossed black letters. She snatched the card, and tucked it into the bodice of her dress, and stashed the colones in her skirt pocket. Her eyes glazed over as she made her way forward into the church.

More than anything she wanted to go and sit beside the beloved old woman, hold her hand, and tell her how much she loved her. Yet, she simply could not command her legs to walk the seven meters to where Analena lay drooped over a wooden pew. Instead, she moved forward, straight down the aisle, and out the door. Once outside, she ran through the smoldering village, zigzagging through fallen debris, and back to the cottage. Her mind a blank, she filled two sacks with few pieces of clothing, a blanket, some food, and healing herbs.

A thought stirred. *Maybe there is someone still alive. Maybe someone needs help!*

Instead of moving, she collapsed onto the floor amid a deep resounding buzz all around her. The front door creaked open, but Mera didn't notice. She rocked back and forth, with her knees pulled tightly into her chest.

"Get the girl, Ángel," a sharp bark commanded from outside the door. "And see if there's food."

Chapter Thirty-Three

1962

Thai-Laotian Border

Water trickled onto Lance's hat and spilled over the brim. There was nothing to do but get wet and wait out the storm as powerful winds whipped trees and plants and dumped a pounding rain. Lance squatted under a short palm tree. The fronds were wide enough to provide at least a small respite from the downpour as a loud and resounding din drowned out the natural rhythm of the forest. Suddenly, the bush beside him trembled. He reached inside his jacket and directed his fingers around hard metal. His eyes glued to the moving branches. He aimed his pistol forward, keeping it inside his jacket, as the branches parted to reveal a bright-eyed and very wet Sawm. Water poured down Sawm's face and onto his shoulders while his lips parted in a wide smile that highlighted his high cheekbones. Lance's fingers relaxed their grip from around the pistol. He removed his waterproof jacket and motioned for Sawm to come close as he stretched the tarp-like wrapping to cover both their heads. He gathered up the smaller man in a warm embrace.

"Damn, it's good to see you!" Lance spoke in English, and Sawm mimicked the sounds joyfully.

"Gud, gud!"

It had been almost twenty-four hours since Lance had last seen Sawm, and he was elated to have this loyal man back at his side. There was still no sign of Miles and Fue. Their location might be kilometers in any direction, but Lance trusted his friend and was confident Miles would show up at some point, alive and well. But would there be a breathing, living boy with him?

Suddenly, Lance swung around and punched his fist into a nearby tree as hard as he could. The knuckles of his fingers bled. He swore under his breath as he replayed his departure from the underground world. Crawling through yet another narrow tunnel and making his way back to the temple, he realized the network of routes he uncovered was far more extensive than he first thought. The second tunnel exit and trapdoor were several kilometers from the temple. If not for the guide Volker provided, he knew he might have circled for hours to return to his backpack, compass, and a general sense of location.

On the way back to the temple, his newly appointed guide led him down dummy roads that ended abruptly into a bush or a wall of stone and paths that wound around in circles. It all seemed more like a labyrinth than a route to any specific place. He felt certain the big German purposefully instructed his guide to navigate the return trip so that he might acknowledge the ingenuity and determination of the guerillas and drug lords.

His mind raced. These people devised an elaborate scheme to fool any intruder. Thousands could successfully live underground if, as he suspected, other underground villages existed across Laos and Vietnam.

Lance unzipped his backpack for the first time since leaving the underground village. Inside, a package of exactly 100 $100 bills was wrapped in thick plastic coverings. Several survival items had been removed to make room. He couldn't find his binoculars, first aid kit, and one of his pistols.

Damn it, this is a complication I don't need! I don't want this guy and his organization on my back for the rest of my life. I'll have to complete the exchange whether intel advises it or not. Shit!

The downpour eventually ceased like a full-on faucet suddenly choked and silent. The squawks, birdsong, cicadas, and cacophony of a thousand creatures returned to fill the void.

Sawm and Lance walked together in single file late into the afternoon. With each step, their feet sank into the thick mud, at times up to their ankles.

A familiar hoot echoed sharp and clear three times.

"Over here!" Miles called out.

Miles had the boy concealed in between an outcropping of shaded trees. He was still unconscious, thanks to the morphine. Lance neared and lowered himself onto his knees. He put his ear down close to the boy's chest.

"He's breathing! Fucking A, Miles! You're my goddamned hero!" Lance swiped his hand across his forehead and bowed his head.

"Sod off. Don't get all sentimental on me. We've got upwards of ten clicks of thick jungle and a pissed Pathet Lao out there!"

"The damn Pathet Lao had Sawm by the throat! The timing of the tiger was ... damn it, there's no way to explain it. It played out just like a fucking dream!"

"Are you saying the bloody tiger came back around?" Miles stared at Lance with his mouth open.

"It's a goddamned miracle that we're all here in one piece. And I've had another little adventure along the way," Lance said.

"Shit, mate, what happened?"

"I passed out from dehydration, I think, and then some Laotians found me. I am damn lucky it was not the same ones we're running from, but I nearly got my arse obliterated. I have been looking over my shoulder every step of the way since I was let go."

"No shit! What did they want, then?"

"I'll fill you in, later, mate. But, damn it, it was a close call."

Lance held the boy's hand and tapped Fue's cheek. The boy's head barely turned in response. Suddenly, his body launched up and to the side as he dry-heaved saliva onto the forest floor.

Lance supported his body and spoke softly, "Let it go. You are safe now. We've got your back."

Fue's eyes trembled, and his body shook from head to toe. Lance continued to hold the boy as Fue choked and coughed.

"He's coming around. We'll stay here till four a.m., and then we're on the road. You may have to give him a shot of adrenaline. See if we can get him on his feet."

Two kilometers from Xob's village, Lance called a halt. "Fue needs rest. We'll stop here," he said, reverting to Hmong as he turned to look for Sawm. But Sawm was already trotting toward the village. A few hours later, he returned. He led a group of six warriors and one healer into their makeshift camp. The village healer stooped low to examine Fue and spoke. Lance nodded and quickly translated for Miles.

"Sawm and I have to go back to the village. Xob is waiting for us. Can you stay here with the boy and step in as needed? These men will protect the camp. They'll accompany you back when Fue is stronger, but I think what's needed now is a different kind of healing. Their herbs and their magic."

Miles placed his hand on Lance's shoulder. "Happy to oblige, mate. Now, get out of here!"

Sawm and Lance returned to an ebullient village. Women sang as they chopped, rinsed, and collected food. The men were dressed in ceremonial clothing. Their weapons were set aside for the moment. In the center of all the activity was a raging fire, where gifts and prayers to the ancestors would be offered.

How the fuck do they know?

The preparations must have begun a long time before Lance and Sawm collapsed into the village, exhausted and relieved to accomplish their mission. Lance dropped onto the ground, prepared to sleep for the next forty-eight hours. Slowly, he opened his eyes. There were half a dozen young boys staring down at him. One tugged at his arm, and another pulled at his foot.

"Let me sleep!" he murmured.

"Xob calls you to his hut," one boy said. The others echoed him.

"All right, all right."

Lance reluctantly stood and followed the flock of young Hmong to the elder's hut. Xob sat as his usual place and motioned for Lance to come and sit beside him.

"You have brought my grandson back from the land of the ancestors. He is reborn. His future is rewritten in the stars. Tomorrow, Fue will receive a new name, and you, my son, will sit by my side. Your name will be woven into the stories of our people. Many generations from now, the grandchildren will sit by the fire to hear of your great courage and the mystery of these days."

Fue returned to the village as two men supported his weight. The procession was slow but sure. Miles trailed behind and shook his head.

"Bloody hell," he said. "I don't know what the hell they did, but they got Fue up on his feet and moving. I'm buggered! He's been talking all the way here, like he took command of the whole group."

The men disappeared into a hut with Fue as Lance leaned up against a tree and closed his eyes. Miles collapsed down beside him. It was almost midnight when Lance, spread-eagle on his back under the tree, awoke to a light tapping on his shoulder. The bonfire cast a dull light over the central village. The entire population of women, children, and elders congregated around the fire, and their voices were hushed. Xob emerged from the main hut, resplendent in ceremonial clothing. There were strips of silver braided into his hair, an embroidered cloak draped over his shoulders, and a wide red sash around his waist. Just behind Xob, Fue stepped forward, his legs wobbly like a newborn calf. But his head was held high, and his eyes were set in a determined gaze. He wore a brilliant turquoise shirt with exquisite, embroidered designs running up both sleeves, a red bandanna wound around his forehead. He sat down next to his grandfather. The seat to the left of Xob was vacant.

Lance rubbed sleep from his eyes as a gaggle of women surrounded him. Two women pulled on his arms, and unbuttoned his shirt, and wrapped him in an embroidered black cloak. Another woman placed a wide green sash around his waist. He allowed the women to poke, prod, and ready him for what was to come. A young girl approached and took his hand, encouraging him to stand and follow her. She led him to the vacant spot to the left of Xob.

The village medicine man was the first to speak. He recounted the remarkable courage of Xob's grandson, a boy who traveled to the edge of the spirit world and back. Next, Sawm stood as all eyes became riveted on him. He wove a story like a finely stitched cloak, his narrative sweeping and intricately detailed. When he described the incident with the tiger, not a whisper could be heard. The only sound came from the crackling and snap of the bonfire. The children cried out for him to tell it again when he finished, but instead, he pointed to Lance, who was forced to stand and repeat the tale. He felt vastly inadequate. The storytelling ability of the Hmong was legendary, and his own recounting paled in comparison. One by one, everyone involved told the tale as Xob threw pungent herbs into the fire and prayed to the ancestors.

Lance was invited to stand in front of Xob, then quickly dropped onto to his knees. Xob threw more herbs into the fire before speaking.

"From the day of the tiger, you are known as Koob-Meej, the honored one and friend to the Hmong. You are a respected member of my family."

Next, he called for Miles to come forward. Miles immediately dropped to his knees and bowed his head. Xob placed his hands on the large man's shoulders and spoke.

"The buffalo are gone. This is a sign that you, great white brother and friend to our village, must return to your people."

He reached behind him and withdrew a thick silver necklace, which he placed around Miles's throat. Miles backed up slowly and kept his head down until he was able to take his seat among the crowd. His raised his hand to his chest as his fingers explored the thick silver bands that rested on his bare skin.

The men helped Fue to stand. Lance lowered back into his seat and watched as Fue stood in front of his grandfather and chief. Xob again sprinkled aromatic, dried plants into the fire and chanted prayers of respect for the ancient ones and appreciation for the abundant gifts of Mother Earth. Sparks jumped and crackled.

"From the day of the buffalos' parting, you are known as Yeej, the victorious one, the one who returned from the edge of the ancestors' world. My grandson is no longer a boy connected to his mother's hut. Tonight, Yeej joins the village men. His strength and courage are for all to see."

The young man turned to face the village, his legs trembling but his eyes clear and focused. Lance sat transfixed by the scene in front of him. The boy was nowhere to be seen. In his place, there was a young man who would one day lead his people.

In the days that followed, Lance conferred with Xob, the village council, and Yeej, who was now a respected and participatory member of the tribal government. The young man's body healed slowly, but he began to show intimations of a commanding presence. He listened intently to the wisdom of the elders before proffering any ideas of his own, but his perspective was always intuitive and imaginative. Lance reminded himself that Yeej was the same young boy who wrestled with him and swirled a dance of pure joy at the gift of a small wooden elephant.

Koob-Meej was invited to the council meeting and was seated to the left of Xob, in a place of honor. The assembly was comprised of village elders and the respected men of the village. Every decision to impact the welfare of the village also needed to consider the welfare of the generations to come. Each council member's opinion and ideas were given the utmost attention and respect. Yeej was too young to be considered an elder, but everyone knew where his place would be in time.

The talk returned to the coming of the big brother and how to fight and resist the encroachment of the ones without honor. Koob-Meej restated over and again the purpose of the big brother, their strength, their firepower, and their numbers. He informed the council that in a short time the cadre would arrive, and training would begin for the men of the village. And he, Koob-Meej, must return to his chief.

Chapter Thirty-Four

1962

Thai-Laotian Border

The twin-engine Dornier banked low and right over the luxuriant, canopied forest as the pilot lowered the flaps before chopping the power abruptly over the touchdown spot. He set the plane down on a narrow ridge of a landing strip.

The pilot kept the engine running while motioning with his left hand out the cockpit window. Lance emerged from behind thick vegetation and ran toward the plane, bag slung over his shoulder. He climbed through the open back door, hopped over an array of burlap sacks filled with rice, and crawled over into the front right seat. Immediately, the aircraft began to rotate in a half circle to point the nose down the hill in preparation for a short taxi and take-off. As the plane crossed the short, narrow strip, the pilot reached full speed and quickly gained the necessary altitude to clear the thick canopied jungle.

"Sorry for the rush!" the pilot shouted. "I need to make one more drop before I return to base with you. Hope you don't mind. That's four bags of rice for a neighboring village. It's just a short diversion, but I could use your help, if you would, for the drop. I usually have a local helper, but there was some big village hoopla. I couldn't get anyone at the last minute. Since I was picking you up …"

The pilot's voice rose above the engine's deep hum, and Lance nodded while looking at the dark green landscape with carved-out fields. The river wound in and out of lush tropical growth. Within twenty minutes, the airplane descended over yet another small village nestled into the mountainside.

"Want to give me that hand now? Roll the top one over and out. Hang on, I'll give a yell when we're over the spot. It's important to time it right, or the bag ends up in the trees. Then, they split open, and it's a fucking downpour of rice everywhere!"

Lance climbed to the back and felt the hot, humid air rush in. He glanced forward, waiting for the signal. They flew direct and low over the open field, a square indentation in the otherwise thick forest.

"Now!"

Lance kicked the top bag over and watched as it plummeted toward the earth. The pilot circled up, around, and back over the same patch of land. He shouted again, and Lance pushed the next bag out. On the third go, the next bag plunged downward. Suddenly, a black figure darted across the field in direct collision course with the falling object.

"Shit! The last bag landed on something ... someone," Lance yelled.

The pilot circled back and came in for a closer look.

"Damn it, we need to go in. I don't have the fuel for this. I hope they haven't used the stash we left. We hide it, they find it, and we end up negotiating for our own damn fuel. They're resourceful little shits."

Lance returned to the right seat.

"Could you make it out?" the pilot asked

"I couldn't tell for sure, but it sure as hell looked like a body on the ground."

The plane scooted to a halt, and both Lance and the pilot jumped out from either side of the aircraft onto the grassy field. They ran across the field to where the last burlap bag of rice had fallen. Lance could see the outline of a black silhouette as the pilot muttered.

"Shit, shit, shit!"

Emerging from the forest, the villagers swarmed the field, and voices rose in a crescendo.

Fifty yards away, the pilot doubled over laughing.

"It's a goddamned pig!"

"Damn, that was a direct hit!" Lance pushed his aviator glasses up onto his head and stared at the dead animal, who had taken the unfortunate blow from the sky.

"Shit, the Hmong dress in black sometimes. Black pig. It sure looked like a goddamned Hmong. But I sure as hell am glad it wasn't."

All at once Lance and the pilot were surrounded by a crowd of exuberant Hmong. Men slapped them on the back and pointed excitedly toward their village. Several broke free of the crowd to examine the fallen pig. They looked at its eyes and hooves and felt the width of its girth. Finally, they tied the pig's hooves together and placed a thick plank under the ties. They hoisted the apparatus with the pig onto their shoulders and then weaved their way toward the forest's edge and the village. Two Hmong who remained in the field grinned broadly. They spoke in a Hmong dialect and pointed once again to the village. Lance translated quickly to the pilot.

"We're invited to the village for a celebration," Lance said. "It's considered extremely rude to decline. Don't count on going anywhere until morning. I need to send a message to base not to expect us until tomorrow."

The pilot openly stared as Lance resumed his conversation with the Hmong.

"You speak their lingo? Now that's a fortunate turn of events. Ask them about fuel. Can we get some fuel? Our own damned fuel, to be precise."

"Tonight, we're the honored guests. It's eating, drinking, and probably not much sleeping. We are a blessing from the sky in their eyes. So is the pig. Put aside any talk of fuel until tomorrow and just roll with it, if you will. We don't really have a choice."

"The name's Dave." The pilot extended his hand, firmly shaking Lance's.

"It was a goddamned pig! Let's show them how to have some fun."

They roasted the pig in a dugout pit, cut it up, and shared the meat. The two pilots formed a circle with the villagers all seated around a large wooden vat filled to the top with a dark liquid. A film of tiny insects was visible on the surface.

"No fucking way I'm drinking that. I don't care who I offend!" Dave pulled his knees in close to his chest.

"Damn, last time I drank that brew, I got into a shitload of trouble!" Lance spoke to no one in particular.

A wooden cross lay across the mouth of the container, and from it dangled a string. It looked to be a kind of measuring device that dipped deep into the liquid and indicated how much alcohol remained. A long, hollow reed was passed from one person to the next. Each person took a large swig before passing the reed to the next in the circle. Lance sucked on the reed, all eyes upon him. The alcohol burned his throat and brought a deep sensation of warmth to his lower belly.

"Shit, the stuff's pure disinfectant. No microbe can survive that!" he said.

Dave took a tentative sip and quickly passed the reed to the next person, but like an echo, the reed reappeared in front of him to a roar of approval from the circle.

The sun was already halfway down toward the horizon when Lance opened a blurry eye. Both pilot and passenger lay unconscious in the dirt outside the large round house. Village life bustled around them. Women chatted amicably as they rinsed rice, chopped chilies, and prepared for the evening meal.

About the size of a small beagle but with the wiry coat of a terrier, a little brown dog gently licked the corners of Lance's mouth. Instinctively, Lance raised his arm to block the dog's tongue and abruptly sat up to a massive pounding in his head. He felt in his shirt pocket and extracted a piece of gum, popped it into his mouth, and began to chew. The dog sat back on its haunches. His right eye was razor-sharp blue, and his left was a soft brown hue. Both eyes were intent and focused on the man chewing and staring into space. Not to be put off, the little dog circled around for a renewed approach. He nudged his wet, black nose under Lance's arm. Lance, not yet fully awake, scratched the dog behind his ear as he pressed the gum around his tongue.

"Where did you come from, little fella? With a bath and a haircut, you might just be a keeper."

Dave was slower to wake up. Flies and no-see-ums buzzed around his eyes and mouth. He swatted absently into the empty air and suddenly jumped to standing.

"Fuck!" Dave brushed his hands in a wild circle. Lance stared into open space, quietly massaging the little dog's ear. "What the fuck are you doing? That mutt has got to have at least twelve diseases. Get him out of here!"

The pilot aimed his foot and kicked. The little dog yelped and ran back a few paces, only to turn around and sit, his tongue hanging from his mouth.

"Shit, we slept half the afternoon. They're gonna have my ass. We have to get airborne and back to base before the light is gone. Can you talk to our new friends and see about the fuel?"

Lance stood, every muscle in silent protest, and swept deeply embedded dirt from his clothing. "Sure thing, boss." He walked toward the round building, followed closely by the little brown dog. A half an hour later, he reemerged with a huge grin. The dog sat attentively, waiting at the entrance, and rose to follow him as he exited. "They'll bring the fuel to the field. I hope you've got something in the plane we can give as gifts."

"Rice, I've got a lot of rice," Dave said.

The little dog trotted a few feet behind.

"Go on! Go back to the village. You can't come with us," Lance said and bent to scratch behind the dog's ear.

The little dog sat quietly, waiting. He allowed a small distance to separate him from the retreating men, and he jumped up to follow again. Every time Lance took a step forward, the little dog advanced and then sat. His tail swished left and right, sweeping the ground.

"Dave, is there anything in the plane we can give this little fella?"

"Kick his mangy ass. That'll do it."

Lance leaned over to massage the dog's neck.

"Sorry, boy, looks like you are out of luck. What should I call you? How about Amigo? We said we'd call our dog that."

"All right, there's some beef jerky in the cockpit, in the righthand compartment. Give it to him and let's get the hell out of here."

A gaggle of villagers carried a large wooden container and set it next to the aircraft.

"We'll have to siphon. Good thing it's not my first rodeo. I gave them another two bags of rice," Dave said.

Lance hopped into the front seat and popped open several compartments, looking for the jerky, as Dave siphoned the fuel into tanks.

"We're all set. It's a go," Dave said.

Lance fed the jerky to Amigo, whose ribs penetrated outward through matted fur. He set the remainder of the dried beef on the ground and hopped into the right seat. The engines already hummed. Amigo abandoned the food and leaped up. His jump was not quite high enough to reach the open back door, so he poised himself to try again.

Dave started the engines and began to gather speed, rumbling down the field for takeoff. The plane rose quickly above the small field, rising toward a hazy orange sun.

"We'll be over the village where I picked you up in a few minutes. Then it's about forty-five minutes to Chiang Rai. Got any plans when you get back to civilization?"

"Debrief and roll with the protocol. Actually, I hope to have a few days off before I head back to the States."

Lance's hand involuntarily moved to rest on his backpack. His mind instinctively thought to the bundle of neatly packaged cash inside. *And shit, maybe a quick trip to Bangkok!*

He considered the problem from every possible angle. There was no solution without substantial risk. He should, of course, turn the problem over to the team, but he hesitated. How would they handle it, and where would he end up? Volker's organized crime syndicate had mafia written all over it and, without a doubt, a giant reach across southeast Asia. Either way, he could never return to Thailand. If he did, he'd instantly be embroiled in the underground world of drugs and warlords. Deliver the goods and get out of town. That was the simplest solution to the conundrum he faced. *I'll have to get word to Isabela. Maybe we'll set up a little house by the sea in El Salvador. There could be worse places.* After returning to the States and freeing himself of his responsibilities there, he knew he did not want to live in America. The possibilities of where he might go with the mafia on his back seemed stifling. And Isabela would not be safe. That was not an option. No, he had to deliver the package, leave the cash payment, and get the hell out of there. If he disappeared for long enough, they'd eventually forget about him, he reasoned. The words shot straight out of his mouth.

"There's this woman, a hell of a woman…"

A loud rustling toward the back of the plane made Dave turn to look over his shoulder.

"What the hell was that? Can you check it out?"

Lance climbed to the back and stepped over several burlap sacks of rice. Wedged alongside the interior wall, a trembling and panting ball of matted, wiry fur peeked one blue eye out from behind several bags of rice. The dog jumped into Lance's lap as he squatted to investigate the noise.

He yelled up to the front loud enough, he hoped, to override the deafening engine's roar.

"Looks like we've got a stowaway!"

The sun sank toward the horizon as smoke from burning rice fields thickened the air to an orange-brown haze. The westward flight plan had little visibility, necessitating a lower-than-normal altitude to follow the landmarks. The twin-engine Dornier transmitted a monotonous drone as the aircraft kept to the right of the winding river below.

"We should see the convergence of the Kok River in a bit and straight into Chiang Rai," Dave said.

The left engine sputtered, missed, and continued its drone.

Dave checked mags on each engine and the fuel selector.

"Damn shitty fuel we get out there in the villages. We get all kinds of water in the tanks. Mostly just condensation. Nothing to worry about. It happens all the time."

Suddenly, the left engine lost all power. The left propeller wind-milled from the airflow generated from forward aircraft speed. Dave leaned in, checking the fuel mixture lever as the aircraft began to lose speed. Lance sat forward, instantly alert. Adrenaline pumped as both pilots began checking the gauges. The airplane was loaded with enough rice for another few villages, so there was no guarantee the bird would fly well with just one engine.

Dave flipped on the fuel boost pump and opened the fuel cross feed valve to transfer fuel from the right tank to the left tank. A few heartbeats and the left engine roared back to life with an erratic rumble. Both men breathed out as one. The clouds glowed orange in the setting sun.

"Nice flying, boss! You didn't miss a beat. Got enough fuel in that left tank to take us all the way in?" Lance asked.

"On a wing and a prayer, we should just make it. If there's an issue, we'll drop the rest of the rice," Dave said, his eyes focused on the aircraft gauges.

Lance reached in his pocket and pulled out the miniature carvings of the elephant and jaguar. He rubbed the elephant in between his thumb and forefinger and held onto the jaguar with his pinky.

CHAPTER THIRTY-FOUR

"Whatcha got there?"

"What, these?" He opened his fingers and displayed the elephant and jaguar carvings in the palm of his hand. "I meant to give them to the kid, but he's focused on important village issues now. I just found them in my pocket. I whittled them. It passed the time out there. I made about ten of them. I've never seen a kid get so excited about a damn piece of wood. Each time I carved one, the kid had the same reaction. He jumped up and did a dance of pure joy. You should have seen it! It got so I couldn't wait to make the next one, just to see his dance. This same crazy kid will be stepping up to take charge of his people when the old one passes."

Amigo began to whimper from just behind the right seat, and the tip of his nose quivered nervously.

"It's all right. You're okay, fella." Lance reached his hand back and massaged the little dog's neck.

"What the hell are you planning to do with the mangy mutt? I don't imagine whoever you're working for will allow you to keep it. Not with this kind of work."

Dave turned to look at his passenger and raised his eyebrows. Lance withdrew his hand from the dog and scratched behind his own neck.

"Like I said, there's this woman …"

"Always a damn woman," Dave mumbled.

"She misses her dog back home, so, maybe I'll clean him up and surprise her. I hope to have those few days off when I get in. He might just keep her company until I get a few things sorted out. Maybe I'll give her these."

He opened his hand again, displaying the tiny animal figures. He started to say something more and then thought better of it. Dave picked up the slack.

"Sounds like the woman has a hold on you. Maybe you should run the other way?"

"Maybe I should," Lance said quietly. "It sure as hell would make things a whole lot easier. Trouble is I've never met anyone like her. I've been focused on the military my whole adult life, and I never considered anything else." He paused and forcefully blew out a breath before continuing. "I don't completely understand it, myself, but my priorities have changed, and I'm at a loss as to where this leaves me."

"She must be one hell of a woman."

The silence in the cockpit deafened as both engines went eerily silent. The only audible sound was the sweeping swoosh of the propellers.

"Pull up, pull up!" Lance shouted.

Dave rechecked the gauges. "Shit!"

He attempted to restart the left engine, but there was no response. The airplane was rapidly losing altitude and gliding down toward the thick canopied jungle at an alarming speed. The jungle, which had been thousands of meters below, quickly loomed large and menacing. Lance checked and rechecked the panel, quickly referencing each position to Dave.

"We have to find a place to set her down. There's a ridge just up ahead. That's our best option. It's a triple-canopy jungle. We're going to hit some trees. There's no way to avoid it." Dave eased back on the stick, sacrificing airspeed to gain altitude, and feathered both propellers to stretch the glide. As the plane approached the treetops, he slapped the flaps to full. "Hope to hell this works!"

Metal scraped against the branches of trees as the aircraft shuddered, shook, and plummeted downward. They sank to the right as the aircraft disappeared into the treetops. The right wing broke sharply in two, and finally, the aircraft came to a tenuous stop, supported by branches like some giant Christmas ornament. Something penetrated the right fuselage just behind the right seat window. Smoke billowed up from the back, and flames shot from the engine. The cabin instantly filled with a searing heat. Lance grabbed the handle of his door, but it was hot to the touch and wouldn't budge. Smoke and sharp plumes of flame began to overwhelm the interior of the aircraft. Lance flew out of his seat and moved toward the back of the plane, but he immediately jumped back into the cockpit, as brilliant flames and a searing heat scorched his hair and nostrils.

"We need to get out of here now! This bird's going to explode!" he yelled.

He saw Dave struggling unsuccessfully with the escape hatch. It wouldn't budge. Lance's eyes darted around the inside of the cabin, assessing conditions, while his hands felt around the windows and struggled again with the door. Suddenly, he looked down and noticed for the first time a tear in the fuselage, just behind the copilot seat.

"There's an opening over here! I'm going to try and crawl through it."

Amigo jumped onto his lap. Lance grabbed him and threw him out the hole. Then he wriggled himself headfirst, but his shoulder jammed in the opening. With superhuman strength, he grabbed the outside of the fuselage and yanked. The upper part of his body now hung upside down, dangling down the side of the aircraft. His hands burned, but he didn't feel it. Without a pause, he wriggled his hips free, and suddenly, his legs and feet followed, plummeting him into an air dive down into the depths of the jungle. Branches scraped his arms and legs as he grabbed for anything that might cushion his rapid fall. He fell onto a tree branch and, for a moment, breathed a sigh of relief. But it was only seconds before the branch cracked under his weight, wavered, and broke violently in two. Lance fell another seven meters onto the forest floor.

LOTUS

He was stunned for a moment and then stared back up from where he had just fallen. Dave leaned out through the cracked opening of the burning aircraft, assessing conditions. The heat, however, from the inside of the aircraft began to scorch the back of his head and body.

Lance yelled as loud as he was able.

"She's going to blow! Get out now! Grab onto the trees! It's long way down!"

Dave looked behind him one last time as the rear of the aircraft burst into a series of small explosions. He shoved his arms out, ducked his head free, and pulled his body through the tight space. He grabbed for the first solid tree branch, hoisted his legs around it, and shimmied down the branch until he reached the trunk of the tree. He glanced toward the ground and swore.

"Shit!"

There was upward of nine meters to the ground. He glanced back at the burning airplane hanging in the trees and began to rapidly climb down the tree.

Another small explosion burst forth from the tail of the aircraft, and Dave, his heart racing, let go of the tree and dropped the last four and a half meters to the ground. He tumbled head over heels down a steep embankment. Ten meters further up the hill, Lance tried to get up, but his legs were unresponsive. His face and hands were deeply burned.

When Dave's somersaulting descent finally came to a stop, he immediately stood up. Blood oozed from just above his right eye. Suddenly, the dark forest was illuminated by a bright explosion of light. Dave made his way up the hill as Lance called out his position. The light of the exploding aircraft filled the forest in a halo of fire.

"Damn, I can't seem to move my legs," Lance said. "I won't be going anywhere until helps comes. You doing okay?"

"It's going to be a long night. There's no way a rescue team can even begin to look for us until daylight. I sure as hell hope the bad guys don't get here first! We'll have to wait until morning to see if there's anything salvageable from the plane. They'll have a rescue team assembled at first light when we don't show up. We need to make it through the night, okay?"

"Roger that."

"This is the last time I am going camping with you!" Dave said.

He kept their conversation to a light banter as he felt around the trees for leaves with dew or any water collected on them. He found nothing. He realized his passenger was seriously injured, and although he himself was upright and ambulatory, he considered he might be in shock and had possibly sustained injuries of which he was, as of yet, unaware. He made a firm decision to stay in one place until the morning.

"I'm not saying that any part of this situation is lucky, but I'll count the blessings where they fall. It looks like some kind of scaffolding, built for God knows what purpose, rammed through the fuselage. Anyway, who the fuck cares? It saved our asses. There was a leak. The damned mechanics sealed the escape hatch. It takes forever to get spare parts out here. Otherwise, the bird is out of commission, and the big guys never want to hear about that."

Dave continued to speak into the dark night while Lance drifted in and out of consciousness.

"The little fuckers added water to the fuel."

Dave attempted to rest, but within minutes, his eyes popped open wide. He jumped up, slapped his shoulders, and ran his hands over his body as if an army of fire ants swarmed all over him. Images of poisonous snakes and spiders filled his head, any one of them capable of making this night his last night on earth. Minutes dragged like hours. Every so often, he checked on his passenger and crouched low to bring his fingers around Lance's wrist. Each time, he breathed a sigh of relief when he heard a light, labored breathing and felt a faint pulse.

The jungle was alive with a primal beat that resounded all around them. Dave attempted to rest, but each time he tried, he was jolted wide awake by the swoosh of bats flying low overhead, the cry of some wild animal, or the crackling of a branch falling from a tree. Every time, he jumped to his feet and swerved around in a wild circle. He knew it was pointless. He couldn't see a damn thing.

The rattle of an owl called out, and a branch dropped with a thud onto the ground. With each noise and unfamiliar sound, Dave's heart pounded. He glanced at the face of his florescent wristwatch. The numbers had barely moved. *Will this night never end?*

Dave's head spun to the left. A rustling in the branches made the hairs on his neck stand straight up. He shot up and spun around. A furry object shimmied past him. Dave hopped up and down, unable to suppress a shrill howl. He was instantly answered by a yelp. Dave breathed out a sigh of relief as he bent down and felt the tail of the little brown dog.

"Shit, you mangy mutt! You scared the living daylights out of me. Come here."

It was two a.m. The ooo-eee-ooo-eee of the cicadas' song rose to a deafening crescendo. Lance was suddenly wide awake and tried to speak. He coughed twice and then tried again, but his voice was faint.

"My backpack. Will you look for it in the morning? Make sure you bring it, okay, boss?" Lance's breath was raspy and labored, and Dave strained to hear. "Isabela," he whispered. "Go see her for me, will you? She is staying at the Thai Guest House in Chiang Mai. I'll make it back, damn it, however long it takes. Don't forget to tell her about my dream … just now, I dreamed of a young girl with the face of an angel and wild auburn hair. Tell her that one day we'll have a beautiful girl. Reach in my pocket, won't you? Give her the elephant and jaguar …"

Lance's words faded into a mumbled incoherence that Dave couldn't make out. He leaned in closer and spoke into Lance's ear.

"Hang in there, chief. You tell her yourself. Do that for me."

Amigo favored his front right paw, which no longer supported him. With fierce determination, he hopped on three legs to place his snout on Lance's belly. The little dog's head rose and lowered with the erratic rhythm of Lance's breathing. He snarled when Dave approached and tried to separate him from the injured man.

Dave woke to the clicking, pulsing sweep of a helicopter circling the crash site. Amigo remained in place on Lance's abdomen, with only his ears pricked and his head turned toward the sky.

"They found us! Thank God, they located the crash site!" Dave yelled out as Lance rocked his head back and forth without responding. The helicopter circled the area as it waited for the rescue team. Amigo suddenly jumped off Lance's abdomen and began to bark furiously, hopping in a protective circle.

The helicopter pilot looked down below to the crash site as he spoke to the operator seated behind him.

"Do you see anything?"

"Nothing but ashes. I doubt anyone could live through that! Wait, circle around again. I think I saw some movement," the copilot said.

He continued to look out the window and then shouted, "There's a survivor, and he's walking! What the hell? There's a dog running around!"

PART II

"The lotus flower blooms most beautifully from the deepest and thickest mud."

Chapter Thirty-Five

1962

Washington, D.C.

Anne Jameson jangled the car keys in her left hand as she reached for her briefcase with her right. She was ten minutes late for the morning commute into D.C. and hoped the traffic on the Beltway would not further delay her arrival. She swore under her breath when the doorbell rang. The only way to the car was out the front door, which she opened a crack. Two gentlemen stood before her, both in dark business suits. One wore a short khaki raincoat over his suit, and the other donned a black fedora hat. The one with the hat quickly removed it and held it at his waist.

"Hello, ma'am. May we come in?" The man observed the tall angular woman as he waited for her reply.

Anne glanced quickly at her watch. "I'm in a bit of a rush. What do you want?"

"I'm afraid there's been a bad accident," the man with the short khaki raincoat said.

Anne allowed the door to swing open, and the two men entered.

"I am sorry to inform you that a bush plane carrying your husband and a pilot is believed to have crashed into the jungle in southeast Asia yesterday. The aircraft is missing."

The man with the hat let it fall to the ground as he reached for the young woman's arm. She teetered on T-strapped black heels and looked as if she might crumble onto the floor. Instead, she straightened her back and took a breath.

"Is he alive?" she said.

"The last communication from the aircraft was at five o'clock local time yesterday. I'm afraid there has been no further contact. They were flying over dense jungle."

"Please, I need to know the pertinent details. Have a seat in the living room."

Anne disappeared into the kitchen and reemerged with a tray carrying three waters, no ice.

"Please understand, Mrs. Jameson. Your husband was involved in a highly classified mission. There can be no record. We can only divulge that a twin-engine plane carrying two passengers, your husband and a pilot, disappeared while flying over the jungle in southern Laos yesterday. With this kind of accident, we can only hope for survivors. The official story is that they were flying humanitarian aid to outlying villages with Air America. Of course, no effort will be spared to recover any remains."

Anne reached for a glass of water, a slight tremble to her fingers as she brought the glass to her lips and took a sip.

"Take me to whoever is in charge. Immediately!"

"I'm afraid that's not possible, Mrs. Jameson. We will be here all day, as long as it takes. As soon as there is information it will be communicated directly to us. It's nighttime in Asia now. There won't be additional intelligence until this evening, which is tomorrow morning for them. He was in a very remote area where communication is sketchy in the best of times. Unfortunately, there is nothing to be done right now but be patient and wait."

Anne stood and paced the living room as if she were a leopard in a zoo enclosure too small to contain it. She forcefully kicked off one shoe and then the other, finally standing in front of her large mahogany desk at the back of the room. She rummaged through the top drawer and pulled out a yellow, lined writing pad and a perfectly sharpened pencil.

"May we sit down?" the man with the khaki raincoat inquired as both men stood just inside the living room doorway.

"Sit wherever you want." Anne spoke as she lifted the receiver to a black rotary desk phone. Her index finger decisively dialed each number.

"Susan, cancel all my appointments. I won't be coming in today."

She released the receiver and let it settle back onto the cradle while scribbling notations on the yellow pad.

"I want to know exactly where the plane went down and what time of day or night. I need to make sure there will be no effort spared for the rescue operation. I will be flying to the closest major airport tomorrow. Please let whoever is in charge know that I will be on a flight first thing in the morning to wherever the hell my husband is located. Have I made myself clear?"

It was ten p.m. when the phone rang. Anne jumped up from her slumped position on the desk.

"Mrs. Jameson?"

"Yes?"

"There is one survivor. We repeat—there is one survivor, and he is ambulatory. There is no way to know yet whether the survivor is the pilot or passenger. The rescue team is cutting back the jungle from several miles away, and when they reach the crash site, the helicopter will lower a gurney for any survivor or body. They'll fly to a clinic in Chiang Rai for immediate observation and most likely will be transported to Bangkok. The doctors there are better equipped to deal with any extensive injuries."

"I will be on the first flight to Bangkok in the morning."

"With all due respect, ma'am, we don't know if your husband is alive." Anne held the phone receiver away from her ear as the agent continued. "Please, wait until we have all of the information."

Anne brought the phone back close to her lips, "I'll be on a flight to Bangkok tomorrow!" she repeated and set the phone down with a bang.

Anne checked her watch and leaned down to close to her brown leather Luis Vuitton suitcase. It was five-thirty in the morning. She dragged the bag to the front door just as the doorbell rang. Expecting a taxi to the airport, Anne opened the door. Instead, standing just outside the front door, holding his fedora in his hand, was the agent from the day before.

"Mrs. Jameson, we have good news. Your husband is alive, as is the pilot. Your husband, however, is badly injured."

Chapter Thirty-Six

1962

Bangkok, Thailand

The staccato-click of black high heels echoed, sharp and precise, down the white marble hallway. A young nurse seated behind the desk looked up as Anne approached.

"I need the room number for Mr. Lance Jameson."

The young nurse responded in Thai and indicated that Anne should take a seat. Anne remained standing. Her clothing was crumpled and her eyes reddened from the transpacific crossing.

"Get me someone who speaks English!" she said, articulating each word.

The nurse retreated and after ten minutes reappeared with an official-looking Thai dressed in a formal business suit.

"Please, may I be of service?" he said.

"Thank God, someone who speaks English. My husband was brought here two days ago. There was an airplane accident. His name is Lance Jameson."

"Yes, your husband is here. He is in Room 112. Please have a seat, ma'am. I need to get permission for your visit from the doctor."

"I just traveled halfway across the world and have come directly from the airport. Tell the doctor to meet me in my husband's room. Thank you."

Anne ignored the hospital official's strident protest and checked her surroundings. *Where the hell are the patient rooms?* Her eyes swept the waiting room and, within seconds, located the correct direction in which to walk. She quickly moved toward a hallway and signage that indicated Rooms 100-126.

"No one is to visit this patient without special permission from the authorities!" The official followed anxiously behind the incessant click-clack of Anne's high heels as she progressed down the hall.

Dave, the pilot, slumped in a white plastic armchair in the far corner of Room 112, with his chin heavy on his chest. His head shot up as Anne barged into the room. Lance lay unconscious on a bed designed for shorter patients. His feet were elevated and bandaged, and his face was burned and black, like seared meat.

"I want to see the doctor. Where is my husband's doctor?"

Anne's eyes darted around the room but avoided the man whose body was bandaged from shoulder to toe. A nurse followed her into the room and shook her head. She motioned for Anne to leave the room immediately, an instruction which Anne ignored. Two American officials appeared outside the doorway. They peeked in the room.

"Mrs. Jameson? We're from the U.S. embassy."

Dave stared hard in Anne's direction.

"Can we get a goddamn interpreter in here? I want to know how my husband is doing. Is that too much to ask?" Her hand shook as she wiped beads of sweat from her forehead. "Who is he?" She pointed briefly in Dave's direction.

Dave continued to stare at the woman without responding.

One of the embassy officials replied, "Please step outside so we might speak in private." He waited a moment as Anne followed him out the door.

"Dave is the pilot," he said. "Fortunately, he was not seriously injured. He suffers from post-traumatic stress, however, and hasn't left your husband's side. We'll talk with him in a few days and get the full story. He should recover and be just fine."

"I don't give a damn about the pilot! What about my husband?" Her eyes once again darted inside the room and then quickly back to the embassy emissary.

"We've spoken to the doctors. Your husband has extensive injuries to his right eye, right hand, and pelvis, which is broken. His burns, as you can see, are quite severe. It's been touch and go the past few days." He paused before continuing. "Please be assured that your husband is in very good hands and is receiving the best possible medical treatment."

"I want him flown to Washington as soon as he is stabilized. Dr. Paul Bazos is one of the finest orthopedic surgeons in the country, and he is a family friend. I'm sure he can provide us with the specialized care my husband needs. My husband is not going to a military hospital."

"We cannot be responsible for his welfare if you move him too soon. When he is stable, the doctor's recommendation is that he be flown by military transport to the burn unit at Brooke Army Hospital in San Antonio, Texas. They have a lot of experience with injuries such as those sustained by your husband. Because he is technically a civilian, they are not required to extend this opportunity. You will not receive better care anywhere. Everything will be taken care of. However, if you miss this window, well, there are a lot of injured soldiers on the wait list."

Anne unsnapped the clasp of her purse and withdrew a cigarette from the slim silver case that held only four. Her hand shook as she fumbled with a matching silver lighter. Both lighter and case were engraved with the cursive initials *AMJ*. Anne inhaled deeply and slowly blew smoke from her nostrils.

Chapter Thirty-Seven

1962

Chiang Mai, Thailand

The taxi screeched to a halt in front of the Chiang Mai guesthouse as Dave leaned forward to extend his payment for the ride. He jumped out but turned back and opened the back passenger door. He grabbed the red leash that lay across the backseat and pulled. Amigo, bewildered and immobile, did not budge a millimeter. He was shampooed and disinfected, and his matted fur had been sheared close to his skin. He looked more like an overgrown rat than a dog. His front right paw was thickly bandaged with no allowance for the leg to bend at the knee, and a shiny red collar hung loosely around his neck.

Dave tugged on the leash, and Amigo flopped onto his side. His bad leg stuck out and into the air. Instead of moving, he began to chew at the bandaged leg. The driver pointed to his watch and shifted gears. Dave gave one last yank.

"Goddamned dog!" Dave dove into the back seat, scooped the small dog up into his arms, and slammed the door shut. "All right, you mangy mutt, you've got one chance, so don't blow it. You better hope this chick likes you. I sure as heck wouldn't. Otherwise, you're on the street. Do you get my drift? No way I'm living with a vermin-infested … just because you're cleaned up and survived the crash doesn't make us friends, got it? I don't like dogs. Are we clear?"

Amigo nestled his head on Dave's shoulder and closed his eyes. Dave continued to mumble into the dog's left ear as he approached the front desk. "Please, is there a young woman staying here by the name of Isabel? I am sorry, I don't have her last name."

"Yes, there is a Miss Isabela. Your name, please? We will contact her and let her know you are in the lobby."

"Actually, she won't know my name. Just tell her I am here on behalf of Lance. Lance Jameson."

The front desk clerk dialed the room. It rang several times before Isabela answered.

"Miss Marquez, there is a gentleman in the lobby here to see you. He is here on behalf of a friend. Lance Jameson? He has something for you."

"¿Perdón?" *Pardon?* "Who?"

"I believe he said the name Lance Jameson." The clerk looked directly at Dave for affirmation. Dave shifted the small dog in his arms and nodded yes.

Isabela ran through a number of people she had met since coming to Chiang Mai. There were not that many. Her mind quickly considered the students she met in the art school, parties she had attended, friends and even friends of friends. She was quite sure she had never heard of a Lance Jameson.

"I am sorry. Perhaps the gentleman has confused me with someone else? I do not know a Lance Jameson."

"I am sorry," the clerk said. "The lady does not know the person you refer to."

"Damn!" Dave shook his head while repositioning the dog onto his other arm. "Just my luck. Stuck with the goddamned dog! Please take my card, in case she suddenly connects the dots."

Dave reached into his pocket, dropped his business card onto the desk, and pushed it toward the clerk. He eyed the lobby bar. *A cold beer sounds good while I figure out what to do with the mutt.* Amigo whimpered and slid his head along Dave's upper arm.

Isabela stepped into the lobby and looked left and then right. She saw no one. The front desk clerk pointed to the bar.

"He's sitting at the bar. He's the only patron holding a dog. If you need assistance, Miss Isabela, we will remove him from the property immediately."

"This is not necessary. Thank you."

Isabela approached the man with the small dog and smiled. She wore a white silk blouse with a small gold pendant that hung in the vee of her neck, exposing her vibrant golden skin and the small round curve of her breast. The light fragrance of jasmine preceded her. Dave looked up as Isabela extended her hand.

"The desk clerk said you asked to see me. Is there perhaps someone else staying here who you mean? I haven't heard of anyone by the name of Lance Jameson."

Dave inspected the woman. Her eyes were kind and gentle but somehow curious and penetrating all at once.

"Well, I'll be goddamned," he said. "I'd give it all up, too!"

"¿Disculpe?" *Excuse me?*

"Lance Jameson. He wanted you to have the dog. He said you missed your dog back home. This one is to keep you company until he's able to make his way back."

"Jameson? You are a friend of Jimmy?"

"Whatever. Lance, Jimmy ... he was in an accident. Actually, we were in an accident together—a plane crash, specifically. He's pretty banged up. They have him in a hospital in Bangkok. He has already been there for ten days, unconscious," Dave said.

"I'm sorry, what are you telling me?"

"Don't worry. They expect him to recover. Otherwise, I couldn't have left. It was a miracle that we survived. I was just released myself yesterday. The dog here, he was in the accident too and, until this morning, was in a veterinary clinic in Bangkok. The U.S. government paid his entire vet bill. That's a new one for me! We flew up from Bangkok this morning to see you."

"Your friend, how does he look?" Isabela said, trying to understand the man with the dog.

"What does he look like, you mean? You wouldn't recognize him now, I'm afraid. His face is deeply burned and swollen."

"His eyes?" she said.

"Whew, I couldn't tell you. That's not something I'd notice or remember." Dave presented the dog with extended arms and then quickly gathered Amigo back into his chest as he stood halfway up, indicating the seat across from him with his free hand. "I promised to bring you the dog. It's the one goddamn thing I could do."

Isabela bent over and lightly scratched Amigo behind the ears.

"Cariño, pobrecito. ¿Por que estás tan delgado?" *Sweetie, poor little thing. Why are you so thin?*

"He said to tell you he named him Amigo, that you'd like that. No, that you'd remember that."

Isabela's head shot up. "You know Jimmy? Why are you calling him Lance?" A single tear slid down her cheek as she searched Dave's face. "Please, you know Jimmy? Where is he?"

"I wouldn't recommend you visit him just now. They're going to transfer him to the States any day, and he wouldn't know you were there anyway. He's in a medically induced coma. He won't regain consciousness before the move. So if you go, he'll most likely already be gone. He told me to tell you he will find you wherever you are, so stay."

"The name of the hospital, por favor. I will get a piece of paper."

Isabela approached the front desk and returned with a pen and paper. Dave scribbled the hospital name and address on the paper.

"You won't reconsider? I told you it's a mistake to go. There are all kinds of American and Thai government officials lurking around. There's even a British officer, but what he was doing there is a mystery to me. By the look of things, your friend Lance was enmeshed in some highly covert, I mean, secret activities."

"The British man, he is Mr. Nigel Hawkes?"

"Nigel Hawkes, yes, that's right. You know him?"

"Por favor, keep Amigo for me. I'll come back for him."

"Sure thing. I'll keep him fed and watered for you." Dave extended his card.

DAVE JOHNSON, *Pilot*
Air America

"Look, I don't like to interfere in anyone's affairs," he said. "Everyone has to go their own way, but if I were you, I'd wait to hear from him. Enough said."

"Thank you, Mister Johnson. I'll call you when I come back. I'll come get Amigo, okay?" Isabela turned to leave.

"Wait, there was something else," Dave said.

Isabela swung back around. "Yes?"

"There's something he wanted me to tell you. It makes no sense to me, but he was quite insistent about it."

"Dígame." *Tell me.*

"While we were stuck at the crash site and hoping to be rescued, he rambled on about some dream he had about this girl with crazy hair. He said she was radiant and looked just like you, but she had his eyes. You have to realize he was in an awful lot of pain and barely coherent. I didn't know what to make of it, honestly, but I thought I'd pass it along. Maybe it's a comfort."

Isabela thrust her arms around the startled pilot and hugged him. When she pulled away, his shirt was wet with her tears.

"Gracias." *Thank you.*

Dave watched as the elegant young woman walked out of the bar and disappeared into the elevator.

"Damn it! I'm stuck with the damn mutt."

Chapter Thirty-Eight

1962

Bangkok, Thailand

The first flight to Bangkok arrived on time at nine in the morning. Isabela wiped sweat from her forehead as she exited the airport and walked toward the taxi stand. The day was already uncomfortably hot. She jumped into a taxi and stared out the window as a light mist blurred the crowds of people hurrying toward their destinations. Silently, she began to pray. She begged God, Jesus, and the angels to protect and save this American man whose destiny was now irrevocably enmeshed with her own. The traffic was backed up for kilometers and moved at a snail's pace. It was almost eleven when the taxi finally pulled up in front of the hospital.

"Please, I'd like to see a patient."

"What is the patient's name?" the nurse's aide asked.

"Jimmy Calhoun."

The aide checked and then rechecked her roster. "I am sorry, but there is no patient here by that name."

"Please, can you check again? I was told he is here."

"No, I am sorry," the aide said.

Isabela thought for a moment and then remembered the pilot.

What did the pilot say Jimmy's name was at work? Jameson, he said his name was Lance Jameson.

"Disculpe." *Excuse me.* "Can you check a different name? Lance Jameson."

"Let me see, Lance Jameson. Yes, we did have a patient by that name, but he was released two hours ago. He's being transferred. Are you a relative?"

Isabela looked down and shook her head slowly, her chest barely rising as she began to sway. The nurse stepped around the desk and led the obviously distraught young woman to the waiting room. All at once, Isabela leaned forward and rested her hands on her thighs. She took several deep breaths. The nurse placed her shoulder under Isabela's arm and eased her upright before guiding her to a nearby seat.

"Stay here until you feel better," the nurse said. "Is there someone I can call on your behalf?"

"I will be all right. Can you tell me about my friend's condition?"

"It's against hospital protocol, but you seem genuinely concerned. I think it would be fine to tell you this. Your friend, Lance Jameson, was badly injured in a plane crash. The doctor recommended that the patient remain a few more days here in Thailand. He hoped to stabilize the patient's condition before transferring him on such a long flight to America. But the patient's wife insisted that he be transferred to the States today. I can assure you your friend is receiving the best medical care."

Isabela's head fell onto her lap as she began to cry.

"There, there. Everything will be all right. You'll see. Go home now. There's nothing for you to do here. Let me call someone for you."

Isabela shook her head and abruptly broke free of the woman's arm. "No, thank you. You are very kind."

Isabela slipped out the door as the grey-haired nurse stood and watched her blur with the incoming crowd. Long after her shift, she couldn't quite shake her concern for the young woman.

Outside the hospital, taxis by the dozens sped down the street. A few slowed to offer a ride. Isabela ignored them all. Her mind went blank as her chest caved in and her breath was reduced to short inhales. The dense traffic merged into indistinct colors and jarring noise. *The doctors recommended the patient remain a few more days, but his wife insisted. Wife? Wife?* The insidious mantra thickened into a shameless, palpable recognition.

A white Toyota came to a stop in front of Isabela. The front passenger door was thrown open wide as the driver leaned across the front seat.

"Miss Marquez, please get in."

In a concerted effort to refocus her attention on the man in the car, Isabela blinked hard.

"Nigel Hawkes, do you remember?" the man said. "I had the pleasure of meeting you in Chiang Mai. Please, allow me to give you a ride. I'd like to make sure you return safely to Chiang Mai and back to your country as soon as possible. I'm afraid it's a highly complex and fragile situation. I am terribly sorry you became involved, through no fault of your own, I might add. Damn Jameson. It's most unprofessional of him. It's quite unsafe for you to remain in Thailand."

Nigel parked the car, climbed out, and went around to the sidewalk where Isabela stood. He guided her into the passenger seat and slid into the driver's seat.

"I have you booked on a flight to Chiang Mai at four this afternoon. In the meantime, let me get you something to eat. Things always looks brighter after a nice meal. Perhaps I might answer a few questions."

"Where did they take Jimmy? How can I see him?"

Nigel sat across from the young woman in the small Indian restaurant. Her eyes were blotchy and red.

"Jimmy is being flown back to America, where he will receive the best medical care, rest assured. He will recover, but it will take time. It will take months of hard physical therapy and a lengthy hospital stay. You would do best to forget all of this and return home to El Salvador," Nigel said.

Isabela listened intently as tears streamed down her face.

"You are a complication that we did not anticipate. A lot is at risk. We cannot guarantee your safety unless you return home immediately. Take a week to close up your affairs and then return to your family."

"Por favor, which name is correct?"

"You won't see him again. What does it matter?" Isabela gazed directly into Nigel's eyes and did not look away. Her plate of curry remained untouched. "His name is Lance Jameson," Nigel finally responded. "Now, please, I am at your service."

"Did he ask for me?"

"I'm afraid he was in no condition to inquire after anyone. He is still unconscious and in a medically induced coma until his burns and injuries can be treated in the United States. It may be years of recovery. His wife will be at his side. Do you understand?"

Isabela pushed her chair back from the table and stood.

"Gracias, Señor Nigel. Jimmy, I mean, Lance is gone. Please do not concern yourself with me. I will stay in Chiang Mai. We do not need to meet again."

Isabela walked out of the air-conditioned restaurant with her shoulders straight and her chin lifted. Nigel, alone at the table, swore under his breath.

"Bloody hell, I don't need this."

Nigel picked up the phone and gave a number to the operator.

"Shepherd, we've encountered a bit of a snag. We can manage the girl, but Lance's cover was compromised. Yes, the drug cartel. I've had reports of maggots and lowlifes sniffing around. I'm afraid they've stumbled a little bit too close to our world and our activities. Of course, these are only the underlings, but I believe they answer to a larger force that could prove damaging. If they obtain solid evidence of our presence in Thailand, it won't be long before the Pathet Lao, Chinese, and Russians know it, along with the rest of the world. They tried to recruit our agent, Lance Jameson. The girl and Jameson were seen in the Chiang Mai bazaar together. There was no denying their affection for each other. She's a possible target now. I strongly urged her to return home, but I'm afraid she won't listen."

The disembodied voice snapped, "Well, use the girl then. Set it up. If your intel is right, they'll come for the girl. We'll be waiting."

"Shepherd, we can't involve a civilian. She's an innocent. The entire cover could be blown."

"She's already involved. The team needs to be ready. With a little luck, we'll intercept the gang without her being aware of any of it. It's what you do best."

Nigel quietly set the phone back onto the cradle, and he sat for a moment, pensive.

Chapter Thirty-Nine

1962

Bangkok, Thailand

The broad avenue was lined with hundreds of shops selling trinkets, food, radios, clothing, and alcohol. Small stands outside the shops were crammed full of medicines available without a prescription, toys, finely cut fruit, and grilled meat and vegetables. The market was packed with customers, and they moved like a wave through the crowded streets.

Isabela didn't head toward the airport when she left Nigel Hawkes. Instead, she walked the old streets without purpose or direction, but with each step, she became increasingly aware of the heavy weight of anxiety crushing her shoulders and chest. She could hardly breathe. The heat bathed her in sweat. After a few hours of aimless wandering, she snapped suddenly awake. *I need to find a hotel. It's getting late!* Isabela took in her surroundings. Everything looked the same. Hundreds of shops all crowded together. She could be anywhere. She kept walking, looking out for a hotel, a guesthouse, or any place that was clean and safe. She crossed the street, and her eyes were drawn upward to where a red blimp hovered in midair above a grand Chinese restaurant. She remembered this place! *Yes, there was the small Shell station down the street from the restaurant. La escuela! The Bangkok Patana International School and Señora Bérnard!*

The old French teacher held the key and the solution to her predic-
ament. Isabela jogged to the curb and waited for the traffic to pass.
She veered to the left and crossed two more streets with a renewed
sense of purpose and intention.

Jimmy Calhoun. Lance Jameson. Por supuesto! Of course! The old teacher
would not know Jimmy Calhoun because that was not his name. His real
name was Lance Jameson. The school was located just behind the black,
cast-iron gate. She glanced at her wristwatch and increased her pace.

The administrator informed her the students had left for the
day, but she might still catch the French teacher before she headed
home. Cécile Bérnard looked up as Isabela approached her office
door. The room and the educator together wafted a musty essence
that brought to mind old trunks in an attic, stuffed with linens
tucked away for decades.

"Señora Bérnard? Do you remember me? I came to visit you
last month?"

"Oui, bien sûr, Mademoiselle Marquez." *Yes, of course, Miss Marquez.*
"It is a pleasure to see you again. How may I help you today?"

"When I came to see you last month, I asked about a student
named Jimmy Calhoun. At the time, I didn't know my friend had
a different name when he was young. Please, can you check for a
boy named Lance Jameson?"

"Well, that is a name etched in my memory! Do you happen to
know where he lives now? Is he back in Thailand? I always wondered
what became of him. Excuse me for just a moment while I go and
retrieve his file."

The French teacher returned to the office holding a manila file
two inches thick.

"Of course, I remember young Lance. It's impossible to recall
every student over thirty years, but certain ones stand out. He was a

difficult child when he first arrived. He understood French perfectly, but he only answered in the indigenous language his nanny spoke with him. It was a good six months before he admitted a passable English comprehension, so he was under my direct supervision for the first year. I was a new teacher, mind you, just learning the ropes. In the beginning, I did not appreciate that he was such a brilliant boy. It came to mind more than once that teaching him was somewhat like trying to domesticate a wild, unbridled horse."

"I am trying to find his Amah, his nanny."

Miss Bérnard reopened the file and scanned several pages before drawing one out.

"We were all so horrified at what happened. The child was finally acclimated and doing well. He excelled in academics and was one of those rare students who had only to see something once before it was committed to memory. He became quite the athlete too. After that, he had a much easier time with the other boys. The faculty was pleased with his progress, especially me. He was quite challenging as bright students can sometimes be. I must admit, he stretched my patience on more than one occasion. As I recall, one night, I went home in tears. I questioned my choice of vocation entirely that night. Yet I grew as a teacher by having him in my class. By his third year, he was one of my favorites. I think he came to appreciate me as well."

The slight, elderly woman tapped her finger on the desk as details of the past came into clear focus.

"The day our relationship solidified was a Friday, as I recall. His nanny came to pick him up when he was expecting his father. Young Lance shared with just about everyone that his father was coming from abroad to see his rugby match. He was so excited, and that was an energy hard to corral in my little classroom." She paused to push her glasses farther up her nose. "In the courtyard after school,

Lance was throwing rocks. Not at anything, mind you, but forcefully down into the dirt. I watched him from my second-floor classroom window for about fifteen minutes. After a while the nanny left, and on my way out, I stopped and stood beside him."

The French teacher paused.

"And?" Isabela said.

"I remember telling him that I thought his disregard and anger were reserved solely for my teaching method. But then I said, 'Perhaps there is something else?' A deep silence ensued. I waited, quiet as a mouse. It seemed like an hour passed with just the two of us standing side by side without a word. It was the boy who broke the impasse. He had just learned from his nanny that his father would not make his rugby match. His father was still in the Philippines. I said, 'That's quite the disappointment.' There was another interval of silence before I had the brilliant idea to ask the boy about rugby. I said I'd heard about his prowess on the rugby field. I asked him if I might come to see his game one day, and he immediately challenged me by asking if I even liked rugby. It was all I could do not to gather him up and promise him the world would be right again one day. But instead, I asked him to fill me in about the rules and the strategies. I told him I'd like to appreciate the finer nuances of the game and be an informed spectator."

Cécile Bérnard paused, her head now turned away from Isabela as she looked out the window.

"Did you ever go?" Isabela asked.

"He asked me to come to his game the following morning, and I invited him for an ice cream. Over two chocolate-dipped ice creams, he talked about the rugby matches he played in and what he liked about the sport. I told him the only detail I knew about the game— get the ball through the goalposts! I recall he was quite exasperated with me and said, 'You don't know much about rugby, do you?' I told him, no, I didn't, but that's what made it so interesting. Then he proceeded from memory to recite everything he knew about the sport and explain the finer nuances of the actual plays. It was like he was waiting for just this opportunity to explain rugby rules to someone. I remember to this day the rules of the game. There are two forty-minute halves and fifteen members on a team. The most important part, he stressed, is that the players have to play fair!"

"There needs to be more teachers like you," Isabela said. "My friend was lucky to have met you!"

Cécile Bérnard returned her gaze from the window to Isabela and patted her arm.

"I came to his game and genuinely became intrigued with the sport. I went to more than one. I sat by his father a few times too. He was quite the gentleman, as I recall. As an added benefit, Lance stopped giving me a hard time in class, which I very much appreciated. But it turns out it was the boy who helped me the most. He gave me a gift that has served me well over my entire teaching career. I learned from young Lance that there is a key to every student. It's always different. Each child is one and only, but if you can somehow recognize where the child's passion lies, and the lens through which the world is seen and experienced, then that's where you will meet their particular genius. Of course, you miss some of them, but when you hit the mark, especially with a gifted child such as young Lance, teaching becomes nothing less than extraordinary."

Cécile Bérnard smiled and offered Isabela a cookie from a plate of several behind her desk. "A gift from my students!" Her eyes turned inward as she set the plate of cookies down and placed her hand lightly on Isabela's forearm. Isabela accepted a cookie and took a small bite, her attention captivated by the unfolding story.

"And then tragedy struck," the French teacher continued. "The school was informed that Monsieur Jameson, the boy's father, was killed in a car crash. The headmaster asked me to be present when the boy was brought into the office. It was a peculiar circumstance. The student's mother died when he was very young. Now, he was a total orphan. There was only the father and the nanny on the student's contact list. So, it fell on the school to impart the dreadful tragedy to little Lance. The school was held accountable for not contacting the authorities when the two of them disappeared."

"Why?"

"The headmaster failed to contact the American Embassy when the boy was left alone in a foreign country. This all came out when the grandfather became involved and hired a private detective. Maiv Lee, the nanny, was arrested for kidnapping Lance, and the school became overly concerned about its liability exposure. Unfortunately, our headmaster did not step forward for several months to speak on her behalf. To our collective relief, she was released after some time. Madame Lee was the real parent in the child's life and the school's main contact. She came to the parent-teacher meetings, performances, and even the rugby games, which I'm sure she understood not at all. Yet she was as proud as any mother I ever saw."

"Did she ever return to the school?"

"After her release, she came by every day. There were times I caught a glimpse of her from my classroom window. Every day, it was the same thing. She'd wait outside the gate until every child left the school grounds. The poor woman's heart was broken. We informed her the boy had been sent to America to live with his grandparents, but that didn't seem to deter her. It was several months before she finally gave up. She walked away one afternoon and never came back. All I can supply is her name, Maiv Lee, which I've already given you. I don't know how helpful that will prove to be. From my understanding there are only eighteen Hmong last names and clans. I suppose you could start there. How long are you staying in Bangkok, my dear? I know a Hmong family, and I can perhaps make a few inquiries on your behalf."

"That is very kind," Isabela said. "I will leave Bangkok tomorrow and fly back to Chiang Mai. I am going to stay a few weeks in Thailand. May I leave my number with you in case you learn anything more?"

Torrential rain greeted Isabela when she returned to Chiang Mai, and the downpour showed no signs of letting up. She stood at the windowed alcove of her room, out of sight to anyone on the street. She parted the blue flowered curtain with the tip of her finger and watched as raindrops dribbled down the windowpane and formed rivulets that merged together at certain points. Across the street, locals and visitors alike scrambled to open an umbrella or hurry toward their destinations. An older gentleman trotted across the street. One hand held a newspaper over his head and the other grasped a leash attached to a large, dripping wet, black Labrador, who pulled him along with no regard to whether the man could keep up with it. Isabela's gaze did not leave the man and the dog until they rounded the corner out of sight.

She had not left her room for the past four days. The remnants of soup and toast from room service were set outside the door. Clothes were strewn in a heap on the backside of a pale blue armchair, and the sheets on the bed were crumpled into a knotted bundle. Suddenly, it was as if someone had upended a bucket of ice water on Isabela's head and shocked her wide awake. *I'll call the pilot* was the first, the only, idea that occurred to her in almost a week. Somehow, with that thought, she could breathe again.

Dave sat across the table from Isabela at a small noodle stand near the main gate to the old city, Tha Pae.

"I have no idea what Lance was up to. I was just the pilot who was sent to pick him up. But I'll tell you this. You don't go to those kinds of places for a vacation. We received watered-down fuel from the locals. I should have been more aware, but we had a lot to drink the night before. I'm not making excuses. It was my responsibility and my watch. I should have checked. All of it is my damned fault."

Amigo, sleeping at the foot of the table and lightly snoring, suddenly sat up, wriggled, and shook himself. He sprang up into Isabela's lap, and his bandaged leg dangled over her thigh. He stared intently up at her face. Isabela carefully adjusted him to sit fully on her lap and allowed the injured leg enough space to hang, she hoped, without causing discomfort.

"I'm sorry I don't have more information I can share with you," Dave said. "Lance and I talked on the plane before everything went south, before both engines quit and I lost control of the aircraft. After the accident, he was pretty beaten up and in and out of consciousness. During the few lucid moments when he was awake, he asked me to visit you and bring you Amigo."

"Is there anything more?"

"I almost forgot, yes ..." Dave reached into his pocket and pulled out the miniature elephant and an equally small jaguar. He opened his hand, displaying both. "He told me he was going to give these to a boy, but he wanted you to have them now. He said he'd find his way back to you and for you to wait. I'm sorry. There's nothing more. He was only awake for a short time, and I was focused on getting us both through the night alive."

Chapter Forty

1962

Chiang Mai, Thailand

Isabela knocked lightly on the door.

"The door is open."

"Katya, are you busy? I can come back later."

"Isabela? Don't be silly. Come in."

Isabela entered the room and slowly sat on the bed.

"You must have fallen in love or something," Kate said. "I haven't seen you at the studio or here at the guesthouse either. Where the heck have you been? What am I thinking? You'll be heading back to the big wedding and Tomás soon. But hey, I do have news to share! I have been seeing this most gorgeous and, should I mention, wealthy Brit. His name is Sean. He's fabulously articulate, funny, and quite cultured and refined. He's at ease with the 'haute-monde,' but get him away from that scene for a minute, and he's very natural and down to earth. It's an interesting juxtaposition I don't often remember encountering in the very wealthy. Heck, I'm not talking love or anything, but I've been having a ball. I've let the classes slip, which is unfortunate, but I'll get back to them. I am living in the moment, and it is delicious!"

Kate continued to deliver a sweeping monologue while applying mascara. She turned to emphasize a point and stopped mid-sentence. Isabela stared at the floor where a giant fly sat near her left foot.

"Isabela, you haven't heard a word I've said, have you? What on earth are you looking at?"

Kate's attention was instantly riveted down to the large insect, its wings shimmering a rainbow of color in the early afternoon sun. Kate squinted and lowered her gaze to fix on the insect. It pointed directly at Isabela, then began to rotate clockwise, forming a perfect circle before arriving squarely back, once again to point its body at Isabela. After a moment's hesitation, it moved once again in the opposite direction and slanted perfectly toward Kate. A peculiar, pregnant pause followed before the fly lifted its wings to take flight.

"Isabela, did you see that fly? It's huge! I haven't seen one like it since we've been here. Actually, I've never seen one like it. It just did the most bizarre dance. I'd say it was very strange behavior for a fly. I don't know. Am I imagining this? It seemed like it was communicating something specific about you to me. Something I should tell you because you obviously are too upset to pay attention. What on earth is the matter? You look like you lost your best friend, which, by the way, is me. I know we've been estranged lately, but look, I still love you madly. You are the best friend I've ever had!"

Isabela shook her head and stared at the floor.

"What on earth happened?" Kate said.

"Katya, no se que hacer." *I don't know what to do.* Isabela's body began to rock as heavy sobbing overtook her slight frame. Kate dropped her mascara brush to move closer. Gently, she put her arm over Isabela's shoulder and waited for the sobs to abate. "I can't go home now! She is with me. She is the most important, but I cannot disappoint my father. I don't see a way out. Please tell me what to do!"

Kate continued to hold her friend. "Don't you worry," she said. "Everything takes time. You'll be fine. I promise. Whatever it is! Do you remember the Dutch girl, Katherine? She's the student with the perfectly straight bangs across her forehead. Well, the rumor is she was knocked up. You really are sequestered in there with Prapat. You miss all the scandal. Anyway, one day she was with us and the next day gone. I mean, her side of the room was completely cleared out, and not a hairpin was left behind. She didn't say goodbye to anyone except her roommate, who was not forthcoming with details. I filled in the blanks. You don't just disappear from a program like this."

Isabela pushed away from Kate.

"Look, I'll help you figure this out, whatever it is. Has Prapat been inappropriate? I wouldn't be at all surprised. He is a man, after all, and the two of you spend hours locked away in that studio. It doesn't mean you have to quit, though. Come and study with the rest of us. That'll teach him."

"No, por favor, Prapat is my teacher and always a gentleman. I am …"

"Then what? You have a boyfriend? Had a boyfriend by the look of things?" Kate said.

"I met him in the bazaar. You saw him once. He was at the party with the embassy officials, recuerdas?" *Remember?* "The tall gringo. Muy guapo." *Very handsome.*

Kate leaned in and strained to hear what Isabela was telling her.

"There was an airplane accident, and he was badly injured. They sent him back to America to recover. There is no way to see him. There is no way for me to know if he is all right. I am alone." A light wheezing ensued as Isabela labored to breathe evenly before speaking again. "Tell me where to go. Tell me where we can live quietly. I need to leave Thailand, but I cannot go home now. I have to disappear. She is my life now."

"Bela, I have no idea what you are talking about! You are not making sense. Slow down, start at the beginning, and don't worry. We'll figure this out."

Isabela spoke for an hour while Kate listened. The story slowly unraveled.

"He's a married bastard, and he wants you to wait? Well, that's not happening! With a little money, anything is possible. And you know I have access to a lot of it. You can have an abortion, then go back home, and no one will be the wiser. You are not alone. You hear me? This is my fault! I left you alone when Prapat chose you. You were without a friend, and I am beyond mortified. You've lived such a protected life on your ranch in El Salvador. Bastards! Men will say absolutely anything to have a moment's gratification. What was I thinking? I am so sorry, Bela."

Isabela shook her head vehemently, "No, no, the baby is why I came."

"Double bastard, I hope you burn in hell! All right, all right. We'll go somewhere. Where? Have a baby and find it a good home. Okay, a challenge I'll admit, but everything is a puzzle. We just need to find the right pieces. You'll have to make up something big to satisfy your mother and Tomás. But then you go home and live your life. Do you hear me? I can't be responsible for destroying your life. I couldn't live with myself. We'll have to leave Thailand in a few months and go somewhere where your Salvadoran passport won't be a problem, somewhere where there is good medical care.

We'll just have to stay away from the ex-pat community. Give me a minute. I'll figure this out."

Isabela wrapped her arms around Kate's neck. Her wet face nestled into her friend's shoulder.

"I am so afraid, and I haven't slept in a week. But, Katya, the baby stays with me."

"Shh, okay, we have time. And you will change your mind once you realize what a crazy bad idea that is. It's total lunacy. Remember where you live? The all-Catholic El Salvador? You are the only child of a very prominent and well-respected family."

Isabela cried harder now. Her face was streaked with tears and showed splotches of red.

"Okay, let me think," Kate said. "First, we have to find a place where you can have your baby. I know you have your own money, but you have to let me take care of this. I brought you here, and I will see this through to the end with you, whatever you decide."

"Miss Marquez, Cécile Bérnard speaking. I have some interesting news to share. I was having lunch with a colleague the other day and happened to mention your visit and my old student. It's quite the coincidence, but she told me Maiv Lee visited the school last year! Can you imagine? After all these years, she wanted to leave her contact information. My coworker happened to be in the office and took down the woman's information, filed it, and didn't think a thing more about it. We have Maiv Lee's address! She lives in a village up near the Burmese border. It's about a three-hour bus ride from here. Do you have a pencil to write this down? You will have to take a bus to Mae Sai and a taxi the rest of the way to the village.

Unfortunately, there is no way to contact Mrs. Lee by phone. Once you arrive at the village, the best way to find a person is to ask around. Will you let me know if you find her? And please, when young Lance comes back into town, tell him to pay a visit to his old French teacher. We'll go out and get some ice cream!"

"Gracias, thank you! This is the most wonderful news! I will go tomorrow and find Maiv Lee!"

Chapter Forty-One

1977

El Salvador

It was the curve of her spine and the soft bow of her head that rattled a memory loose. Ángel lingered just inside the door, hypnotized almost by the girl sitting on the floor of the small cabin. She rocked back and forth. Ángel could almost hear her silent screams ricocheting inside his head. The recollection wavered—his mother bending down to kiss him goodbye and his little sister pulling on his shirt, afraid to walk alone into the one-room schoolhouse on her first day of class. He shook his head once, hard. He willed himself to act and bent to grab the girl under the armpits and pulled. Mera didn't resist. Instead, he allowed her dead weight to drop to the earth. Ángel let go of the effort to raise her up and withdrew a pistol, placing it at her back.

"I'm sorry, but you've got to move. He'll shoot you if you don't!" Ángel said.

Ángel supported the girl as her legs engaged, and she slowly stood. She turned her head and noticed the young man with a pistol in his hand aimed to the right of her and at the ground. Ángel smiled, as if meeting a pretty girl at a village gathering. He nodded and shifted his weight to tap the muzzle of the gun lightly on her hip.

"Lo siento, señorita. Vamos." *I am sorry, miss. Let's go!* Ángel's voice was low, for her ears alone. He pushed her out the door and then returned inside the cottage, intent on gathering any food he could find. He ignored the plants hanging on the ceiling and in jars and concentrated instead on the potatoes, chicken, and grains.

Outside the cabin, the other man waited. He stepped out from the shadows and seemed to emerge directly out of the pile of wood stacked on the porch. Mera adjusted her eyes to the light. Which way should she go? It didn't matter. Run! Run far away from here. She turned to leap off the porch, but a hand shot out and grabbed her by the hair.

"Not so fast, señorita."

She refused to look. The man from the woodpile set his rifle down and, with the other, raised her chin. Mera looked in every direction except forward. She recognized him immediately. He was the one called Dino, the man with the two-toned dragon tattoo that spiraled up his upper arm.

"You are a pretty one, aren't you? Maybe I'll keep you for myself!"

Ángel swung the door open and threw out two sacks filled with potatoes, rice, and vegetables on the porch.

"Hurry up, tonto!" *Stupid!*

"Jefe, give me a minute. There's a plucked chicken, ready for the taking."

Dino released Mera's hair, and her head dropped like a puppet no longer sustained by a string.

"Get what you can quickly. We need to leave the village before the military catches wind of what happened today."

Mera walked in between the two men. She stumbled over a rock or a root every so often. Her senses were on hyper alert. She knew the forest well and waited for a sign from the birds or the insects or a moment when her captor might light a cigarette or step aside to relieve himself. She knew it would only take seconds for her to disappear inside its darkness. But the forest was silent, and the tall one, Dino, was focused and sharp. The only light came from a flashlight behind her and in front of her. Her hands were tied behind her back and made balancing difficult with the fast, hard pace. Ángel cut back the forest with his machete as they moved quickly forward, both men confident of their direction. They pushed Mera into a trot until she lost complete sense of time and her surroundings. Even though it was dark, she sensed that she was now in a completely new and foreign area of the forest.

It was impossible to determine how deeply into the night they were when she began to hear faint voices in the distance. *Will these people help me?* Her heart sank as her captors moved toward the light of several campfires. *These are not friendly voices. Would there be a chance for escape?*

The kidnappers guarded Mera between them and emerged into a glowing light. Tents were scattered across the clearing. Mera's eyes were drawn to the women in the group, particularly a blonde who sat on the lap of a heavyset man with black stubble on his chin. He fondled her breast, and she threw her head back and laughed. The man pushed her off his lap when he saw the three entering the camp.

"Dino, we've been back for three hours. What took you so long?" He stared at Mera. "Ah, I see you brought me a gift," he said.

"Sorry, the girl is mine," Dino said.

"Go ahead, flex your muscles, Dino. We leave tomorrow before dawn. It's a pity I don't have time to enjoy the girl tonight. Bring her to the women. Then come and see me. I'd be very careful if I were you, Dino."

The man stood and disappeared into the largest tent.

Dino pushed Mera backward toward the outer rim of the circle. He motioned for Ángel to follow.

"Ángel, take the girl to my place. Sleep in the woods. Tie her to a tree or tie her to you. I don't care. In the morning, you'll find the way. Get her away from here. This is the last time Carlos gets to humiliate me in front of the men. He thinks he can take what is mine, but very soon, I will be the one who gives the orders. I'll come for the girl tomorrow night. Carlos is a fool. It's only a matter of time. You'll see." He spat on the ground. "And don't touch the girl. She's mine."

Chapter Forty-Two

1962

Thai-Burmese Border

Kate leaned into the window of the silver-and-red bus headed for Mae Sai. Isabela sat next to her on the aisle. The fan hummed but emitted negligible cool air.

"Once again, why are we subjecting ourselves to this miserable bus ride just to find the old nanny of some derelict, deceiving bastard?"

"I told you. You didn't have to come."

"No way will I let you travel alone. Not now. You are responsible for my one and only niece or nephew to be. I know you think it's a girl, but there's no way to be sure. So if it's a boy, you can't be disappointed. Okay? I don't know why you wouldn't let me hire a private car, if you're dead set on this pilgrimage."

"No, por favor, you do too much. I like to ride the bus. It's simple."

"Well, I, for one, don't understand why anyone would choose to suffer when there's no need, but okay. I'll write it off as a research project and leave it at that."

"Do you think I'll find her?" Isabela asked.

"Who? Oh, right, the nanny. Hell, I don't know. I wish she hadn't decided to move to the other side of nowhere."

"What can I say to her? Maybe she'll have some idea how to get in touch with Jimmy? I mean Lance."

"Isabela, you strain the limits of friendship. I'll swing to the ends of the earth for you, my dearest. But for the bastard? I won't lift a finger. If this little trip helps you find resolution, I will sit on this damned bus for a week."

"I don't deserve a friend like you."

The two young women descended from the bus. A long row of taxis lined up on the opposite side of the road, waiting to pick up fares from the bus station. One driver, all the way at the back of the long row of cars, suddenly pulled out of line and made a dramatic U-turn. He screeched to a stop in front of the two startled women. Several drivers waved and yelled profanities in his direction.

"Looks like we've got our ride!" Kate grinned. "I like his style!"

The taxi raced down the rutted road and darted swiftly to pass buses, trucks, motorcycles, and cars. Kate gave up on asking the driver to slow down. Each time, he happily complied with a wide smile before revving the engine and shooting around the next approaching vehicle as if it stood still. Isabela steadied herself by holding onto the seat in front of her, while Kate, who was much taller, swore and held her hands up on the ceiling to cushion the lurches and sharp jerks.

The driver screeched to a halt and motioned ahead to the small village nestled in the trees.

"This is far as car go. You walk now!"

"We had a deal. You take us all the way to the village!" Kate's voice rose as her cheeks, already flushed from the heat, darkened.

"No missy. Car get stuck. You out. Walk now!"

"Goddamn it! Hell, these shoes are useless! Bela, you up for this? The road is pure mud."

CHAPTER FORTY-TWO

"We came so far, Katya. You wait here. I'll take my shoes off and go alone to the village. It is not so far."

"Damn it." Kate removed her pumps and placed them under her arm as she slid down the seat and out the door. She poked her head back in through the window. "Bela, take the taxi back into town. I'll check around for the nanny. If we're lucky and she's in this godforsaken village, I'll try and bring her back here. Come back with the taxi at five. Okay? No way you're walking through this mess. We can't risk it, capisce?"

The road narrowed further still. A steep drop on the left and a sheer wall of slate on the right lined the muddy pathway. With each step, Kate sank up to her ankles in a kissing sludge. Dirt splattered her hair, face, arms, and legs. She knotted her skirt just above her knees, but a reddish loam splotched her white blouse. Mud oozed through her toes. Every twenty steps or so, her foot sank deeper into the mud.

"Goddamn it! Fucking asshole, bastard, shit, shit, shit, motherfu …"

Several inches of mud clung to the bottom of Kate's foot, upsetting her center of balance. She wavered like a flag in the breeze and tried to steady herself, but in a slow-motion roll, she fell forward into the muck. She was suddenly immersed from head to toe in a reddish, ochre dye. She began to shake and laugh hysterically. Tears splattered her cheeks, and wild undulations rocked her body.

She didn't hear the wooden cart squeak to a halt ten meters away. She didn't see the old man squinting at her. One of the old man's hands was on the haunches of a large water buffalo, and the other shielded the sunlight from his eyes. The large animal shook its head, and the bell around its neck clanged and clinked.

Kate swung her head around. The ancient villager was clad with rubber boots that reached up above his knees. He nodded at the back of the cart laden with sacks of rice and removed a stick from his belt to swat the animal into a forward motion. When the cart was just alongside Kate, he jumped up on sacks of rice to extend her a hand. Kate scrambled onto the cart.

The water buffalo was surefooted and strong and did not hesitate at her added weight. Forward movement creaked along at a turtle's pace while the sinewy villager walked alongside, prodding the animal with a swat to its hindquarters every so often. Kate suppressed the urge to hug the old man when they arrived in the village. She made several attempts at communication, but the old man only smiled and answered in a strange dialect she assumed was the language of the nanny. The old man continued deeper into the village and lifted his hand in farewell.

A small stream gurgled on the outskirts of the village. Kate moved toward it, kneeling to scoop water onto her face. The clear water immediately darkened to a reddish brown. She waded up to her knees. She rinsed her arms and legs and wrung out the ends of her clothing. She ran her fingers through her thick, snarled hair. Kate smiled and reimagined her father's most certain outrage. There was nothing she enjoyed more than exploiting the boundaries of his parental jurisdiction.

Small huts nestled on the hillside, chickens pecked at the ground, and a mother sow trotted through the village followed by nine diminutive piglets. Everything was neat and orderly. Smoke billowed from a larger building set in the center of the village.

My guess is that's the kitchen. And where the kitchen is, that's where I'll find the ladies of the town.

Several women sat cross-legged outside the building, while aromas of cooked meat and vegetables wafted through the air. Large bamboo sieves filled with uncooked rice, with the purpose of filtering pebbles, twigs, and other foreign objects from the grain, were lifted up into the air and lowered. Vast kernels of rice were tossed up to form billowing clouds that fell back into the sieves. Over and over, rice kernels formed a multitude of shapes and patterns as the women's expert manipulations tossed the grains up in a rhythmic cadence. The women chatted amicably and never missed a beat.

Kate, mesmerized by the flying grain and the women's dexterity, forgot for a moment what she was doing there. All at once, the throws of rice ceased, and eight pairs of dark brown eyes riveted upon her.

"Hello," Kate said. "Bonjour. Does anyone speak English? Français? I am looking for someone named Maiv Lee."

The women began to speak quietly among themselves while glancing periodically up at the foreigner. A matron pushed her daughter to stand, and the daughter walked up to Kate with her hands on her hips.

"Bonjour, je m'appelle Paaj. Vous cherchez Maiv Lee? Elle est très malade, mais ça va. Je vais vous emmener vers elle." *Hello, my name is Paaj. You are looking for Maiv Lee? She is very sick, but it's okay. I will take you to her.*

The young girl smiled and took Kate by the hand. She led her passed the seated women, who resumed the rhythmic throws of rice and easy chatter. The girl wound deeper into the village, past thatched-roof huts, and, finally, beyond the periphery of the village. At the end of the pathway, a one-room shed stood on spindly stilts two feet above the ground. Kate noticed that the wooden supports hardly seemed adequate to sustain the dwelling. A small three-step ladder leaned against the open doorway.

Paaj, Kate's newly appointed escort, ignored the ladder and leaped up onto the small porch. She indicated with her hand for Kate to wait. Paaj ducked her head in the doorway and disappeared. The

minutes stretched beyond what seemed appropriate. Kate paced
and swore under her breath while she looked again at her watch.

Cultural considerations aside, propriety be damned. Kate took
a deep breath, straightened, and moved purposefully forward. *If the
nanny is in there, I'll be damned if I go back without something to tell
Isabela.* Just as she was about to leap up onto the porch, young Paaj
reappeared in the doorway and motioned for her to come inside.

The room was semi-dark, and a thick, embroidered tapestry
divided it in half. On one side, kitchen utensils hung from the walls,
and a small stove stood in the corner. Paaj indicated she should sit.
Kate looked around for something, anything she might use to sit
on, but there was nothing. At this point, she mused, she was much
dirtier than the floor, so she dropped down to a squat and leaned
against the side wall. She adjusted her body in a cross-legged posture
on the bare floor.

A thin voice wavered from the other side of the embroidered curtain.

"Bientôt je rejoindrai les ancêtres. Je t'attendais." *Soon I will join
the ancestors. I have been waiting for you.*

It was an old person's voice, scratchy and weak. Definitely the
nanny, Kate decided. The disembodied voice wavered, faded, and
then bolstered like radio waves coming in and out of range.

"J'ai quelque chose pour l'enfant. C'est toi qui dois le garder,
pas la mère, tu comprends? Gardes-le jusqu'a ce que la fille soit
grande. Ne l'ouvrez pas. C'est la fille qui rétablira l'équilibre." *I
have something for the girl. You have to keep it, not the mother. Do you
understand? Keep it until the girl is grown. Don't open it! It is the girl
who will restore the balance.*

"Paaj, viens ici. Prends la boîte. Donne-le lui." *Paaj, come here.
Take the box. Give it to her.* The nanny coughed and said something
unintelligible while Kate strained to hear. Then the nanny's voice

grew louder as she said, "La fille saura. La fille est le centre. Elle est le cœur de sa famille." *The girl will know. She is the center. She is the heart of her family.*

Paaj emerged from behind the curtain and extended the small box to Kate, who had not said a word. The container fit into the palm of one hand and was covered in a thick twine that wound around the small case until it completely covered it in a voluminous wrapping.

Kate's mind raced. *How does this woman—out in the periphery of nowhere, with no phone, and no modern communication whatsoever— know about Isabela, the baby, and me? She never once mentioned the bastard. What is up with that? Well, there has to be a logical explanation. Everything can be explained with enough research and investigation. Even the makeup of the atom came to light with brilliant minds focused on it.* Kate breathed away the gnawing discomfort that challenged her carefully orchestrated universe.

"Madame, please. My friend, Isabela, she needs to know… she has questions. Did the school ever tell you where the boy, Lance, went to live in America? May I tell her something about you?"

"Non, jeune Lance et moi, nous ne retrouverons pas dans ce monde et la mére ne saura pas connaître l'enfant. Chacun doit forger son proper chemin. C'est dûr, mais c'est la verité. N'oublies pas et ne te décourages pas. Tout se pose et ensuite tombe. Il est sans conséquence." *No, young Lance and I will not see each other in this world, and the mother will not know the child. Everyone must forge their own path. It's hard, but it's the truth. Do not forget, and do not be discouraged. Everything arises and then falls. It is of no consequence.*

Maiv Lee's voice tapered to a thin, shaky timbre. Kate moved closer to the tapestry so she could better hear. She peeked through the opening into the dark shadows of the other room. The old woman rested on a mat on the floor. Her head and chest were lifted and leaned against Paaj, who held her up against her chest. The old woman labored to breathe. Kate quickly drew back, her heart beating fast.

"Vas maintenant. Je suis fatiguée." *Go now. I am tired.*

Paaj emerged once again, shooing Kate toward the exit. Kate resisted and stood in place, ignoring the young girl while staring at the dark, embroidered division.

"What do you mean, 'the mother will not know the child?'"

Paaj grabbed her hand and pulled her toward the door. "You have to leave. Don't come back. She has given you everything."

The old man with the water buffalo agreed, for a small fee, to take her back to the rendezvous point. Paaj negotiated on her behalf. Grateful she wouldn't have to navigate thick mud in the receding light, Kate doubled the fee. It was almost six-thirty in the evening when the slow-moving cart finally arrived, laden now with just the old man and his charge.

The taxi driver turned off the engine, and Isabela's head leaned on the back of the seat with her eyes closed. She must have dozed off when she felt a light tapping on her arm. The driver pointed toward the road. The metallic clanging of a bell resounded from down the muddy path. Isabela climbed out of the car and peered. A faint outline of the cart lumbering toward them could barely be seen in the darkening sky. It was another ten minutes before the cart came to a stop ten meters from where the taxi was parked. Kate accepted the proffered hand and jumped to the ground.

"That was, by far, the weirdest encounter I have yet to experience in this world!"

"Did you meet her?"

"Yes, I found her. And no, I didn't exactly see her. I'm so sorry. She's near death and quite incoherent. It won't do any good to go back."

Kate's fingers reached into her pocket and encircled the small box. The texture of the twine rubbed against her fingers. She counted how many times the string wound around the box. To Isabela, she said, "I'm sorry this turned out to be a wild goose chase, but you have to know you did everything you could. Let's get out of here. Okay? I'm starving!"

Chapter Forty-Three

1962

Chiang Mai, Thailand

The meeting took place in an abandoned building outside the old walled city. Nigel Hawkes was seated next to the American liaison officer, John Shepherd, who presided over the assembled team.

"Gentlemen, there's been a breach. So far, intel hasn't confirmed the source of the penetration or how deep it goes, but we are taking every precaution. Effective immediately, all leave is cancelled. All officers and civilian contractors are restricted to base unless specifically on assignment. A drug cartel has been making serious inquiries about one of our agents. The operative is back in the States recovering from injuries sustained in a plane crash. They've made it a priority to locate him. They have launched an Asian-wide search for him since he disappeared from the scene. In their search, they've stumbled a little too close to our activities."

"What do they want with him?" someone asked.

"He was undercover for us and was introduced to a Laotian warlord a few months ago. It doesn't answer the frenzied activity to find him, so there's something else involved. The agent is in a coma. We'll have to wait to get answers. In the meantime, we should proceed as if our entire operation has been compromised," Shepherd said.

"Is there anything else?" Nigel said.

"Jameson, the operative, was involved with a young woman from El Salvador staying here in Chiang Mai. It was innocent enough at the onset, but potentially dangerous to our mission. Jameson and the girl were seen together, and we believe the young woman is now a possible target. They may try to obtain information from her. Crispin, we have a room reserved for you at the Chiang Mai guesthouse where the young woman stays. She's one of many possible targets and perhaps a less likely one, but keeping a tail on her is still a priority until we resolve this.

"She has a predictable schedule. She stays at the guesthouse at night and in the daytime goes to a local art studio. She eats most of her meals at the hotel or in the restaurant across the street. Sean, you and the team continue frequenting ex-pat hangouts, parties, local bars, hotels, and the Sunday bazaar. Blend in. Any lead, no matter how small, should be reported back to base. Dismissed."

Crispin sat in the back corner of the hotel restaurant eating a bowl of oatmeal with brown sugar and a sliced banana. He had brilliant blue eyes and copper hair wound in tight curls close to his head, and his skin burned bright red in any kind of sun. He had a round face and dimples that deepened when he smiled so that people tended to take an instant liking to the massive Scot, who never missed an opportunity to add wit to the dullest conversation.

He glanced at his wristwatch. It was seven twenty-five in the morning. She was late. She always came to breakfast at seven and ate toast with butter and marmalade, a cup of tea with milk, and a little papaya or mango. He took one last spoonful of his oatmeal and pushed the chair back from the table.

Something was amiss. For the past month, he'd sat at the table nearest the kitchen, quietly observing the Salvadoran woman. Although he never approached her or spoke with her, he was nonetheless a little bit in love. She never missed an opportunity to thank the staff, bussed her own dirty dishes, and stayed a few extra minutes to inquire after everyone's welfare. Every day, she smiled at the Scot as she passed by.

Crispin approached Abijah, the head morning waiter.

"Good morning, Abijah. Y'er selling bacon on the black market again, aren't you? We'll have to report the infraction to the highest authority."

Abijah grinned and slapped Crispin on the back. "Friend, your share is big this time. With all this money you can buy a boat and sail the world. You'll have no more cares!"

"I wait for the day!" Crispin said. "My friend, by chance have you seen the Spanish woman this morning? You know, the bonny one who sits at the table by the window?"

"You mean Miss Isabela?"

"Yes. I was concerned she might be ill?"

"I'm sorry, it was all quite sudden. She and her friend have gone. The staff only learned about her planned departure early this morning when we came to work. There was hardly time to say a proper goodbye. We all love Miss Isabela. She is such a kind young woman." Abijah paused, his gaze pensive. "One morning, Miss Isabela brought her dishes into the kitchen. She came up behind me, put something into my hand, and then whispered close to my ear, 'for your Anna.' I opened my palm, and there was this beautiful glass rabbit. You see, she learned my little daughter Anna loves rabbits. Miss Isabela even invited my Anna to come to her room and paint with her. One time, the two of them spent half of a day drawing rabbits." Abijah's eyes moistened. "I hope everything is all right."

Crispin smiled and looked pointedly at Abijah. "Was anyone with them? Did she happen to say where they might be headed?"

"I'm sorry. They didn't mention where they were going. But an American man joined them just before they left. Miss Isabela gave him the little dog. She told him that she will come back for the dog, but it might take some time."

Crispin excused himself, went to his room, picked up the phone, and dialed.

"Nigel, Isabela Marquez and her friend left early this morning. The hotel staff doesn't know where they're headed. I don't know how I missed this. There was no indication of departure. I'll check the manifests with the local airlines, trains, and buses. It can't be too hard to track down two foreign women. One last detail, there was an American man with them this morning. Miss Marquez gave him her dog."

"That'll be Dave, the pilot. Reach out to him and report back."

Chapter Forty-Four

1962

Brooks Army Facility, Burn Unit, San Antonio, Texas.

His eyelids opened halfway and took in the room around him. Everything was stark white. Not a single flower, picture, or personal item adorned the sterile backdrop. A quiet hum of indistinct conversation mingled with phantasmal shadows that hovered haphazardly around the periphery of his consciousness. A hospital, but where? He was attached somehow to a body he was disinclined to acknowledge while agonizing spasms cried out from a finger or a hip. Each pain was more piercing than the next. A familiar voice, melodious and kind, neared.

"Mr. Jameson? Can you hear me? He's waking up. I'll call the doctor." The female voice tapered off and disappeared.

Lance tried to focus. Where had he heard that voice before? The woman's voice was like a lullaby and somehow soothing and familiar. The doctor approached the hospital bed with a clipboard in hand.

"Hello, Lance. I'm Dr. Thomas. I'm very pleased to see you are awake and conscious. How are you feeling?"

"I've felt better. How long …?" His voice broke.

"You've been in a coma for two months, medically induced for quite a bit of it. You sustained some pretty severe injuries in the crash."

Screaming scrapes of dense metal, branches snapping in two, brilliant, shooting flames, and a smoke-filled cockpit suddenly drowned out his present-day awareness. Lance coughed, and his body began to shake.

"Mr. Jameson, you are on the road to recovery. You had us very worried for a while, but your progress has been extremely positive. You are healing quite nicely, which says a lot for your health condition before the accident. We'll increase the morphine for the next day or so. We want to keep you comfortable. You have a long road ahead, but we expect you to recover with time."

"Where am I?"

"Brooke Army Medical Center in San Antonio, Texas. It's arguably the best burn center in the country. Your treatments will be ongoing, but we want you to rest now. We'll speak again in a few days to discuss the therapeutics in detail. Don't try to talk too much. Sleep whenever you can. That's the best medicine."

The doctor scribbled quickly onto the chart and then handed it over to the nurse before taking his leave. The young woman glanced at the notation and pulled up a chair. She had wide brown eyes set in a sweet, oval face with a small cleft in the middle of her chin. Her dark hair was cut in a chin-length bob with bangs that rested on top of thin, arched eyebrows. Her white uniform was buttoned up to the neck where her stethoscope hung loosely.

"I am really happy to see you are awake, Mr. Jameson! A lot of us have been pulling for you! My name is Hanna. I've been one of your nurses while you were in the coma. Is it okay to take your vitals? I can come back later if you'd prefer?"

"You're Asian?"

"My parents are from China, but I was born here. I'm a stranger to both lands, I'm afraid."

"We have something in common then. I've been an alien since the day I was born."

"Where was that?" she asked.

"Thailand. I grew up speaking a funny language—Hmong. Do you know it?" Lance closed his eyes as his breathing became labored.

"No, I can't say that I do, but you shouldn't try and talk. What you need is rest."

"Okay, tell me about you, then. Pretend you're telling a story to a baby. Distract me from this horrendous pain."

Hanna injected the morphine-filled syringe into a hollow tube attached to Lance's arm. She watched as her patient's muscles began to soften and his face relax before she responded.

"At home, we speak only Mandarin. My family adheres to strict cultural norms. I think they think we still live in China! I've never been. In school, I was always drawn to play with the American kids."

"Hanna, not very Chinese?"

"My Chinese name is Li-Hua, but I insisted on an English one when I was six. I have an inquiring nature and do best when I have room to explore. My parents, on the other hand, are completely traditional. I like to tease them because it's so easy to get a rise out of them, especially my father. He has absolutely no sense of humor when it comes to his daughters."

She smoothed the sheet and adjusted the angle of the bed.

"Are you warm enough? It can get cold as an icebox in here. There you go. You'll be feeling better in a few minutes. Do you know that your wife has been around to see you every evening? She is a formidable lady and oversees your care with precision. She and my father would get along well. She's kept all of us, including the doctors, on their toes." Hanna smiled, her eyes warm and encouraging. "So, what is her first name?" she asked.

CHAPTER FORTY-FOUR

"Who?"

"I'm sorry, your wife. Don't get me wrong. Around here they call her, um, the minotaur. I'm not sure the metaphor is accurate, but she is a force to be reckoned with. I shouldn't be saying this, but I'm curious. Before you woke up fully, you kept murmuring a woman's name. Isabel?"

"Can you keep a secret?" Lance said.

Hanna leaned in, touched the stethoscope lightly to his bare chest—pa-tom, pa-tom.

"I've always been a curious girl, and yes, your secret is safe with me."

"Isabela ..." Pa-tom, pa-tom, pa-tom, pa-tom, pa-tom. "I want to find my way back to her, to Isabela, but it's complicated. My wife, as you have seen, is quite capable of handling her life without any help from me. However, it's delicate. I'd like to avoid embarrassment and hurt and will stay as long as it takes for her to agree to part amicably."

Hanna's eyes were wide as she listened intently to his words.

"Will you help me? I want to get a letter, maybe several to Thailand. Obviously, I am unable to write, so I need an accomplice." He attempted to raise both bandaged-covered hands off the bed. He was only able to lift them half an inch before wincing and lowering them back down. "You see?" he continued. "I am totally at your mercy. I do understand if you decline. I promise I won't bring it up again. It's just somehow your voice, your presence, has been with me this entire time, like a melody. I don't know you, but that doesn't seem quite right. You don't seem like a stranger."

"Mr. Jameson, I need to think about it—the ethics of it, you understand? I will keep your secret, I promise you that, and I will consider your request, but I can't guarantee anything. What's most important is that you rest and concentrate on healing."

"Call me Lance, okay?" Lance's voice drifted off as his eyes closed.

The burn treatments were excruciating, but he was lucky. His entire facial area had been charred, blackened like a marshmallow in a campfire. However, those burns were second degree and did not affect the deeper tissue of the skin. Within a few short months, the burns began to heal, and his face was once more recognizable.

A third-degree burn on his left hand was the most troublesome, and several times, it had to be treated for infection. His physical therapy began with mostly small movements, moving the digits of his fingers and relearning how to pick up an object and move it a few inches to the left, right, up, or down. The progress seemed slow and tedious, but Lance approached his physical therapy with determination.

Chapter Forty-Five

1962

Brooke Army Facility, San Antonio, Texas

It was already late afternoon when Hanna wheeled her patient back to his room following an hour-and-a-half of intense physical therapy. It had been a month since Lance first opened his eyes. He was healing from the two surgeries to reset his broken pelvis, and now he was laboriously progressing from tentative first steps to taking several laps around the physical therapy room, albeit still dependent on a walker. Hanna spoke from behind the wheelchair.

"Mr. Jameson ... Lance, I've given your request a lot of thought, and I've reached a decision."

"About what?"

"Isabela must be beyond worried. All this time without a word from you. Let me know what you want to say. I'll take the notes and transcribe everything at home. Did you know I used to be a stenographer? Well almost. I was set to graduate at the top of my class but decided at the last minute it wasn't the work for me. My father was hopping mad. All that money and time. I told him I'd repay him every cent, and I will. I'll take care of mailing the letters. Don't thank me. You can pay me back when you get out of this place."

"You are my personal angel! When I'm better, if you ever need anything, know you have a friend. I mean that sincerely," he said. "It's not just the letters. You've been my counselor, confidante, and a genuine healer in this otherwise colorless place. I'm curious, though. How did you arrive at your decision?"

"When you first arrived, it was pretty much touch and go. Sometimes, I'd sit beside you for a while. The staff and I were briefed on the traumatic accident you lived through in Thailand. I'm not sure why, but sometimes we nurses get attached to certain patients. Later, when the doctors reduced the medication and brought you out of the coma, you mumbled a lot. I felt you were trying to communicate a vital message. I listened whenever I could spare a few minutes. There was something about a backpack. You kept saying, 'I have to get it. Don't let it burn!' You got quite agitated whenever you spoke about the backpack, so I'd go get permission and then administer some morphine to calm you. One day, I was alone in the room with you, and I heard it, crystal clear. You said, 'Isabel.' You said the name so softly. It was, well, the tenderness of it that got to me. Maybe it's just a young woman's fantasy, but I imagined whatever you were feeling must be pretty close to what love is."

Chapter Forty-Six

1962

Ko Pha Ngan, Thailand

It was still dark when Kate and Isabela left their guesthouse. Kate secured a room for the day right in Chiang Mai under their newly acquired aliases to wait for the evening train to Bangkok, the first stop on their three-day journey to the island, Ko Pha Ngan. The plan was expertly outlined and prepared. Isabela would spend the last three months of her pregnancy in the beauty and quiet of Ko Pha Ngan. At eight forty-five at night, they boarded the train and took the added precaution to sit in different cars. Though it was still too early to sleep, Isabela draped a shirt over the top of her head as an active discouragement to any fellow passenger interested in conversation. Kate merely turned her head and stared out the window, ignoring anyone and everyone. After the twelve-hour train ride from Chiang Mai, the women took a taxi to the bus station in Bangkok and bought a ticket south to Surat Tani, where they planned to spend another night.

Early the next morning, they boarded the local ferry to Ko Pha Ngan. They wore oversized sunglasses and wide-brimmed hats, trying to blend in yet stay apart from the foreigners, locals, and all the commercial activity that filled the ferry. An American woman from North Carolina edged nearer to Kate and tapped her on the shoulder.

"Where are you from, honey? I am from Raleigh. Isn't it exciting? We've been saving for this trip for five years, and we are finally here! I have to pinch myself." The woman peered into Kate's dark glasses expectantly, awaiting her response. Instead, Kate stood up and walked to the other side of the ferry. The woman watched her retreat and mumbled to herself, "Well, I never …"

Kate reveled in the challenge of going undercover and even joked about applying for a detective job. She created fake identification cards and rented a house under the name of a company owned by one of her father's business associates. It was away from prying eyes. She made sure the house was fully stocked and hired a Thai servant to be a companion for Isabela to take care of cleaning, shopping, and communication. Kate also researched and obtained one of Bangkok's finest obstetricians and hired a nurse to assist in the weeks following the baby's birth. Then she took another two weeks to review her plans to ensure no details were omitted.

"I'll be back a month before the baby's due," Kate told her. "Don't worry about a thing. All the arrangements will be set by the time you arrive. Your student visa is good for another year now, so no problem there. Until I come back, a nurse will visit you once a month. I feel terrible about leaving you, but I think it's wisest for me to go back to Bangkok. I'll be more flexible near an airport, and with a little luck and a lot of planning, I'll have everything lined up and ready for the birth. I'll be the eyes and ears for both of us. Don't worry. I plan to keep a low profile. You're sure you will be okay? Shit, I cannot believe we're pulling this off!"

"Gracias, Katya. Go. I am happy. I cannot imagine a better friend than you!" She patted her belly, which was just beginning to bulge.

"In all the excitement of planning our disappearance, I forgot to ask you," Kate said. "What did you end up telling Prapat?"

"I told him I had to return to El Salvador. I invented a very sick grandmother. I feel terrible that I lied to him. He has been so gracious and kind. He said he will welcome me whenever I am able to return to Thailand, but I'm afraid that will never happen now."

"You haven't changed your mind? This endeavor will require serious creativity for you to go home, live your life, and have your baby at your side," Kate said. "Don't worry. I'm up for it. It turns out I have a talent for cloak-and-dagger conspiracy. Who knew? It's fascinating to disappear and confuse the powers that be and … our families. I need to stay incognito, too. There's no problem where my father is concerned. He's completely self-absorbed and only requires a five-minute phone call every so often. Unfortunately, your mother never will accept your plan. She'll freak if she imagines you traipsing off to Burma to rescue orphans. You need to invent a backstory that sounds less risky. Write home often so your mother stays happy and unconcerned. Send the letters to me, and I'll post them from different cities and towns. Lucky for us, we're just a couple of lowly art students. Are you sure this is the way you want to play it?"

"Go, Katya. We are fine. Do not miss the boat."

Isabela spent tranquil days, lounging on the deck and allowing the murmuring water to caress her and quiet her mind from the seemingly endless thoughts and worries for which she had, as of yet, no solution.

The first month, she was content to sit by the water, read, and help Boonsri with chopping and cooking, but soon, she ached to stretch her legs and explore beyond the confines of the house. At six months, she could still conceal her pregnancy with an oversized blouse and a flowing skirt. Boonsri went daily to the market to buy fresh fruits, vegetables, and any delicacy Isabela might crave on a given day. She brought newspapers and books from the local library. After only a short time, the line between servant and mistress blurred, and the two became easy friends. Boonsri was Isabela's sole contact with the outside world, and Isabela confided in the young Thai woman, who easily accepted her into her heart like a sister.

Boonsri was vigilant at guarding her friend from the curiosity of strangers, as well as her own family. Each week she brought special herbs and roots known by the local women to enhance the health of pregnancy. Boonsri was nervous, though. There seemed to be too many eyes and too many questions. However, she shied away from asserting her opinion when Isabela announced that she wanted to accompany her to the market.

"Miss Isabela, I bring you everything you need. Please, don't come to the market."

"Boonsri, I need to go out and be around people, just for a little bit. I don't know the people here, and the people don't know me. I won't talk to anyone. Don't worry."

At the market, Isabela was immersed in the marvelous colors and aromas. Plump mangos, lychees, and giant papayas lined the shelves of one stall, while another brimmed with avocados, bright red peppers, tomatoes, cucumbers, and oddly shaped vegetables unfamiliar to her. Others offered delicacies from the sea, such as giant tentacled octopi and scaly red snapper. Their gills expanded wide and retracted. The fish jerked and flapped in crowded buckets of water, making vain attempts to swim. Isabela felt happy and carefree while out and mingling with the locals and, for a moment, was able to forget the fears that plagued her sleep. Boonsri nudged her forward, hurrying to complete the morning purchases.

"Miss Isabela, we cannot carry more. We go home now?"

Several stalls down from where the women just concluded their last purchase, a man, his blond hair slicked back and glued to his head, stepped out from the stall and squinted. His eyes followed the two women as they walked away from the market.

"Boonsri, let me carry some of that. The bag is bigger than you!" Isabela said.

The man backed farther out of the stall to look from a more advantageous angle. He knew he had seen the one woman before, but where? She was quite striking. Most men would notice her.

Avery watched the two women walk down the road and away from the market. He followed, careful to keep out of view as he racked his brain. He knew he'd have it in a minute. He never forgot a face. Suddenly, the smoke-filled nightclub with its wide terrace came sharply into focus. Immediately, he remembered the two lovers gazing at the moon. *Well, what do you know? The man, Jimmy Calhoun, the one they'd all been looking for, might be right here on Ko Pha Ngan! Finding him will definitely get me noticed. Out of the little leagues and into the big leagues. This might be just the opportunity I've been looking for.*

When he first started running errands for Volker, the big German, Avery thought that's where the hierarchy ended. But he quickly realized he'd stumbled upon a crackerjack of illicit activity, and Volker was only a small fish. Foreign governments vying for power and money in quantities his mind could barely fathom were tossed around like pocket change in conversations he overheard. The Chinese were backing the Pathet Lao in an attempt to gain control over the entire Asian peninsula. Thailand would be the first country to fall, and his people were in on the game. They had the money.

Avery didn't care about politics. What he cared about most was money. He knew money was power, and he wanted to make a lot of it. He wanted to get even with all those in his past who mocked, ignored, or dismissed him as a loser. It was as simple as that. In his mind, he saw himself negotiating with the big honchos and making deals to overturn the power structures of countries. Not that he cared who might prevail. He just wanted to be in the game and, specifically, on the winning side. Bribery, kidnapping, forgery, and smuggling, those were just the beginning. Then Volker gave him a job: find Jimmy Calhoun, the American photographer, who had disappeared out of thin air. Finding Jimmy Calhoun was his key to entering the high-stakes game of international politics and drug cartels, but so far, he had failed. His fantasy dangled beyond arm's length. Who would have thought he'd get a lead on him here on the islands? Volker sent Avery down here once a month. His job was to ensure that the hashish smuggled onto the island and held secretly in a house awaiting distribution was the same quantity that left the island.

He thought again about finding Jimmy Calhoun. *People don't just disappear like that! A stroke of luck, that's what this is! I won't let this opportunity get away from me. Succeeding in a job like this is what it takes to get noticed.*

Avery followed the women, strolling down the road like a tourist enjoying the view. The women veered off the main road onto a smaller dirt road that hugged the coastline, passing the heavy sack of vegetables back and forth between them. Avery dropped back now, careful to stay hidden but close enough so he didn't lose sight of their direction. He watched as they turned into a wide, semicircular driveway and disappeared into a house that appeared to stretch out over the water.

Chapter-Forty-Seven

1962

Special Operations Facility

Chiang Rai, Thailand

Crispin ducked his head into the makeshift office and withdrew it promptly when he saw Nigel on the phone. Nigel waved with his free hand, gesturing for Crispin to enter.

"Come in. I'm just finishing up," he said. "What do you have?"

"The two women, Isabela Marquez and Kate Morgan? They haven't left Thailand."

"Are you certain?"

"Ninety-five percent. We've checked airline manifests, trains, and buses. Their names aren't anywhere. No signs or indications of foul play, coercion, kidnapping, or the like. There'd be communication and demands. There have been none. High probability they're hiding out and do not wish to be found. It's not easy for two foreigners to disappear in a small country like Thailand."

"That's all you have?"

"That's about it."

"Most unfortunate. However, our priority is the mission. We need every man. The Americans will be here within weeks. Keep the channels open. If information surfaces, we'll act on it. Otherwise, stand down."

Chapter Forty-Eight

1962

Ko Pha Ngan, Thailand

"Hello, Volker. Avery here. I've got something."

"Don't waste my time. What is it?"

"I recognized a woman at the market today. I was doing business, ya know, checking out the distributors. Anyway, when I first saw her, she looked familiar, but I couldn't place her. I'm pretty good with faces, so I knew I'd have it in a minute. Then there it was. Six months ago, she was with that guy you've had me looking for. You know, the photographer Jimmy Calhoun? When I saw them together at the nightclub, he said she was just a date, but I watched them. He looked smitten, involved, if ya know what I mean. I've checked out the island. He's nowhere to be seen, but I thought you'd like to know. I know where she's staying. I cased the house, and it's an easy hit. Just the two women are staying there."

"So far we've got nothing. A whole lot of nothing!" Volker spat into the phone. Avery immediately distanced the phone and held it away from his ear, as if the saliva traveled through the wire and sprayed out through the earpiece.

"What do ya mean?"

"Get the girl, Avery. Just the girl. Do what you want with her companion. Bring the girl to Bangkok within the week. We'll see what she knows. If she doesn't know anything, well, there are other ways to make a dime. Don't disappoint me."

Avery staked the house for three days before he made his move. He watched the young Thai servant leave daily for the market at nine a.m. She returned between ten-thirty and eleven. Avery didn't like the idea of making a hit in broad daylight. The authorities would be notified within hours, and the girl would be wide awake and hard to keep silent. No, the middle of the night was the best option. Hopefully, he would be in and out without the servant waking. If not, well, that was unfortunate.

"Please, Boonsri, go home tonight and see Chatri. I know Katya wants you to stay each night, but I am good. I am sorry you've been away so long from your boy."

Boonsri felt a tug at her heart. Her mother looked after her only son. She knew he was well cared for and happy, but she still ached to hold him, listen to his voice, and feel the softness of his skin next to her cheek. She smiled warmly and pressed her palms together in a slight bow; the anticipated joy of holding her son in her arms eclipsed the worry and fear for her friend.

Isabela smiled at her friend. "Don't worry. It's only one night. I'll be fine. My little one is not even born yet, and I can't imagine being away from her!"

Kate called every few days to brainstorm. How to get Isabela home? How to smooth the ruffled feathers of an angry mother and an abandoned fiancé? How to return to a somewhat normal life, one that included the child living with its mother? Together, they envisioned innumerable possibilities, but in each scenario, a fundamental flaw arose, necessitating a return to the drawing board.

One lazy Thursday afternoon, Kate telephoned, unable to suppress her exuberance. Isabela distanced the receiver to several inches beyond her ear.

"Bela, you are going to love me! I have the answer. It's the perfect plan. This one will work! I am going back to El Salvador! I've already booked the flight. I'll be back in a few weeks with all the fine details. Remember I told you I spent the semester of my junior year in a village twelve hours from San Salvador? I was placed with a family there, and they were incredible. At the time, I liked them better than my own family. It's because of them that I learned Spanish so well. I am going to find you a family like that one! One that is loving and kind and who will take care of the baby for a year or so. You'll have to be apart for that time. Can you do it? I'll fly the baby back to El Salvador when it's a few months old. It'll have an El Salvadorian and an American passport. That's one benefit we can request from the deadbeat dad. If we have to, we'll get in touch with your British acquaintance. I'm pretty sure he'll have the clout to pull off this one small request, or we'll threaten to reveal whatever it is they're doing. After you've been home a year, and repaired your relationship with your parents, and hopefully, smoothed things over with Tomás, you'll make arrangements to work with orphans in the same village. No one will question your desire to do this as you have always volunteered to help with poor kids. There, you'll fall in love with your own child, a half-British, half-Salvadorian orphan with a sad, sad story. You'll insist on adopting. What do you think? Pretty ingenious, right? Okay, there's some ifs, but we have time. I am going to come back from El Salvador with the perfect family."

Isabela's face was wet. "Katya, can we do this? Will it work? Gracias a Dios! But I can't marry Tomás. I have to tell him that it can't possibly work."

Chapter Forty-Nine

1962

Ko Pha Ngan, Thailand

Avery observed the Thai servant board the bus and then waited another two hours after the lights went out. He worked the back lock until the latch gave and the door glided easily open. He removed his shoes to avoid noise and set them just outside the door. He slid across the floor, careful to stop at the slightest creak of the floorboards. There were several bedrooms, but he knew the side of the house she went to at night. The door to the bedroom was wide open. Avery looked down on the sleeping woman. Slowly, he bent and placed a cloth over Isabela's mouth.

As the thick, chloroformed rag was forced over her mouth and across her nose, Isabela's eyes flew open. She struggled to get free, but the vapors did their work. Isabela's body went limp in less than a minute. Avery tied her hands and feet together, forcing her body into a fetal position, which made her an easy fit for the large shipping box packed onto the back of the rented truck he parked a few streets down the road. Once he was sure his victim was unconscious, he ran down the road and slid into the truck. Quickly, he drove it around to the backside of the house and out of view.

Avery was sweating, and his heart raced. *Shit! I've got to get her onto the truck and down to the boat. I can't have her waking up until morning.* He fumbled through a small bag tied to his waist and pulled out a syringe. *This should keep her quiet for the next twelve hours until I get her to the mainland.*

It felt like cotton candy filled the cavity of her skull. Isabela tried to stretch her legs, but her knees were shoved up against her belly. She couldn't figure out what prevented her legs from extending. The fog in her brain was thick and heavy. She nodded off and then jerked wide awake as the floor beneath her began to wobble. Her head banged against something hard, and her whole body jolted. Light streamed in as the crate was opened. Isabela squeezed her eyes shut to block out the blinding light. The pressure in her bladder was a dam about to burst. She tried to open her mouth to speak, but something was taped across her mouth. Jumbled, random thoughts began to arrange into coherent order. *What's happening? ¿Dónde estoy? Where am I?*

"Get her out of there," Avery commanded.

Strong arms lifted her under her arms and pulled her out. Her hands were still bound to her feet.

Isabela could see about four feet from the floor now. There were four plastered walls, the legs of a metallic table surrounded by four chairs, a dirty mattress on the floor in the corner. Her eyes moved cautiously around. Before she could suppress it, a hoarse gurgle sounded in the back of her throat.

"We're going to take the gag off. Don't bother to scream. No one will hear. Otherwise, we'll put you out again. Understand?" Avery's tone was quiet and unemotional.

Isabela nodded her head once, and he removed the gag from her mouth.

"Por favor? Please, I need to use the toilet."

Red sneakered feet moved closer and released the tie between her legs and feet, as well as the one between her feet and hands.

Isabela tried to stand, but her feet buckled. Liquid tricked down her leg, which turned into a flood as she began to sob great heaves without tears. Her hands, once untied, flew wildly in all directions. She sat now in a puddle of her own urine. Nothing made any sense.

"My baby. Please do not hurt my baby." Her words slurred, tantamount to gibberish.

Isabela sat at the metallic table, with an empty glass of water before her. She asked for another.

Volker, the German with blond hair shaved to almost bald, entered the room, followed closely by Avery. The German wore a thick gold chain around his neck, and his biceps bulged under the tight-fitting white shirt. The first three buttons were open to expose his dark, hairy chest.

"Hello, my dear. How was your trip?" Volker laughed, amused by his own humor. "Let me introduce myself. My name is Bob. Now, please be polite and introduce yourself." Volker's heavily accented English was grating and guttural. "You do understand English?"

Her hand flew up to the leather cord around her neck where the little wooden elephant and jaguar dangled. It was still there. She remembered Dave placing the small wooden carvings in her hand and saying, "Lance wants you to have these now." Tears welled in her eyes, but she willed her attention back to the man sitting across from her. Her teeth chattered.

"Sunee, get over here. Take her to the toilet and get her cleaned up. She smells."

Volker addressed the small, thin Asian man who stood in the shadow of the doorway. Sunee approached quietly, took her hand, and then walked silently down the hall to a bathroom. She used the tiny bar of soap to sponge wash her face, under her arms, and behind her neck. Sunee stood at the door with his eyes averted. Still, her cheeks flushed and reddened. She did the best she could under the circumstances.

Isabela's heart raced as her thoughts began to clear. *What was I thinking? I was in the house with a made-up name. No one will know where to look. No one will know I am gone. Katya! But no, Katya is in El Salvador.*

She struggled to hold back a floodgate of overwhelming emotion. The Asian man handed her a skirt and a blouse, albeit two sizes too large. But, still, she was grateful to have something clean. She turned her back to the man, removed her soiled clothing, and stepped into the clean ones. When she was done, he lightly nudged her forward, back into the room with the metal table, where the German and the one called Avery waited.

"Let's start with your name and how you know Jimmy Calhoun? All we need is the whereabouts of your friend, and you are free as a bird. Simple enough?" As Volker spoke, his gaze probed her eyes and then her entire body.

Isabela felt raw and exposed. She wrapped her arms close in, against her chest, in a vain attempt to make herself smaller. She tried to concentrate, to remember. Slowly, she recalled how Jimmy rushed her away from the island. Why? Why did Jimmy need to leave the island so suddenly? Something about drugs and guns. She had seen the man, the one standing behind Bob, before. Where? Suddenly, images arose like a dream. Jimmy holding her hand. Jimmy telling her, "I need to keep you safe. He can't know you mean anything."

Emotion welled up as her breath caught in her throat. She stammered, took a breath, and spoke.

"My name is Isabela Marquez. I am from El Salvador. I study art in Chiang Mai. I came to this island to rest. Please! I'll give you money."

"Very nice, Isabel. We'll discuss money in a little bit. We need to know about Jimmy Calhoun. I'm sure you know the photography is just a cover? We'd like to know where he has gone. Give us the information we want and you are free. Not too much to ask under the circumstances, is it?"

"Por favor, maybe he is someone I went out with, once, twice? I do not remember." A hand flew across the table and knocked Isabela off her seat. A bright red blotch immediately rose to the surface on the right side of her face where he hit her.

"Isabel, we know you know him better than that. I do not have a lot of patience. You will tell us what we want to know." Volker edged nearer, his face only inches from hers now.

Isabela searched her memory. Detailed scenes rushed in and out of her awareness, and she finally realized there was no harm in telling this man what she knew. Jimmy was far away and wasn't coming back. This man would never be able to find him.

"If I tell you, I am free to go?" she said.

"That's a good start," the German replied.

"I don't know where Jimmy is. He told me he was a photographer. He was in an airplane accident, and his wife sent him back to America to a hospital. You see, I didn't know he had a wife! How was I to know?" Isabela began to cry as she held her head in her hands.

Volker looked at her pointedly, squinting his eyes. He took her chin in his right hand and forced her to look him straight in the eye. He reached into his pocket, withdrew a medium-sized switchblade, and clicked it open. He paused just long enough for the woman to absorb this object into her awareness. The silver blade was stained with dark blotches. Slowly, Volker traced the blade along the right side of her mouth up to her left ear without leaving a mark. Isabela's body tightened as she closed her eyes.

"You wouldn't lie, would you? I can ruin that pretty face," he said. "No. You are telling the truth. Maybe not the whole truth, but you don't have the information we are looking for." He dropped his hand and turned to Avery. "All right, she doesn't have anything." Volker looked off to the side and scratched his ear. "But since we have gone to so much trouble to extract her, I'd like to see what happens when we dangle the bait. Avery, one more mess-up and you are out. Remember, our organization doesn't let you go with a severance package. You get my meaning? Get up to Chiang Mai and dangle the bait. Let the underground know we have the woman."

Isabela's eyes widened, but she remained quiet. No use arguing integrity, not here, not with this man. Her own skill was all she could count on. The hours spent sitting in on negotiations with her father and all kinds of people might just be her saving grace. *Gracias, Papá!*

She observed each of the four men. Volker, the hulking German, might have made a decent businessman. He demanded order and precision within the group. Volker courted a woman, and his voice softened when he spoke of her. Isabela took note.

Avery, the man she had seen with Jimmy, reminded her of a hawk, circling, patient and ready to strike. She often caught him staring at her as if he was assessing the appearance of rare prey. He stalked not her precisely, but the opportunity she represented. He was a pseudo-sycophant who carried out the wishes and desires of his superior while biding his time.

The second German, Albert, was short and boxlike. His rarely washed blond hair appeared brownish-grey. He was a person who thrived on strictly following orders. He was ready to call out anyone who he deemed his inferior. In their small group, that was young Sunee. Sunee was the odd man out and reminded Isabela of a younger Prapat. He was elegant in his movements and graceful like a dancer. She wondered what experience had brought him to be part of this sad group.

Isabela knew she needed to stay awake and very, very alert. One moment could be her only chance. She suppressed the deep emotions that threatened to engulf her, knowing she could not give in to self-pity. At night, they handcuffed Isabela's leg to Sunee's leg. She lay on her side on the wide mat, her body turned away from him, and willed her breath to calm. For his part, Sunee also stayed on his side. His back only lightly touched hers, and his breath was barely noticeable. At first, it took Isabela hours to sleep in this awkward position, but eventually, she drifted off.

Chapter Fifty

1962

Washington, D.C.

Kate hummed as she boarded the Pan Am DC 8 jet departing from San Salvador to Washington, D.C., with one stop en route. She had met and located the perfect family. The stars aligned in immaculate order. It felt almost as if it was meant to be. Scientifically inclined, Kate disparaged esoteric belief, a sharp delineation with Isabela's faith-based background. With an IQ in the top three percent of young American women, her worldview depended heavily on science and mathematics. It was Kate's belief that there could be no mystery of universal proportion that could not be unveiled by intelligence and a thorough investigative mind, yet she had to admit there was something unusual about the ease in which all these pieces came together.

She was led to the family within the first week of setting foot in El Salvador. It was a synchronistic progression of events that seemed miraculous. The father dreamed of purchasing a small farm with livestock. The amount of money required to make a family's dream come true in this third-world country was negligible to Kate. The father agreed to her terms and said he would embrace the baby into their family for as long as was needed. When someone from the family showed up to reclaim the child, he would make sure everything went smoothly. He only asked that the agreement between them be kept strictly confidential. He would tell his wife about the arrangement and the gift from God that had fallen from the heavens, but his children and the village would hear a different story.

Money was exchanged and the agreement signed. All was in place. A self-satisfied sigh escaped Kate's lips as she passed through customs at Idlewild International Airport in New York. She really was quite good at this. She planned to stay a week in the United States before flying back to Thailand. There was still plenty of time. Isabela would be fine now. Everything was covered.

The two men in dark business suits approached from a no-entry airport door to flank her on either side.

"Katherine Morgan?"

The tall, angular man in the navy-blue suit extended his card. "Thomas Baker, Central Intelligence Agency. You are wanted for questioning in the disappearance of one Isabela Marquez in Thailand. Please come with us."

"What? Isabela is a Salvadorian citizen. You have no jurisdiction!"

The tall man answered by taking her elbow and purposely propelling her forward.

Kate sat in the small, overly lit interrogation room for five hours now. The room was stark, furnished with only a table and two chairs. There were no pictures on the four whitewashed walls. Tom from the Central Intelligence Agency sat across from her.

"One more time. We need to know the location of your friend, Isabela Marquez. You *will* remain here until you have given us her information. Sam, get Miss Morgan a sandwich and a Coke, and we'll begin again. Do you have a preference? Tuna or turkey?" Sam, the second CIA officer in the room, looked expectantly in her direction. Kate glared back.

"Get her turkey, then," Tom said.

"I am a U.S. citizen. I know my rights. You can't hold me here. I want to speak with my lawyer. This is crazy. I haven't done anything wrong. I don't know where my friend went. Last time I saw her was in Chiang Mai, months ago. Look, one call to my father and you will regret holding me here. He's a very powerful man."

"Falsifying documents in a foreign country is enough to hold you indefinitely. The CIA protects American national security, at all costs. Do you understand? I hope there will be no further need to convince you of the legitimacy of this interrogation. I'm going to ask you one more time. Where is Isabela Marquez?"

Kate blew out her breath. A piece of paper slid across the table and teetered on the edge.

"There are extenuating circumstances ... she doesn't want to be found right now. Okay? She's fine, more than fine. But I need to know what interest you have in my friend. She's just an art student traveling abroad."

"An art student who, however innocuously, trespassed into areas of concern regarding our national security. Your friend's life may be in danger. Every hour you delay, her safety becomes less assured. Please, Miss Morgan, her location?"

Kate's lip began to tremble subtly. "If I tell you her location, her circumstances, do I have any assurance this information will be kept strictly confidential?"

"She needs to leave Thailand immediately and return to her home country, preferably. Any extenuating circumstances beyond this are of no concern of to the U.S. government. You have my word on that. So, please, start at the beginning."

"Can I have a cigarette?" Kate asked.

"You're a smoker? That's not in your file."

"I see. You've checked me out with that fine-tooth comb of the CIA. Since you seem to know so much about me, I only have a cigarette when I am very, very nervous. You can add that to your file."

"We know you have a very sharp mind, Miss Morgan. We know that you were able to hide your friend in a foreign country. Under different circumstances, I'd applaud your ingenuity. But this is an extremely delicate and, I might add, dangerous situation. We need to know your friend's location."

"Look, what I say or don't say may have far-reaching implications for my friend's life. However, I understand I really don't have a choice. Do I? I'm going to read between the lines here, so correct me if I'm wrong. Isabela fell in love with one of your operatives in Thailand. She's an innocent and was completely unaware of the nature of your agent's work. Our illustrious government doesn't want its people to know about whatever the hell it is up to in the far east. How am I doing so far? Warm?"

Tom, a manila file open on his lap, scrawled a few notes in the margin on one of the papers before glancing up with a neutral expression. Kate, emboldened by his lack of denial, continued to speak.

"Your agent disappeared or was reassigned elsewhere, but not before leaving her a gift. That's right—she's knocked up. She's the only child of a prominent El Salvadoran family and Catholic. She can't return to her home in this condition. The father is AWOL, so she's on her own. She's been hiding out until the birth. We've worked out a plan, and it's a pretty good one. We could use your help with papers, U.S. passport and all. It really is the least you can do."

"Location?"

"Will you keep her condition private? Her family really cannot know about this, or it will ruin her life."

"There's a lot more at stake than your friend's reputation. However, if she leaves the country and stays with the family you located, she's no longer a concern of ours."

"Well, then?" Tom lightly tapped his pen on the open file.

"She's in a house on the island of Ko Pha Ngan. The house is rented under the name of the Alexander Gardner Foundation."

"Thank you, Miss Morgan. You have done your friend and your government a big favor and maybe saved her life. Leave the rest to us. Do not return to Thailand. For the time being, your visa has been revoked. We'll ask you not to contact your friend until she is safely out of the country. That's all."

Kate stood. Her face was bright red, and her heart beat erratically.

"There's one more thing, if you would?" Tom stared directly at the young woman.

"I've told you what you wanted to know, and you've returned the favor with a slap in the face. It's not likely I'll share anything else with you."

"Miss Morgan, the Central Intelligence Agency of the United States government would like to extend an opportunity to you. Provided you score as well as we think you will, we may have a job for you. If that would be of interest?"

Kate slowly sat down. The events of the past six months, even for her wild and independent self, had been extremely stressful. The sequence of happenings that led her to sit across the table from an agent of the most clandestine branch of the U.S. government was mind-numbing. Several minutes passed before the silence was broken.

"We think you fit the profile, and … you would be serving your country," Tom added.

Kate's face broadened into a wide grin. Over the past few years, she pursued studies in international affairs, finance, literature, art, and botany. Inevitably, her enthusiasm waned, and she was left bored and dissatisfied. She looked across the table at Tom.

"Hell yes!"

Tom extended his card. "Come in at nine tomorrow. We'll set up the screening and interviews and see how the cards fall."

"Isabela … you really will take care of her? Get her back to El Salvador and keep her condition private? I'll give you everything I've worked out. The Rodríguez family agreed to take care of the baby. They already received compensation. Isabela needs a quiet, secluded place to stay with good medical care throughout the pregnancy. Once she gives birth, she can go home."

"I'll tell you what. Come in tomorrow and we'll see how you do. If you are unable to help your friend due to employment with our esteemed government, then I'll personally make sure your criteria are met."

"I have your word?"

"My integrity is on the line, young lady. Count on it."

Chapter Fifty-One

1962

El Salvador

Ivanna Marquez hung up the phone and stared out across the veranda. Pablo Marquez strode into the room and approached his wife. He kissed her cheek before heading toward the kitchen.

"I am starving. Come with me and let's get something to eat," he said.

"Something's wrong. I can feel it," Ivanna said.

Pablo turned and looked at his wife. "What, my dear?"

"It's Isabela. There is something wrong with my child. A mother knows. I haven't been able to get in touch with her for weeks. The last time we spoke, she said she was going to be traveling to some remote areas. Remember, she said it may be difficult for her to call, but she would send postcards. Postcards! I have been patient, but this is too much! You need to go get our daughter and bring her home. I don't know why, but Isabela is not telling the truth. My daughter has never lied to me, but without a doubt, she is lying now."

"I will make a few calls to my contacts in Chiang Mai," Pablo said. "There's probably no reason for concern. It's only a young woman stretching her wings and getting a first taste of independence. We'll keep a closer eye on her. She'll never have to know. Please do not worry, my dear. Our Isabela is a very intelligent young woman. If there's anything amiss, I will be on the first flight to Thailand. You can be sure of that."

A few days later, Pablo set down the phone and called for his wife.

"I spoke to my contact in Chiang Mai a few days ago. He was informed by the front desk staff that Isabela left Chiang Mai several months ago with her American friend. The staff was not informed of their destination. I pulled some strings and had the airline manifests checked. She has not left Thailand, so that is good news, perhaps."

"Please, go find her. And bring her home!"

Chapter Fifty-Two

1962

Ko Pha Ngan, Thailand

Crispin tapped lightly on Nigel's door, cracked it open, and ducked his head. He waited for an invitation to enter.

"Come in, Crispin."

"New development on Isabela Marquez and her friend. They have Kate Morgan in custody in New York. The CIA picked her up at Idlewild, coming out of customs. They are questioning her. No word on how the two disappeared, but we have Isabela Marquez's location. She's on the island of Ko Pha Ngan under an assumed name. And Nigel … the situation is delicate. Apparently, Jameson's going to be a father. One more glitch. Mr. Marquez, the girl's father, is in Chiang Mai and is asking around for information concerning his daughter. It appears Miss Marquez hasn't informed her family of her whereabouts either."

"The situation has become complicated. The local drug cartel has put out the equivalent of an all-points bulletin. Locate one American photographer Jimmy Calhoun and bring him in alive. There's a reward on his head." Nigel paused before continuing. "The drug mafia doesn't go to this kind of trouble just to recruit someone. Something's happened, and our agent Jameson is not in a state to fill us in on the details. We need to tread very carefully here. Go to the island, pick up the girl, and get her to Bangkok. Make sure she's on the first flight out of the country. Don't leave her side until she's on that flight and you've seen it take off! I'll let her father know she's no longer in Thailand when you give the word. Bloody hell, Jameson!"

A private boat awaited to take Crispin to Ko Pha Ngan because the local ferry departed only once a day. Crispin whistled as he flagged a taxi and hopped in, calculating the turnaround time to reach the home, have Isabela Marquez gather a few things, and get back to the boat. It should be a piece of cake. He had the return flight to Bangkok booked for later in the evening, as well as papers from the Thai government revoking one student visa effective immediately. Isabela Marquez would have no choice but to comply and leave with him.

The taxi pulled into the semicircular driveway and parked. The driver was paid half in advance and asked to wait. The man happily leaned back in his seat, closed his eyes, and rested, content and appreciative of today's stroke of luck.

Crispin knocked on the door. There was no sound of approaching footsteps. He waited a minute before walking around to the side of the house. He jiggled the doorknob and found the door unlocked.

"Hello?" he called.

The house was quiet. To all appearances, no one was home. He stepped inside to a breathtaking view. Floor-to-ceiling glass windows framed an ocean of azure, crystalline waters. He heard a shuffling sound and the opening of a door from the back side of the house.

"I'm sorry," he said. "The door was … " Crispin turned and pointed toward the side doorway he had just entered.

"Please, no one is home." Boonsri waited quietly, with her hands in a prayer position at her chest.

"I am here to see Miss Isabel Marquez. Is she at home?"

"You are Jimmy?" Boonsri's voice was soft, hopeful.

"No. I'm a friend. I must speak with her. I am to accompany her to Bangkok and make sure she is on a flight back to her country. Her visa's been revoked. Will you tell her that? Be assured we have her best interests in mind, so please, have her come out and speak with me. I won't leave without her."

Boonsri fell onto the floor in a heap and hugged her knees, rocking forward and back.

"I only go one night to see my son. I come back in the morning, and she gone. All her things still here. Miss Isabela do not leave like this! I promise Miss Kate I don't tell anyone. I don't know what to do! I try many times to call the telephone in Bangkok for Miss Kate, but no one answer."

"Bugger it!" Crispin removed a handkerchief from his pocket and tendered it toward the distraught servant. "Pull yourself together now. You'll be no help to your friend if ya keep blubbering. Here." He leaned down, wiped her face, and extended a hand to pulled her up into a chair. "We'll go over everything. Tell me what you remember. What time did you leave, and then when did you return? If we're going to find her, every detail is important."

The young Thai spoke for twenty minutes, stopping only to take a breath and wipe her face with the back of her sleeve. Crispin interrupted twice and then allowed her to finish. He monitored his voice to an even pitch before speaking.

"Do you have a phone?"

Boonsri pointed to the kitchen and followed closely behind him. Crispin let the phone ring ten times before Nigel answered.

The connection was poor, so Crispin raised his voice and clearly articulated each word.

"Isabel Marquez is gone. Her clothes and her personal things are still in the drawers. The servant is distraught. She left for the night and says she came back early, but the house was empty when she returned. What do you want me to do?"

"Bloody hell! Check the island and get back to me. We'll have to work with the Thais on this. What do the kidnappers want? If they know the girl is connected to Jameson, it complicates the mission. So let's hope it's a human trafficking abduction." Nigel tapped the phone receiver on the desktop as he considered the complexity of the situation.

"Isabel's father is a prominent citizen of El Salvador and is very well connected. If he's apprised of the situation, he will complicate our efforts and won't be easy to control," Crispin said.

"Damn it, we don't need this! The mission is primary. There can be no compromise."

Chapter Fifty-Three

1962

Brooke Army Facility, San Antonio, Texas

Hanna looked forward to passing her shifts in the company of the tall, lanky patient with his sharp wit, astute perception, and easy banter. He teased her constantly, and she learned to return the humor with equal animation and lightheartedness. On weekends, when Anne Jameson arrived, their warm familiarity ceased on a dime. There was never a need to say anything. Hanna instantly converted from confidante and friend to strictly professional nurse tending to her suffering patient.

Anne fluffed up his pillows, rearranged everything on the shelves, and inquired about his progress. What did he need? Invariably, her heels clicked on the linoleum as she stalked the nurses' station with a list of infractions and required items. She rarely spoke about her week, except to say that it was busy. She always tended to a thousand minutiae, and she was disinclined to burden Lance with the details. He needed to focus on getting well. That was his job now.

Anne had recently been appointed to the position of executive vice president in her father's multinational corporation. She assured her father and the company's board of directors that she would be more than able to conduct business from the company's satellite office in Dallas, where she stayed during the week. She hopped on a flight to San Antonio every Friday evening to visit her husband and oversee his care.

Hanna cautioned herself to practice vigilance. Anne Jameson was sharp. Hanna mustn't leave a scrap of notepaper anywhere in sight. She also realized with a pang, however, that Mrs. Jameson loved her husband in her own intelligent and efficient way.

One Friday evening, Anne stopped by the nurses' station just as Hanna prepared to go home for the night.

"Hanna, how did it go this week?"

"He's surpassing all of the doctor's expectations. He'll be ready to walk without the walker tomorrow or the next day. Don't quote me on this, but it's looking like he might be able to get out of here in ten days, or maybe two weeks at the latest."

"What fantastic news! I will need to set up his therapy and doctor appointments then. I will arrange to take a short leave of absence until my husband is fully capable of getting around by himself."

"That's wonderful, Mrs. Jameson. You must be so happy. I know it's been a long road. I'll be off to go home now. We'll see you tomorrow. Betsy is the night shift nurse. She's on until seven. Anything you need, just ask her."

"Thank you, Hanna. Have a good night. One more thing before you go. Now that my husband is doing so much better, has he received any visitors? Letters? I want to screen, I mean, protect him from any upsetting situation or people. You understand? I'd like all visitors to be okayed by me. I've let the hospital administration know that all correspondence addressed to Mr. Jameson is to be held in the office until I pick them up. I'll give them to him when he is fully recuperated. Please let the nurses know. Thank you, Hanna. Goodnight."

Chapter Fifty-Four

1962

Unknown location, Thailand

Two months into her captivity, Isabela was all belly. Her round abdomen protruded, and the oversized clothing was a much better fit on her otherwise slight and delicate body. At eight months pregnant, Isabela felt tired and emotionally spent. Since the last move, she was restricted to a small closet during the day, her child's life threatened if she made the slightest noise. Isabela complied. She followed her captors' instructions and never complained.

For the greater part of each day, she was alone without light, in absolute and complete solitary confinement. She studied her captors' habits and movements and tried to decide which one of them was the most vulnerable. Which one might leave a door unlocked? Or possibly take pity on her plight?

Volker was a brute, but he was not without a bizarre set of ethics, demanding a strict adherence to rule and protocol. She was oddly grateful that he was protective of his asset and didn't allow anyone to physically harm her. He was the leader of the gangsters here and, as such, was determined and focused. He answered to a higher power, though, by the name of Sisto. Isabela was unsure whether Sisto was a person or an organization, but she believed Volker and his group were a small cell in a larger network.

Avery, the man who taken her hostage, was the least savage in the end. Late evenings after the others were gone, when he opened the door to the closet, he'd walk next to her, showing a kind of twisted empathy, asking if she needed anything and inquiring if the baby was okay. If the key turned in the lock, his face instantly changed color and contour, chameleon-like, back to a cold, hard exterior.

Albert, the other blond German, was short and heavyset and perfectly polite. At first, she focused on him as the most civilized and approachable, but all too soon, she realized that his behavior was a ruse. He did anything to look good and achieve recognition for a job well done.

Last, there was Sunee, the young Vietnamese man. She never heard him speak more than a short yes or no, but he executed instructions with immaculate precision. Isabela was most afraid of him. He was the piece that didn't fit. What series of events or circumstances had brought him to be with the two Germans and the sleazy American man? Money? A desperate life crisis, the remedy for which he would clearly risk everything? The two Germans and the American barely took notice of him, except to bark instructions. Isabela had nothing but time. She observed the characters and behaviors of her captors and determined that Sunee was dangerous. He would just as easily slice his boss's throat as hers.

She listened very carefully to her captor's conversations, especially between Volker and Avery, and paid attention to their movements. Every few days, Volker sent Avery out to scout for information. Early on in her captivity, Avery returned from a particularly lengthy absence. She strained to hear the subdued voices and brought her ear to the wall, her full attention focused on each word spoken.

"The Americans are sniffing around," Avery said. "They've been very, very careful and haven't mentioned the girl by name, but I think she's important to them. Maybe your guy, Jimmy Calhoun, was an agent for them? Or the girl knows something that endangers their interest? What do you want me to do?"

"Put it out there. We'll exchange the girl for Jimmy Calhoun, and … 10,000 in U.S. dollars." Volker's voice tapered as he stood and moved into the kitchen. Isabela strained, but she could no longer hear the conversation. Slowly, she withdrew her ear from the wall. Her heart pounded.

Jimmy and 10,000 American dollars! Isabela's heart sank as she considered the enormity of the sum and the pure impracticality of Jimmy Calhoun showing up from his hospital bed in America. She searched her brain for something to offer her captors to satisfy their demand, but try as she might, no workable solution was forthcoming.

The last move was the tenth in two months, and now, from her new location, she could hear the crow of a rooster and the bleating of goats. *We must be farther north.* It was cold in the mornings and evenings. She was purposefully compliant, showing an eagerness to do as she was told.

The baby kicked and made its presence known while the minutes ticked by, each second excruciating and interminable. Isabela began to pick at her arm, scratching the many bug bites that afflicted her daily. She and her child would die here. There was no way out, she imagined. Conversations from the other room blurred to a meaningless hum.

Her captors supplied her with a bowl in which to relieve herself. The odor was rank in the warm afternoon hours, but she became used to it. They gave her food in the mornings and at night. During the day, she was supplied with nothing more than a small jug of water, which she rationed to only a few sips every half hour or so.

Another day of darkness loomed as the door to the outside room closed decisively behind her and locked. She suppressed a violence and rage she didn't know lived inside her. She suppressed the urge to scream, pound, or kick down the door. She breathed out, willing herself to calm, and then slowly lowered her cumbersome body onto her back and closed her eyes. When she was able to find a comfortable position, sleep was a welcome relief from the endless hours of the day.

She found herself in the middle of a clearing, the only open space in an otherwise impenetrable forest. Slowly, she turned and searched for a pathway. There was none. Instead, she heard a rustling from the west, where the sun set. In between dense foliage, flashes of midnight black circled and menaced. She moved quickly and retreated in the opposite direction. She froze. There were muscular carnivores from this side too! She tried the north and then south. The beasts loomed in all four directions. Her heart thumped against her chest as she frantically searched for an escape route, but there was nowhere to run! No way could she outrun the feline! It would be a thousand times faster. She lowered into a squat and held her hands over her head in a vain attempt to hide.

The scene shifted. A bevy of black leopards surrounded her, each with a unique design of rosettes camouflaged in the midnight fur. The largest one neared, regal and dominant. It nudged its snout under her chin and licked her face. She threw her arms around its neck, and the tension in her body softened its grip. The muscular cat laid its head on her lap as she stroked its neck, drowning in its tawny eyes.

Three cats drew near. One dropped onto its haunches and began licking her toes. The dominant one snarled, a warning for the others to keep their distance. She sat up abruptly, tossing the majestic cat off her lap, and opened her arms. She fell back into a giant pile of felines and giggled. They licked her face, her arm, and her belly.

Isabela woke to the baby's kick—one, two, three, pause. She instinctively placed her hand on her abdomen. Images of lithe black cats remained in her mind, and the sensation of rough tongues brushing her toes and her face tickled her skin. Her dreams became more stable and vivid, while her ongoing reality adopted a more surrealistic quality. Sometimes, she wasn't certain whether she was awake or asleep. The dream world and the real one overlapped and intermixed. More than once, she thought to herself, *Now I am back in that place, the one I thought was a dream.*

The loss of a solid and absolute real world began to unnerve her. *Am I losing my mind?* Isabela tried to bring her attention to the ground beneath her. She raised her hands to feel the texture of her hair and her skin. She counted her fingers and reached down to feel her toes. Her attention narrowed to a thin strip of light that crept under the door, exposing an inch of a sunbeam. She realized it had been there every day, but she hadn't noticed it. She began quietly to pray. When the door to the closet opened in the evening, she was still praying. From that day forward, from the moment the door closed in the morning until evening when it reopened, she kept her eyes glued to the light seeping under the door while her lips repeated prayers from her childhood.

The Lord is my Shepherd; I shall not want.
He maketh me lie down in green pastures.
He leadeth me beside still waters.
He restoreth my soul.

Yea, though I walk through the valley of the
shadow of death, I will fear no evil,
For You are with me ...

Volker and Avery disappeared more frequently now, at first for only a few hours and then later for days. Volker left the young German, Albert, in charge of the hostage. Now the firm close of the front door and the grind of the deadbolt snapping into place made the hair on Isabela's arms stand straight up. Albert's rule in the absence of a higher authority marked a silent progression from sycophant to tyrant. With each departure, he became bolder and more confident.

"What I can do as soon as the brat is out! But why wait? Shh, shh, just a little more time."

His hand reached under her skirt and stroked her leg. Isabela flinched and drew her feet as close to her belly as she was able. Just then, Sunee emerged from the bathroom and took in the scene—the open closet door and the German almost on top of the pregnant woman. The German edged closer to Isabela and turned to stare at Sunee in a silent dare, and deliberately reached his hand under Isabela's blouse. Isabela pushed herself further up against the closet wall.

"Ayúdame, por favor!" *Help me, please!*

Sunee averted his face and floated away. Albert turned back toward the woman, released his hand from under her blouse, and held it across her throat. With his free hand, he thrust her skirt up to her waist and forced his stubby fingers around her cotton undergarments. Isabela cried out.

"Por favor ..." *Please ...*

"Keep your mouth shut, or when the brat comes, I'll make so it doesn't live, yah? An accident."

Isabela swallowed hard to hold down the vomit that rose in her throat. She forced her lips into a weak smile. The short German removed his finger and unzipped his pants and began to stroke himself. Isabela closed her eyes and bit her bottom lip, praying fervently for the protection of her unborn child. Her eyes opened momentarily to glimpse Sunee in the periphery of her vision, a phantom in the doorway of the living room.

Albert shoved his hand over her mouth, forcing her to suck air in through her nose. She held her breath and passed out, while her awareness floated up toward the ceiling, disembodied, weightless, observing the scene below.

Per Volker's protocol, at one a.m., Sunee attached the handcuff to Isabela's ankle and then to his own. This time, however, he lay with his torso facing the young pregnant woman. Light snoring from the room where Albert slept rose and deepened. Sunee reached over and lightly placed his hand on Isabela's arm and squeezed. Isabela felt her body freeze, a silent revolt to the impending violation.

Men without honor cannot touch my spirit or my heart.

Sunee's hand slid down the side of his body and released the handcuff, which he had purposelessly left open. His hand moved to undo the restraint around her ankle.

"Qué pasa?" *What's happening?* Sunee stood to tug on her arm as he held his finger to his lips. Isabela followed the direction, and her heart pounded. *Where does he want me to go? It can't be worse than here.*

Sunee reached for her hand. He quietly moved across the living area and into the foyer. The German guzzled whiskey like water all evening, and his snoring grew louder. Sunee unlocked the deadbolt knob, and a sharp clack echoed throughout the small house. The rattling breath stopped on a dime, and an uncanny silence ensued.

Sunee squeezed Isabela's hand, and she froze in place. The German wriggled onto his side, and rhythmic wheezing snorts began again. Sunee pushed the door open wide to let Isabela pass in front of him and then slid out after her.

It was a moonless night. Sunee removed a small flashlight from his pocket, illuminating a narrow fringe of light, just enough to see a few feet in front of them. Isabela's step was a waddle now, but with adrenaline, she kept up with the slender man. No words were exchanged. The two moved in tandem and with determined effort. Isabela followed, unsure of his motive and where he led her. To freedom or another prison? Would he sell her to the highest bidder? Take the money to fund his cause? She pressed herself to a fast pace, increasing the distance between herself and the small dark closet. Her chance of escape and hope for her child were far better here, on the run, than locked inside the closet. They walked throughout the night for indeterminable kilometers. It was still dark when the first birdsong trilled in the pre-dawn hour.

As soon as it's light, I'll find a way to distance myself from him. I'll find someone to help me. Until then, I will pray.

Isabela pushed to keep up, but it was harder to breathe now. She took quick sips of air as Sunee urged her to walk faster. The incessant pace of the night finally weighed on her. The muscles in her legs weakened, and her abdomen was heavy. Pain shot through her groin, and she doubled over until it subsided. Sunee glanced back and said something in a language she didn't understand. The pain rose, intensified, and then abated. *Por favor, not now!*

She picked up her pace, intent on reaching someone, anyone, who might help. Sunee stopped and pulled her off the road when he saw a car coming, the first they'd encountered that night. The vehicle sped by, but instead of moving back onto the road, Sunee motioned with his hand across a field. She could just barely make it out in the greying dawn. Her feet squished on … rice paddies? Her abdomen tightened, and pains shot across her belly in consistent, five-minute intervals just as dawn edged the sky to a light pinkish-orange.

They emerged from a field that smelled of freshly reaped grain. In the distance, a small village was just visible as a cluster of thatched-roofed huts on the side of the hill. Sunee pointed to it, and his eyes brightened. The distance, however, seemed impossible to Isabela. The contours of his face pale and cryptic face were now visible. *What did he want?* A contraction shot across her midsection as she leaned onto her thighs and stifled a scream. As soon as she was upright, Sunee pushed her into a forced trot.

They were less than a kilometer away, out of the rice paddies and on more solid ground, when an intense pain shot across her abdomen. She dropped to her knees. Sunee gesticulated toward the village and took off running. Isabela sank onto her hands and knees, panting, and then she dropped completely onto the ground.

Sunee returned, leading the Montagnard villagers to where the semi-conscious woman lay on the earth. Twigs and stones pressed into her skin. Her body felt like one solid, blasting pain as the baby's head, turned posterior, became stuck in the birth canal. She laid on a woven blanket as six men carried her, writhing, the kilometer to the village and into a small, thatched hut where several village women awaited. The men retreated.

Only candles lit the interior, and pungent herbs smoldered and stung her eyes. A middle-aged woman with callused hands reached toward Isabela and felt the crown of the baby's head. She withdrew her hand and began to press on Isabela's abdomen while Isabela screamed. The Montagnard's midwife chanted in the strange tongue of her ancestors, and still the baby did not come.

Chapter Fifty-Five

1962

Chiang Rai, Thailand

The U.S. Marine Colonel Edward Mitchell and Nigel Hawkes shook hands. The American Marines would continue clandestine air reconnaissance over Laos and Vietnam—all sanctioned by the Thai government.

Crispin waited outside the door as Nigel and the colonel exited.

"Sir, when you are finished, I'd like you to have a look at this," Crispin said.

Nigel shook the colonel's hand and turned to Crispin. "We're all done here. What do you have?"

"We just received communication from a Montagnard village along the border. They have a foreign woman in labor, and there is concern that the woman is in trouble. Nigel, this might be our girl."

"I want to attend to this personally. Order a helicopter and get the coordinates. And get me someone who speaks the dialect. I want to be airborne within an hour."

The aircraft hovered, searching for a spot large and clear enough to land, and then lightly set down just below the small village nestled against the hillside. The whirling whoosh and thump of the Sikorsky Sea King rotors quieted as the blades decelerated, circling slowly, to become once again individually defined. The pilot shut down the engine and settled back into his seat.

Nigel carefully stepped down, holding on to his hat that threatened to blow away. He was followed closely by the French interpreter, who was all he could drum up on such short notice. The village was a short climb up the hill, but a muddy and steep one. The interpreter reached the top within minutes while Nigel struggled, slipped, and grabbed onto any solid sapling or bush. He used his prosthetic leg for leverage and his good one to propel himself forward. The interpreter checked over his shoulder, then slid back down, and proffered his hand. When the two reached the outskirts of the village, Nigel was breathing hard.

"Thank you."

The interpreter spoke with the first villager they came upon, and the local man quickly led them through a maze of identical-looking huts. Nigel limped to stay close, but the stump of his left leg throbbed near the amputation site, just below the knee joint. Children appeared out of nowhere, surrounding the small entourage with loud voices and curious laughter. The self-appointed guide indicated with a nod at the designated hut set apart from the others.

Nigel bent down to enter the opening and adjusted his eyes from the bright light of day to the subdued interior. Isabela lay on her back, with one arm slung over the baby, who lay across her chest. The baby was still covered in a bloody mucus. Nigel recognized the Salvadorian woman immediately, although her face was gaunt and drained of color and her hair was matted. The poised, self-assured woman he had met with Jameson was completely redrawn. He approached the mat where she lay and slowly lowered himself beside her.

"Miss Marquez, we've had a bloody hard time locating you. Congratulations. By the look of things, you and Lance have a beautiful baby. I'd like to ask your permission to get the two of you to a hospital in Bangkok straightaway. I don't know how you managed to escape your captors, but we are very pleased you did."

Isabela lifted her arm to reach for Nigel's hand. He squeezed it and continued to hold on. Her voice shivered.

"She is perfect, yes?"

"Splendid. Absolutely exquisite. As beautiful as her mother."

The corners of Isabela's mouth raised a fraction.

"Promise me you'll bring the baby to her father. My parents cannot know. I am not the same. I want them to remember me the way things were. Please tell Jimmy her name is Mera ... Mera."

Isabela's grip on Nigel's hand tightened.

"Tell him I'm not afraid. We'll see each other on the other side of the boat line."

"There, there, my dear. Everything will be just fine. I will let Lance know he has a beautiful baby girl just as soon as he's stable. In the meantime, let's get you both on the helicopter. A baby needs its mother. You'll raise her yourself. Promise me that."

She tightened her grip until he thought perhaps his fingers might break. The source of her strength was a mystery. Her head moved slowly to the left, and Nigel bent closer. Her voice was labored and hoarse.

"Promise me?"

Blinking hard, he forced himself to smile while holding the delicate palm and lightly pressing damp hair from her forehead.

"Yes, love," he said.

"Don't you see it?" she said.

"See what, my dear?"

Isabela attempted to raise her head, with her hand lifting halfway.

"The temple. It's all around us. It's so beautiful."

Nigel looked around the small earthen hut, taking in the four indigenous women, the small doorway, and light streaming through cracks in the walls.

"Yes, yes, my dear. I see it."

The village midwife approached from the opposite side of the mat. She lifted the woven blanket. Isabela lay in a pool of her own blood. The village woman washed away the blood and applied a poultice of herbs between her legs. She poured water over her hands and gently washed the baby's face, arms, and legs without removing her from her mother.

Nigel still held Isabela's hand while he unclasped the walkie-talkie from his belt and barked into it.

"Get a stretcher up here, stat!"

Isabela's breath was raspy now. Her hands and feet turned an odd shade of blue as oxygen retreated from her extremities.

Nigel picked up the walkie-talkie again and shouted, "Where the bloody hell are you?"

Isabela's right hand released its grip, and Nigel saw she held two tiny carved animals, an elephant and a jaguar, on a thin leather cord.

Nigel rarely spoke about the cloudy, windswept day he spent in the small, thatched hut in the Montagnard village. It was the day he held the young Salvadorian woman's hand and watched her take leave of her body. He had the strange urge to jump in and go with her, so sure was he that she was on her way somewhere better.

The pilot and medic entered the hut with a stretcher and approached the mat. The medic leaned down to feel for the pulse on the young woman's neck. He shook his head and looked up at

Nigel, who stared at the wall. Nigel returned his gaze to the mat, where the village midwife gently separated the baby from its mother and wrapped her in a soft goatskin.

Nigel extended his arms to take the child. The woman handed the baby to him and turned back to the dead woman on the mat. As Nigel exited the hut, he felt a light tap on his shoulder. The midwife placed the small wooden carvings into his free hand and turned to join the village women, who gathered around Isabela's body. A soft chanting arose. Nigel placed the carvings into his front pocket and stooped low to press the child close to his heart. At the doorway, he stopped and looked back.

"Bring the body as soon as they are finished," he said to the medic. The man nodded and followed him outside.

"Do you want us to bring her now?" the medic asked.

"Wait until the women are done. We still have a few hours of daylight."

Chapter Fifty-Six

1977

El Salvador

Ángel nodded once and guided Mera forward, shining the flashlight so both could see the path. He moved quickly, urging her to move faster when her pace slowed.

The night seemed endless, a continual darkness that seemed to foreshadow only doom and destruction. Did an hour pass? Or was it three? Surely, the sun should rise soon! Mera stopped suddenly and collapsed onto the ground. She didn't care anymore. Let him do what he would do. Ángel turned and knelt down beside her. He spoke close to her ear, as if someone might overhear.

"We can't stay here! We need to keep moving! My brother is no friend of Dino's. I'm hoping he'll help both of us."

She glanced over her shoulder, but there was only darkness. Her body trembled, and her teeth tapped rapidly, despite the heat and humidity.

"Do whatever you want. I'm not walking anymore." She spoke with no inflection or emotion.

Ángel shone the flashlight on her wrists and placed it under his arm as he worked to free the ties that bound her hands together.

Mera shook out her hands to stimulate blood flow back into them. Her heart began to race at the opportunity that seemed to present itself, but still she was unsure. Ángel was only inches away from her. The snap of twigs crackled as Ángel stepped anxiously from one foot to the other, and Mera could feel his eyes riveted upon her in the darkness. She calculated her next move. With renewed energy, Mera jumped up and grabbed Ángel's hand. He quickly took the lead, still holding her hand as they moved northeast.

After a while, she found the rhythm and joy of movement returning. They kept walking, trotting, and stopping periodically as Ángel checked the compass heading to readjust their direction. He noticed the girl kept up without the need to rest, so he made the decision to keep going until they reached his brother's house. He knew his older sibling was not to be trusted, but he might help them for a price.

Ángel couldn't say why he suddenly ignored Dino's instructions and risked everything for a strange girl. He didn't have hope for himself anymore. He had already committed monstrous acts that could never be fully redeemed. Maybe it was because of the way he found her, kneeling and broken. He trotted through the woods, wondering all the while how the hell he would pull this off.

When it was finally bright enough to see the outline of the girl without the flashlight, Ángel switched it off and stopped to reassess their location. Rumblings of tires on gravel instantly brought his index finger to his lips. He recognized the area. They were half a kilometer from his brother's house. It was important to be vigilant now. There were too many prying eyes. Dino might have friends in the neighborhood. The girl stayed close behind him. He could feel the warmth of her breath on his neck. As they neared the house, he motioned for her to stay low and out of sight, and then with a last look around, he walked quickly to the door of his brother's house. José sat at the kitchen table, with the stub of a cigarette in his left hand and a can of beer indented by his right.

"¿Hola, como estás, hermano?" *Hello, how are you, brother?* Ángel greeted his half-brother with as much affection as he could muster.

"Ángel? What are you doing here? Where are your mercenary friends?"

"Don't worry. I'm alone. I need some help and … I have money."

José's eyes narrowed. "What kind of problem are you bringing to my door?"

"I need a place for the girl to stay a few hours while I figure things out," Ángel said.

"What girl?"

Ángel motioned toward the edge of the forest. He reached into his pocket, pulled out some colones, and extended the wad of bills to José.

"I'll come back for her tonight. I promise we'll be out of your house then."

José pocketed the money and lit the stub of his cigarette. "Just one day. Then I forget I have a brother. Understand?"

José watched as Ángel brought the girl in from the forest. Her dark hair was matted and wild. Mud splattered her legs, and there was a large bruise on her right cheek. She was unusually tall, but quite attractive. His eyes slithered, calculating the boon that just landed on his doorstep. He motioned for the girl to come inside.

"Bring her upstairs. She can sleep. By the looks of her, she won't wake up until you get back. I'll get her something to eat later."

Ángel took Mera upstairs and down the short hallway. "I'll be back for you as soon as I can."

Mera eyed the mat on the floor, and as soon as the door closed, she dropped her skirt and blouse and threw them in a heap at the bottom of the mat. Quietly, she lowered herself onto the mat. Within minutes, she was fast asleep.

Ángel lunged down the stairs two steps at a time, moving quickly through the house toward the front door. José eyed Ángel from his seat at the kitchen table and took a last drag from his cigarette.

"Thank you for the cash," he said. Ángel stopped and turned to face his brother as he spoke. "I'll take it as a down payment. Get back here by ten. Otherwise, the deal is off—"

"Gracias, hermano!" *Thank you, brother!* Ángel forced his lips to smile. "I'll be back as soon as I can." He closed the door quietly behind him and walked quickly toward the bus stop a quarter of a mile down the road.

Chapter Fifty-Seven

1962

Near Brooke Army Facility, San Antonio, Texas

Hanna opened the mailbox and pulled out two advertisements, a couple of bills, a birthday card, and a large manila envelope folded to fit into the small box. She quickly sorted through the mail and sucked in her breath, jamming everything but the large manila envelope back. Red stamps with dancing gold tigers adhered to the top right corner. Thailand!

The thick envelope was addressed to Lance Jameson, in care of one Hanna Chang. She held the envelope for a minute before opening it, imagining his excitement to finally receive the long-awaited letters. Should she stretch it out and bring him one every day? She swallowed hard. The twelve letters were tightly bound with a light blue ribbon, the envelopes postmarked and dated with U.S. stamps and addressed in her own looped black script. A white piece of paper was folded three times and lay atop the bundle. As Hanna reached for it, a small business card fluttered to the floor. She bent over, picked up the card without looking at it, slowly opened the sheet, and scanned the contents.

Dear Mr. Jameson,

We are so terribly sorry to inform you that Isabela Marquez will not be able to receive your letters, and we therefore return them to you. We held your correspondence in anticipation of Miss Isabela's return to our guesthouse. However, it is with the greatest regret we inform you of a terrible car accident up on the southern border of Laos. We are burdened to inform you that Miss Isabela died instantly in the crash. Due to the severity of the accident, her body was cremated, and her remains were returned back to her home country, El Salvador, accompanied by her father. Mr. Marquez left his business card, and we have included a copy of it here in case you would like to contact the family.

Everyone at the hotel loved Miss Isabela, and we share your profound grief at her very untimely death.

Please accept our deepest condolences,
Mr. Gamon Pradchaphet, The Chiang Mai Guest house

Hanna pressed her back against the wall and slowly lowered herself to the stone floor. She held the letters close to her chest and stared out across the hallway. Fifteen minutes passed before she heard the key to the front door engage and her mother enter the corridor.

"Hanna, 你在做什麼呢？快從地板站起來!" *What are you doing? Get up off the floor!*

Chapter Fifty-Eight

1962

Brooke Army Facility, San Antonio, Texas

Anne approached her husband's bed and lightly kissed the top of his head, smoothed the sheets around him, and tucked them tightly. Lance, propped up by several pillows, winced, but didn't protest.

"Hello, darling. I just heard some fantastic news from the young nurse, Hanna. We'll have to wait for the doctor to confirm, but it looks like we may finally have a release date. I've taken care of everything so you just need to concentrate on healing."

"Hello, Anne. Actually, I've already had a word with my doctors, and they seem to be in agreement that if I continue to progress, a mid-June release date is realistic."

"That's wonderful, darling. Then it's all set. I've asked my father for a leave of absence until you are stronger, to begin as soon as you are released."

"Anne, do you have a moment? There are things we need to discuss."

"Can it wait a bit longer? A few days? I have an early appointment tomorrow morning, and it looks like I'm going to have another jam-packed week. Let's bask in the anticipation of your homecoming before we jump into logistics. All right, darling?"

"I'm afraid it can't wait. I've procrastinated beyond redemption. Please, sit down." He sighed before continuing. "I want a divorce. I hope it can be an amicable one, but I won't protest if you feel the need to drag me through the mud. I want you to know that you have done nothing wrong. You have been incredible throughout this whole mess. If there's blame, it falls entirely on my shoulders. I take full responsibility. I hope one day you will forgive me. I understand if you don't. Whatever I can do to make things right, I'll do it. I am forever in your debt and beyond appreciative of everything you have done for me over these past months. I can't begin to imagine how hard it must have been for you to consult with the doctors, hospital, and government agencies, all the while, working your full-time job. You have protected my interests at every turn. You are an accomplished, competent and, I might add, extremely beautiful woman. I am forever amazed at what you make happen. Anne, any man would be lucky to have you."

"Any man but you?" Anne said. "Lance, darling, please don't say anything you might regret. You have been through an incredible ordeal, an agonizing nightmare. We both have. I simply will not listen to any crazy thoughts you entertain. Later, when you are home, you'll see everything will be just fine. It may take some time, but our life will one day resume its expected course."

"Anne, please listen carefully. You are a wonderful woman. I mean that sincerely. There was a time when I thought we shared a similar vision and ambition." Lance paused and purposefully pulled out the tightly tucked sheets. "A lot happened in Thailand, not just the crash. The experience and my time there rekindled something I thought was dead and buried in me, but it turns out, it's the very essence of … I'm sorry I was not physically able to speak to you sooner, but none of this has to do with my condition, the crash, or a passing fancy. As soon as the mission was complete, I was going to come back and present you with the same request. I will agree to any and all demands. I want you to have the house and all our shared holdings." Lance readjusted his position, winced, and then looked directly into Anne's eyes. "I won't be coming home after my release from the hospital. I am asking for an amicable divorce. I won't fight you on anything. None of this is your fault. Say what you will to the court and let the proceedings be set in motion. When I leave here, I've arranged to go to a rehab facility until I am strong enough to fend for myself. You are off the hook. Just hire a lawyer. Have him draw up the papers, and I'll sign them."

Anne stood up, smoothing sheets and pulling the thin blanket up around Lance's chest, tightly wrapping his lower body once again like a mummy.

"We'll speak of this another time, darling. I'm sure when all the facts come to light, you'll see things quite differently. For the moment, I'll have no talk of divorce. In fact, I am going to forget you even mentioned it. If you feel the same later, we'll speak again, but I don't think you will. Rest now, my darling."

"All right, Anne, as long as it takes for you to come to terms."

Anne stepped into the hallway as her thoughts drifted back to her encounter with the British special ops agent, Nigel Hawkes, almost six months ago. Mr. Hawkes had approached her and initiated a polite conversation. At the time, her husband was still in a medically induced coma while they monitored his condition in the ICU for complications from first-, second-, and third-degree burns.

Nigel said he "was just passing by, a few days' stop" on his way back to southeast Asia from England. He wondered if he might have a word with her. Would she like to join him for a glass of wine later that evening? Anne accepted. She had many questions and logistical concerns. Perhaps she would finally get some answers surrounding the accident and any possible wrongdoing on the government's end. What she hadn't anticipated, however, was learning that her husband had an illegitimate baby.

Nigel said he was wont to interfere in the personal affairs of his officers, but the situation required unusual action. The child's mother was dead. While the child was currently being cared for, the responsibility for the child now rested solely with her father. He realized this was a shock and, of course, would give her time to digest what he just told her. But the fact remained: the father must be informed of the child's existence as soon as he was awake, stable, and cognizant.

Anne remembered her next words precisely. "I don't need time, as you say, to digest this unfortunate development. These things happen. I'm sorry it happened to us. My husband's condition is my primary concern. When he is brought out of the coma, he will require months of arduous therapy. I will not have him concerned about anything other than his recovery. I'm sure the infant has a family. An aunt, an uncle, grandparents? I'm quite sure they'll take the baby in, especially if it comes with funds for its care."

Anne recalled Nigel's quick response and breathed a sigh of relief.

"The child is being well cared for. There's no need for you to concern yourself about that. I respect the burden of your husband's care and recovery. Once he is home and out of danger, however, can I have your assurance that you will inform him of the child?"

Her response, she recalled, was authoritative and purposefully dismissive. "We will cross that bridge when my husband is able to function and respond in an appropriate way. Until then, please respect our privacy. For any and all concerns regarding this matter, please contact me at my office."

Chapter Fifty-Nine

1963

Washington, D.C.

Anne glanced at her watch. Damn! It was already five p.m. Her last client of the day, Mr. Benson, had a propensity for detail and demanded nothing less from the organizations and companies with which he conducted business.

"Will you excuse me for just a moment? This is going to take a bit longer than I anticipated. I need to let my husband know I'm running late."

"Of course."

Anne dialed, calculating when she would reach home. The phone jangled, yet with an odd, hollow quality. After eight or nine attempts to connect, she gently set the phone in its cradle, arched her neck to one side, and sighed.

"Mr. Benson, where was I? Ah yes, we need to be sure there are no surprises when we meet with Miles Laboratory on Monday. We want to be sure the negotiations swing in our favor."

The usual thirty-minute drive from the office to home inched like the second hand on a clock with a dying battery. Anne recalled the events since Lance was released from the hospital three months ago.

He took up cooking and, surprisingly, drawing. There *was* something to say for a spouse who stayed home. Not forever, mind you, yet after a laborious day of interminable negotiations, it was quite agreeable to come home and have dinner on the table. She smiled. When her husband put his mind to something, you could be sure it would be mastered. Last evening, he emerged from the kitchen with a sizzling Dijon-encrusted salmon atop wild rice, accompanied by a medley of sautéed vegetables, and there was a chilled bottle of Pinot Noir on the table. It was one of the most enjoyable evenings she could remember.

After arduous months of physical and occupational therapy, her husband's recovery neared the ninety-percent mark. He was now ambulatory, and although his hips gave him trouble at night, he only walked with a slight limp. Best of all, the skin on his face had regenerated, with negligible scarring, and only his left hand still required daily manipulations to alleviate nighttime stiffness. Another few months, she mused, and everything would return to a semblance of normality. Of course, he still spoke of leaving from time to time, of going their separate ways, but she felt assured he would come to his senses and settle back easily into the life they envisioned for their future.

Lance told her about the affair and his infatuation with the woman. Anne was not naïve. She understood aspects of the male character and especially servicemen so long away from home. She presumed and even expected dalliances with other women. Men, in her view, were weak creatures. It was natural and to be expected. She believed his candor and her ability to forgive these small transgressions were basic prerequisites for a successful relationship. If he hadn't been upfront with her, well, then that would have been a problem. But he had come clean. She anticipated their relationship would only get stronger, having withstood this particular bump in the road.

She wasn't sure how he learned the woman in Thailand had died. She considered telling him but, after thorough reflection, realized nothing good could be accomplished in her being the bearer of sad news. Eventually, the news would reach him. It was much better for it to come from an unbiased source. A little patience and everything would fall into place, back to the way it was.

However, she knew the precise moment he learned of her death. It was the day he agreed to come home. Of course, he was disheartened. That was to be expected. The death of someone young who you'd once known intimately was always a shock.

Lance moved into the guest room on his discharge day. They both agreed it would be best for the healing process. He was awake most nights, the bedding knotted, twisted, and, more often than not, hurled to the floor. One night, after consuming a half a bottle of tequila, her husband returned to their bedroom and performed the sexual act with mindless brutality, but it was a start. She straddled him, using the aggressive energy to her advantage, and they finished, both covered in sweat and breathing hard.

Now, she hoped she might be pregnant. The timing was right. She had always planned to have a baby. It was what one did, but they both agreed to put it on hold until they'd reached the stratum of power and influence they anticipated. Once they had a baby of their own, she reasoned, some foreign child, born out of wedlock and far away, would become just a check to write every once in a while—a child that belonged to someone else.

I'll wait before informing him about the bastard child. We need time to get our relationship back on track. I'm sure when he is able to see the situation from my point of view, he will understand my hesitancy to burden him with an obligation he was in no position to handle.

However, the crash was a serious setback, and one had to be flexible. Given the situation, the timing of a pregnancy could not be more perfect. She smiled and turned the car into the driveway. Strange, there seemed to be a vacuum, a hollowed emptiness, that followed her up the steps. She inserted her key into the lock and opened the door. The house was dark, except for the hall light in the passageway.

"Lance?"

Anne entered the living room and looked around, apprehension gnawing at the edges of her stomach. Obviously, he had gone out, but why hadn't he left a message? Ah, maybe he had, and her brainless secretary forgot to give it to her. Damn her! She proceeded into the kitchen. A single sheet of white typewriter paper stood starkly against the green marbled countertop. She thumbed on the switch and slowly retrieved the paper to scan the contents. She read the note three times, then four, her breaths becoming more painful until she could barely breathe at all for the massive thumping of her heart.

Dear Anne,

I have left. I am sorry to depart in this manner, but, in my feeblest defense, I have tried to talk to you on more than one occasion, and you just wouldn't hear it. Although we began our relationship with a similar vision and life purpose, things changed, at least for me. This has nothing, yet everything, to do with Isabela, the woman I met in Thailand. Although she is no longer in this world, she, along with a rich tapestry of encounters, struggles, and occurrences shaped a different universe for me—one I choose to walk alone. You are a resourceful and competent woman. I hope our separation will be a mere blip in your life. I'd like to know that you will be happy and live the life of your dreams.

I left divorce papers signed in the office desk drawer and copies with my lawyer, Jeffrey Oliver. Full ownership of the house, cars, joint bank accounts, and all personal household contents have been transferred into your name. I retain ownership of my father's inheritance. Please do not look for me. The Lance Jameson you knew no longer exists.

For all it's worth, I do love, respect, and appreciate you beyond measure. Thank you for everything we shared and all you have done for me these past months. I do not await your forgiveness; hate me if you will, but I will always hold you in the highest esteem.

Lance

Anne folded the note in two and collapsed onto the sofa. At eight o'clock the next morning, when the sound of the phone shattered the silence, she was still in the same spot. Anne pushed herself up and moved quickly across the room, lifting the phone to her ear.

"Hello?" She held her breath.

"Anne? Nigel Hawkes here. How are you, my dear? I hope this is a convenient time? If not, I can ring back later."

Anne exhaled slowly before responding. "It's okay," she said.

"And how is our boy? I was most pleased to hear of his progress. On that note, I wonder if the subject we spoke about last time we talked has been broached … about the child? If he isn't au courant, I'm afraid I must insist he be apprised of the child's existence and location. Decisions must be made. The deference is to the biological father as the child's mother is dead. I respected your privacy and Lance's condition. However, now that he is home and you are both back in Washington, I really must press the issue."

"I'm sorry we waited, but it's a moot point now."

CHAPTER FIFTY-NINE

"Come again?"

"Lance walked out yesterday."

"I'm terribly sorry to hear that."

She swallowed hard, a surge of bile rising steadily up her throat.

"I don't believe even you will find him. It's all in the note. I think he's been planning this ever since he learned of her death, maybe even before that. He said not to look for him." A quiet sob escaped.

"Would it be best to ring back later?"

"No, it would be best if I could hand the phone to him. Other than that, now is as good as later."

"All right then, what was in the note that makes you think he disappeared?"

"*Don't try and find me ... the Lance Jameson you knew no longer exists.*"

"My dear, I'm afraid if Lance does not want to be found, that's the end of it. He's learned from the best."

"The baby ... I can write a check and cover expenses for the child."

"Thank you, Anne. That is so kind of you, considering the circumstances. However, I'm afraid the responsibility is now mine. Money was never the issue. The child has a wealthy benefactress who set up a trust in her name. It's quite substantial."

"You know Lance in a way that I never did. Do you expect he will resurface and return to his old life?"

There was a pause on other end of the line before Nigel spoke. "I am sorry, my dear. I know you've been through your own personal nightmare. I sincerely hope he will, for all our sakes."

Chapter Sixty

1977

San Salvador, El Salvador

Mera waited at the rural bus stop, shooting intermittent, nervous glances to her left, right, and even behind her. She hopped from one foot to the other, ready to leap on the cherry-red bus to San Salvador that rumbled toward her. The bus, enhanced with a super-sized Jesus that smiled benevolently from the rear, slowed to a stop. She stuck her hand in her pocket and touched the wad of colones she'd taken from the padre's room. She hoped it would be enough to disappear in a city of so many people.

Her father had never allowed her to visit the big city. He said it was too far away, too busy for a young girl, but he promised he would take her there one day. She had pestered him with a thousand questions every time he returned from a trip. How many automobiles? How many people? She was fascinated by the idea of a million people. He told her it was hard to breathe in the city. Now, she hoped she might find some kind of work in the city to make enough to sleep and eat while she searched for David, Rosita, and her father.

Her mind returned to her narrow escape from Ángel's brother's house. She probed her shoulder with her fingers, which still ached from the second-story drop onto the ground. The fall had stunned her for a moment. Despite the pain, she recognized the need to distance herself quickly from José, and even Ángel, even though he had helped her. She remembered running and using the afternoon sun's western arc as her directional guide. A car had sped down the country road across from her hidden vantage place, but she suppressed the urge to run out and wave it down. Instead, she remained hidden. After watching it disappear around the corner, she continued running for several kilometers along the forest's edge. She only dared to emerge from the woods when a young couple holding hands came into view. Their lips barely parted from kissing each other long enough for them to take a breath.

"Please, do you know where I can get the bus to San Salvador?" she asked, glancing over her shoulder and then to both sides. "Is it nearby?"

The young man nodded down the road. "You can hop on about half a kilometer back that way. Out here, it only comes by once a day. But you're in luck. It should be passing by at five o'clock, give or take, which is in about forty-five minutes."

He immediately returned his gaze and lips to his lover as the two continued to stroll in the opposite direction.

Mera returned to the edge of the woods to head back the way she came, keeping her eyes peeled on the road. She reached a vantage point opposite the bus stop and only emerged onto the road when she glimpsed the refurbished and repainted school bus rumbling down the road in her direction.

Mera chose a seat on the bus, careful to remain up front and close to the door. Every so often, she glanced over her shoulder, checking to make sure no one looked at her. Seated next to her, by the window, a young mother nursed her baby. Other passengers slept. Nearby bits of laughter, conversation, and English rock-and-roll music drifted to her from the back end of the bus. No one seemed interested in the girl with mud splattered across her face and blouse. The bus followed country roads and eventually began its precarious climb, navigating narrow serpentine turns for several hours before beginning its long descent. Mera held the baby for its mother. She hummed a song her mother used to sing to her when she was little more than a baby herself. Instantly, she felt her mother's callused hands smoothing the top of her head and remembered the soft tones of her mother's voice. She squeezed her eyes shut to keep tears from spilling down her cheeks. Outside, the rain splattered the window, and she inhaled sharply upon seeing the sprawling lights of the city for the first time. It was a mesmerizing display. She nudged the young mother next to her and pointed, her eyes now bright and inquisitive. The young mother patted her arm and smiled.

Mera stepped off the bus in the terminal, walked a few paces, and stopped. She looked around nervously. Which way? She noticed the woman from the bus with her baby and moved quickly toward her.

"Por favor, do you know a place where I can sleep?"

"Where is your family?" the woman asked. "Aren't they coming to welcome you?"

"I'm alone. I don't have family in the city."

The woman sighed, peering closely at the girl before continuing. "You are welcome in our house for a night. I will tell my husband. Just one night. That's all I can do."

The woman spoke quickly to her husband, who shook his head and glanced over his shoulder to stare at Mera. The woman motioned for Mera to come. Mera hesitated. Her mouth was dry, and her stomach flipflopped. She quickly trotted after the retreating couple with their baby.

The woman showed her to the bathroom and gave her a large shirt to sleep in. Mera left her clothes in a pile on the bathroom floor and then lay on the woven straw mat just outside the kitchen where the woman indicated for her to rest. The next day, a full seventeen hours after Mera fell asleep on the mat, she awoke to the baby crying beside her. She picked up the cloth-wrapped infant and wiped sleep from her eyes. Mera watched as her new friend made tortillas and spooned a plate of rice and beans on top of a warm one. She handed the steaming plate to Mera.

"Eat something and then clean yourself. I washed your clothes. You will need to leave before my husband comes back from work. He will be angry if you are still here."

Mera hugged the woman and thanked her for her kindness.

"Is there someone you can call?" the woman asked.

Mera shook her head slowly, but then Father Guillermo's face and the small, yellowed card he'd tried to give her came to mind. It had only been preserved because it was with the colones she took. She wasn't sure how a small piece of paper could possibly help, but it was at least a start.

Leaving the house, Mera felt oddly refreshed, with her hair soaped, rinsed, and shiny. Some color returned to her face. She retraced her steps through the crowded streets from the day before, back to the bus station. The woman told her there was an office at the bus station where she could make a phone call to anywhere. Just give the clerk the number and they would transfer the call to a private booth in the station.

There had never been a need to use a telephone. Mera's family didn't own one. She withdrew the card from her pocket and looked once again at the strange lettering in English. She couldn't make anything out. She knew how to read. Often times, children several years older had asked for her help in school, but the strange name Nigel Hawkes might as well have been printed in the raised dots of braille.

She waited her turn in line and then timidly approached the man at the desk. She placed the card on the counter between them and spoke. Her voice rose barely above a whisper. "Por favor, can you tell me what this says?"

"Señorita, you need to speak louder. I can hardly hear you."

She repeated, her voice an octave higher, "Please, can you tell me what this says?"

The man picked up the card and read the name. "Do you want to speak with this man?"

"Sí, sí, señor, por favor." *Yes, yes, sir, please.*

The clerk was kind and explained the international calling protocol. The village girl was obviously unfamiliar with the system. Afterwards, he pointed to the booth where she would receive the call.

She jumped when the phone rang.

"Nigel Hawkes speaking."

Mera breathed into the mouthpiece, unsure how to respond. Finally, "Me llamo Mera Rodríguez." *My name is Mera Rodríguez.*

The pause was imperceptible as recollections flooded Nigel's awareness. He responded immediately in Spanish, calculating how old she must be. Fourteen, fifteen? The baby and her mother were a subject he'd firmly tucked away and seldom revisited.

He had done what he could for the child. He procured American and El Salvadoran passports and made sure the baby was supplied with every required legal document. It was the least he could do. The new American operative, Kate Morgan, lined everything up for Mera's care. She located an honest, hardworking family to care for the baby in a quiet, local village. Nigel assigned Crispin to fly the child back to the mother's home country. In the place of covert maps, guns, and ammunition, Crispin's suitcases were filled with diapers, bottles, formula, baby clothes, and blankets. The recollection echoed.

"Bloody hell, Hawkes, y'er not gonna inform the girl's parents?" Crispin asked.

"I gave my word. A mother's dying wish, wasn't it?"

Crispin had not been opposed to the assignment. When his mother passed away years earlier, he had easily assumed the role of parent to his younger siblings. He was adored by all of them.

Two weeks passed caring for Isabela's child before all the proper documentation was obtained in Thailand. He spent another ten days in El Salvador, waiting. He woke in the night to soothe the infant. Crispin grew attached to her in the short time he'd spent caring for her. He swore she smiled at him, even though she was only a few days old. He boasted like any proud parent that she was the most exceptional baby! He informed Señor Rodríguez that someone would come for the child, either her father, her aunt, or perhaps himself. But, when the day arrived to leave the child, as instructed, he set the bassinet down by the front door, knocked three times, and disappeared into the darkness. On his return, Crispin factually recounted the series of events as if it was a post-debriefing from any mission.

It was three years before Nigel was able to visit El Salvador and the small village. In that time, no trace of Lance surfaced. Nigel called in a few favors and, off the record, initiated a search for his operative. He thought he would find him. When he didn't, he could not deny the possibility that Lance Jameson had been murdered.

He arranged to meet Señor Rodríguez after church on a Sunday when the whole family was assembled and happily engaged, playing, socializing, and sharing food. Nigel picked the child out immediately. She stood out among her darker siblings and the other village children. A halo of dark brown curls feathered her face, and he could already see she would be tall like her father. Nigel didn't stay long. He didn't need to. Her little body barely touched the earth, passed from one family member to the next as laughter pealed and resounded in the church courtyard. There was no mistaking a happy and well-cared-for child and a loving family.

He apologized profusely for the terrible lapse in communication. Both her father and mother were dead. Would the Rodríguezes be able to care for and raise the girl? Make sure she was educated? He would provide all financial support necessary for her welfare. Señor Rodríguez shook his head. No, no! They loved little Mera as their own and didn't require any assistance. The farm was doing well, and his family was blessed. Gracias a Dios! The farm afforded them an abundant and full life. Mera would go to school with her brothers and sister when she was old enough, he assured Nigel. She would have every opportunity.

Nigel asked to have a word with the child.

"Hello, Mera. My name is Nigel. You are a very pretty girl. I see you like to run!"

Mera responded by racing to the end of the churchyard and returning, breathing hard.

"I run very fast! Papa says I run fast, like a jaguar!"

"Indeed, you do! Would you like a sweet? I brought these for you." Mera's eyes widened.

"For my brothers and my sister too?" she asked.

"Of course, for all of you."

"Hello, Mera," he said into the phone, wishing the conversation was face to face. "My name is Nigel Hawkes. I was a friend of your mother's. Are you … is everything all right?"

"You knew my mother?" Mera began to cry softly.

"Yes, I knew her quite well."

"They killed Mama … the men with guns. She is gone now."

"Where are you?"

"The phone box at the bus station." Giant tears splashed onto her dress.

"What city?"

"San Salvador, señor."

"Where is your family? Your father?"

"I'm alone. There is no one."

"Do you have money?" Nigel asked.

Mera's fingers delved into her pocket, assuring once again the wrapped bills were still intact.

"Yes, I have some."

"Mera, listen carefully. Find a small guesthouse near the bus station and stay there. Check with the office where you are now each morning. I'm going to transfer money there, and you can pick it up later this afternoon. Find out where the American Embassy is." He spoke slowly, carefully. "When I have everything arranged, I will leave word for you. Then go to the American Embassy. Give your name at the gate and everything will be taken care of."

Mera nodded. Her lips closed.

"Can you do that?"

"Sí … La Embajada Americana?" *Yes … The American Embassy?*

An angle of light caught her peripheral vision and drew her attention from the phone at her ear to the street outside. A young man strolled past the window of the station. His sharp nose and rounded shoulder were oddly familiar and then unmistakable. A twin-toned dragon tattoo spiraled up the man's hairless bicep. Mera doubled over to hide below the booth's window.

"Help me! He is here! He is coming for me!"

"Leave the phone and go to the man at the desk," Nigel said. "I will have someone there to help you as quickly as I can. Stay behind the desk. Do not leave the building!"

"He will kill me if he finds me." Mera's voice lowered to a scratch, barely audible, as if Dino might hear through the walls from the street outside.

Mera slowly raised her head, assessing the distance to the desk and the man behind it. She looked out the window and saw a second young man saunter past the telephone office at the bus depot. She blinked several times to clear her eyes and leaned forward to look closer. When he stopped directly opposite the window and turned his head to look behind him, she noticed that the young man's hair was cropped short. His skin was burnished by the sun, and he looked thinner than she remembered. A low, gurgling sound formed deep within her chest that expanded into a loud wail. The phone dropped from her hand and dangled back and forth carelessly. She jumped up, pushed open the door to the booth, and lunged for the outside just as Nigel's disembodied voice rose to a wiry crescendo through the telephone speaker box.

Nigel slowly set the phone down and crossed the room to rummage through his desk. He pulled out a small black notebook from the top drawer and quickly flipped through the pages until he found what he was looking for. He dialed the international number in El Salvador. After filling in his contact with the pertinent details about Mera, he was assured that the local army would do everything possible to locate the girl and get her to a safe place. Then he made a flight reservation and began to pack. As he set shirts, trousers, socks, and shoes into his bag, his mind wandered back to the days after Isabela Marquez died giving birth in the small Montagnard hut on the Laotian border.

Before what the Americans called the Vietnam War, the interest of the CIA in southeast Asia focused on the incursion and spread of communism. It was considered imperative that the United States gain access to the panhandle in southern Laos, and the CIA needed to enlist the Laotian district commanders. Unfortunately, the district commanders had their own agendas. Their willingness to cooperate with the West came at a price. Nigel had understood that. The CIA supplied the district commanders with military might to protect the area. If they hadn't, the Chinese or North Vietnamese would have moved into the area and taken control. Nigel's job had been to gather intel and pass it along through military channels. He didn't question it. But the expansion of opium production and its distribution throughout the world increased significantly during and after the Vietnam War. Illicit drug abuse penetrated the heart of America. Nigel had plenty of time now to look back and consider the implications of the war and his part in it.

It had not been difficult to locate the young Vietnamese man who helped Isabela escape from her captors. Nigel interviewed the youth personally. He learned Sunee was taken from his family by the drug cartel in his teenage years. Although Sunee worked with the gang for some time, he had no love or allegiance to the band with whom he worked. He worked for the money, and he was able to send some back to his family. Volker had convinced him that his family would be safer with the cartel's protection. In exchange for the names of the gang, Sunee was given immunity and enough money to relocate his family to a remote area. He supplied the team with the names of the gang and the locations of their hideout places. The team picked up the American, Avery, and his German counterpart, Albert, easily. At the time, he wished for the power to put an end to their petty, useless existence. Instead, each was extradited to his respective country to await trial. Locating Volker, the head of the band of kidnappers, had been a lot trickier. The minute Volker had an inkling of the massive hunt to uncover his whereabouts, he dove deep into the underground, like a fish avoiding the lure about to hook him, and somehow managed to disappear.

On the other side of the world, it had been a month before the doctors felt the severely injured American was stable enough to bring him out of his medically induced coma and then another few weeks before a CIA agent was sent in to debrief him. The debrief was a slow and arduous process due to the burn treatment Lance was under and the extreme pain he experienced.

It slowly unraveled that the Laotian district commander Lance visited in the panhandle was expanding his little empire into a massive opium production and distribution kingdom with the help of his new friends, the Americans. Volker and his friends had been only a small cog in a giant wheel.

Nigel remembered sending in the report, implicating the Laotian district commander as an up-and-coming drug lord and the possible uses of American arms and military equipment. There was no response to the report. Later, he inquired about it. He was told that no further action was required.

Chapter Sixty-One

1977

San Salvador, El Salvador

The crowd was thick with cars honking, swerving in and around each other for no apparent gain, idling, and then moving forward in meters, rather than kilometers. Mera thrust her way through the swarm of people, passing workmen and vendors peddling their wares. Her eyes were frantic as she stared out and into the crowd of people. The faded red T-shirt skimmed in and out of sight. An old woman, a sack of groceries balanced in each hand, stumbled as Mera pushed by her, sending two apples and a tube of toothpaste rolling onto the sidewalk. The old lady fell to her knees, screaming obscenities as Mera retreated farther down the street.

She was closer now and could see that he wore blue jeans and rubber boots that reached almost to the top of his calves. Even though he was thin, the muscles in his arms were more defined than she remembered. *It has to be him. Please let it be him!* The space between them shortened until she came up behind him. Her eyes probed for the small birthmark under his right ear. Once she saw it, she sprang up onto his back, without a care who she knocked out of the way. She wrapped her long legs around his waist and cried out.

"David! Gracias a Dios, hermano!" *Thank God, brother.* She squeezed tightly, cutting off circulation to his neck.

David jolted and violently shook his body until the girl reluctantly released her grip and slid onto her feet.

"Gracias a Dios. Gracias a Dios ..." *Thank God. Thank God ...*

Mera searched his eyes. "David?" She stepped back, quietly studied the contours of his face, and noticed for the first time a jagged scar that ran from cheekbone to jaw. "David, qué pasó?" *What happened?*

She ran her finger lightly along the raw, reddened gouge. He slapped her hand away and pushed her forward without a word. She had so many questions she wanted to ask but silenced them at the sight of her brother's set shoulders and the tight line of his jaw. Mera stopped to quietly reach and touch his face again, assuring herself that he was solid, real. They were together now. That was the important thing. Later, he'd tell her what happened. He grabbed her wrist and pulled her arm violently. Mera resisted.

"David, please! I've been so scared. There is a very bad man looking for me. We need to go back to the bus station."

David shouted as the roaring city traffic consumed his words.

"Mera, what are you doing here? You need to go back to the village now. Otherwise, I can't help you. Do you understand?"

Mera remained rigid. Her arm extended fully as David yanked her forward. She lurched a few steps but held her ground.

"David, I have to go back to the bus station and give the man money for the telephone call. There's a man who said he would help me." He squeezed her arm until it drained of blood. "David, you are hurting me!"

"We have to get away from here. Understand? If you stay here, there is nothing I can do for you. Nothing!"

Mera glanced over her shoulder. The clerk from the bus station stood outside the office and scanned the crowd. He held a piece of paper up in the air and motioned for Mera to come when he saw her wave in his direction.

"Mierda!" *Shit!* David cursed under his breath and pressed his fingers tighter around Mera's arm. "Quickly!"

Mera approached the clerk, still attached to her brother. She shook her arm free and extended colones.

"Come inside. I'll get your change," he said. "There is an urgent message for you, young lady."

"Olvídalo!" *Forget it!*

David yanked hard on Mera's arm and propelled them back into the crowd. Mera looked back over her shoulder to extend a quiet wave and quick "Gracias!" to the clerk, although the word was drowned out by the bustle of the late afternoon traffic.

At the corner, David scanned the bottlenecked cars for a possible path through. Out of nowhere, an arm shot through the crowd, and strong, bony fingers clamped like a vise onto Mera's other arm.

"I knew it was a good idea to bring you along." Dino grinned at David. "I'll just take the girl. Thank you. Go find the others. I'll meet you at the casita. We'll have to stay tonight. Jaco has the truck and the shipment of guns." He shoved Mera forward.

The color quickly drained from Mera's face. She took two steps backward, and her eyes moved from the twin dragon-tattooed arm that squeezed her wrist toward David. His expression was unreadable beneath his thick, dark lashes. He let her arm fall, shrugged his shoulders, and disappeared into the crowd. "We meet again, señorita! This was meant to be! I am surprised a little village girl made it all the way to the big city. Good for you! Now do as you're told and stay in front of me."

Mera stepped one foot in front of the other, and her head twisted back. Her eyes swept the street behind her for a glimpse of a faded red T-shirt and knee-high rubber boots. Dino forced her hand to feel the bulge of the pistol under his shirt. She continued to move like a wind-up doll with unblinking eyes. *Why doesn't David come?* She couldn't feel her legs anymore, and the honking of horns and city noise turned into a persistent, unrelenting buzz.

At the casita, her hands were bound and attached to her feet. Her tongue stuck to the roof of her mouth as she continued to struggle with swallowing.

A small, ragtag group of mercenaries milled around inside the casita. Ten wooden crates filled with rifles and ammunition lined the north wall of the front room where Mera was taken. From her position on the floor, she counted a total of six men. One meticulously cleaned his gun while a second soldier lounged on the floor. Another walked into the room and grabbed his genitals, making obscene, leering gestures in Mera's direction. There were loud hoots of approval from his cronies, but no one approached her.

The front door opened, and the chilling sound of Dino's voice filled the room, followed by David's softer tones. In another lifetime, that voice had never failed to soothe her into a restful sleep. She jerked her head up to see.

"Tráeme a la chica." *Bring me the girl,* Dino yelled.

David walked across the room to Mera. "Get up," he said. "The boss wants to see you!"

Mera stayed put, with her legs hugged close in to her chest. David unbound her hands and feet, grabbed her under her arms, and dragged her across the room to Dino's feet. Dino leaned his face down until it was only inches from hers.

"You wouldn't know where to find Ángel, would you? I know he helped you. He's a dead man!"

A kick came out of nowhere. Her body catapulted backwards as she rolled over onto her hands and knees, gasping for breath. David leaped across the room onto Dino's back, pinning his arms. Stunned for a moment, Dino quickly regained leverage and flipped the lighter man off his back.

"Get out of here!" David cried.

Mera remained pinned to the wall, panic-stricken. It took only a moment for Dino to regain control and dominate the smaller man. Mera sprang onto Dino's back and squeezed her fingers around his neck. He threw her easily onto her side with a momentous thrust and grabbed her by the hair. David backed up, breathing hard. He knew the man would not hesitate to twist Mera's neck front to back. It would just take a second.

"Move and the girl is dead," Dino said.

He thrust Mera back against the wall and turned his head, his gaze fixated on David. All activity ceased. Suddenly, a loud bang resonated through the room as the front door blew open. Eight Salvadorian soldiers dressed in green army fatigues burst into the room and swept the space, pointing their machine guns at the mercenaries. A shot rang out, and Dino instantly crumbled to the floor. Then another. David, with his hands up in the air, fell to the ground, clutching the side of his stomach. Mera bolted from her crouched position and ran to David's side. She knelt beside him and gently cradled his head. His breath was warm and his eyes glazed. She brought his hand to her lips.

"I won't let you die!" she cried.

David clutched his side, blood oozing through his fingers.

"Get out of here! There is nothing you can do for me. Go!" David attempted to raise his head and free it from Mera's hold. An officer from the other side of the room called out.

"Take the girl! Get her out of here!"

Two soldiers instantly appeared on either side of Mera. They reached down and pulled her away her from David and up onto her feet. They threw a blanket over her.

"He is hurt! Por favor!" *Please!*

She resisted, and her hand stretched back toward her brother. The two soldiers lifted her up and forcefully carried her out of the building.

"Take the girl to Salma. Get her cleaned up. We'll take care of the rest. We'll need to sort this mess out when we get to the station."

Chapter Sixty-Two

1977

San Salvador, El Salvador

She heard voices. Strange words in a language Mera could not understand drifted in and out of earshot. A middle-aged English woman conversed quietly with a younger, blond-haired woman, who was half her age. Both turned to watch the sleeping girl before speaking. Mera's head pounded. She tried to concentrate and understand the conversation around her to no avail. She soon fell back asleep. The women continued to speak in hushed tones.

"He's quite well known and very well respected. On his way here from England, I've heard tell. Why all the fuss for a little village girl? That's what I'd like to know," the young blonde woman said.

"He must have his reasons. Our job is to comfort and care for the child, not to ask questions. They gave her a shot to help her sleep. She'll most likely not wake until the morning. Keep the room dark and make sure you are here when she wakes. She's been through a terrible ordeal, poor child."

Nigel Hawkes arrived in El Salvador four days after the phone call. He had meant to come back for the child earlier. They all had—he, Crispin, and especially Kate Morgan. But Kate had just begun her career with the CIA and was strongly advised to keep her life simple. None of them had the time or circumstances to care for an infant. After many conversations, Nigel and Kate finally agreed it was better for the baby to be raised in a loving family in her mother's home country.

In the beginning, Lance's injuries were too severe to enable him to make any coherent decisions. It would not have been right to burden the man with information he was in no condition to do anything about. When Lance was finally well enough to speak with others, he disappeared without a trace. Nigel reviewed his actions or lack thereof. He didn't want to interfere in the affairs of a married couple, especially one confronted with so many challenges. On all counts, it seemed quite right to the British covert officer not to mention the child to Lance just yet. He felt he had all the time in the world to let him know. Only later, looking back, did he realize what a grave error he had made.

Nigel took a taxi to the hotel, ate a light dinner, and went to bed early. The following morning, dressed in a light suit, he ate a breakfast of poached eggs on toast, papaya, and black coffee and then headed to the safe house. On arrival, the blonde-haired caretaker led him to the girl.

"Mr. Hawkes? We've been expecting you," she said. "I am sorry to report the young lady is not doing well. She keeps asking to see her brother. We haven't told her anything, I assure you. She won't eat, not a bite in three days. She's been drinking a lot of water, though. Maybe you'll have better luck."

Nigel stood at the door and surveyed the scene. Mera sat on a wooden chair, with her hands in her lap. She was quiet, and only her profile was visible from the entrance. Nigel slowly entered the room, careful not to startle the girl. He lowered his voice.

"Mera, my name is Nigel Hawkes. Do you remember talking to me on the telephone?" he said. "You are quite as lovely as your mother. It's been a very long time since we first met."

Mera's head swung violently to the right to stare at the visitor. "My brother. Do you know where he is? Take me to my brother."

Nigel sighed. "May I?" He indicated the chair. She nodded once as he quietly sat down. "I'd like to reunite you with your brother. However, there are extenuating circumstances. You know he was injured, yes? They brought him to the hospital. I spoke with the doctors, and he is going to be fine. They anticipate a full recovery. Unfortunately, he has suffered substantial trauma over the past year. He needs time, Mera. He does not want to see anyone presently."

Nigel spoke slowly, pausing every so often to make sure she understood his less-than-perfect Spanish.

"Your brother was brought to the hospital under military arrest. It's taken a bit to unravel the players here. The group that kidnapped you and enlisted your brother into their ranks was, most unfortunately, sanctioned by the government. It's an internal war, I'm afraid, and that is bloody and heart-wrenching. In these terrible circumstances, families are often ripped apart."

Mera began to squeeze the fingers of her left hand, one digit at a time. Nigel tentatively placed his hand on her shoulder.

"I'm here to help. I want to get you to a safe place where you can receive proper care and recover from your own ordeal."

There was something in his voice, a reflection of the light streaming in through the window. She recognized the kindness in his eyes. Mera sprang from her chair and onto his lap. She wrapped her arms around his neck and laid her head onto his shoulder. Startled, Nigel remained immobile, with his back straight and rigid. The rhythm of the girl's breath was abrupt and uneven. Slowly, he lifted his hand and patted her shoulder.

"There, there, my dear. Everything will be all right. You'll see. Everything will be just fine."

Chapter Sixty-Three

1977

San Salvador, El Salvador

Nigel cautioned against the visit but finally acquiesced when he realized Mera would not eat or consider moving to a safe place until she had seen for herself that her brother was stable and well. They arrived at the hospital at ten in the morning. Nigel gave her the room number and sat down in the waiting room. He picked up a newspaper and began to read the local news of the day.

Mera, confused by the large building and so many doors, returned to ask which way she should go. Nigel walked her to the elevator, and together, they rode up to the third floor. He pointed down the hallway to David's room and then returned to the main floor waiting room.

Mera positioned herself just outside Room 311 and timidly knocked. David looked up. His forehead knotted. He lay flat on the hospital bed, bare-chested, with a bandage around the waist. There were three beds in Room 311, but only one was occupied. Mera inched in, and her eyes were immediately drawn to the bed next to the wall and her brother's bandages. David was the first to speak.

"What are you doing here, Mera? Didn't you get the message? I don't want to see you!"

"I was afraid we would never meet again! You don't have to fight anymore, David!" Mera said. "Remember I told you there was someone who wants to help? My friend will help you too. We can leave this place, leave everything, and start again. Everyone is gone. You are my only family now. Those men that took you, do you know they killed Mama?"

David stared hard at the wall. He deliberately concentrated on his breath but stopped abruptly. He turned to face Mera and edged himself up onto his elbows, wincing as he threw his legs over the side of the bed. He swiped the back of his hand across the sweat beading on his forehead and quickly lowered his eyes to the white linoleum floor. After a long pause, he spoke.

"The man here," he said, pointing to himself, "is not the brother you once knew. That brother is dead. Get it? Just like Mama. Forget about him! Go and live a good life. That's what you can do for me. Okay? Now get out and don't come back!"

"David, a lot happened to everyone. No one is the same."

"I killed Marcos!" he breathed, and the words reverberated around the room.

Mera slowly edged closer, inches now from his face. "¿Qué? Qué dijeste?" *What? What did you say?*

"I killed our brother. They told me to shoot, and I pulled the trigger. The bullet went straight through the middle of his left eye. There's the truth. It's done! There's no fixing that. Now leave!"

David continued to stare at the floor as Mera slowly backed up, keeping her eyes glued to his face. She separated her lips, breathed in hard, and clamped her mouth shut. She committed to memory every detail of the room. The covers were thrown back, David held the sides of his ribs, the shadows swelled and receded along the stark linoleum floor, and the lone cotton curtain ballooned and flattened with the light breeze from the open window.

Abruptly, she ran out the door and raced past the nurses' station. She ignored the elevator and thrust open the fire exit door. Holding the handrail, she practically leaped down three flights of stairs to burst into the waiting room, startling Nigel, who sat calmly reading the newspaper.

"Why the American Embassy? Why are you helping me? Here there is only death!"

Mera hovered uncertainly; her face blanched of all color. She stared blankly at Nigel, who quietly set the paper to the side.

"Let me take you back to the safe house, my dear. Later, when you're feeling better, I can try and answer your questions, of which I am sure you have many. For right now, please count on me as someone who has your best interests close at heart."

"I want to leave this place."

"You have family here and grandparents you haven't met. I'm sure they will welcome you with open arms."

"No! My family is dead! I want to leave here. Will you help me?"

"When you are rested, we'll talk again. If you still want to leave, of course I will make the arrangements."

PART III

My dreamlike form

Appeared to dreamlike beings

To show them the dreamlike path

That leads to dreamlike enlightenment.

—*Bhadrakalpika Sutra*

Chapter Sixty-Four

1994

Sarajevo, Bosnia, and Herzegovina

Meri crouched low into a squat, a Nikon camera suspended from a strap around her neck. She pointed, and its wide-angle lens nudged out beyond the relative safety zone of the rubble of a partially collapsed building. A cloud of dust rose as a deafening explosion spewed debris nearby. The blast knocked her onto her back as splintered particles flushed the grey landscape. The explosion originated in the cluster of buildings across the street, but still, she closed her eyes as flying bits of wreckage flew through the air near to her.

The fall was reactive, a subconscious response to danger. As the dust settled, she wiped her face with the back of her sleeve, then sat up and checked the camera's lens. It was intact. Without pause, she scrambled onto a knee and adjusted the aperture setting. She instantly captured the scene in front of her in a series of rapid clicks. Where just a moment before the windows held dirt-clouded panes, only shattered glass remained. A random door, blown off its hinges, lay broken across the street. She observed the devastation: muted grey buildings, a darkly silvered sky, and drab clothing hanging on a line to dry. Rolls of color film lined her camera case, but she shot the photos in black and white. There was a striking absence of color in every direction. Locals began emerging from the other buildings onto the street, warily checking for damage and loved ones. The wail of a small child pierced the harsh, windy afternoon.

Meri darted from her shelter to zigzag around abandoned cars and debris, cautiously navigating to the other side of the street. The child, no more than three years old, wailed. Her face was blackened, and her eyes opened wide with shock. Her only protection from the elements was a thick pink sweater with several holes. Among the few who braved the outdoors, none of them seemed to notice the child or, if they did, had more pressing business of their own.

Meri angled the camera, adjusted the focus, and clicked. She zeroed in on the child's eyes. The ravages of war, direct and haunting, mirrored the small child's face.

Meri took the film reel out, placed it in the canister, and stowed both camera and lens into the case. She threw the case over her shoulder and looked to see if anyone appeared interested in the fate of this small girl. She moved cautiously and then squatted to the eye level of the three-year-old. There was no possibility of communicating. Such a young child would not know English.

"Come, Cariña. Everything is all right."

She swept her up, camera case on the left, small child on the right hip, and quickly moved to a safer place. The girl clung to her shoulder in a viselike grip as Meri made her way back across the street. Once assured they were as well protected as possible, she turned her attention to the small being who stuck to her side like glue. She opened her parka and enveloped the girl, pulling her close in, and rummaged through her pack. She pulled out a bottle of water and brought it to the girl's lips. Water dribbled down her cheek. Then Meri heard desperate gulps and liquid gurgling from the child's nose.

"Slow down! Take it easy."

Meri pulled the bottle away from her tiny hands and waited as the child swallowed. She then offered the remaining liquid in equal, absorbable amounts. Still holding the girl, she turned and scanned the area for the safest, most protected spot with the best vantage point. Without hesitation, she slid herself down the side wall of the building to land on hard ground, adjusting the little one from her hip onto her lap. There was no sign of the mother, father, or a relative. After an hour in the cold, both of them were close to frozen. She hoisted the child back up onto her hip and carefully began to make her way to the designated pickup point.

Emmett, the German, who saw himself as Meri's self-appointed champion, had spread out earlier that morning along with a handful of international journalists, each one focused on a specific street. The bulletproof car would arrive at the designated meeting point at exactly 5:00 p.m. It would stop only long enough to load them all in and then speed back to the bright yellow Holiday Inn, where most international journalists stayed in Sarajevo. If you were late, well, it was up to you to make your own way back. Meri shot out into the open when the armored car screeched to a halt for its brief stop. The door was thrown open, and several journalists scrambled in.

"What the fuck! You can't take that kid! What the fuck are you thinking?" Emmett yelled.

"I am not fucking leaving her here! Go!"

Bypassing the front desk and an obvious protocol, she buried the girl close under her parka and carried her up the elevator to her room on the third floor. Still holding the child, she ran tepid water in the bathtub. The almost nonexistent pressure was barely more than a dribble. It took some time, but eventually, the tub began to fill. Gently, she removed her own clothing, then the girls, before stepping both of them together into the lukewarm water. Tenderly, she washed black soot from the small face and ran the washcloth up the tiny, rounded spine. The girl's hair was plastered to her scalp, unwashed for a very long time. Meri placed a small amount of shampoo in her palm and lightly massaged the scalp until she felt assured it was completely clean. She began rinsing, making sure to keep the soap away from the child's eyes.

She had been in the tub holding the little one for quite some time when she noticed the small body was covered in goose bumps in the now-cold water. Quickly, she grabbed a thin towel, the only one provided, and wrapped the girl tightly. She encouraged the girl's fingers to release her grip, and gently settled her under the covers in the bed, and scrambled under the blanket to wrap the child in close to her chest. She didn't move until she felt the girl's soft breath ease into a quiet slumber. Careful not to disturb the girl, she slowly shifted and eased herself out of bed. She threw on a pair of jeans and a sweater and dialed room service.

"I'd like to order dinner. I'll take whatever meat you have and potatoes. Are there sweets? Great! Apple puree then. And a large milk and a glass of red wine. Yes, wonderful, thank you."

The knock on the door was accompanied by the aroma of roasted chicken and boiled potatoes. Meri shut the door quietly, but when she turned to set everything on the desk, the girl sat up and stared with luminous brown eyes at the tray of food. Meri smiled warmly. The child now stood up on the bed, completely naked, with her eyes glued to the tray in Meri's hand. Meri rummaged through her suitcase and pulled out a long-sleeved T-shirt, placing it over the girl's head. It made a perfect nightgown. Then she brought the tray to the bed and indicated the food and the milk. The child remained standing, timid and unsure. Meri sat down next to her and picked up a chicken leg, transferring the meat into the little girl's small hands.

"What are we going to do? I am not sending you back to that hellhole! Not until we find your family or a relative. Got that? What's your name, Cariña?"

Meri pointed to herself. "Meri," she said.

She pointed to the girl her eyebrows raised. Through a mouthful of chicken, the child whispered, "Zhss."

Meri leaned her ear in closer and pointed again to the girl. This time, she swallowed the mass of chicken in her mouth first. "Zhera."

"Zhura?"

The girl shook her head and reiterated the two syllables again.

"Zhera, what a beautiful name!" Meri smiled and hugged her, placing a light kiss on the top of her head. "Where can we find your people, Zhera?"

There was a light tapping at the door. Emmett, the great hulking German, leaned easily against the doorframe, holding a bottle of cheap red wine in his left hand and two chipped wineglasses in his right. In his shirt pocket, a cellophane-wrapped chocolate bunny peeked out, like a Joey peering out from its mother's pouch. Emmett nodded toward the candy in his pocket.

"What do you want, Emmett?"

"Chocolate for the kid, wine for us. Figured you might need some help. It wasn't easy finding the chocolate!"

"Come in, then."

She motioned to the one chair in the corner of the small, square room. The walls of the room were empty, save for a picture of the Miljacka River in springtime, white-blossomed trees lining its banks. Meri took the offered glass of wine as Zhera sank out of view under the covers.

"Can you find some clothes? Little girl clothes?" Meri said, "I've been trying to figure out who to contact. I'm not letting anyone take her until I'm sure she's with her family or good people. I need to find someone who speaks a Slavic language and see if I can get her to open up. Serbo-Croatian or Bosnian, whichever should work. They all understand each other."

"The kid's just a baby. I doubt you'll learn much from her."

Chapter Sixty-Five

1994

Sarajevo, Bosnia, and Herzegovina

In haunting, heart-wrenching notes, a muted Billie Holliday's "God Bless the Child" drifted throughout the small bar in downtown Sarajevo. Just a few die-hard customers lingered over a drink. Meri downed a double whiskey, straight up. She ignored a few attempts engaging her at conversation. She chose this dive for its quiet and its anonymity. She had slipped out of the hotel using the back worker's entrance, wanting to exit unnoticed before Emmett or anyone could caution her to remain at the hotel after the sun went down.

A tall man wearing a brown woolen cap with flaps covering his ears and frameless, round glasses with thick lenses quietly sat down on the empty stool next to hers, although there were plenty of open ones. He ordered a beer without looking at his neighbor.

"Hope you don't mind," he said.

He stared hard at the wall as if memorizing the mirrored reflection of Jameson Whiskey, Smirnoff, and the lagers lined along the bar.

"There are a lot of seats. Why this one?"

He spoke over his shoulder with a quick glance.

"Proximity to others helps me relax, I think. Is it a bother?"

"No."

The second-hand ticked evenly, precisely navigating the face of the antique grandfather clock placed centrally behind the bar. Ten p.m. The bartender replaced the man's beer without being asked and inquired if the lady would like another whiskey. She nodded briefly and abruptly swung around to face her neighbor on the adjacent stool.

"Why did you choose to sit next to a stranger? I like space, usually."

"Need me to move?"

"No, it's fine. I'm just curious."

"A habit. And you? Here? This bar? Sarajevo?"

"As good a place as any to lose oneself. Wherever you go, there you are. That's the shit of it."

"That's halfway to bitter. The proverbial broken heart? A wandering spouse? But here you are in Sarajevo, sifting through the ashes like the rest of us. If you have a mind to unload, I'm quite the good listener. One you'll most likely never see again. I promise it won't end up on the front page of *Time*."

"You're a journalist and not at the hotel?"

"I don't like to move with the crowd. I'm staying with friends, locals, and scrambling for water and food like most of Sarajevo. It's better to sniff out what's real. I believe it's how I am able to uncover the truly interesting stories, like yours." He swiveled the stool to face her directly and extended his hand.

"I'm Ian from Vancouver. You're American?"

She took the hand without committing to further conversation. Her body remained stiff and still half turned away from him.

"Just Meri," she murmured.

"A pleasure to meet you, Mary." He swiveled back to face the mirror and downed the last of his beer, indicating to the bartender to refill. Meri ordered another whiskey, so that two whiskeys sat side by side in front of her. She inhaled one, then the other, and pivoted her chair back around. The Canadian journalist was now framed in her direct line of vision.

"Are you up for listening to a sordid tale, Ian from Vancouver? It turns out I fell in love."

"Okay," Ian said. "And then?"

"I fell in love with a three-year-old girl. She's Bosnian. They took her away today, and there was not a damned thing I could do about it. Ever have a kid look to you with enormous, trusting eyes, as if you hold the key to making her world okay? It's a crushing thing. They took her and placed her in some orphanage, where she will be a thousand times worse off."

"If I may ask, how did the Bosnian girl end up in your care?"

"I was taking some pictures after one of many explosions. She sat abandoned in the street. It was the eyes. I got lost in her eyes. She stayed at the hotel with me almost six weeks before the authorities came and took her away."

"That's rough."

"A long time ago, in another lifetime, I was her. It happened when I was a lot older, though. Same story. Country ravaged by cruel and unconscious humans. I was lucky, though. I was rescued in time."

"Where?" Ian asked.

"El Salvador."

"I'm surprised. You sound and look American."

"I was fifteen when I came to the States. I didn't know my biological father was American. I never looked back. I needed to get anywhere, away from the horror. I was lucky. I had private tutors, school, and a rabid, determined effort to lose anything remotely connected to my country. I didn't rest until I erased my accent."

"Impressive. I've known plenty of folks who change countries, but try as they may, they can't quite leave the vestige of their mother tongue behind. Obviously, you have an aptitude. Did you ever want to revisit your home country, out of simple curiosity?"

"I don't talk about El Salvador."

"Okay. What then?"

"A year into my new life, I started high school. Looking back, it wasn't healthy or normal. My only focus was on education. I had no interest in trying to locate any family, especially the one I grew up with, but also a biological one with a cast of fictitious characters. Then college, graduate school, and a passion for running marathons. That's how I got through the night. I might have gone professional, but I never quite got around to it."

Ian removed his knit cap, revealing wavy, taupe hair sprinkled with grey and plastered to his skull from long hours of restraint. A prominent pharynx protruded from an olive-skinned neck. He ran long fingers along his forehead to lightly massage the top of his head without taking his attention from the woman seated next to him. "And now?"

"Ironic as hell, you must think. Girl escapes a war-torn country, only to place herself in harm's way all over again. It's impossible to explain. But living on the edge is what I do best, it turns out. I tried a more conventional route, the corporate world, but I didn't like my dependency on mediocre employers. It lasted six months. I spent another six months in a quiet NGO, raising money to help countries like the one I grew up in. It wasn't long before I realized the inconsistency of it all." Meri's voice trailed off as she gazed at their mirrored reflection.

"And?" he said.

"There's a cost to keeping the citizens of the USA happy, feeding the mostly overweight population's habit for McDonald's hamburgers."

"What do you mean?"

"I mean it's all one ecosystem. Everything affects everything else. The easy life of rich countries depends on the sweat of the poor countries. The farmers and villagers of El Salvador remain forgotten. The world-power cartels get richer and feed their militaries, who in turn repress and butcher the forgotten and poor. Well-fed in my cubicle, the enormity of contradiction overwhelmed me. Don't get me wrong. There's a lot of wonderful aid happening through these organizations and a lot of incredibly well-meaning people. It just wasn't for me in the end."

"So, you end up traipsing the world looking for another war zone. That seems to me like another contradiction."

"Somehow, I figured if just one of my photographs awakens somebody, anybody, from their comfortable slumber, putting my life at risk is worth it. It's my service to the world, if you will. Unfortunately, people read the paper, see the photographs, and gasp in horror for a day or two, but then they move right along with their convenient little lives. So, what about you?"

"Me?" The corners of Ian's mouth wavered into a half smile as he pointed to himself. "Well, it turns out you might be preaching to the choir. Actually, I've been an activist since my early twenties. K. D. Lang is my hero. Have you heard of her?"

"No, I haven't."

"She's a Canadian singer but also an activist for gay rights, the First Nations people of Canada, animals, and Tibet."

Meri took a closer look at the Canadian. The corners of her lips mirrored his emerging smile.

"Did you did go back?" he said, abruptly changing the subject. "I mean to El Salvador."

"I thought I said the subject is verboten."

"Yes, you did say that." Ian drank a swig of beer and remained quiet.

Several minutes passed, both withdrawn into their own private thoughts. Then Mera spoke. "After college, I did in fact go back. My therapist thought it might do me some good to look the beast in the eye. It turned out to be a very brief stay. I agreed it might be a good thing to do, but every part of my body resisted. From the moment I stepped on the ground in San Salvador, I wanted to leave. It felt as if there was someone behind me, ready to pounce at every corner. Instead of a healing, it was the opposite. It felt like I ripped open a long, tender scar from my collarbone to my belly."

"Ouch. Was anyone with you?"

"I traveled with my aunt. She suggested we leave the city and visit the country and the rainforest. But there, the fear only intensified, coupled with oppressive heat and a shitload of bugs. What was intended to be a week-long trip lasted two-and-a-half days. I vowed never to go back."

"I'm sorry."

"It took me a couple of years to recover from the visit. More therapy and a lot of running! Anything to find peace. I grew up Catholic, but there's no protection in the Church. You need faith, and for me, belief was irreparably shattered one morning in a hospital in San Salvador."

"I see." It was his turn to scrutinize the face of the woman seated next to him. Meri, encouraged by Ian's quiet and attentive manner, continued to speak.

"After a year of unsatisfactory employment, I decided to embark on a walking retreat and visited several countries around the world. I had so many unanswered questions. The Church didn't come close to resolving the contradictions. And funny you should mention Tibet. I began to practice meditation, also at the advisement of my therapist. In the course of things, I came across a Tibetan meditation teacher.

He was the first person who seemed able to shed a bit of light." Meri spread her hands out, as if indicating a vast and crazy world. "Did you ever wonder who you are?" she asked softly. "Like, what the fuck am I doing here, in this world? Why do some people, some countries suffer so much? While others seem to have it all? It isn't fair!"

"No, it isn't," Ian said. "But suffering is universal. Everyone aches or will at one time or another. There's no respite from the human condition."

Meri took another swig of whiskey and set the glass down with a bang, looking to the bartender for another. "I'm sorry. I don't know what possessed me to go down this road tonight."

"I'm an insomniac. I don't sleep until four a.m. most nights. Sometimes it helps, you know, to say it out loud," Ian said quietly.

Meri downed another whiskey. Her words slowed but remained clear enough to follow.

"For three years, I dropped off the planet. I looked for some kind of answer, I suppose, to questions that are pretty disturbing if you take the time to consider them. Where do we go when the body returns to dust? Is there life beyond this constantly changing form? Why am I not the same as I was even a few months ago?"

"Where did you go?" Ian asked.

"I scaled mountains in Peru. I hung out with shamans and climbed into caves high in the Himalayas. I met meditating monks, many of whom had no interest in talking to me and who were totally removed from the outer world. I met imposters, too, ones looking to enrich their positions. Some of the teachers I met were actually more like me and still searching. Then I stumbled upon one who was different. How do you recognize a person who has transcended this world? They still look the same as you and me. They have two eyes, a nose, and a mouth."

Meri paused and took another gulp of whiskey before continuing. "I hired a guide. It took me two weeks to reach that damned cave! I rode buses and bicycles and hiked with my own two feet. I had to crawl to get in. Inside, there was this emaciated being who sat completely still. He seemed totally at peace. In the beginning, he ignored my existence, but for some reason, I stayed and slept in the cave. I brought him food and helped take care of his needs. He didn't require much. What he ate could sustain a mouse. I can't say he ever really acknowledged my existence. But I felt him, later on. There was nothing at all to do. After a while, I did what he did, or tried to. I stayed still and watched my mind, day after day. I had a pack full of food, but it had to be rationed. Food was left below for him, but it was sporadic. Eventually, I ran out of what I brought and became dependent on the gifts of strangers. There were days where half of daylight was spent scrounging for berries. I don't think he cared. He only ate when there was something to eat."

"Impressive. I would have left when the food ran out. What compelled you to stay?"

"It's impossible to explain. There's no recognizable reference point. The closest I've come to describing the experience is that an all-pervasive view replaced my ordinary mind. For just one moment, I understood the illusory and mirror-like quality of this solid-seeming world. And it broke my heart. Our cumulative grief might fill a million oceans. In the end, we all cry the same tears, no matter what damn part of the world we're from, the color of our skin, or whatever the fuck we believe in."

Meri was silent a moment and then continued slowly. "I often think about my time there. I fell in love with this emaciated man who never said a word to me. And yet I felt completely seen and accepted. How do I explain it? It is an incredible relief to let go of the many masks you wear and realize there's nothing at all to strive for. I'd like to think that maybe if I had stayed there, I wouldn't be sitting here in Sarajevo still ruminating and considering the same tired old questions." Meri drank the remainder of her whiskey. The liquid burned her throat and warmed her chest.

Ian remained quiet, but his attention did not waver from her face.

"In the end, I resurfaced and left the cave. You can sit with the most awakened master and still miss the point. No one, it turns out, can do it for you. That's the painful reality for all of us humans. The monastic path wasn't for me. I went back to my life, and the truth that seemed so clear and bright in that Himalayan cave was like sand sifting through my fingers. Yet there are times, even now, when I feel him. I have mornings when he's my first thought and nights when his image wavers behind my eyes. I get the feeling he's not really separate from my own mind, whatever that is."

Together, Meri and Ian stared at the old grandfather clock as if hypnotized, the synchronized second hand tapping the movement of time out loud. The old clock's melodious chime interrupted, a resonating bellow that filled the bar. They both looked up as the large hand covered the smaller one to land evenly on the XII.

"My given name is Mera," she said.

Ian leaned in and studied her expression.

"I was born in Laos in a village of indigenous people on the Laotian-Thai border. That's what they tell me. Nigel, a British secret service guy, and Kate, a retired CIA agent. The two of them are the only family I'm left with, and both are totally unrelated to me by blood. I'm the result of a bizarre union between an El Salvadoran art student who, unluckily for her, fell head over heels for an American agent working undercover in Thailand right before the start of the Vietnam War. There was a plane crash. The American was rescued and sent home. He convalesced, then disappeared, never to be heard from again. They think he became a target of some nefarious drug cartel. Apparently, money he was entrusted with burned up in the plane crash. My biological mother died giving birth to me. It's quite sad. I would have liked to have known her. Both Nigel and Kate told me about her. I checked it out after graduate school. It took that long before I wanted to know anything about them. I wouldn't allow Nigel or Kate to broach the subject when I was younger, and they were very respectful."

"What happened? Why did she die?"

"That's a topic for the history books," Meri said.

"How so?"

"My mother was kidnapped by a drug gang. They didn't actually pull the trigger but are directly responsible for her death."

"Why was the gang interested in her?"

"It was my biological father they were after, but they couldn't find him. My parents' story is enmeshed in the history of the Golden Triangle. My biological father, undercover, visited a drug lord. He was on a mission to help the CIA gain access to a potential supply route in southern Laos in preparation for the impending conflict. We all know how that turned out." Mera was quiet for a moment and then murmured into her shot glass, "It should have been him they murdered."

"What did you say?"

Mera looked up and said, "It's my biological father who caused all the trouble. They should have shot him."

"Did your uncle tell you that?" Ian asked.

"No, it's just my opinion. My uncle thinks he made some clear errors of judgment but usually speaks quite highly of him."

"Then why the condemnation toward someone you've never met?"

"It's always the same story. Men use guns like toys and leave a trail of destruction behind them."

"That's harsh. There must be something good you've heard about your father."

"Actually, yes. Years ago, my uncle introduced me to someone who knew my biological father during his time in a Hmong village in Laos. The man's name was Yeej. He was a Hmong refugee who got caught up in the mass exodus at the end of the Vietnam War. I spent an evening with him, and he was the first person, other than Nigel and Kate, that I felt a deep connection to. He told me my biological father saved his life, and he owed him a tremendous debt. After the war, Yeej's's village was overrun by the Pathet-Lao. Only a handful of them were able to escape. He wanted to return to his village but inadvertently was rounded up by the Americans. He thought he was being taken down river, back to near his village, but was put on a ship to Guam with hundreds of refugees. He kept asking to go back, but of course, the ship had set sail. Yeej and I only spent the one evening together, but I felt his heart, and he knew mine."

They were both silent. Mera sipped her whiskey, and Ian tapped his beer glass with his right index finger to the beat of Creedence Clearwater's Revival's "Have You Ever Seen the Rain?" It was several minutes more before Ian looked up.

"Where did you live when you came to America?"

"I lived with my aunt mostly. She was injured in the line of duty and ended up working in an office, much to her chagrin. She loved fieldwork and was good at it. I stayed with Nigel in England whenever he had time, but he was gone a lot. It was in graduate school when I took an elective class in genealogy. That's when I decided to learn what I could about my family. Nigel and Kate each knew something, but the heart of the story was still a big question mark. My life has huge chunks of history that are simply missing."

Mera motioned for to the bartender to fill her glass again.

CHAPTER SIXTY-FIVE

"Whoa, slow down! You don't want to pass out. Shall I get you a coffee?"

Mera ignored the suggestion and continued speaking. "When I was a baby, it was Kate who found a family to care for me, and it was Nigel's extremely high level of government clearance that allowed me to fly across the ocean and end up with the Rodríguez family, back in my mother's home country. I loved my family beyond words, but that ideal ceased to exist when my mother was killed and one of my brothers was inducted into the El Salvadoran army. The other went off to join the rebels."

Mera's monologue slurred as the end of one word became the beginning of the next. She stared at the empty shot glass as though, with enough concentration and fortitude, the glass might transform into a magic sphere where history reorganized itself.

"He killed my brother Marcos, you know, and I can never forgive that." She slumped her head onto her hands and became still.

Ian pushed his stool away from the bar and stood. He took Mera by the arm and urged her to stand.

"Come on. It's time to go. This joint is about to close. You can stay at my place. It's at least safer than the Holiday Inn, which is sniper alley. That's about the most dangerous corner of Sarajevo. You can sleep with me. It's on the floor, but there's blankets and warm enough if you keep close. It's just around the corner."

Slowly, Mera stood, and for a moment she was the same height as the Canadian journalist. He reached under her arm and supported her weight while moving her forward and out, and into the bitter, cold night. He took his brown cap out from his pocket and placed it on her head. He stumbled under her weight initially, but once he gained the momentum, he moved easily enough down the street.

In the courtyard, behind piles of debris and rubble, the door could have easily been overlooked. He inserted the key and pushed, but the door stuck. He stepped back and pressed his shoulder against it, knocking it with force. Inside, several people slept spread out. One slumped on a worn yellow couch. Another was propped up against the wall with a bottle of vodka still clutched in his left hand. Ian steered his semi-conscious guest as quietly as he could down the hallway and into a small room on the right. The door had broken off the hinge so, after entering and lowering Mera onto a sleeping bag on the floor, he returned to slide the door up against the hinges, creating, he hoped, some semblance of privacy.

"Should get back to the hotel. Damn, it's cold," Mera mumbled.

She pulled the worn sleeping bag up to her chin. Ian knelt in an attempt to arrange the woman, sleeping bag, and another blanket into a somewhat comfortable position and then moved toward the lone window of the room. He pressed it open, hoisted himself up, and urinated. The plumbing in the building hadn't worked for months now. He lowered his tall frame back onto the floor, gathered the sleeping Mera in close, and stole the blanket to throw it over them both. She unconsciously wedged her body into a spoon to nestle in close to the Canadian, who, oddly, fell asleep within minutes.

She walked quickly, rubbing her gloveless hands to keep warm. Her feet were bare. Crimson toes contrasted the grey, dingy snow. She stopped abruptly, stomped her feet, and pivoted in a circle. All around her, the landscape was the same. A bleached sky merged with a reference-less ground. Which way to go?

The faint morning light from the curtainless window cast the bare room in fugitive shadows. Mera, eyes closed, pulled the blanket up to her chin and shivered. Her back ached, and a sharp pain from her left hip made going back to sleep impossible. Her head throbbed.

What the fuck am I doing on the floor? Where am I? Oh right, I came here with the Canadian journalist, Ian. Instantly, she felt a warmth expand in her chest. She wriggled her body around to merge with her sleeping companion. Her mouth reached along his jawline as her tongue probed his ear. Ian's eyes opened halfway.

"You sure?" There was no reply as she wedged in closer. He reached down to lift the thick woolen sweater over her head, then unfastened her bra. She, in turn, slowly unbuttoned his dingy white polo shirt and lightly touched his chest. His skin rose like chicken flesh in the cold of the unheated room. He laid his cold lips into the nape of her neck. She reached up and pulled his mouth to hers.

A knock on the door and then the semi-closed, unhinged door scratched across the thick, wooden flooring.

"Ian? You all right man? It's ten a.m. It's not like you to sleep in. I'm sorry. I didn't know you had company. Tarik will be here in an hour. I've scrounged some potatoes and something resembling meat. Want some?"

"Out in a minute. We'd appreciate anything you can spare."

Ian's friend slid the door back into place. Mera quickly rummaged for her clothes on the side of the sleeping bag.

"Not so quick. Come here."

"I need to get back. I don't suppose there'd be a bathroom?"

"Shh …"

"What about Tarik?"

"Tarik can come back later."

He pulled her in close, and her form softened, compliant. The two were immersed in touching and erotic sensation.

An insistent knock woke them for a second time. This time, Mera grabbed her clothes and quickly slipped into them. She ran her fingers through her thick hair.

"I can see myself out."

"Meet me tonight, won't you? Same place?"

"This is a one-time deal," she said, indicating the makeshift bed. "A commitment to myself, if you will. One time, one time only. That's my rule."

She leaned down and gave him a kiss on the top of his head.

"Just a minute. There's something that may interest you," Ian said.

"What then?"

"A possible contact concerning the girl."

Ian lay on his side, with his head propped up by his arm.

"I need to make a few calls. Meet me at nine tonight. Can you? I'll pass along what I find out."

"Goodbye, Ian." Mera smiled and turned, struggling to move the heavy, unattached door.

"Let me," Ian said. He grabbed her around the waist and moved her to the side.

"There's a method. The damn thing weighs more than the both of us."

When the door was opened wide enough to pass, Ian took her hand and, holding it up in both of his, brought it to his lips.

Chapter Sixty-Six

1994

Sarajevo, Bosnia, and Herzegovina

"Where the hell have you been? I almost had the troops out looking for you. Next time, let me go with you if you get the urge to wander at night. It's not safe." Emmett sprawled on the lobby sofa, his large frame occupying a good portion of the couch.

"Emmett, thanks for your concern, but there's nothing safe about Sarajevo, nighttime or daytime, especially at this hotel. If I wanted comfort, I'd have stayed home."

Mera retrieved the room key from her back pocket, blew a kiss, and continued across the lobby to the elevator. Back in her room, she shuffled through papers and finally found the telephone number she was looking for. She quickly dialed. Several hours and countless calls later, she still sat on the edge of the bed, frustrated at the impossibility of reaching anyone who might have information or authority concerning the little girl. She called room service, ate a light meal, and finally dropped onto the bed to fall into a deep sleep.

When she awoke the room was dark. She glanced at her watch. *Shit!* Ten p.m. She planned to sleep for an hour, then get up, and make something of the rest of her day. She meant to send the photographs back to her employer. What she wasn't planning was a return trip to the seedy bar and Ian, the Canadian journalist.

Not to meet the man, just to get the information. She repeated the mantra as she showered, applied a light lipstick, and brushed her thick auburn hair.

Ian sat on the same stool as the night before and sipped a beer. He glanced at the clock and decided that Mera would not be coming. He indicated to the bartender that he wanted to settle up when the front door suddenly swung open. Mera was bundled to twice her size in a heavy parka, hat, and woolen mittens. Her cheeks were red from walking several kilometers in the cold Sarajevo winter. She relaxed into the relative warmth of the bar and unzipped her coat.

"Looks like we'll need a whiskey," Ian offered.

"Thanks, but tonight a hot coffee will do." She pointed to her head. "Tsunami of a headache."

He gathered up his coat and moved toward an empty table. He pulled a chair back.

"Have a seat," he said. "I thought you weren't coming."

"I thought so, too. You have information?"

"Contacts, really. How to adopt a kid and get her out, if you're that serious."

"I am that serious. What would it take?"

"I have friends here. A few of them are quite influential. It would take a good bit of money and a lot of forms, interviews, and patience. Are you up for it? I've spoken with Jakob, a friend of mine. He said he'll meet with you. He also said to expect it to take a minimum of six months, though it could take a good deal longer. Some things are slower in wartime, but it may be easier in other aspects. Her family needs to be researched to determine if there is any. They'll have, of course, the option to take her back in. In the meantime, help the orphanage. All the kids will benefit, and hopefully, they'll take good care of your girl and keep her fed, if there's any food to be had."

"When?"

"He can't meet you tomorrow, but he has time on Wednesday. It's not the best idea, you know, out on the streets of Sarajevo alone."

"So they tell me. Safety is a relative thing. Damn, that coffee tastes good." Mera nudged her chin in Ian's direction. "So, what about you? What's your story?"

"Me?" he said. "I'm a street kid. I had to scramble to survive. It was all right until my father died. Afterward, my mother did her best trying to raise two boys by herself. She was a good woman, who had a penchant for collecting boyfriends and inviting them home. When I was thirteen and my brother was almost sixteen, she brought home one in particular. This one made life miserable for all of us. He beat her and us. We did what we could to get her to come away with us, but she was addicted to love—the wrenching, destructive kind. It's the only way I've been able to make sense of it. My brother and I ended up on the street. The Sarajevo apartment is a paradise in comparison to some of the places I've slept. Unlike my brother, my days were spent in the library. I never returned to school, but I devoured poetry, history, science, art and just about anything I could get my hands on. I am completely self-taught. It didn't turn out well for my older brother. He forfeited his life to drugs and a cast of lost souls. He overdosed at nineteen."

"I'm sorry."

"Don't be. He made the choice. I found out the hard way there's no escape from the unrelenting human condition. Change, suffering, it's all part of it. In a way, I decided that's what makes it beautiful, worthwhile."

"You want to get out of here?" Mera said.

"And what of the rule?"

"I'm not completely inflexible, as long as we agree that this is not a 'thing.' I just don't feel like being alone tonight."

Ian rose and paid the bartender, who nodded with both of his hands wiping a glass dry.

"I'd use the bathroom now if I were you. The plumbing hasn't worked for months."

Mera emerged from the toilet, and as Ian held up her coat, she slipped into it.

"From the ghetto to consummate gentleman, offering a lady her coat."

"I am but one of your fellow humans, an amalgam of contradiction."

They walked quietly down the sidewalk, navigating random patches of ice. Mera slipped and then righted herself.

"Careful," Ian said as he took her arm and steadied her.

This time, she stepped back as he pushed open the door. Three Bosnian men sat in a circle atop blue woven blankets playing a card game that was illuminated by candles and two flashlights. A bottle of vodka was passed continuously around by the trio.

"Back already? Deal you in next hand?" Armin turned and noticed Mera for the first time. "Who this is?" he asked.

"Meri. She's a photographer from America. She's staying at the hotel. Meri, these are my friends, Armin, Aleksander, and Leon. They are partners in crime, if you will. Revolutionaries to the one. It's why we get along. A pass tonight, my friends. Catch you later."

Leon concentrated on the cards in his hand and spoke over his shoulder.

"Special girl. Does she know you don't bring a woman here?"

"Meri's one of us. She knows Sarajevo, the risk we all take."

Ian switched on a flashlight retrieved from his backpack and illuminated the hallway down to the bedroom on the right and the door off its hinges. He slid the door closed behind them. They both sank gratefully onto the sleeping bag and leaned against the wall, a good distance apart.

"You know Croatian or Bosnian?" she asked. "How come?"

"Bosnian, but just the minimum. I don't like to stay somewhere without a bit of language. Like I said, I'm self-taught."

"I wish I'd known you a few weeks ago. It might have helped. In hindsight, Zhera and I did quite well without a common word between us, though. Would you mind if we just slept?"

Ian reached over and pulled her in close, gathering the heavy blanket around them both.

"Tonight, just talk and a good night's sleep," Ian said.

Mera snuggled against his chest for warmth and rested her head on his shoulder. She laid her hand across his chest, still dressed in her thick, winter parka.

Ian bent to lightly kiss her on the lips but then withdrew a few inches. He murmured close to her ear. "In the saddest moments, when you confront seemingly unbearable tragedy, look to your heart. You are love. Close your eyes. Fall in love. Stay."

"Hm, beautiful words. Source?"

"Rumi, the great Sufi mystic. A nomad who roamed around Turkey in the 1200s."

"I suppose that's hopeful. I don't know."

"It seems like the human condition hasn't changed much, but there's always those rare few. Those scraggly-looking fellows in the other room? I'd count on any one of them to put their life on the line for freedom, justice, maybe even a stray dog. And I'd be there for them. That, in itself, is reason enough to live."

Mera reached up, kissed Ian on the lips, and snuggled her face against his shoulder.

"I suppose so," she said.

"Did you ever go to Thailand? Check out the places where your biological father and mother met?"

"Funny you should ask. I did. It was after I left the cave. The trip was meant to be an investigative one, but I met up with some Swedish tourists and got hopelessly detoured. They were graduate students taking a year off. It turned out they were also heavy partyers. We ended up on this beautiful island in the south, at the opposite end of Thailand and as far from the Laotian border and any possible links to my past as one could be. The particular island has a reputation for crazy, wild parties, and it lived up to it. One particular night, after a bonfire on the beach with spontaneous drums, music, and way too much alcohol, I passed out in the sand. Maybe I needed to reassure myself of the solid ground of existence. I woke up with the first rays of light. I had sand in my ears, eyes, and navel. Instead of going back to the guesthouse, I wandered along the water for a while and then just kept walking. My head was filled with hangover cotton, so I wasn't doing a lot of thinking. After walking for I don't know how long, I heard faint singing that seemed to be coming from above on a hilltop. I was drawn there like a moth to a flame. It was early, so there weren't any tourists around. When I finally made it up to the top of the hill, I discovered a temple with an incredible view of the island's coastline. It was stunning. It turns out the singing was from a group of thirty to forty monks intoning some prayers. I sat on the stone floor and just let the vibration of sound rock me, like maybe a mother would with her newborn child. A gong rang out, and just like that, I was transported back to the cave. Time and distance collapsed. It felt so damn real. My old monk, the one I told you about, remember?"

Ian kissed the top of her head, "I remember."

"Well, he sat in his meditative pose, like I always remember him. But this time, he noticed me. He smiled and reached his hand out, then lightly placed it on my heart. The minute his hand touched my chest, his unspoken words seared into my brain. 'A dream within a dream within a dream.' I opened my eyes and realized I hadn't moved from my place on the floor of the temple. The monks began chanting again, and I was whispering to myself... *a dream within a dream within a dream* ... I still think of it from time to time and wonder."

"Maybe none of this is real," Ian said softly. "Not you, me, or the tears we've all cried."

"The cold in this room sure as hell feels real. Damn, I don't know why I'm thinking about that island. Can you throw the blanket over my feet? My toes are freezing cold. There was something else, a presence. I don't know. Maybe I'll remember in the morning."

"I asked you about Thailand. That's why you thought of it. Association is one of the ways the brain operates. By the way, I remembered something today that might interest you."

"What?" she murmured, half asleep.

"About a year ago, I covered a story in Indonesia and met an interesting man. We both had a lot to drink, so take this with the proverbial grain of salt. The guy ranted on about a plane crash. I believe he said the crash happened along the Laotian border in the 1960s. After all those years, he was still haunted. He was guilt-ridden because he was the pilot. He went on and on about the crash being all his fault and his responsibility. His passenger was badly injured, but he survived. The patient was airlifted out of Thailand, so the pilot lost contact with him. Oddly, his passenger tracked him down several years later. Now this is where it gets murky, but it's probably why I remember the story. His passenger contacted him to find out about a dog. If I have it right, the pilot sent a dog to him on one of the islands in Indonesia. What was the name of the damn island?"

Mera nestled on his chest. "Plane crash? Indonesia?" Mera murmured before falling asleep.

Ian rose and, once again, opened the window to urinate. He quickly returned to the sleeping bag. The room was as frigid inside as the air outside. Awake now, he began to kiss Mera's neck and all the way down each arm.

Mera peered through squinted eyes. Her voice was hoarse with sleep. "Really need to use the toilet. Suggestion?"

"Bucket in the corner is the best I can do. Sorry." Mera slowly rose as Ian switched on a flashlight and handed it to her. "Over there. Turn off the flashlight. It will be almost private."

After a few moments, she was back, her teeth chattering.

"Hard to relax, but mission accomplished. Thanks."

Ian reached for her hand and pulled her back down.

"What the hell time is it?" she said.

"Too early to be out in the streets. Come. It's still warm where you were sleeping."

He leaned to kiss her on the lips, along her hairline, and down her neck as both struggled to remove heavy clothing from the night before and still remain attached to each other for warmth.

After they made love, they slept again. Their breath was visible in the early morning light.

Mera's eyes flew open wide. She began to lightly shake the Canadian asleep at her side.

"What were you saying last night? About a plane crash, a pilot, and a dog? I had this bizarre dream last night, about a hunched-over man and a dog with one blue eye and one brown. I wish I could remember the rest."

"I was talking to the dead last night, wasn't I?" Ian said. "Something kept nagging at me. I couldn't figure out why the story you told me about your biological father and his work in the 1960s sounded familiar. Then it came to me. I heard something strikingly similar a few years back. It may be nothing, but you might check it out. Usually, I have an uncanny memory for detail, but the pilot and I had a lot to drink …"

"Tell me what you remember."

"Last night, I couldn't remember the name of the damn island. But when I woke up this morning, it popped up first thing. The island is called Sumba. It's in Indonesia. The pilot sent the dog to Sumba. There's a man on the island who lives at the western tip. He picked up the dog and transferred it to its new owner, I think. There was nothing regarding the color of the dog's eyes, I'm sure about that. The pilot's name was Dave, but you'd have to ask around for the other fellow who lives on Sumba."

"Can you back up a bit?"

"What part did you miss?"

"The beginning, the middle, and the end!"

Streaks of light crept across wooden flooring. Mera slowly opened her eyes. The bedding was rolled tight around her body like swaddling. She peered out from under the blanket and realized she was alone. Soft conversation filtered in from the front room. Slowly, she stood while keeping the blanket wound around her. She slid through the doorway. Ian leaned up against the wall, the phone receiver held up to his ear and his glasses balanced precariously on the edge of his nose. He glanced in her direction and nudged his glasses into a more comfortable position. There was a blur of Bosnian being spoken and then silence as the voice on the other end replied. He gently settled the phone back onto its cradle.

"You're up! How'd you like to go on an excursion? We'll need to get moving."

"You let me sleep too long. I should get back."

"I didn't have the heart to wake you. You looked so peaceful, despite the cold. I made an appointment. Don't argue. It's all set up. We're going to pay a visit to your Bosnian girl at the children's home. I made you coffee."

"How did you …?"

"I have my ways. Connections. Here, drink this."

Mera sipped watery, sweet coffee, feeling a warmth spread across her lower belly. Fines lines deepened around her eyes, and her lips instantly curled downward. "That's terrible!"

"Come on. Drink up. It'll warm you. There's a bakery around the corner. If we're lucky, they might have some bread."

"The orphanage is all the way across the city. How do we get there?" she asked.

"Like I told you, I have friends in high places." Ian dangled a lone car key in his left hand. A smile broadened across his face as he once again pushed his thick-lensed glasses up along the bridge of his nose.

Outside, Ian nodded his head at a car.

"She belongs to Aleksander," he said. "And we can count on her being fairly reliable, by Sarajevo standards, that is. Once upon a time, she was a shiny apple red. She's not much to look at and dented on about every side. The passenger door won't shut, so you'll have to hold it closed. Ready?"

The faded red car only slowed at the stoplight, then accelerated, and shot past an intersection at a fountained plaza. Ian leaned forward, his gaze shooting from the small, cobblestone street to the buildings above and back again. Mera held onto the side of the semi-closed door with one hand and with the other back into the seat. She raised her voice to combat the ever-changing drone of the engine as Ian shifted gears, swerving to avoid abandoned cars and random debris without losing speed.

"Ever hear of the Dakar Rally?" she yelled.

"Sure, most challenging road race on the planet."

The tires suddenly seemed to lift off the ground as the car hit the curb, narrowly avoiding a black cat that darted across the street.

"Well, you'd be good at it!" Mera tightened her grip on the door handle and let out her breath as the car righted itself and, for once, slowed.

"I learned a few things living on the street, and it's come to be helpful. I do what I can to avoid becoming just one more statistic on the pages of the fallen journalists. Look, sorry for the wild ride, but there are snipers just about every … Get out of the car!" Ian yelled. Mera let go of the car door, which sprang open. Ian shoved her shoulder, pushing her out. Mera ducked and rolled hard onto the pavement. He jumped out the left side, ran around the back, and grabbed her hand. He urged her back up the street they had just driven down. Several minutes later, when Ian slowed, both of them were breathing hard. The car was carelessly parked, with only two of its wheels on the sidewalk. It was the only vehicle in sight. Mera bent down and rested her hands on her knees.

"What was that?" she said.

"I didn't mean to go down that street. It's notorious. Come on. We'll come back for the car. The kids' home is just a few blocks from here. It's safer on foot."

They rounded the corner just as the darkened building came into sight. A gaunt, elderly woman poked her head out to look down the street and just as quickly withdrew it back into hallway.

"Let's go. She won't wait long."

Ian picked up Mera's hand and trotted forward, his eyes constantly sweeping the surrounding buildings, streets, doorways, and windows. The woman beckoned them to come quickly when she saw them approach. Inside, she motioned for them to follow while speaking quickly with Ian.

"She says we're late. We can't stay long. They'll be moving the younger children to another building for the night."

They passed several rooms, each equally bare of furniture. In one room a few blankets were strewn on the floor, and several older boys took turns bouncing a semi-deflated soccer ball against the wall. The woman led Mera and Ian through the one room and into the next. There, fifteen to twenty small children either sat, rested, or chased one another. The absence of any toys for the children was apparent. Mera quickly surveyed the room and its occupants and did a double-take. She didn't recognize her at first. Zhera leaned against the wall and held the hand of a small boy. The girl's hair was shaved close to her scalp like all the children. Zhera dropped the boy's hand and ran across the room. Mera fell to her knees and swooped the small girl up in her arms. She held her tight against her chest. Ian squatted down next to them. A soft, wheezy voice was muffled against her armpit. Ian quickly translated.

"She wants to come with you. That's all I can make out." Mera pushed Zhera away from her chest to gently smooth her hand over the girl's forehead as she peered directly into her eyes.

"I'm going to get you out of here. We're going to live together where there's lots of sunshine, okay?" Mera turned to look at Ian. "Make her understand. She needs to know I'm coming back for her. Then remind me why I shouldn't grab her and run out of here right now. Who would stop me? This place is horrible."

"Well, for one, you might be kicked out of Bosnia at any moment. Two, the hotel is in the most dangerous part of town. Where would that leave your girl? Better to follow legalities and extract her with documents."

"It breaks my heart to leave her. I hate for any of these kids to be here."

Mera hugged Zhera close to her heart as her attention was drawn to the small boy who had been holding hands with her. He inched away from the wall and now stared in their direction.

"Who is your friend?" Mera asked in English.

Zhera responded by burrowing her head in deep, and her little hands gripped tight onto Mera's neck. Ian repeated the question in Bosnian and pointed to the boy. Without releasing her hands or removing her face from Mera's sweater, the child answered softly.

"Adin."

"Hello, Adin!" Ian swooped down and lifted the boy up above his head and swirled him in an arc, round and round in a circle.

"Again!" the boy screeched. Within moments, the room full of children narrowed to form a tight circle around Ian. Several pulled on his arm, while others tried to jump on his back.

"Slow down. One at a time!"

Mera set Zhera down. Together, she and Ian swung the children in big circles and gave them piggyback and airplane rides. Sweet laughter pealed and filled the drab room. The matron watched, with her lips a thin line. Finally, she pointed to her watch and motioned for the children to line up. Mera hugged Zhera, and her eyes filled with tears. Zhera started to cry in earnest.

"Mera … Mama!"

The matron plied tight, little fingers from around Mera's neck as she hoisted the wailing child onto her hip. Mera held up her hand.

"I will be back for you!" she said.

The children filed through the door and down the stairs. Zhera, still held by the matron, stretched out her little hand.

"Come on," Ian said. "We have to get back and see if the car's still there."

Miraculously, the battered, old car remained undisturbed in its hastily created parking spot. Ian quickly inserted the key as Mera stared out the window, quiet since leaving the children's home. The engine sputtered and died. Ian tried again. On the third try, there was no engine turnover at all.

"Quick, jump in the driver's seat. The battery's dead, and we're sitting ducks here unless we can get this thing started. I'll push."

Ian jumped out as Mera climbed into the driver's side. Fortuitously, the narrow cobblestone street had finished its climb and now began a gradual descent, down toward the river. Mera popped the clutch as Ian pushed, the small car picking up speed to a fast roll down the road. Ian ran alongside the car and finally jumped into the driver's seat as Mera climbed out of it, still guiding the steering wheel with her left hand. After a moment, the engine roared back to life. Mera held onto the door as they sped down the narrow streets.

"Do you mind dropping me at the hotel? I think it's just a mile or so from …"

The shot came out of nowhere, the windshield splintering into a spiderweb design on the driver's side. The car swerved up onto the sidewalk and bounced back onto the road, making a sharp turn onto a side street.

"You okay?" Ian asked.

Mera stared at the single hole in the left side of the windshield as if hypnotized by the pattern of cracks emanating from its center. Her attention turned to the driver, who shot a glance in her direction.

"All in one piece," she said. "If you ever decide to register for that Dakar Rally, use me as a reference!"

The bright yellow building, the Holiday Inn, emerged into sight just up the road.

"Turn left. You can access the parking garage from down the street," Mera said.

Ian turned and maneuvered the car down the ramp into the garage. He slowed to a stop in front of the stairway access, jumped out of the car, and held the door open as Mera climbed out and stood.

"Thanks for the …" In mid-sentence, Mera noticed Ian's left arm drooped at his side. He tried to support it with his right hand. "Let me see your arm."

"It's nothing."

Tentatively, Mera pulled Ian's jacket down his shoulder. His white shirt was splotched with a wide red stain.

"Let's take a look at that."

"It's nothing. Don't worry about it."

"You are not getting back in the car until it's checked out. If nothing else, the hotel has antibiotics and painkillers."

Once in the hotel, they rode the elevator to the third floor. Inside her room, Mera removed his jacket and shirt. On his upper arm, a raw, meaty chunk of flesh lay exposed.

"It looks like the bullet only grazed the arm, but that wound looks nasty. Lie down. I'll get the first-aid kit."

Ian slowly lowered himself onto the bed. It was almost forty-five minutes before Mera returned. She cleaned the area, poured iodine onto a clean cloth, and pressed it over the open wound. Ian winced. Slowly, she nudged her arm behind his back and eased his head up. She held a glass of water up to his mouth and dropped two pills, an antibiotic and a painkiller, onto his tongue. He lowered back down onto the bed. Gently, she wrapped his arm in gauze.

"Rest now and we'll get someone to look at that later. Okay?"

"Just a scratch."

It was already dark when Ian opened his eyes in Mera's hotel room. Photographs crisscrossed the room, suspended with tiny clothespins on strings attached to the side walls. The photos were all in black-and-white. Ian pushed himself up with his good arm and threw his legs to the side. He stood up as Mera looked over her shoulder.

"Sometimes I use the bathroom as a makeshift darkroom. How are you feeling?"

"Good as new. Thanks for the care. I'd offer my recommendation if you ever have a mind to enter the medical profession."

He considered each photograph one by one and stopped in front of a particularly haunting image of a woman. She hung drab laundry out to dry, her greying hair merged within a slate sky. The ordinary act of hanging laundry defied the devastation all around her.

"This one," he said.

She came to stand beside him.

"This woman … can you believe it? She invited me in for a cup of tea. I politely declined, but she wouldn't let me refuse. She spoke a little English. We had a sweet visit. Why is it that those who have the very least seem to be the most generous? In the hope she might be able to get some food for her family, I left an envelope with some dollars on the counter. What she and countless others come home to every night haunts me. Will her family be alive tomorrow? Will her house be standing?"

"Every act of kindness means something," Ian said, placing his good arm around her shoulders and drawing her close. "Come. The suffering of the world and its inhabitants will be here tomorrow. Might you direct just a sliver of that massive compassionate heart in the direction of one poor, wounded Canadian?" He placed his lips on the top of her head, and they both leaned down toward the bed.

Mera entered the bar at ten p.m. It had been two months since she'd been back to see Ian.

He sat at his usual post. There was a woman seated beside him. Her hair was bleached blonde, and her eyes were heavily coated with a thick black eyeliner and blue mascara. Otherwise, she was quite pretty. He glanced at the door when she entered and then returned his attention to the blonde. Mera sat down at a table against the wall. She ordered a whiskey without looking in Ian's direction and leaned back into the chair. A few minutes later, Ian sat down across from her.

"How did it go with Jakob?" he asked.

"How's the arm?" Her eyes drifted to his left shoulder.

"Good as new." He lifted the arm and rolled it in a giant circle.

"That's good. I was worried about infection."

"I was fortunate for excellent medical assistance provided on the scene."

"I came to thank you. Jakob set up some interviews and briefed me on the channels required to get Zhera out of the country. He's an amazing resource. I have a fair chance to get her out. It wouldn't have happened without your contact. I'm sorry I waited so long to tell you how much I appreciate your help."

"My pleasure." Ian pushed his chair back from the table and stood to return to the bar and the blonde, who was now turned in their direction, staring. He swung back around.

"I thought you were gone. Otherwise, you would have come, right? What's it been? Two months?"

"I wanted to come earlier. It's just that, well, I couldn't. I'm sorry."

"If you had come later, I might not have been here. I'm thinking of disappearing for a while."

"I'm glad I came then. I have to leave Sarajevo. I've been ordered out, myself and several journalists. I wasn't expecting that to come so soon."

"What will you do?" he asked.

"I researched the island. You know, the one you told me about with the pilot and the dog? I think I'll fly to Indonesia while I'm waiting to hear about Zhera. There's too much coincidence to at least not try. I might find a few answers. Anyway, that's the hope."

"Sounds like goodbye."

"It's always goodbye. I've learned that lesson well."

"How are you getting out?"

"We won't know until the last minute. We have to move when they say go. It's a tricky business, getting out of Sarajevo. I'm sure you're aware."

"You know I went back to the hotel and asked for one Mera Rodríguez. They said there was no one there by that name. Of course, they wouldn't allow me to wander up to your room."

"I'm sorry. I use my father's name, Jameson, for travel. It's what's on the very valuable American passport. I'm sorry you went to the trouble, and I wasn't there."

"There was a big German fellow. I was sure he knew who I was talking about. I thought he was going to pick me up and bodily throw me out of the hotel. He seemed somewhat possessive."

"That would be Emmett. He means well, but his affections are misplaced. He's been told, more than once."

"I'm easy to find if you change your mind."

Ian slid his business card across the table. Mera quietly stared at it for close to a minute. Slowly, she walked her fingers across the table and laid them on the card.

"Memories …" She spoke softly, more to herself than the man. "It's hard to distance yourself from the story."

"What do you mean?" Ian stared into her eyes.

"Life. It's a crazy, fucked-up hypnotism." Her fingers quickly snatched the card and dropped it to the bottom of her purse.

"I take that as a positive sign." Ian nudged his glasses up his nose. "You want to spend the night? I can offer five-star accommodation!"

The blonde woman, seated at the bar, threw her stool noisily back with a dark glance to the table in the corner. Ian placed his arm on Mera's shoulder.

"You're leaving. What's the harm? I've missed you."

Leaving her whiskey unfinished, Mera slowly put on her coat.

"That's the thing. I … missed you too. But I can't. I'm sorry. I hope I didn't …" She nudged her head in the direction of the front door, which closed with a bang.

"No problem. See you around." Ian continued to watch as Mera followed the blonde's exit. She turned at the door and lifted her hand for a moment before letting it drop to her side.

Chapter Sixty-Seven

1994

Sumba, Indonesia

A navy-blue Volkswagen decelerated. The slowing crunch of tires on rocky dirt crackled in the hot, muggy afternoon. Mera stepped out and closed the door. She glanced at the hastily scribbled directions that circumnavigated the perimeter of the local dive-shop brochure and then looked to the east, where the lane ended abruptly one hundred meters from the edge. Thirty feet below, waves crashed against a rocky coast, and the spray crested up in a giant arch. The small farmstead, located to the left side of the lane, was the only habitable accommodation here at the tip of the island. *This has to be the one.*

The main house had a thatched grass roof and was nestled at the edge of the tree line. Several smaller structures were scattered around the property, including a fenced area for livestock. A pig, two goats, a horse, and a burro cohabitated in the enclosure amicably. To the right, there was an open-air garage consisting of a roof, back wall, and three open sides. Inside it, a 1964 Yamaha motorcycle in mint condition leaned against its kickstand.

Mera swept her sunglasses up on top of her head and shaded her eyes from the bright sun with her right hand. She waited a few minutes, hesitant. The door to the main house creaked open to reveal a man with thick, silver hair. He leaned on a wooden cane. He stretched and emitted a shrill whistle. A small brown dog jumped to attention and was at the man's side within a moment. The man straightened. In tandem, the dog and man turned toward the woman standing at the edge of the property. Immediately, the dog took off running, broadcasting its strident warning, its sharp barks amplified in the quiet of the afternoon. In seconds, the little dog breached the distance to within a meter of Mera and circled, nipping at her heels. Mera leaned over, calm, and allowed the small animal to smell her hand.

"Hello, Cariño. What a sweet one you are. Take your time. Have a good sniff. I mean no harm."

The small dog, calmed now, eagerly wagged its tail and allowed its head to be massaged. The silver-haired man lifted his hand to his forehead and peered intently in the woman's direction. He shook his head as the sun was now directly in his eyes. Beams of light made the woman's image waver and become transparent as a mirage.

Mera stood up and swept the back of her hand across her forehead while walking toward the building. The man waved and called the dog, who immediately returned to his side.

"Hello!" She raised her hand in greeting.

"I'm sorry. The sun was in my eyes. For a moment, I thought you were someone else," he said. "But of course that couldn't be. I'm afraid you've reached the end of the island. You must have missed your turn. Sumba doesn't get many visitors this time of the year, at least out our way."

"No, I believe this is the place—the house where the road ends. If you go any farther, you'll drop off the cliff. Anyway, that's how someone described it. I'm sorry. Steve, from the local dive shop, gave me directions here."

"Well, then, how can I help you?" the man said.

"I am looking for a man, but unfortunately, I have only a brief description. Steve seems to know everyone on the island, the full-time residents anyway. He narrowed the possibilities to three. Since you are the only farmhouse at the end of the island, I thought I'd start here."

"If he lives on Sumba, I probably know him, too. I've been here a long time."

"The man I'm looking for brokered a dog for a pilot named Dave and a man who used to go by the name of Lance Jameson. It was some thirty-odd years ago. I know it's not a lot to go on."

"Lance Jameson? No one here by that name. What do you want with him?"

He shuffled his weight as a sharp pain shot up his left leg. The man leaned deeper onto the cane, and the tip wedged into a groove on the ground where he stood.

"Damn leg, gives me trouble when the humidity rises. I don't know that I can help you. It's a struggle to remember what happened yesterday, much less thirty years ago."

"Have you heard of the pilot? Or anything about a plane crash in the early 1960s along the Thai-Laotian border? I'm sorry. This is probably a wild goose chase, but I've been cursed. I have to see it to the end. Here's the thing. Dave, the pilot, mentioned a man on Sumba to a friend of mine. The two met in a bar in Jakarta a few years ago. As the story goes, Dave had a dog sent to Sumba. The dog was picked up and delivered to one Lance Jameson somewhere in Indonesia."

The man's eyes withdrew. Only the crashing of the surf below, a faint rustling of leaves, and several bird cries disturbed the quiet afternoon. Mera shifted uneasily and cleared her throat, a gentle reminder of her presence.

"Lance … Lance hasn't gone by that name in decades," the man said. "No use trying to resurrect the dead. No good will come of it."

"I've traveled a long way, if you know something?"

"Come inside, weary traveler, and have a lemonade. It's too hot out here this time of day." *Odd mix. American, British, a hint of south of the border.* "Atibu, we have a visitor," the man called. "Do we have something cold? Lemonade?"

A slight Indonesian woman in her early forties, her black hair braided and draped down to the small of her back, emerged from the kitchen with a radiant smile. "Hello," she said, "lovely to meet you. Will you excuse me for a moment? I will bring a cold drink."

"Thank you, Atibu. We'll have a seat in the living room. I'm sorry. What was your name, miss?" the man asked.

"Meri, Meri Rodríguez."

"A pleasure to meet you, Mary. Will you stay and have lunch? It's a rare occurrence for a visitor to make it out our way."

"I don't want to intrude …"

"No, it's our pleasure. Please stay. Atibu here, she's the heart of this humble abode. My name is John Smith." He extended his hand.

"John Smith?" Her gaze was direct.

"I'm sorry the place is a bit of a mess. Like I said, we weren't expecting company. Give me a minute to clear these papers."

Mera waited a moment until the seat was free and then easily dropped onto the cushioned beige couch.

"Thirty years, that's practically an archeological dig," John Smith said.

"I have been researching my roots. I was told there's a man on Sumba who might have known Lance Jameson." She paused, inspecting the man's face for any sign of recognition. His expression remained neutral.

445

"Go on," he said.

"A year ago, I gave up the search and resolved to let the whole thing go, but a chance encounter with a journalist a few months ago reignited my interest. The journalist told me a story he'd heard, something about a plane crash in the early sixties on the Thai-Laotian border and a pilot named Dave who may have had a connection to the man I've been trying to locate, Lance Jameson."

"And why do you think Mr. Jameson might be able to help you?"

"I believe he knew my mother."

"Your mother's name? If I happen to run into him, it would help if I could pass along a name."

"My birth mother is not the mother I knew as a child. I learned quite late in life that my real mother's name was Isabela. I never knew her. She died, unfortunately, at the time of my birth."

"Her name ... the last name?"

"Isabela Marquez from El Salvador."

John Smith looked up sharply. "That's impossible. Isabela died in a car accident in 1962. She never had a child."

"You knew her?" John's gaze wandered and came to rest on Mera's left index finger and thumb that played with her left earlobe. He was silent.

"Yes, it's true she died at that time," Mera continued, "although not in a car crash. That was the made-up story—the intelligence cover-up, if you will. The truth, what I've been told at least, is that my mother died giving birth to me in a small village in Laos, along the border. When I first learned that my family, the family that brought me up, was not my biological one, I had zero interest in learning anything about the parents that gave me life. Many years later, after college, it became more important. My uncle told me my biological parents were an American on assignment in Thailand and a Salvadoran woman who was an art student studying abroad for a year. It's all I wanted to know for a long time. When I changed my mind, I became determined to learn it all. My uncle told me what he knew, the truth from his perspective. Dave, the pilot, is the only link to Lance Jameson."

"I'm sorry you've gone to all this trouble. It's probably a very bad joke."

"Not likely. My uncle doesn't have a humorous bone in his body."

The man focused on the woman's face, her eyes, hazel with a slight downward tilt. He pushed back his chair to stand and shifted uncomfortably. His hands settled on the back of the chair.

"Your uncle's name?"

"In truth, he's not my uncle. I call him my uncle because he is the one who saved me. His name is Nigel Hawkes."

Dust particles danced on beams of light that flickered in through the front window as the late afternoon sun shifted lower in the sky. The room darkened imperceptibly. The man squeezed his hands into fists and slowly released them.

"How old are you?" he asked.

"Do you know these people? Does anything sound familiar?"

"Your age, please?" he asked again, softer this time.

"I am thirty-two. Now, please, can you help me?"

Color drained from the man's tanned, leathery skin and made his face appear yellowish. He took a step back and swerved to face the wall, away from her. His arm shot out, and in one full swipe, a blue plate, a cup, a vase with pink flowers, and a stack of papers flew up in a tornado. Papers hovered in midair and then fluttered to the ground as the heavier items crashed. Pieces of vase splintered and dispersed in a puddle of pink petals, coffee, and water.

Mera's attention jerked to the right, her eyes drawn to the broken debris on the floor, and slowly revisited the man standing in front of her. Tears began to form in her eyes. *What the hell is this?* Her heart thumped erratically against the inside of her ribs. He swung back around to face her.

"I was in the hospital when I learned Isabela died. I was not long out of a coma and still not able to wipe my own ass. I couldn't continue … I had to make sure there was no trace of my old self … Lance Jameson. And there was a price on my head. I couldn't let the innocent get hurt. It was my fault, every damn misstep and error. It doesn't matter that I didn't intend for any of it to happen. All that money up in flames! What was I to do?" Lance stopped abruptly and stared into space.

"What money?"

"Even after all these years, there isn't a day that I don't think of her."

Atibu reemerged from the kitchen, wiping her hands on her skirt. Her eyes moved slowly from the visitor to the man and back again.

"It was the accident. The plane lost both engines. We hit the damn trees. It couldn't be avoided. Dave did an incredible job flying that piece of junk. It's only because of him we both made it out alive, and I can tell you I've flown with all types." He turned to look at her.

"How long has Nigel known … about you?"

"Since the day I was born. He was with my mother when she died. He saved me then and again years later. He rescued me from the war in El Salvador."

"Goddamn it, Nigel!"

Lance stepped nearer to extend his hand. His fingers lightly brushed the smooth texture of her jaw, as if to feel the credibility of its density. She immediately stood and took a step back, as if burned by the contact. A tear rolled uninhibited down his cheek.

"I didn't know. How was I to know? Nigel didn't say a word, and later when he might have, I was already gone. Please, tell me you have been looked after. I can't believe I didn't see the resemblance. You look so much like her."

Lance's arm lowered and hung awkwardly by his side. He glanced up as if to memorize the outline of her.

"My darling girl, you have no idea what you mean to me or that you have found your way here."

Mera studied the lone coffee cup, tilted on its side, as dark liquid dripped onto the white linoleum floor. Her eyes remained riveted to the debris on the floor as her next words were pronounced in a lugubrious monotone.

"You are Lance? My biological father? Don't worry. Please, I don't need anything from you. I just want to know something of my mother, how you knew her, or why all of this happened."

"A few dinners and four days on a tropical island. That's all it was. And yet." He splayed his fingers to stare at the knuckles. "My life was irrevocably changed. I owe her a debt beyond measure. Can you … will you stay?"

Sunglasses lowered to cover her eyes. Mera quickly turned away from the man.

"I'm sorry. I wasn't expecting this." It was her turn to wave her hands aimlessly to flop back down by her sides.

"Please, say you'll come back."

She was halfway out the door when she turned. "What about the dog? Why did the pilot send you a dog?"

"It was two years before Dave and I met up again here in Indonesia. In the beginning, he only kept the dog out of loyalty or guilt that I was the one seriously hurt. He didn't like dogs, especially village dogs like Amigo. But, by the time I met Dave in Indonesia, he and Amigo had been together for close on two years. Over time, they bonded. Even though I wanted the dog, it would have been wrong to reclaim ownership. The dog was devoted to Dave, and I think he loved the mutt equally. He took the little guy everywhere he went. He was the craziest-looking mongrel, one brown eye and one blue. He looked more like an overgrown rat, one who hadn't eaten in a long time. Amigo was going to be our dog, Isabela's and mine."

It was Lance's turn to stare at the spillage broadening across on the linoleum floor as Atibu bent to clean it up.

"It was Dave who told me Isabela went to the hospital after the accident. She was looking for me, but by the time she arrived, I was already halfway to a medical military transport back to the United States. Over the years—and you can't possibly imagine how many times I've wondered about the timing of it—I've imagined how things might have, should have, turned out differently. The way he talked about her, I believe Dave was a bit in love with her, too. Who the hell wouldn't be? Maybe it was for her that he kept the damn dog."

Mera fumbled in the side pocket of her purse, extracted two items, and opened her hand. "And these?"

The elephant and the jaguar lay side by side in the palm of her hand. Lance stared at the carvings a long time before speaking.

"She told me once she thought the elephant and jaguar represented our strange encounter and love."

Atibu stood, the dishrag still in her hand, dripping brown liquid. Gently, she took Lance's arm and guided him back to the couch, where he collapsed with a sigh. "That is the way it is and not a damn thing we can do about it."

Atibu ran her fingers through his thick silver hair. "He's tired now. Come back later?" Mera remained at the door, with one foot in and one foot out. Her fingers gripped the wooden carvings until her fist turned white. Lance continued to talk in a monologue directed to the wall.

"We agreed, finally, that he would breed our little friend to a bitch with excellent references. He said he'd send me the pick of the litter and damned if one day there weren't a pair of the cutest damned puppies waiting for me at the airport." He paused, and the room was eerily quiet. "What were you saying? You're looking for Amigo?" Lance mumbled, "Amigo's outside. I'll call him for you. I'm sorry, I don't think we've met?"

"I'm Mera."

"Mera, yes, of course, Isabela's daughter."

Mera looked to Atibu. "Is it okay? I'll come back later if you think it's best?"

"He don't sleep now. You can stay. He get tired, and he don't make sense. But he want you to stay." Atibu turned and quietly withdrew to the kitchen.

Mera stepped purposefully back into the house and sat down next to Lance, who continued to speak to the wall. She took his hand in hers and interlaced her fingers with his.

"Go on. It's why I've come."

Gentle pressure on his fingers prompted Lance's head to lift. He looked fixedly at the girl with eyes so like his own. Tears rolled down his face unabashedly.

"I'm not the same. Not the same as when I knew your mother. I'm sorry."

"My given name is Mera. Isabela told Nigel to make sure I was given this name."

"Mount Meru is the center of the universe. That's what the Buddhists say."

Atibu called from the kitchen. She set three plates out on the lanai. Several platters were heaped with rice served on banana leaves, grilled chicken skewers, lime and peanut sauce, and an abundant green salad with a glass of lemonade at each setting. Mera rose and walked outside to sit under the shaded palm tree. Lance got up slowly and limped across the room, leaving his cane by the door.

"It smells delicious. Thank you!" Mera said.

"Damned hip has never been right since the accident. If I stretch it out for an hour or so, I can straighten up to almost my old height, but by the next morning, there I am again, crooked and bent like the old man I am." He smiled and tapped his leg. "I'm grateful I can still walk. My pelvis was broken in two places. I can't see out of my left eye." His eyes set on the young woman seated across from him. "I want to hear about your family, the family that raised you. Was your life happy? Did they treat you well and love you?"

"My family was wonderful, the best anyone could hope for. Unfortunately, it all shattered when I was fifteen because of the war."

Mera sat with her legs drawn under her seat. She felt uncommonly relaxed and at peace. For the second time since leaving El Salvador, she recounted the story of her childhood, and her words flowed. She talked for hours. Lance wandered the room, stretched his back, mumbled words only he could hear, cried, and then he sat down again. Once she started to talk, she found she couldn't stop. In the end, what mattered was the kindness in his eyes and the peace she felt in her heart.

Before there was discernable light, a rooster crowed.

"I'm suddenly starving," she said. "Is there anything in the kitchen I can make?"

"I'll wake Atibu. She'll make us something."

"Don't wake her. I can manage."

"Do you like pancakes? There's mix and syrup, I think."

Atibu appeared from the bedroom, wiping sleep from her eyes.

"Go back to sleep, Atibu. This beautiful young lady is making pancakes!"

Lance began to cry again as he pulled the pancake mix from the shelf and the butter and milk from the refrigerator. He lit a match at the stove, and immediately, a bright, bluish flame ignited.

The following morning, Mera returned to the hotel to pick up her things while Atibu set up the guest room. Little did she know it would be days before she would be able to return to the small farm at the edge of the island. Lance scanned the dirt road hourly, pacing, mumbling, and then forgetting what he was doing outside.

When Mera returned to her hotel room, the message light flashed and cast a reddish hue on the back wall. There was an urgent message from her lawyer in New York. The orphanage in Sarajevo was hit by a missile one early afternoon and sustained one casualty, a care worker. The blast shattered the windows of the orphanage and collapsed two of the outlying buildings. In the aftermath, the west wing, where the children slept, was badly damaged, and it was determined the entire orphanage was beyond repair. But the children were all accounted for. Immediate funds were needed to care for the orphans, who were relocated with families who could scarcely afford to feed them. Due to the volatility of the situation, the authorities indicated a willingness to move Zhera's adoption process along in the interests of getting at least one child to a safety zone. It was several days before Mera was able to work out the logistics of transferring funds to New York. On a wing and a prayer, the money would find its proper destination with the next attaché, journalist, or diplomat. It was abundantly clear that after the difficulty of getting out of the city, she would not be allowed to return to Sarajevo anytime soon.

It was four days before Mera was finally able to return to the small ranch at the end of the island. This time, Lady, the dog, bounded up to meet her and wagged her tail in a furious greeting. Lance opened the screen door and allowed it to slam shut behind him. As he recognized the car, a wide smile broadened across his face.

"You've been gone a long time. I was worried you wouldn't come back," he said.

"Well, if you'd get a phone, I might have been able to call and let you know. It is 1994. I, for one, would feel better if you'd get one installed. Then we could talk all the time." She picked up her suitcase in one hand and took his hand in her other. Together, they entered the farmhouse.

"Never wanted one, but if I get to talk to you, I might consider it," Lance said.

Mera stayed for several weeks and helped tend the animals and weed the garden. Every evening, they all watched the sun lower onto the horizon and disappear. Dusk was her favorite time of day. She, her father, and Atibu all quietly sat around the bamboo table with a glass of wine or a fruit juice. At times, they spoke. Other moments were quiet. The raucous cries of blackbirds sharing their last lament before dark punctuated the silence.

In the garden, among the growing things, her father's mind was clearest. He had a way with plants. His produce was larger and more colorful than any she had seen anywhere on the island or elsewhere.

"When I first discovered Sumba, I felt I had to do something useful, so I flew a bit, cargo flights to the mainland mostly. There were just locals here back then and an incredible quiet. It's still pristine, but the invasion is coming. The hordes always find places like this in the end. I wish they'd leave us alone."

They walked back to the farmhouse. She leaned her head on his shoulder and said, "I want to show you something. I've been holding onto it. Kate gave it to me when I turned twenty-one. It's this funny box wrapped in string. I know it's odd, but I didn't open it until a few years ago. That was my state of mind. She said an old woman gave it to her years ago in Burma. The old woman accurately predicted my birth and sex, without ever having met my mother. I guess the whole thing felt too heavy, just another something I didn't want any part of. I believe it's quite valuable. I'm supposed to know what to do with it, but honestly, I don't."

Mera went into her room and returned with the box wrapped in twine. Carefully, she unwound the binding until the string dangled and touched the floor. Inside, a large emerald rested atop a bed of cotton. As a boy, Lance had seen gems laid out across the kitchen table each time his father returned from a business trip. He never learned the details that a master jeweler would know, yet his father showed him how to spot a genuine, valuable stone and those gems that deserved a closer look.

He leaned in and picked up the emerald, feeling the heavy weight of it in his hand. He held it up to the light and saw that the color was evenly proportioned and transparent. Green light shimmered and reflected on the white wall. From every angle, there was no flaw.

"That's one of a kind. I wouldn't be surprised if it's fifty carats or more. Priceless. Where did it come from?"

"From Kate. She said your old nanny gave it to her, Amah? Maiv Lee? I'm supposed to know what to do with it."

"My father was a gem dealer. He bought and sold them all over southeast Asia. I don't know. You could sell the thing and make a lot of money," Lance said.

"Is that what you think I'm supposed to do with it?"

"When I was a boy, Amah talked about my father's gems. She'd shake her head and look me straight in the eye. She'd say, 'Those rocks can steal away the people's heart.' As a kid, I wondered what she meant. How can a pretty stone have that kind of power?"

"What else?"

"When I was ten, Amah accompanied my father to her village. One of Amah's friends came to stay with me while they were away. There were gems up there in those hills, she told him, so he might have thought he could do some trading." Lance knitted his forehead into three distinct lines. His gaze remained fixated on the perfectly cut green emerald in his palm as his mind wandered back. He paused several minutes and said finally, "I remember this stone!"

"You've seen it before?"

"I think so. It was a long time ago, so I can't be sure it's the same one," Lance said, "but this might be the gem that caused all the trouble in her village."

"What do you mean?"

"I don't really know, but Amah made me swear never to tell anyone about it." He continued to stare at the stone that had apparently resurfaced from his childhood.

"Amah took the stone from the village for a reason. She didn't give a rat's ass about things or money. It wouldn't have been that. There's no way to know her motivation. The important point is for you to take it and follow the tracks."

"What? How could she have possibly known about me? I wasn't even born yet."

"Amah had a sixth sense about her. She always knew about events before they happened. I'm not surprised she knew about Isabela and her daughter." Lance's gaze turned inward, and he was silent for several moments before he spoke again. "I'm so sorry. I should have felt you like Amah did. What kind of person abandons his daughter? Maybe the damn thing is cursed. Get rid of it. Keep it. I don't know! Isabela died because of a rock? They all died because of this thing. There has to be some mistake. Take it away. I don't want to see it."

Mera snatched the emerald from Lance's hand and returned it to its box.

"Don't give it another thought. I'll figure something out. Maybe I'll sell it and give the money to the orphanage in Sarajevo when the war's over, when they stop blowing each other up."

"Damn thing is cursed. Get rid of it!"

"I have to leave soon. I need to get back to Washington and see about the girl. Remember? I don't want to go, but I really have to be where my attorney is more accessible."

"What girl?" Lance said.

"Zhera, the little girl I am trying to adopt out of Bosnia. I told you about her."

"I see. Yes, you told me about the girl. I don't want you to leave. Please don't go."

"Maybe I can bring her here, if all goes as planned."

"El Salvador. We need to go there, the two of us. I need to tell them I'm sorry," Lance said.

"It took months to get my sanity back the last time I went to that country. I won't go back. I don't want to see any of them. I'll go anywhere in the world you want, but El Salvador is off the map."

"We need to go right away. Pack your bag!"

"Let's go back inside and have a lemonade. I'm not leaving today or tomorrow. Let's wait a bit and see how you're feeling."

Mera couldn't be sure if Lance played the fool, or if his early senility was closing in. At times, his speech elicited perfect recall and sharp observation, while at other times, he made no sense at all.

The following morning, Lance rose as usual at four forty-five a.m. He began his day with a cup of coffee and went to sit on the veranda as the cicadas chirped and the birdsong announced its morning presence. Each species had its unique tone and melody. Lance looked up as Mera joined him on the lanai.

"Early morning is the best damn time of the entire day. Can you feel it? The rhythm, the balance of nature. Man thinks he's in control, and nature has a good laugh. Best we can do is join the chorus and let go. That's why we have to go to El Salvador, my girl."

From that moment, it was as if Lance's entire life purpose was to travel to El Salvador. He brought it up at breakfast, lunch, and again in the evening as they sipped fruit juice and watched the sun kiss the ocean. Atibu shook her head and looked to Mera, her eyes softening as they both turned in his direction. In the end, one day in the garden, Mera finally agreed to make the trip.

"It's always good to have growing things near you," Lance said. She dropped to her knees to pull weeds, softening the soil with a trowel. Lance knelt beside her. "It's like this." He scooped out the weed at its root and let the dirt fall through his fingers. "The weed is not bad," he said. "It wants to live too, but it will choke the life out of the plant if we let it. The root needs room to grow, to prosper. That's why we have to go to El Salvador. Pull out the weeds so that you can breathe and prosper."

Chapter Sixty-Eight

1994

San Salvador, El Salvador

They hoisted their bags into the bed of the dirt-splattered white Hilux truck while Atibu hopped into the driver's seat. For the fifth time, she reminded Mera of the three medications Lance should not be without, the time of day they needed to be taken, and what to do if he became agitated. It took several days for Mera to convince Atibu that Lance was strong enough to fly halfway around the world and another four to convince herself she was capable of handling whatever situation might arise with a return to a country she vowed she'd never to set foot in again.

Atibu remained at the airport and waved goodbye to the small airplane as it rumbled down the runway and lifted off the ground into the air. She continued to watch as it vanished into the clouds and then quietly walked back to the truck.

The Boeing 737 began its slow descent over San Salvador as the flight attendant passed out landing forms. For the third time in three days, Mera filled out her father's forms while his head rested gently on her shoulder. When he disappeared so many years before, Lance procured a passport and birth certificate that were expertly forged. He hired craftsmen employed by governments to create aliases for their agents and who could be relied on for their absolute discretion. Lance assured Mera there was no difference between his passport and hers.

Mera knew the forgery was excellent, but she was all too aware of the country they were traveling to. A numbing chill shimmied up her spine. Her fears turned out to be unwarranted, though, for on this particular day, only a few passengers lined up to wait their turn at Immigration. It was only a short thirty minutes before their bags wound around the circular baggage claim carousel. A driver waited outside the customs hall. *Mr. Smith* and *Miss Jameson* were printed in bold black lettering on an erasable chalkboard. He drove them directly to the Real InterContinental Hotel, where a room with two double beds and a view overlooking the swimming pool awaited. Mera kicked off her shoes and sank gratefully onto the bed. Lance, however, paced the room. He opened the curtains to peer at the lighted pool below.

"Papa, it's ten p.m. Whatever you have planned is going to have to wait until tomorrow. I'm spent. Let's sleep."

"Papa" slipped easily off her tongue. Lance leaned down to squeeze her hand. She closed her eyes and fell instantly asleep, only to awaken three hours later. Lance's bed was untouched. A tan armchair had been dragged halfway across the room to the window. Her father sat in the chair, gazing out beyond the pool into a starless night. Mera threw her sheets back and slowly pushed herself up. With a slow exhale, she rose and walked to the window. She took her father's hand and gently guided him to the bed.

"Sleep now," she said.

He was showered and dressed when she opened her eyes again, and there was a pot of coffee brewed and waiting. He poured coffee into the paper cup and offered it to her.

"Cream? All they have is this powdered stuff," he said. "Here's the address. I found it right there in the directory, under 'Pablo Marquez.' Isabela always spoke so highly of her father. She described the ranch, the sweet-smelling flowers, the birds, and wildlife in such meticulous detail, like a landscape portrait." Lance's eyes suddenly teared.

"That sounds nice," Mera said.

"Let's go. The ranch is only fifteen kilometers outside of the city. We can take a taxi."

"First, shower and breakfast. Then taxi. Okay?"

Mera slowly showered, the beat of her heart a loud thumping in her chest. She ran the brush through her thick hair and counted—450, 451. At 1000 strokes, she quietly set the brush down and came out of the bathroom. It was clear that she couldn't send Lance to the ranch by himself. She would have to go with him. Just being in the damn country made her skin crawl. How much worse could meeting phantom relatives be?

I'll make this trip for him, to resolve the past and put it to rest. But I'll hold my breath until we are on the plane and taking off out of here.

She insisted they eat a big breakfast. She ordered scrambled eggs, toast, bacon, a slice of pineapple and strong coffee for both. She watched as he swallowed three pills. That accomplished, there was nothing left to do.

Lance jumped up from the table and paid the bill. In full command of the moment, he pressed her elbow forward. Mera stood and took a tentative step, her forward movement as stymied as if the weight of a thousand stones pressed upon her shoulders and back. Her nervous system was on high alert. Inside the InterContinental Hotel, one could imagine and quite easily believe you were in any country in the world. El Salvador was no longer at war, but combat zones were not what she feared. The hauntings came from a completely different source. She worked a very long time to subdue the inner demons. It was many years before three therapists gave her a clean bill of health. But, in the end, she knew the dragon merely slept, ready at a moment's notice to open its wings and char the landscape with the fire of its breath.

"Ready?" he asked.

Her breathing intensified as the hair on her arms stood straight up.

"Let's stay in the hotel another day. We can research a few things."

Lance was already halfway across the lobby and talking with the bellman.

"Hurry up," he said. "A taxi is waiting."

His voice carried across the lobby, and Mera trotted to catch up, afraid he might hop into the taxi and take off without her. Inside the taxi, Lance reached across the seat to hand the driver the address. The taxi honked and darted through the traffic, passing the bus station and hospital. Each time she recognized a place, albeit ones transformed and modernized, she quickly looked the opposite way and willed the images to fade. It was another twenty-five minutes before the taxi pulled up in front of the hacienda. Mera made arrangements for the driver to wait. She told him they would not be long.

"Over here. I think the front door is down this path," Lance said.

It was hard not to succumb to Lance's childlike enthusiasm. The knock on the heavy, mahogany door was answered almost immediately. The servant smiled and politely inquired who they wished to see. Mera stayed quiet as Lance spoke in negligible Spanish.

"Queremos ver a Pablo Marquez." *We want to see Pablo Marquez.*

"Un momento, por favor." *One moment, please.* The maid left the door slightly ajar and quickly retreated. A man who appeared to be in his early fifties opened the door wide and extended his hand. He spoke in a perfectly enunciated English.

"How may I help you?"

"We are hoping to speak with Pablo Marquez. Is he at home?"

"I'm sorry. You must not have heard. Pablo Marquez passed away two years ago. I am his nephew, Enrique Marquez. Please come in. My aunt, Pablo's wife, Ivanna, is on the veranda. Would you like to speak with her? She is in her eighties now, but you would never know it."

Lance shook his head, "I waited too long. We are terribly sorry to learn of his death. Yes, please. May we speak with his widow?"

"Who shall I say is calling?" Enrique said.

"Lance Jameson. This is my daughter, Isabela."

Enrique looked at him for several seconds.

"Me llamo Mera." Mera stepped forward to offer her hand. "I am his daughter. That part is true." She smiled, a light flush broadening across her cheeks.

The three walked across a gleaming marble floor that opened onto a wide verandah. Pink-tufted trees canopied the deck as a flock of parakeets squawked and rose in a flutter of wings to land on a tree across the hillside. Ivanna Marquez sipped an orange juice as she read the morning's newspaper. Her snow-white hair was cropped to chin length, and a black headband pulled her hair off her forehead. Stray wisps fluttered across her forehead as a light breeze swept across the porch. She looked up as the trio approached the porch.

"If you came to discuss business, you will have to speak with my nephew. I see you met Enrique."

"This is a personal matter," Lance said. "We were hoping to speak with your husband, Pablo Marquez. Sadly, we just learned we are two years too late. We are terribly sorry for your loss. Please, may we have a moment of your time?"

Mera hung back to lean against the railing and stare into the tufted pink flowers, swallowing hard to relax the pressure rising up her throat. *What's the good of all of this? Disturbing an old lady with a past that haunts us all?*

Ivanna rose, her eyes hidden behind dark glasses. She removed them and held out her hand. Her fingers long and elegant. Lance stared at the blue-veined hand and began to cry.

What have I gotten myself into? Mera pushed harder into the railing, shrinking back from what was happening in front of her.

"Oh dear. Enrique, have Theresa bring tea. We'll move to the living room. We will be more comfortable at the table."

They sat on comfortably stuffed, green-striped chairs situated around a wicker-and-glass table. The servant set the teapot on the table with a stack of toasted bread. A small silver pot held butter and another one strawberry jam. Lance wiped his eyes with the sleeve of his shirt, leaned over, and took Mera's hand. He introduced himself once again and then Mera, correctly this time.

"Can't you see it? The resemblance to Isabela?" he said.

Ivanna Marquez turned in Mera's direction and stared at the young woman. Mera felt blood rise up her throat. Known for her daring and careless abandon in war zones, she was a photographic journalist who risked her life for that one perfect shot of the face of a child or the bloodied remains of a fallen soldier. Here, she found herself completely immobilized. Ivanna Marquez straightened.

"My daughter died a long time ago. I am an old woman. I am not foolish."

"I should have come earlier," Lance said. "It shattered me, you see. Not just my body, which was wrecked. It was my spirit. When I was finally able to sit up and look around, I didn't want to disturb you in your grief. I figured what was the point? I couldn't bring her back."

Señora Marquez's hands began to visibly tremble. She opened her lips as if she was going to say something, but abruptly closed them. Lance glanced in her direction and continued to speak.

"I didn't see it at first either, how much she looks like her mother. All those years, she was growing up right here in El Salvador!" He paused. "I came to ask your forgiveness. It was my fault. If Isabela hadn't met me, maybe she would still be alive ..."

Señora Marquez shifted in her seat. One blue veined hand, the skin papery thin, reached for a delicate, green-flowered china cup and brought it to her lips.

"I was the one who took her to the island," Lance continued. "It wasn't safe. I should have known with that kind of work you can't have a private life. Isabela was an innocent. We had such a wonderful time. Those days on the island were the best few days of my life. How could I know she would choose to go back there? But that's where they took her."

The old woman quietly set the china cup back into its saucer. "I am not well. If you will excuse me, Enrique will see you out. I hope you enjoy your visit to our country," Ivanna said, her hands visibly shaking.

"Come, Papa, it's getting late. We need to get back." Mera commanded her voice to stay even. Despite the effort, it rose and wavered uncertainly.

Ivanna walked out of the room as Enrique entered from the veranda.

"I am terribly sorry. I had an important call. Please excuse my aunt. She tires easily. How may I be of service?" Enrique said.

"The taxi is waiting. We are just leaving," Mera said.

"I took the liberty of dismissing the taxi," Enrique said. "I have business in town today. It will be my pleasure to drop you off at your hotel."

The shiny black Toyota sedan rolled up in front of the Inter-Continental Hotel. The thirty-minute ride from the ranch was filled with Lance's comments on the beautiful countryside and Enrique's polite descriptions of the area through which they passed.

"How long will you in be our country?" Enrique asked.

Mera responded in a rush, "We'll be leaving in a few days. Just as soon as I make the flight arrangements."

"I want to see the countryside. I want to explore where you grew up, and I'd like to wander the city. We'll need at least a few weeks, maybe months. I am looking forward to getting to know this fascinating country," Lance said. He extended his hand up into the front seat. "Thanks for the ride. It was a pleasure to meet you!"

Mera jumped out of the car without a goodbye.

I'll give it four days. I'll show him the city and take him to the nearby beaches. That should do it. No way will he coax me farther than an hour's drive from the airport. I've told him all about my history here in this country. He should understand that there's no fucking way I'm going back there!

On the third day, tourist maps in hand, father and daughter wandered the old city. They visited the National Palace, La Plaza del Salvador del Mundo, and the Basilica Sagrado. If it was in the brochure, Lance wanted to see it. After a while, infected by his ebullient joy at every turn, Mera began to enjoy the time roaming the sites. She never dropped her guard, though. She checked behind her every few minutes and constantly scanned the crowd.

Lance seemed determined to enter every small shop, especially ones that peddled local trinkets, weavings, and handicrafts. He took his time and talked with the shop owners, the locals, and even the tourists. He felt the texture of blankets and held the work up to the light. He complimented the shopkeepers; theirs was the most beautifully crafted and designed. And he bought something from each one of them. Mera entered the shops, glanced at the arrays of colorful handicrafts, and quickly exited to wait for her father outside.

"I would kill for an ice cream," Lance said. "What do you say? There's a cute little shop. I bet they have a dozen flavors to choose from."

Mera exhaled and followed Lance into the store. Rows of canned goods, toilet paper, and bottled water were arranged side by side. Shelves were filled with carrots, onions, broccoli, radishes, avocados, pineapples, and papayas. Six colorful piñatas hung from the ceiling. There was a life-sized Tinkerbell and a giant Mickey Mouse among them, dangling from the ceiling. It was impossible to enter the shop and avoid bumping into at least one of the colorful papier-mâché characters. Lance searched the store for the freezer. When he found it, he slid the glass cover open and stuck in his nose. Popsicles, ice cream sandwiches, and chocolate-covered ice cream bars lined the bottom rack.

"What do ya know, I used to have these as a boy! I love 'em! Do you want one?" He pulled out an orange creamsicle and grinned.

"Sure, whatever you're having," Mera said.

She glanced around the store. No clerk was visible. A moment later, a young boy darted out from the back room and jumped behind the counter. On the counter, prominently displayed, was a bucket filled with an assortment of Chiclet packets, the kind that held only two pieces. Lance dumped the contents of the bucket onto the counter.

"Upping my supply. These are hard to come by on Sumba!"

"Marco! ¿Desempacaste el envío de leche?" *Marco! Did you unpack the milk delivery?* a throaty voice called out from behind a beaded doorway at the back of the store. Lance counted out chewing gum packets and engaged the brown-eyed boy in an earnest conversation regarding the obvious merit and superiority of spearmint-flavored gum. The two sorted through the small packets. They lost count and began again.

Mera unwrapped her creamsicle and took a bite. She watched the interplay of man and boy in an exchange that needed no translation. There was a soft tinkling as the doorway beads at the back of the store parted. An adult male with a broad face and stocky build walked through it. Mera's eyes shot to the back of the store and froze. Orange syrup dripped onto her fingers, and vanilla ice cream began to melt and form a puddle at her feet. She stared at the man and dropped her remaining ice cream to the floor. Her eyes locked with the man's. Mera swerved to face the front door, a bitter taste rising up her throat. She rushed outside and began to run. The boy raced around the counter to clean up with the rag in his hand.

Lance stared at the empty space recently occupied by his daughter. Slowly, he looked up and observed the broad-faced man, who rubbed his eyes with the back of his hand.

Mera raced through the crowded streets and, only after several blocks, stopped and stood still. *I need to get him out of there!* Slowly, she turned and retraced the steps of her crazed run. She hesitated outside the shop.

He's changed! His face is wider, and he's not much taller than Mama. It looks as if he enjoys a few beers, judging from the gut on him. I'm different, too. I'm a lot taller than he would remember. Maybe he didn't recognize me. She fidgeted and glanced every few seconds at her watch. She was ready to grab Lance's arm and propel him away from the small grocery as soon as he exited. Customers entered, and purchased their items, and exited with their bags full of produce. Lance was not among them. *What is he doing? I can't believe he expects me to go in there and get him!* She edged to the side of the door and peeked in. Her father straddled a three-legged wooden stool. Standing next to him, the young boy rested his arm casually on Lance's shoulder. Their heads were bent, and they both looked down at something Lance held in his hand. Across from them, an older, more mature David smiled cautiously. His skin was brown and toughened from the sun. Tiny lines were etched on the side of his eyes and in between his eyebrows. In a futile attempt to keep her tone even, Mera called out from the doorway. Three sets of eyes looked up to the front.

"Papa, we need to get back. It's getting late."

"Nonsense, I've just met these wonderful people. Please sit with us."

"I can't, Papa. We spoke about this."

"You can," Lance countered.

David took a tentative step toward the front entrance way and shifted from one foot to the other, all the while looking down at his feet. Eyes still downward, he started to speak, stopped mid-sentence, and then slowly began again. "Mera, I know you don't want to see my face. I can't tell you how happy I am to see you and know that you are well."

"Come, Papa. We need to go!" she almost shouted.

"Wait, Mera, I need to thank you …" David said.

"I'll wait for you outside, Papa." Mera inched backward out the door. She stopped abruptly as a stream of unpunctuated narrative suddenly burst forth from David.

"Your friend, Señor Hawkes? He helped me just like you said he would. He showed up when I was being discharged from the hospital. I thought I was being sent back to the military, but instead, I ended up in a rehabilitation center in Mexico for children of war. It happened at the direction of Señor Hawkes. I refused to go, but they forced me. You see, I was afraid. I thought it was a setup. I didn't trust anyone or anything for a long time, but the people there were so kind and very patient. In Mexico, I was able to heal from more than just a few bullets in my ribs. And it's thanks to you and Señor Hawkes."

Mera stared at the floor and repeated, "Come, Papa. Let's get out of this place."

Lance patted the boy on the back and said, "Es un buen niño de verdad! Muy inteligente! Somos amigos desde ahora." *He's a really good boy! Very smart! We're friends already.*

David kept talking, his sentences rolling one into the other. "When I left Mexico, Señor Hawkes loaned me the money to buy this shop. Can you believe it?"

Suddenly, the oversized Tinkerbell piñata began to swing erratically and bounce against the ceiling. It fell down and rose up in the air again. Several cans of evaporated milk clattered to the ground. Mera held onto the doorway as the ground beneath her feet began to roll and tilt.

"Earthquake!" Lance yelled. "Get down! Stay low!"

Young Marco immediately sank to the ground and held his arm over his head. David rushed to the front of the store and swept Mera off her feet. The walls of the building shook as objects on the shelves banged against each other. A deafening silence ensued as all motion ceased. Mera felt warm breath in her left ear. David slowly pushed himself up from his crouched position and held out his hand. Mera ignored it.

"Fuck!" She stood up and dusted herself off. Lance rushed to the front and hugged her close.

"I just found you. I can't lose you again."

"Papa, I'm fine. It was just a small tremor."

David retreated to watch from the back of the store. His right arm wrapped around his son's shoulder.

"While you were outside, David introduced himself. I'd like to get to know your family, Mera." Lance said, "This is meant to be, fortuitous. What do you say?"

Mera continued to dust herself off. Her expression remained impassive and self-contained.

"We can't waste this opportunity," Lance continued. "Close up shop, David. I want to take everyone to the best restaurant in town. We just survived an earthquake. That's a sure sign we need to celebrate!" He grinned.

"They don't speak English, Papa." Mera brushed dirt from her father's shirt and wiped a smudge from his face with the back of her hand.

"I learn a little English," David piped up from just in front of the beaded doorway.

Lance's eyes began to tear. "I am so sorry, love. This is my fault. I should have protected you. How was I not able to feel your presence? All those wasted years! I wish I had come back for you." He wrapped his arms around her and pulled her close. "You'll see. Everything will be all right, my love. Don't blame the boy. He's a good boy."

Mera straightened and looked her father in the eye. "There's nothing you could have done. You didn't know I existed. I'll have dinner with Beelzebub himself if it keeps you from feeling sad."

"I want you to meet your nephew, a fine boy. His name is Marco."

Lance made all the arrangements. He asked the concierge for recommendations and called each establishment to discuss the menu. After a long deliberation, he finally chose the Atrio Restaurante. At eight o'clock, the taxi swung by the shop where David, young Marco, and David's wife, Yorleny, lived behind the beaded doorway. David's wife was a thirty-five-year-old Salvadorian woman with brown eyes, black hair, and a ample bottom that filled out her tight blue jeans.

All three jumped into the back seat with Lance. Young Marco sat on his father's lap. Mera climbed into the front passenger seat and immediately stared out the window.

David held his wife's hand but did not initiate conversation. Lance rambled, filling the quiet with stories that not even Mera understood well. He spoke in English and broken Spanish, addressing Marco, David, and no one in particular. His enthusiasm bubbled.

They pulled up in front of the restaurant. Inside, a preset table for five was set with a small card in the center of the table, *"Reservada."* Lance insisted Marco sit next to him. Mera jumped into the seat on her father's other side and grabbed the menu. She buried her face in its contents like it was a novel she couldn't put down. Several minutes passed. The air was thick, heavy. Even Lance was silent. The waiter's quiet approach and subsequent request for drink orders was a welcome respite. Lance only glanced at the menu and then looked at David.

"What happened after the war? What did Nigel do?" he said.

A single white rose, the centerpiece of the table, seemed to command all of David's attention. He spoke softly to it, ignoring the people seated around the table. He began, determined to speak with the little English he knew. The process was achingly deliberate and slow. He told of how he had been flown out of the country to Mexico for the therapy for children caught in war zones. The organization provided an education as well. It was not until he returned to his home country that he learned his benefactor was Señor Hawkes. Señor Hawkes loaned him the money for the business, and from then on, his life was different.

David expressed his sincere gratitude for the help he received. Together, he and his wife worked day and night to make the shop prosper. Finally, a year ago, they had managed to repay the loan back in full. The store was now completely their own and a business to leave to their only son. David was aware of the blessings he received and was committed to working with the children. He wanted to pass along the incredible lessons he learned in Mexico. He realized God had given him a second chance. So many people died during the war, and he survived. Why? The only answer that made any sense to him was a sacred duty to teach and help young ones.

"It's wonderful. Isn't it, Mera? Nigel's been busy! We have to thank him," Lance said. He then ordered mini lobster tails, gallo-pintos, rice, and a beautiful salad for everyone.

Mera snuck a glance in her brother's direction. Her mind raced. Nigel helped David? Why hadn't Nigel said anything? Oh, right, she made Nigel and Kate swear never to bring up her brother's name in her presence. Mera slowed her breathing. For some reason, the old monk from the cave seemed to oscillate within the air itself. *If you want to be free, let everything be as it is. Everything you see, feel, and touch has no more substance than clouds in the sky that form, change, and disappear.* Mera was afraid she might pass out. Feelings of grief and rage threatened to overwhelm her. She closed her eyes and allowed the intense emotions to enfold her. Lance glanced in her direction and then turned to speak with young Marco.

"I love sports. I used to play rugby when I was a boy," Lance said. "Do you play fútbol?"

Marco's eyes lit up. "Yes, I am a defender!"

Out of nowhere, a lone pinto bean sailed across the table to land in David's inky black hair. Immediately, two brown pintos returned fire, one skimming the top of Mera's head and landing somewhere on the floor behind her. The other stuck to her blouse for a brief moment before it tumbled onto her lap. Mera's shoulders began to shake as she squeezed her eyes shut in an attempt to keep tears from running down her cheeks. The aroma of her mother's favorite chicken-and-rice dish suddenly filled her senses. She could feel the rough texture of her father's handcrafted, wooden table under her fingertips. Marco's voice echoed clear and bright, admonishing her for kicking him. Everyone joyfully speaking at once. The memories, so long denied, became a floodgate of images and sensations, and suddenly, Mera could breathe again.

After dinner, they returned to David's shop and the apartment hidden behind the beaded doorway. A blue Formica counter with three stools separated the kitchen from the living area, where several chairs and a couch all faced a small television. To the right, the room extended into another living area filled with several stuffed chairs and another couch. All the furniture was covered in protective plastic sheeting. Yorleny began to remove the coverings, but Mera stopped her.

"I always feel more at home in the kitchen," she said.

David took out a bottle of white wine from the fridge. Yorleny set five cups of assorted sizes on the table with a plate of butter cookies. Mera leaned in to listen to Yorleny, curious to know more about the woman who captured David's heart. She deliberately avoided conversation with her brother, but every so often, she stole a glance in his direction. Marco fell asleep on a stack of pillows on the floor.

Mera accompanied Yorleny into the kitchen and hopped up to sit on the counter. Her legs dangled down over the side. Conversation drifted amicably over recipes and childhood stories of David as a boy.

"It seems like another life, but at the same time, the memories are so vivid and clear," Mera said. "David and I used to wade in the river. Often, we'd lose track of time and were scolded for being home late. But it was a happy time. If I close my eyes, I can still see the green moss on the riverbank, hear the gurgling of tiny waterfalls, and imagine the vanilla smell of the tree trunks. I used to wrap my arms wide around the trunk base and inhale its aroma. So many species of wildlife came to drink from the pools of water that formed along the banks. David was the only person I ever trusted to take there. We discovered exquisite butterflies, insects, and brightly colored birds, and those are only a fraction of the wild species that we encountered. One unforgettable day, we came head-to-head with two jaguar cubs. The one cub and I locked eyes, and I fell immediately in love. I would have followed both cubs back to their den. I had no sense of fear back then. David always watched out for me. He yanked my arm and broke the spell. A few minutes later, the mama jaguar growled, and the cubs trotted back to her. David probably saved my life that day!"

David wandered into the kitchen, followed closely by Lance. Yorleny smiled as she saw her husband approach. David leaned back against the wall. Every so often, he glanced in his sister's direction and finally spoke.

"Rosita lives just outside of town, Mera. She had a hard time during the war, but she's happy now. She is married and has three children. Our families have dinner together every Sunday. I haven't told her you are here, but I know she will be so happy to see you and know you are well."

"Estoy tan feliz! Ese es una tan buena noticia … Y Papá?" *I am so happy! This is such wonderful news … And Papa?*

David slowly exhaled. "Lo siento mucho, Mera." *I'm so sorry, Mera.* "Papa died. I searched for him when I returned from the rehabilitation center. It was many months before I learned he was killed."

Slowly, Mera moved toward David and placed both hands on his chest. She stared down at his scuffed brown boots next to her brand-new Teva sandals.

"No fue tu culpa, David," she whispered. *It wasn't your fault.*

Chapter Sixty-Nine

1994

El Salvador

The night was black—no moon or starlight lit the way. She ran. Branches scratched her arms and face, but she dared not stop. Every so often, she glanced behind her and stifled a sob. It was drawing nearer. She caught whiffs of the fetid odor of its breath and sensed tentacles of dark energy pressing relentlessly toward her.

Suddenly, the dragon was directly upon her, fire spewing from its mouth. All she could see was its red-hot eyes and rivulets of bloody stripes running up its side. She tried to hide behind a cluster of rocks, but nothing escaped its panoramic view. A tornado of smoke erupted from its nostrils, and rocks immediately tumbled out of the way. She stumbled, and her breath came in short pants as she attempted to hide behind trees. The dragon expelled a gust of fire from its mouth and lit the forest into a blazing inferno. She ran faster, zigzagging to escape the searing heat as sparks landed in her hair. Her hand slapped at the burning on her head. She scrambled up the mountainside, higher and higher, but the dragon was right behind her.

The light of the fire below illuminated the night in all directions. Without warning, she was unable to move her arms and legs. Her eyes were the only part of her body still under her command. Her heart pumped harder inside her chest. The beast drew nearer. Its dark red tongue was inches from her face. Her eyes darted to the left and landed upon a sheer wall of dense rock. She drew in her breath sharply as the realization dawned—neither she nor the dragon cast a shadow. Her mind and body softened. None of this is real, she whispered to herself. "I am dreaming!" Her arms and legs immediately responded to her intention. She turned slowly to face the beast and tentatively reached out her hand to touch its gooey, dark shoulder. The beast roared and sprouted a multitude of tentacles. Huge suctions cups attached themselves all over her body, sucking out her life force. She felt her throat constrict as she splayed her arms in a wild circle to dislodge the beast's multi-armed hold. Slowly, she breathed out. It is not real, she reminded herself. She allowed the feelings of dread and anxiety to embrace her without running away. Suddenly, like smoke dissipating into the wind, the beast vanished.

"What now?" she wondered. Easily, she lifted off the ground and flew past the darkened clouds that obscured her view and rose up into a clear, starlit night.

Mera sat straight up and stretched her arms in a wide arc as she slowly breathed out. Images from the dream were still easily recalled. She smiled to herself and noticed Lance seated by the window.

"Where's my cup of coffee?" she said.

"You're up? How'd you sleep?"

"Great … I had a frightening dream, but strangely, I woke up inside of it."

"How so?"

"I faced down my demon and then flew away. I feel amazing!"

Lance walked over and kissed the top of her head.

Lance, Mera, Yorleny, and Marco all piled into David's truck. Traffic was negligible on this Sunday as they rumbled down several bumpy dirt roads before pulling up in front of a small adobe farmhouse. Rosita, a pile of clean laundry at her side, quietly hung shirts and pants on the line to dry in the sun. Her children, Alejandro, Maria, and Eliani, all played in the yard.

Mera watched the scene from inside of the truck for several moments before pushing herself out and into the bright, sunlit day. A rooster crowed, and two-year old Eliani screeched, as she was chased by her older siblings. Rosita peered at David's truck, a damp shirt draped across her arm. Suddenly, matching the pitch of her baby's cry, she dropped the white shirt onto the ground and broke into a sprint. Her short legs spun like bicycle wheels. At barely five feet, Rosita threw her arms around her younger sister's waist and did not let go. When she finally released her grip, she stood back and patted her sister's face. Her mannerisms were indistinguishable from their late mother's.

Rosita prepared several chickens, fried yucca, a cabbage, cucumber, and carrot salad, and heaping bowls of rice and beans. When her husband returned from the field, Rosita pushed Mera forward and cried, "Mi hermana, mi hermana. Gracias a Dios, ella es viva!" *My sister, my sister. Thank God, she is alive!* She immediately broke into tears.

Marco and Alejandro played football in front of the casita. Unable to run after the ball, Lance leaned on his cane and searched for wood fragments. After the boys were done playing football, he enlisted their help to collect soft chunks of wood with a straight grain. He demonstrated the type of wood that was easiest to work with, then took out his pocketknife and began to carve a miniature horse.

"Anyone want to give it a try?"

Marco held out his hand as the others looked over his shoulder. "Remember, make sure the wood is dry, and carve in the direction of the grain in the wood. That way you're working with the wood." The boys each waited for a turn. Lance only had one knife.

"I'll bring each of you a good, sharp knife and a sharpening stone. Your tools have to be worthy of the art pieces I know you will find inside each piece of wood."

"It's my turn," Alejandro cried as he squeezed his brother's wrist.

"Art cannot be rushed," Lance said quietly. "Let your brother have a little more time. When it's your turn, you can take as long as you need."

They stayed until the sun went down. Mera hugged her sister and promised to return as often as she could before it was time to leave the country.

Back in the hotel room, Mera collapsed on the bed and pulled the sheet up over her head. From under the covers, she said, "I thought I came here for you, so you could find peace. Yet all along you knew. Didn't you? It was me who needed to come back here. I was the one consumed by rage."

Lance fidgeted with the drawer to the nightstand, rummaged inside, and opened small boxes, one by one, to inspect the contents.

"I was sure I left it in here. Where's the darn thing? I want to make sure Fue gets it!"

Prescription bottles filled with pink and yellow pills flitted across her mind. *Damn!* In all the excitement of the past few days, she had forgotten Lance's medication. She pushed herself up and went into the bathroom. She opened the prescription bottles and took out three pills. She filled a glass of water and handed the pills to her father, who was still opening drawers and sifting through his open suitcase.

"I don't want those things. I only took 'em to make Atibu happy. They don't do a damned thing. In fact, I feel more muddled when I take 'em."

The phone jangled loudly. Mera, still holding the pills, answered with her free hand. The desk clerk politely advised her of a visitor who waited in the lobby.

"You stay here. There's someone downstairs. We'll revisit the pills when I get back."

She dropped the contents of her hand onto the nightstand and headed downstairs. Enrique stood by the elevator. A small smile played at the corner of his lips.

"I have been to the hotel three times since your visit to the ranch. My aunt is most anxious to talk with you. She hopes you will accept her apology for the reception last week. Your visit was a bit of a shock for her."

"I'm sorry. The visit was my father's idea. We should have left well enough alone. We'll be leaving soon."

"She doesn't sleep until midnight. Might you come now?"

"It's been a long day. My father is not well."

"Then we will expect you in the morning? You can breakfast with us. I really can't leave unless you accept."

"Is ten a.m. all right?" she said.

"That will be perfect. Thank you. We'll look forward to seeing you in the morning then."

She inserted the key into the lock to enter a frigid room, the air conditioning set at its coldest setting. Lance slept beneath a pile of extra covers pulled from the closet. Mera shut off the air conditioner, opened a window, and slipped off her clothes to put on a long T-shirt. She turned off the light without washing her face and lay staring at the dark ceiling. The dull glow from the swimming pool below suffused the closed curtains. Scenes from the past few days streamed in and out of awareness, one replaced instantaneously by the next. Sleep was impossible. She threw the sheets to the back of the bed and slid down onto the floor, crossing her legs. Her back lightly touched the side of the bed. After an hour of sitting in the lotus position, she readjusted her position, stretched out her legs, and breathed slowly.

Her awareness expanded. She felt the sensation of rough stone on her bottom and sand scratching the soles of her feet. The sweet scent of jasmine filled her awareness. The old monk wavered in front of her as she watched a montage of images and emotions arise and pass like an old movie reel.

Steam escaped through the crack beneath the bathroom door. Mera opened her eyes. She threw off the covers and reached for the cup of coffee she knew would already be brewed. Lance came out of the bathroom dressed in a T-shirt and shorts.

"Good morning, sleepyhead. Sleep well?" he asked.

"It took me a while but then total blackout. How about you?"

"Like a baby. What shall we do today?"

"Enrique came by last night. He said his aunt would like to meet with us this morning. I told him we were leaving in a few days, but he insisted we come by the ranch for breakfast. I wonder what she wants. I really hope our presence doesn't upset her all over again."

"Maybe she'll show us some of Isabela's paintings."

"More than likely she'll ask us to stay the hell away from her ranch! Let's get a taxi and get this over with."

The phone rang once again. Lance leaned in to answer it. "Enrique is downstairs. I told him we'd be down in a few minutes. You're sure you're okay with this?"

The trio walked onto the veranda where a table was set with five place settings. Already seated were Ivanna Marquez and her great-nephew, Andrés, who rose and pulled out a chair for Mera. Ivanna remained seated and did not extend a hand.

"I have spoken with my nephew and great-nephew, Enrique and Andrés. Enrique will moderate on my behalf. My nephews and I are in complete accord." She glanced in Enrique's direction and nodded to him to begin.

"My aunt was disturbed by your recent visit and expressed her deep concern that there will be another attempt to stake a claim on the ranch. After my Uncle Pablo passed away, the ranch and all its properties were transferred to myself and my son, Andrés. Any attempt to stake a claim on these properties will be dealt with in a court of law. We will not hesitate to bring legal proceedings against anyone who attempts to gain proprietorship."

Lance leaned forward, giving Enrique his full attention. Mera began to rise from the table just as the maid poured a steaming cup of hot coffee at her setting. She thought better of it and sat back down.

"We have more than enough money," Lance said. "All these things?" He waved his hand around the terrace. "You can't take any of it with you when you die, so what's the use of hoarding? I like Sumba. I've lived there almost my entire adult life. You have a beautiful ranch, but I don't want to live here. Mera here, my daughter, lived through a very traumatic past in El Salvador. She survived the war. She didn't want to come for a visit, so I'm quite sure you couldn't convince her to live here even if you wanted to. I hope she'll come to see me in Indonesia and bring the girl. What I'd like, if you would be so gracious, is to show her a few of her mother's paintings. Have you kept any? She was most proud of her piece *Parrots in the Jungle*."

Ivanna's posture drooped. She looked up sharply and stared at the young woman, who was lightly tapping her father's arm, entreating him to leave.

"It is most cruel to deceive an old woman with memories of her only daughter. I have cried all the tears. Now the well is dry. You will not succeed any further with this nonsense. If my daughter had a child, we would have been informed. After my husband's death, there have been numerous attempts to make a claim on the ranch. It is a very valuable piece of real estate. We believe that both of you are the newest attempt."

Mera observed the old woman, the blue-veined hands and the slight tremble of her lower lip. She fought back the strange urge to gather up the frail woman and hold her tight against her chest. Instead, she let go of her father, breathed slowly, and looked Ivanna in the eye.

"I'd like to know something of my mother," she said. "She died when I was born. In return, we'll tell you what we know."

"Come. Sit here next to me, and let me have a look at you," Ivanna said. "You are so tall! Tell me why you think my daughter was your mother." Mera glanced at Lance, who leaned over and patted her arm.

"Go ahead. She won't bite."

"I couldn't have asked for a more loving mother. The mother I grew up with was a woman named Maria Rodríguez. She was the most loving woman anyone could ever hope to meet." Mera's eyes began to well. "I never dreamed that the family I grew up with was not my biological one. You see, it was the war. The war shattered the only family I ever knew into a thousand broken pieces. I was left alone. A British man, Nigel Hawkes, rescued me. He told me he knew my mother, but as it turns out, who he meant was not the mother I knew as a child."

Ivanna listened to the story of Isabela's life in Thailand pieced together through information acquired from Nigel, Kate, and Lance. Ivanna's composure never wavered, though her expression modulated between mild shock and horror.

"Isabela kidnapped? Pregnant? A prisoner? Our granddaughter grew up in a poor farmer's family?" Her face drained of color as she held onto the sides of her chair.

Ivanna scrutinized Mera's face. Her mouth puckered at the edges. Mera readjusted her posture as her fingers instinctively reached up and began to knead her left earlobe. Ivanna leaned forward and scrutinized the young woman in front of her. She noticed the contour of Mera's face was oval like her daughter's, and the tiny gap in between the young woman's two front teeth was identical to her deceased daughter Isabela's. Several minutes passed. A flock of parakeets' chitter rose to a sweet crescendo, while the tufted pink flowers of the nearby trees trembled in the light breeze of the morning. Ivanna straightened. Only her eyes revealed the internal turmoil she felt. She spoke each word slowly.

"Who is responsible for keeping our granddaughter from us? Who allowed her to grow up in poverty? Someone must be held responsible!" Her gaze spanned the room and landed on Lance. Her glance was pure ice, but captured within it was the depth of grief and suffering she had endured.

"Nigel did what Isabela asked him to do. We can't fault him," Lance said quietly.

Ivanna closed her eyes. Her body remained stock-still, almost rigid. After several minutes, Mera glanced at her father and whispered, "Do you think she's fallen asleep?"

Abruptly, Ivanna opened her eyes. "I would like to show you my daughter's paintings. If you will follow me, I'll take you to her room."

Isabela's room had been left as if she might walk in at any given moment, her age effectively frozen in time. Sketches lay on the table. Paintings half done and completed were pinned to the wall. There was a musty, dank smell to the room, and dust covered the table tops.

"I've forbidden anyone but the servants to enter the room," Ivanna said. "They are instructed to air it out once a month. I haven't had the heart to enter."

Lance walked among the paintings and lightly touched them. He held one up to the light and then another.

"Could you bring yourself to part with two of these? One for myself and another for Mera?"

"Take what you want, but I want my granddaughter to stay. A lifetime has been robbed. Pablo would have nothing less." She directed her attention to Lance, daring him to contradict her. In her gaze was the condemnation of a thousand mothers who had lost both their children.

In the spirit of compromise, Lance and Mera extended their visit one month and moved from the hotel to the ranch, allowing for Ivanna to know her daughter's child. In turn, Mera learned Isabela's childhood stories.

Chapter Seventy

1994

Chicago, Illinois

The plane took off slowly and climbed above active volcanos, lakes, rivers, and the vast Pacific Ocean. Mera looked out the window and had a strong intuition she wouldn't see the country where she'd grown up again. Images from her visit to El Salvador popped into her mind. Ivanna, not one for tears, brushed her granddaughter's hair. She tried to convey on the head of a pin everything she might have said over the years about etiquette, comportment, and the prominence of the Marquez name. The eighty-two-year-old grandmother caught herself staring unabashedly at the beautiful young woman. Her face revealed mannerisms and traits she never thought she'd see again.

"I am eighty-two years old. Please do not forget me."

Mera remembered the emotional goodbye at the airport. David, Yorleny, Marco, Rosita, and her family, all of them, crowded around her as Lance stood with his hand on Marco's shoulder. Ivanna stood apart, her gaze vacillating between the horizon and the small group of family congregated around Mera. David's little daughter, Maria, burst into tears as her brother, Alejandro, lifted up the folds of her skirt, yanked her hair, and then quickly ran away. Ivanna moved into action, leaned over, and wiped a mucus dribble from Maria's nose as the little girl coughed and sniffled.

"There, there, my dear. Pay him no mind. It's just the pranks of little boys. A young lady holds her head high and carries herself with dignity. Come, come, that won't do. Dry your tears. Will you have an ice cream? We'll all go for an ice cream after the plane departs." Sticky, little fingers reached up and grabbed hold of a slender, blue-veined hand.

The plane rose, finally, to reach 35,000 feet. Mera took her father's hand and rested her head on his shoulder.

"How did you know, Papa? I couldn't get beyond the pain. Seeing David again, I realized love has always been present. It was my heart that shut down, and I buried myself inside the rubble. Things are the way they are, and it's okay."

He squeezed her hand. "My girl, I knew you'd make it back to me."

She woke to the slowing of the engines and an announcement over the PA system.

"Ladies and gentlemen, in preparation for our descent into O'Hare International Airport, please fasten your seatbelt. We will be landing in approximately thirty minutes."

Lance's head suddenly lurched back, and his eyes rolled up into the top of his head. Saliva dribbled out the side of his mouth. Mera reached over and grabbed his wrist to feel for a pulse. She pressed the stewardess call button and yelled down the aisle, "Is there a doctor?"

An anesthesiologist was the first to answer the call. A few minutes later, a heart specialist made his way up from the back. The anesthesiologist was already performing CPR in the aisle. Once a heartbeat was established, oxygen was administered. An ambulance met the airplane, and for the second time in his life, Lance was transferred from an airplane to the hospital.

There was no room for Mera in the emergency vehicle. She grabbed a cab to follow the ambulance until the cab driver became stuck behind traffic. Mera urged him to hurry. When she finally arrived at the hospital, Lance was sitting up in the bed and cheerfully making jokes with the nurses.

"I didn't mean to give you a scare," he said. "Apparently, I suffered a mild stroke. Nothing to worry about. We haven't a care in the world."

Mera lifted the covers and climbed into the hospital bed, snuggling in next to Lance. The bed was barely big enough for one large patient, and it bulged beyond its limit with the two of them. Mera's tall frame hung off awkwardly. She wrapped her arms around her father's chest. As the stress of the last few hours abated, Mera quietly dozed. The night nurse eventually entered, introduced herself, and approached the bed to take the vitals of her patient.

"Shh. Come on this side. Don't wake her."

Rays of morning sun filtered through the window. Mera shifted and jumped up. She stretched her arms above her head and covered her mouth with her hand as she yawned. "I am going to find the doctor."

"Well, good morning to you," Lance said.

She returned twenty minutes later with Dr. David Mueller into tow. He listened to Lance's steady heartbeat, checked his reflexes, and shone a light into Lance's retinas. He carefully looked over the chart.

"You've suffered a mild stroke. I see you were informed last night? We'll put you on a blood thinner. We want to avoid future episodes, but from everything I can see this morning, you don't appear to have suffered impairment. I am going to okay a light diet—clear soup and a little fruit. We'll see how that goes. We'll observe you for twenty-four hours, and if all goes well, I don't see why we can't get you out of here by tomorrow morning."

The doctor smiled briefly before moving into the hallway to continue his rounds. Mera sat on the bed and took her father's hand, lightly massaging his fingers and palm.

"If I knew I would get such caring attention, I might have feigned something earlier," he said.

"Papa, don't joke, not about this. I was in a panic. I thought I'd lost you!"

"Never happen. You're my girl. We'll always find each other. There's proof of that now."

A food cart was steered into the room, carrying a tray of chicken broth and several pieces of fruit. Lance immediately reached for a slice of watermelon and took a bite.

"They're wont to starve a man in this place. Want a piece?"

Suddenly, his hand shot up to his throat, and all color drained from his face as he gasped for air. Mera dropped the slice she was holding and threw him forward, hitting him hard on the back. But nothing she did helped. She jumped from the bed and ran into the hallway.

"Help!"

A nurse entered from the doorway and immediately placed a code blue. The on-call doctor administered CPR while Mera, shoved to the back, darted her eyes from the monitor to the frenzied activity around her father's bed. A second doctor administered paddles to initiate an electric shock. Mera slowly moved forward to stand between the two doctors and took her father's hand.

"Please stand back so we can do our work." The nurse once again pressed her backward, but Mera resisted.

"I don't want him to be alone. Please!"

Instead of heeding their advice, she moved in closer. Finally, they let her stay, cautioning her to stand back as the shock was administered for the third time. Suddenly, Lance opened his eyes. A light blip danced across the monitor.

"Where's my girl? Come closer, sweetheart. Can you help me sit up?"

"I'm here, Papa."

The doctor nodded in her direction and took hold of Lance under the arm. Mera did the same on the other side, and together they lifted him into a more vertical position. Lance stared into hazel eyes so like his own and smiled. He slowly breathed in and gently exhaled, and his body went limp into the arms that supported him. Dr. Mueller immediately began CPR once again and initiated electric shock three more times. A faint blip on the monitor relaxed into a steady, even line. The doctor slowly shook his head.

Mera chewed on the knuckles of her hand as she viewed the scene in front of her. Amid the machines, the paddles, the code blue, the nurses scurrying in and out, and the doctor rubbing gel over Lance's chest and applying the defibrillator paddles, calling out 'stand back,' she found herself watching her father's face. She observed him breathe in and then slowly breathe out for the last time, as if he was consciously letting everything go. A pervasive peace filled the room.

The medical staff quietly withdrew. Mera bent down and gently kissed her father's forehead while she ran her fingers through his thick white hair.

"I love you."

Mera called Kate, Nigel, and her lawyer. What was needed to fly her father back to Sumba? They all advised her to fly the body to Washington. Nigel would see to it that Lance received a burial in Arlington with full military honors.

"He ran away from all of that. He wanted to go home. Atibu wouldn't be able to come to Washington, and I know he'd want to be with her near the garden, the ocean, the dog, and everything he loved. I'll send him back as John Smith just like he came."

"Do yourself a big favor," her lawyer advised. "Have him cremated here and then take his ashes to Sumba. You'll avoid a lot of red tape." There was a pause before her lawyer continued. "I'm sorry. The timing is awful, but I thought you'd want to know. There's been information from Sarajevo. The city is completely surrounded. The Serbs have closed off all access and are trying to starve the Bosnians into concession. It's become impossible to get anything or anyone out of there. It will take a miracle to follow through with your application for adoption under these circumstances. For the time being, I'd advise working with the humanitarian organizations. They're the only ones able to get something through, as difficult as it is."

Chapter Seventy-One

1995

Washington, D.C.

A steady rain lashed against the windowpane. Mera stared out the window at puddles formed in the street and dirty water splashed onto cursing pedestrians. She held a blue ceramic urn in her lap as the rain dripped rivulets of changing patterns on the window. The door to the coffee shop opened slowly, and Nigel, leaning heavily on two canes and bundled in a great black coat, his cheeks rosy from the cold, entered to slowly make his way over to the corner table. Mera leaned up to kiss him on the cheek.

"Dreadful weather, isn't it? My dear, I came as soon as I heard. Bloody terrible business. I wish I was able to get here sooner. I am terribly sorry you had to manage all this alone."

"I had help. Kate arranged the cremation with a funeral home. I wanted to bring him back to Sumba, where he lived all these years, but I was advised against it. All his documents are under a made-up name, so officially, there's no known relative. I realized it would be a nightmare to sort it all out. I'll fly the ashes back instead."

She lifted the urn and placed it on the table between them. It was Nigel's turn to stare at the changing patterns of rain on the window.

"I imagined we'd cross paths again one day, your father and I, but not like this. It's a bloody shame. After all these years, blown away before you had a chance to know him. He was a fine man, your father."

"Somehow, it's all right. The time we spent together was brief, but there were no walls. It's like we'd known each other all along. I know it sounds crazy, but even in that sterile hospital setting, he died so peacefully. I am comforted to know he lived the way he wanted and had few regrets. His death was heartbreaking but also beautiful."

"What will you do now? Any progress in Sarajevo? I wish you'd let me help. I still have a few avenues for an old bugger like myself. I've heard there's a tunnel being constructed in the city. It's a project of bloody desperation! The people have no supplies and are digging twenty-four hours a day with shovels and pickaxes. The city's been completely cut off. If the project is successful, the tunnel will link the city to the Bosnian-held territory on the other side of the airport. They're hoping it will become a way to get in supplies and food and quite possibly a few lucky ones out."

"I wouldn't want to ask you to call in a favor that huge. Is it possible?"

"I'll check into it. In the meantime, you're off to Indonesia?"

"Tomorrow morning. I'll stay as long as it takes for her, for Atibu, to be okay."

"Right, right. Hell of a mess this, isn't it? I took the liberty of letting Anne know. I hope I did not overstep?"

"Thank you for dealing with that."

"She was quite upset. She loved him too, in her own way."

"Yes, I know."

Chapter Seventy-Two

1995

Sumba, Indonesia

Lady bounded from a sleeping position to meet Mera with joyful yelps. Her whole body wagged with her tail. Atibu waited on the step, wiping her hands on her dress, with her eyes peeled in Mera's direction. When she saw that Mera was alone, an undulating, torturous wail escaped from deep within her belly, as if the sound arose from the Earth itself.

Mera stayed on and worked with Atibu in the garden. They cooked, fed the animals, and cared for Lance's prize vegetables and roses. Every day, they watched the sun drop toward the horizon to spew its evanescent golden light. She waded along the water's edge. The waves pounded in, waters reversing in a swift, vibrating retreat. Mera felt her toes connect deep into the sand as the waves washed gently over her feet.

One particular evening, without a word exchanged between them, Mera and Atibu took the urn from atop the kitchen table and walked down to the ocean's edge just as the sun beat its way to the horizon. The sky was tinged with violet, lavender, and plum hues. A storm hovered several miles away as a light mist formed a halo of a double rainbow. One at a time, they dug their hand into the urn. Mera moved slowly into the water up to her waist. She held up her hand as dust merged with the wind and sprinkled back into the great ocean below.

"Goodbye, Papa."

Atibu waded only up to her knees with the blue urn held under her arm, hugged close to her chest. Her other hand dug into the ashes and held a handful up to the sky. Mera stood perfectly still. She observed the evening dance across the sky, and the beautiful Indonesian woman opened her hand and released the contents. Clouds of ash billowed around them. Was it something in the way Atibu held her head? Or was it the soft breeze blowing wisps of hair across her face? Or perhaps the long-legged white birds hunting for dinner in the moments of receding water only to quickly skedaddle back up the shore? Or the way reflective rays of sun shimmered and danced? Whatever brought it about, a forbidden memory, a beloved face stole across Mera's mind and whispered, "You will wander far from here."

Mera remembered the smell of healing herbs brewing on an old woodburning stove, and she was instantly transported back across the years to Analena's small cabin. Two old women, Analena and Amah, separated by a vast ocean and countless years. One known, the other hidden and mysterious, but somehow in Mera's mind, the two were one and the same.

The emerald flashed across her mind, accompanied by an all-encompassing, expansive view. The words formed instantly in her mind. *It's not about you. All phenomena are connected and inter-dependent. All things arise and then disperse.*

She shook her head. *Fuck, what was that? Where did that come from?* She edged closer to Atibu to dig her hand into the urn for the remaining ashes.

In the morning when she awoke, Mera jumped from the bed and opened the top drawer to the bureau. Right where she left it, the small box lay wound in string and settled in the drawer underneath blouses and undergarments. Carefully, she unwrapped the ties and removed the stone. She held it up, and green light splintered and reflected geometric patterns on the wall. She moved the stone in every direction. Light shone through its facets. The purity of the stone and its intrinsic value stole across her mind. *I could make a lot of money selling this stone.* Quietly she replaced the stone back into its box, rewound the string, and placed it in her suitcase.

Chapter Seventy-Three

1995

Thailand and Burma

The flight from Jakarta to Bangkok was a quick three hours and thirty minutes. Mera arrived in Thailand at four on a Monday afternoon, two months after her father's death. Kate had supplied her with the name of the village where she encountered the nanny so many years before. Mera was determined to find and speak with any and all living relatives of Maiv Lee.

The first village was a wash. No one there had heard of Maiv Lee. Mera then rode all-night buses to even more remote villages. She hiked kilometers on foot to reach villages tucked high in the mountains where the only access might be a small path that curved and hugged the mountainside. Each time, the villagers shook their heads. They didn't know anyone by that name, but would she stay and have some tea? Inevitably, talk would graze the subject of the war and the horror left behind by the retreating American force. The Hmong, who had risked their lives to help the Westerners, were abandoned to their tragic fate. They were tortured and persecuted for having helped the enemy. So many were gone. It was impossible to remember the little old lady who had left her village long before the war started. After so many villages and too many stories of horror, Mera was exhausted. Although there was no one around to hear, Mera's voice rose to a high pitch and echoed across the low-lying valley below.

"What am I doing? I need to get back to a semblance of a life. Papa, I tried to figure out what to do with the damn stone. Get it to its rightful owner. But too many years have passed. As much as I've tried to do the right thing by you, I don't have the answer. I'm sorry." She sat down on a rock and wiped sweat from her face with the back of her hand. "I'm done," she said to herself. "I am going back to Washington. Fuck the stone."

Mera straightened and began the slow descent to return back down to the village. Just then, a small bird flew across her path to alight on a nearby branch. The color of its wings was a resplendent blue and its chest a burnt orange. Mera stopped to watch it. *Are there bluebirds in Burma?* The little bird chirped its melodious and soothing notes and then swiftly flew up and out of sight.

Moving up the trail and headed in the direction she came from was a man who appeared to almost fly up the mountainside. At first, she assumed he was a young boy. Who else could move with such long strides and without pausing for a breath? As he drew nearer though, she stopped. She was surprised to see the man was not young at all, but quite old-looking. An elder. She moved to the side of the trail to let him pass, somehow troubled by his apparent ease and agility. Something didn't seem quite right.

"Hello!" he piped up cheerfully in clear, bright English. "Mighty fine day!"

Mera watched the diminutive man. Her mind was tired and jumbled. *How is an old villager, out here in the middle of absolutely nowhere, speaking to me in perfect English?*

"Yes," she said. "I suppose it is."

"I see you've been traveling. Don't worry. You don't need to go any farther. This is the place. Come on, I've been waiting for you."

He continued past her with a springy step. She scrutinized his face. His cheeks were luminous and surprisingly unwrinkled. Only a few hairs graced the top of his head, and he had a single long grey strand of hair that hung from a mole on the side of his cheek. His eyes were a brilliant brown and sparkled like moonlight on water. Mera instinctively turned to follow him without questioning her choice. She began the long, hard climb back up the hill.

The old man moved effortlessly and sprinted through the trees. He darted up and around bushes and eventually came upon a smaller path. She hadn't noticed this one before. The small path wound deep into thick pines and disappeared. Mera was breathing hard. The old man kept getting farther ahead. He stopped and turned to beckon her with his hand. *Damn it, with all that's been going on, I haven't been running regularly. I can't believe I am having trouble keeping up with this old man.*

She followed him up the winding, switchback path. Every so often, she stopped to take a breath. She wondered why she had so easily followed this stranger's lead and was hurrying up the trail behind him. After almost an hour of a hard climb, she arrived at a rock ledge that overlooked the village below. The old man was nowhere in sight. Slowly, she sat down and dangled her legs over the precipice. She rested her hands lightly in her lap. Just behind her head and out of nowhere, a loud buzzing noise shocked the silence. Her heart ricocheted inside her chest. *What the hell was that?* The buzzing wound quickly from behind her to just a hand's length in front of her face. Its wings shimmering with a rainbow of colors in the afternoon light, a tiny hummingbird hovered and seemed to stare directly into her eye. It departed just as quickly as it arrived.

Mera shook her head. She relaxed her shoulders and surveyed the small village nestled below, where tiny goats grazed on the hillside and the crow of a rooster echoed and resounded up the valley. She closed her eyes as her breathing quieted. After a while, she eased onto her back. Clouds drifted together with her thoughts, merging then dispersing. She opened her eyes. The clouds formed angels, elephants, and airplanes … then nothing at all. The old one whispered in her left ear. She sat up and withdrew the small box from her pocket, unwinding the string that bound it for what she hoped was the last time. The old man was now seated on the stone outcropping next to her. The emerald sparkled in the bright sunlight. She extended her hand to place the stone on the ground between them.

"I think this is for you."

"Well, I don't want it. That's just a rock," the old man said.

"What am I supposed to do with it, then?"

She stole a glance. The old man was seated on her right, solid and real. Lulled by the warmth of the sun, Mera's eyelids felt heavy. She allowed them to close as her shoulders relaxed and her breathing slowed. The old man suddenly jumped up, his foot inadvertently kicking the stone. It rolled quickly and hovered precariously close to the edge of the precipice. Mera's eyes flew open as the precious stone wavered and then decisively spiraled into a gravelly, clinking descent. She sprang up with her heart in her throat.

"I have to get it!" she said.

"Forget the rock. Look!"

"Look at what?"

His finger tapped in between her eyebrows and then in the middle of her breastbone.

"Hmf, you are quite hopeless. It's all in here, not out there."

The old man's finger probed deeper into her chest. Mera's heart exploded and shattered into a thousand pieces. The indiscriminate suffering of the world was palpable, searing, and defied resolution.

"How do we live in the world?" she heard herself murmur.

"With all of your heart!" He paused for a moment, then added brightly, "Don't be attached to any of it!"

"That's a contradiction."

The old man giggled and peered directly into her eyes. "Everything is change. Don't you see! Ride the waves with complete and utter equanimity." He leaned over and tickled her. He kissed her on the cheek and the top of the head and then tickled her again. Her heart felt battered inside her chest and began to ache.

"You have to ask the right question. See? Don't take yourself so seriously. It's not about you! There's nothing solid about you. There's nothing substantial about anything at all! Relax! Get out of the way! You will see things as they are."

Without warning, her mind began to expand. Boundless. Clear. The empty, vast potential of all things intrinsically interconnected and whole as a vast ocean continuously expressed its endless waves.

"That's it! Now you see, it's quite simple."

She felt the searing heat of the sun on her face, arms, and legs. She sat up slowly and looked around. The old man was gone. The stone, however, was back up on the ledge and shimmered in the sunlight. Mera leaned over and replaced the emerald back in its box, moving without any idea of where she was headed. Halfway up the hill, she paused for a breath and looked around her. The path disappeared into the thick vegetation. Which way should she go?

The path appeared to end here. Instinctively, she crouched down on her knees, and moved the branches aside with her left arm, and shielded her face with her right. Straight ahead, a sheer wall of rock loomed. She was about to turn around when sunlight flickered in between two large ferns. The rock in front seemed one with the stone wall, but on closer observation, there was a narrow opening between the two. She wedged herself through the narrow opening. The smell of fresh dirt filled her nostrils as pebbles skinned her knee. She slithered down, close to the earth, using her arms to pull herself through the opening between the giant slabs of stone. Slowly, she pushed herself to stand.

Inside, a huge cavern opened. Stalactites hung from a thirty-foot ceiling, forming a perfect, natural cathedral. Light filtered in from a thousand cracks along the top of the grotto. Walls of embedded stones shimmered and mixed with the natural light. She was unable to control a deep inhale of breath. Slowly, she squatted down. She removed the box from her pocket, opened it, and then placed her fingers around the green stone. Pushing herself to stand, she turned in a full circle and surveyed the inside of the grotto. Her fingers grazed the left wall, and she moved tentatively forward to sense, rather than decide her direction. Her hand explored along the smooth stone and jagged rock. In the darkest corner of the cave, she stopped abruptly and rose up onto her tiptoes as her fingers probed where her eyes could not see. The stone fit perfectly inside a small cavity in the rock. Gently, she withdrew her fingers and let go.

She retraced her steps along the grotto wall, back the way she came. Before dropping onto her knees to once again pull herself through the narrow opening between the rocks, she swung around and sat, committing the extraordinary beauty of the place to memory.

Then she scurried down the hill and stopped at the ledge that overlooked the valley. She reached up to touch the diminutive elephant and jaguar that hung on a leather strap around her neck. Mera lifted the necklace over her head, and held the carvings between her fingers, and then brought them gently to her lips to lightly kiss each one. With an easy flip of her hand, she tossed the tiny carvings. The elephant and the jaguar soared high up into the air in a giant arc and tumbled down into the abundant rainforest below.

Back in the village, she asked around. She did her best to describe the old man with his wrinkle-free skin and his uncanny agility. Had anyone seen him? No. No one in the village matched that description. All the old ones were wrinkled and bent. She asked if he might be from another village? The villagers looked at her and shook their head. A tiny smile played at the corners of her mouth. She waved to a small group of women, who beckoned her to join them for a cup of tea, then moved along down the trail.

Chapter Seventy-Four

1994

Narita, Japan

On a stopover in Narita, she placed a call to her attorney in Washington.

"Where have you been?" he asked.

"Long story, but I'll be back stateside in just about fifteen hours. Twenty-four before I'm back in D.C. I thought I should check in."

"I've been looking for you. I have news."

"What then?"

"Your little Bosnian girl, Zhera? She's out of harm's way. You can thank your friend Nigel Hawkes for that."

"How?"

"From the information I was given, it's impossible to consider getting anyone out of Sarajevo, much less an orphan girl without papers. Contrary to incredible odds, little Zhera's out of the country and has her passport and adoption paperwork. All of it. Your friend Mr. Hawkes has some serious global connections. He didn't do it alone, however. There was a Canadian journalist who helped on the inside. I'll give you the details when you're back. It's a pretty incredible story."

"Where is she?"

"I thought maybe you'd like to keep going. Take the nonstop flight from LA to London when you get in. That's where you'll find her. I'm sure Mr. Hawkes will appreciate you showing up as soon as you're able."

Mera lightly placed the phone back on its cradle. She rummaged into the side pocket of her purse with her left hand. She felt a pen, loose coins from several different countries, and a white business card. Her fingers zeroed in. She held the card up to the light.

IAN HAYDEN, *Journalist*
Vancouver, Canada

Mera's eyes shifted out through the airport window to the tarmac where a United jumbo jet slowly reversed. The ground personnel visually signaled the pilot with handheld illuminated beacons to ease the aircraft out from its gate to begin its transpacific crossing. Crowds of people swarmed the airport. All nationalities were indistinguishable in their rush to catch a flight, meet loved ones, or simply check in at a nearby hotel. Mera's fingers lightly brushed the card's raised black lettering as she moved toward her flight.

Acknowledgements

My sincere gratitude and appreciation to friends and family who offered insight, ideas and knowledge to bring Lotus to life. It is not possible to thank them all but I would be sorely remiss if I didn't mention a few here.

Bob Durham, for sharing stories of his time in Laos during the Vietnam War. Jim Trotter, for his advice and proficiency in all parts aviation. Margi Ness, for captivating my imagination with tales of her time as a Donut Dolly during the Vietnam War. Ned Rifkin for his love of language and his thoughtful edits, and to my very first readers who agreed to tackle the manuscript in its infancy and share their impressions and ideas: Dian Doody, Tim and Wendy Stokes, Brandyn Dente, Bernice Hill, Barbara Longo, and Margi Ness.

To editors, Theresa Boyar and Cindy Draughton, who helped me take a lump of clay and mold it into something recognizable. For the editors at Paper Raven Books: Brian Dooley, Heather Pries and M.A. Hinkle. I am exceptionally grateful for their expertise and thoughtful edits. And to the staff of Paper Raven Books who patiently walked me through the steps necessary to bring a novel to the light of day!

Lightning Source UK Ltd.
Milton Keynes UK
UKHW051552130223
416650UK00013B/993/J